The Thornham Copyist

The Seventh Catrin Sayer Mystery

ALLAN JONES

THE CATRIN SAYER MYSTERIES

*This book is a Kindle Direct Publishing paperback.
The series is also available as e-books from
Amazon Kindle eBooks and other suppliers.*

CONTENTS

"It's the way I look. I've never been trained as a fine artist.
I've never developed a natural style because I don't have one.
It is totally representational.
It is a completely different discipline."

Susie Ray, copyist, quoted in an interview
published in 'The Telegraph' in 2017

PROLOGUE. THORNHAM

The silver Range Rover moved steadily north with the wide, open fields of North Norfolk stretching out on either side of Chosley Road, a minor road south of the picturesque village of Thornham. Anyone paying it any attention could guess at the purpose of the lone occupant. A man of some wealth, obviously; either an avid bird-watcher on his way to Titchwell Marsh or perhaps a visitor to a country estate of the landed gentry or the *nouveau riche*. The Sandringham Estate belonging to the Royal Family was less than fifteen miles away.

However, the vehicle turned into a farmyard just before the village and in response the residents, an older couple, came out of the front door and stood side-by-side, waiting as the driver got out and sorted things from the back seat that he wanted to bring with him. From their expressions the visitor was expected but he was more of a business acquaintance than a close friend. The man was in his late-fifties, well-dressed in a casual sense and self-assured it seemed, although he walked from the vehicle with some effort. He made the move forward to shake hands formally with the couple.

This was clearly not a regular encounter. There was no natural sequence of warmth and welcome between them. They seemed caught between the formal and informal; the faces, the body language, the reserve in the handshakes. There was a sense of relationship but also a tinge of disappointment in the eyes of the couple, as if he was a bearer of bad news.

So it was a little surprising that the woman impulsively moved forward to hug the man briefly, as if she relented on some prior decision and her natural spontaneity took over.

The farm had some modern structures; the storage sheds for equipment were obviously built within the last twenty years but the main farmhouse was from the early nineteenth century. A hundred metres or so set back on the property was a cottage of similar age, but with additions.

On closer inspection it could be seen to have evolved from two adjoining smaller cottages; tiny homes by modern standards, but ones that were built to house large families of farm workers in a bygone era. The original occupants of such humble dwellings used to be the mainstay of agricultural production before mechanisation made North Norfolk an area with one of the lowest density populations in England. Some recent renovations had taken place, including the addition of a large north-facing window quite out of character with the cottage and a modern vestibule area facing towards the yard.

The three people headed directly over to the cottage rather than enter the farmhouse, keeping a measured pace considerate of the younger visitor's slower step.

Two hours later, the man left alone carrying a large, flat parcel. Earlier in the week there had been a foretaste of the autumn and winter to come, with strong winds stripping still-green leaves everywhere. Today the wind wasn't that strong or cold but the man's eyes were streaming. In the months ahead the locals would be reminding each other that the last stop these north-easterlies made before blasting Norfolk was Norway and the cold North Sea.

He placed the parcel in the back seat of the Range Rover cushioned in a blanket he had brought expressly for that purpose. Then he wiped his eyes before driving away slowly south again.

PART 1. THIEF

1 GERDA

It was Leo's response to Gerda Lentz at the hotel near Brands Hatch that brought Lyall out of his oppressive sense of guilt. Leo had introduced him as 'his associate, his prospect'. That was a step up from 'hangaround' in the vocabulary of the biker world. Gerda was in her late-forties, really attractive and hard as nails, Leo said. Be very polite.

Lyall was the perfect gentleman that morning.

His waking hours in the days before the meeting had been plagued by the memory of breaking Seb's rib, looking at his friend standing there and swallowing hard, waiting for the single blow. Lyall hadn't even hit anyone with a knuckleduster before. Sure, he had put one on and felt the fit and heft of it but the one that Chas had handed to him was a wicked-looking thing; a straight steel bar rough-welded across the top of a stock four-ring set of knuckles. It wasn't fancy or decorated with stupid images; it was a working tool, designed to wreak damage.

"One hit, and don't you pull it, Lyall. I want to hear it," Chas had said, pointing at the spot, "Just here. Ready, young Sebastian?"

Lyall had nodded vigorously, nervously, showing his compliance with the instruction, trying not to hear the fear in his friend's terse response.

"Yes, Chas. Thanks, Chas." Seb drew in a deep breath.

Lyall had glanced at Leo Altman, his own patch member, his club sponsor really, for final confirmation. Leo had just nodded once, his lips pursed. Then Lyall gave it all he could and above the explosive, exhaling groan from Seb, he heard the floating rib crack.

Chas Drummond and Leo Altman were long-time patch members of a motorcycle club in North London called the Centurions. Originally named the Edmonton Centurions, after the area in North London where it was founded, it quickly contracted its name; too many people in their world jumped to the conclusion that they were a satellite of some club in Western Canada.

The Centurions were independent and didn't want to be associated with anyone. In fact, club discussions about affiliating with one of the largest 'outlaw' biker clubs, the Outlaws, had been going on for years.

It had about thirty members, with double that number attending many rides, events and private gatherings. Around the core of patch members were the circles of prospects and hangarounds; men spending the time to sample the life and values of the hard-core biker world and the women tied to the biker life.

As he hit Seb, Lyall had every hope of making it up a grade soon, to the level of 'prospect'. Selfishly, he knew, he thought this hit on his friend may be just the step he needed. He would never know until he was told by Leo, of course.

Seb, the hangaround that Chas mentored, was being disciplined for breaking the rules. Drummond had heard on the street something about himself only known within the club. It took no time for him to find out that Seb had been in a bar and let it slip, showing off. Now the word was out there that Chas had a 'juvi' record, an assault charge at age fifteen, long before he ever joined the Centurions. It wasn't a big issue given Charles Drummond's later encounters with the law, but it was a breach of trust.

They had been standing around talking and drinking when Chas asked Seb about it. Chas was stocky but four inches shorter than his tall, young disciple. Within a few seconds Seb was making his apologies repeatedly as Chas went to a drawer and pulled out the knuckleduster. Seb stopped talking, looking scared as he realised he was in for it. But he made no effort to move away or leave.

Chas had said, "Seb, you take the hit or you walk out now. If you walk, never come back here. Don't ever be seen within viewing distance of the front door. Your choice."

"I'll stay; thanks, Chas, for giving me the chance."

He was almost begging for it.

Chas had first fitted the knuckleduster on his right hand then thought for a moment, looked at Leo and said, "Alright if I borrow Lyall?"

Leo had smiled and nodded. "Lyall, help the man."

Chas had taken the weapon and handed it to Lyall.

After the blow, Chas said softly, "It's going to hurt a lot for a good long time, Seb. It will constantly remind you. We don't talk about brothers out there, nor do we gossip about them and what they do in here. It's about respect."

He looked across to Leo. "Can Lyall take him - ," he pointed at Seb, "to the Middlesex? I don't want him to puncture a lung or do something stupid."

Leo was the perfect example of courtesy. "Of course. Lyall, go home and get the car. Take Seb to the hospital and make sure it's OK."

Lyall and Leo had ridden over to the clubhouse on their bikes. 'OK' meant that whatever happened at the hospital, the injury was recorded as no more than an accident.

When Lyall got back to take Seb to the North Middlesex Hospital, his friend was outside, alone, in tears, leaning against a wall. They hadn't thrown him out, for which he was grateful, but his shame was overwhelming him; inside he couldn't look them in the eye. On the drive to the hospital he couldn't stop talking, even though it increased the pain; he had been terrified of being exiled and discarded and remorseful about the way he had let Chas down. To be accepted as a patch Centurion had become his life; his dream, one he shared with Lyall.

"I could hear it break as he fell and hit the wall," said Lyall, talking to the triage nurse in admissions as his friend was having difficulty talking now.

Two days later in Brands Hatch, on a windy, cold day in early October, Leo had included Lyall in this meeting, his first serious business issue for the club. He knew it was linked somehow to 'The man from Norfolk' as Renée, Leo's wife, referred to him. Six months ago Leo had gone north to a town called Swaffham, Renée had said, and returned with several transport boxes, each with a painting. This was the second delivery. Leo and another patch, Henry, had delivered one painting to Harwich four months ago.

Today, Leo and Lyall were in dress-casual clothes, looking neat; no biker wear, Leo had said. In the hotel room Leo had greeted Gerda Lentz with a warm smile and a hug. Lyall, as he had been forewarned, shook her hand politely.

"My associate, Lyall Beddows. A prospect, a good one; so far."

Leo hadn't said anything before this about Lyall's status in the Centurions being upgraded but glanced at him to see the effect; the look of pleasure sweeping across Lyall's face. Gerda didn't miss it, either.

She admonished, "Look out for my good friend Leo, Lyall. He will look out for you, too. It's our way."

Lyall had been struck by the woman's excellent English, without any trace of accent. Leo had warned him. "She is German but speaks English and French fluently. You would never know."

Gerda was the wife of Oskar Lentz, Leo's opposite number. Leo was the president of the Centurions. Oskar was president of the Munich Demons, or München Dämon, a club fully affiliated with the Outlaws franchise worldwide. The

Outlaws, with the Hells Angels, constituted two of the largest, most organized and feared biker organisations around.

Leo placed the transport case on the table and opened it. "There you are. Amsterdam as it was, by Johannes Klinkenburg."

The older, silent woman in the room came forward ignoring him, picking up the painting, taking a first look. After a long half-minute, apparently satisfied with first sight, she stood it near vertical, resting against the back of the open transport case.

Gerda watched her then smiled. "So do you like the painting, Leo?"

"I don't give a rat's arse for it, Gerda; not my thing. It's just money to me, trading money."

Gerda laughed. Lyall thought they must know each other pretty well; he, after all, had been told to be polite and don't swear at all.

She replied, "It's Johannes with a soft 'J", like a 'y' at the beginning. You are no art expert, let's face it. Nor me. But my colleague is. Let's see if you have bought the real thing before I call Oskar."

The older woman was more interested in the painting than the people. She pulled out from her own solid-looking briefcase a fifteen-inch tablet computer, a flash unit of some sort, a slim tripod and a laser measure. By her efficient actions she obviously knew what she was doing with this mix, even if it mystified Lyall. Within a minute or so she had set up the computer on its stand and checked and adjusted carefully the distances between the corners of the painting and the corners of the computer. Lyall could see that she wasn't that worried about the precise alignment along the centre line of the painting but was ensuring that the two were in parallel as far as possible. She held the flash at an angle then pulled a small fob remote from her pocket. The flash triggered and the woman waited.

Lyall, curious, edged along the wall a little for a clearer view as Gerda said to him, "High-tech stuff, eh?"

He just nodded.

The first image on the screen was a photograph of the painting, but not taken in this room. It was on a wall, on display. Then a superimposed black and white skeleton of the image appeared. The woman pressed some soft keys on the computer screen and the images started moving, aligning and realigning. Finally they stopped and the woman looked carefully before resetting it again.

After three further flashes from different angles, three repeats of the process, she pressed other keys and they were left with a simple outline screen of fragments of the image, as if the original pencil or charcoal layout marks had been discovered. Along certain sections there were red lines, very thin generally but a little broader in places.

Gerda spoke in German to the woman whom, Lyall suddenly and belated realised, hadn't been introduced. Then she spoke to Leo, pointing at the screen.

"The red marks are deviations between the archive image that is our reference point and your painting."

"And?" said Leo, evenly.

Lyall was impressed by his patch's coolness under pressure. His own heart was pounding although he tried to hide his apprehension. He knew there was big money at stake. Stolen paintings used as transaction currency in the drug trade weren't small change items.

Gerda talked further with the woman, several interactions, with Lyall and Leo looking on, waiting.

"We accept it," Gerda said finally.

She pulled out her mobile, rang a number and spoke in German, listened, then closed the call.

"Five minutes. How is Renée?"

The older woman was packing up her equipment as Lyall watched Leo and Gerda socialize about their respective families.

"She still loves to bits your Princess Di, Leo?" Gerda asked.

Lyall was blown away by the juxtaposition of conversation about a dead princess in the middle of a deal like this. But almost by intuition five minutes later Leo pulled out his own mobile and made a call. Other than, "It's me," he listened.

"Great, 'bye," he said finally, before closing the call. He stood up straight and moved forward.

"We received the payment, thank you. Gerda, it is good to see you again - and do business with you and Oskar. I always liked the times at your clubhouse and your people. When we have a ride over in future some time…"

She laughed. "Leo, you liar! The Centurions never get past Brussels these days on their summer ride and you and Renée never come on to Munich. You should. Or make a separate trip. We will have a good time together; Oskar said I was to invite you."

She glanced at Lyall. 'Bring Lyall; he can meet some nice German girls!"

She winked at him and Lyall smiled.

Lyall nodded at the older woman who still said nothing to him and shook hands again formally with Gerda. Leo moved in and gave Gerda another hug. The German said, "One more thing; can you take the transport case back?"

Gerda moved to the closet and pulled out three bags emblazoned with 'Portobello Street Market'. Discarding a cheap framed tourist print into the expensive transport case, she nonchalantly transferred the Klinkenburg painting, wrapped in the market stall tissue paper, into the bag.

She put on a mock 'German' accent. "Now we German ladies go home with our shopping. We love your London markets and your funny policemen in their hats."

London sounded like 'Lon-done'. God help anyone who asks her about the purpose of her trip, Lyall thought. She would talk their hind leg off.

Leo just laughed.

Later, as they drove out of the hotel car park, Leo asked Lyall, "When they were talking, what was it about?"

"Gerda was questioning the differences between the two images, the red line areas she mentioned. The expert said it was minor, to do with the parallax issues of the different cameras used; they were consistent with others, in her experience, not troubling."

Why Europeans always assume that English people don't have other languages, I don't know, Leo thought. He had asked Lyall to accompany him primarily because he had spent time living in Germany in his early teens. And it gave him another chance to assess his new prospect. Lyall had done well.

"Fancy some lunch, Lyall?" Leo asked, knowing his acolyte would say 'yes' no matter what he felt like if he thought Leo was hungry. Leo knew a pub in Shooter's Hill which always had one or two Outlaws among the regulars. Better there than a place where he might inadvertently run into a Hells Angel. Not that there would be any bother, but the tension would give him indigestion. Leo was still fit but closer to fifty than any other milestone; not the young buck he used to be.

~~

Back in central London that lunchtime, Detective Inspector Catrin Sayer of the Metropolitan Police Art and Antiques Unit was buying lunch at The Queens Larder, a pub restaurant just south of Euston station.

Last week she had heard the news that Keith Marshall was leaving the Met. DI Marshall had taken a job with the Greater Manchester Police Serious Crime Division at the same rank, it was said. It had leaked through the grapevine out of the blue and had surprised her. Keith was one of the people in the Met she thought of as a permanent fixture.

It came on the back of similar news; there had been an official announcement that two senior Met officers she had worked with, Superintendent Jack Taylor and Assistant Commissioner Sandra Hunt, were also to retire soon. They had the years of service in place and there had been whispers beforehand about their planned departures. So that news was not much of a surprise. But Keith?

Sayer had joined the Met at age twenty-one after completing a Fine Arts and Art History degree at Aberystwyth University. Twelve years later it was hitting her that as her career developed, younger faces were arriving and older colleagues were leaving.

Marshall had been her first boss when she moved from uniformed duties with the drug squad in Brixton into a detective constable position at New Scotland Yard. He had taught her a lot. Keith wasn't ambitious, she knew; he just liked the work in the unit.

In Sayer's time in the little Art Crime Unit in Serious Crimes Command, she had risen to the rank of detective sergeant. After a subsequent stint as a uniformed security aide to Assistant Commissioner Hunt, she had received a promotion to her currently post with the prestigious Art and Antiques Unit in Specialist Crime Command, as head of the Art Team. There the focus was on major art crime, much of it with international links.

Time was passing. One day, she began to realise, it would be her turn to consider that path. But being three months pregnant now she had more imminent life events to consider.

She had heard Keith's news coincidentally when she was going to see his sister Liz, who owned the gallery that sold the art produced by Catrin with her friend Jean Hughes. Jean and Catrin had been friends since their schooldays in Pontypridd in South Wales. Over the years, Catrin, a ceramic decorator, and Jean, a talented potter, had worked together on original 'one-off' works.

For Jean, these were a counterpoint to the regular pottery lines sold at the boutique pottery in Spitalfields, the Cymbran Kiln, she owned with her wife and business partner, Melanie Farrell. Sayer-Hughes art now had the serious attention of a number of local and foreign collectors.

When Catrin raised tentatively the news about Keith, his sister was matter-of-fact about it.

"He has been with the ACU for a long time now. He needs a change. He told me about it last week."

She paused. "You know he had a bad time as an army officer earlier on, before he joined the Met? The UN Bosnia thing? He told me he discussed it with you back when he was your boss."

Catrin nodded.

"I think he realizes that he needs less pressure now, more time to himself nearer to where we both grew up. He wants to get out into the hills to enjoy the countryside up there and the new job will let him do that. The pressures will be different away from a job in central London."

Before Keith left, Catrin took him to lunch at 'The Queens Larder', the pub where they had first really talked to each other. They had only met once before that occasion and during that meal Marshall had been coaching her for a difficult interview; to get Superintendent Jack Taylor's buy-in for her to join the Art Crime Unit. She had chosen the location for the farewell meal to remind them both of times past.

Keith seemed quite at ease with his career change decision. At one point he said, "I don't think art crime will carry the same weight much longer in the priorities of the Met, despite Neville's success in asserting its economic importance. They need to beef up resources for counter-terrorism particularly, but everything is changing in policing these days; all this cybercrime, the rise in knife violence, the growth in gang culture. I want to go back north but I also want to stay ahead of the changes that I think may be coming."

Detective Chief Inspector Neville Coltrane was Catrin's boss, the head of the Art and Antiques Unit.

He added, "And you need to think about what you want to do, too!" Marshall glanced down at her stomach. Catrin wasn't showing really, but had made her pregnancy known to people at work only a week or so earlier.

She smiled. "Funnily enough, Chris and I are clear on that. After the birth and a little recuperation for me, Chris wants to take parental leave and look after our baby; then I will take mine after him. But after seeing our little one, if I can't be parted that soon or there are complications, we will switch timings. We have it all worked out, you see?"

Chris Treneer, her husband, was a civilian employee at the Met, a computer and e-crime specialist.

She added, "Then of course, with Melanie and Jean and their baby, Lili, we can start a crèche at the Kiln."

Melanie and Jean had married nearly eighteen months ago and Melanie had set out immediately to become pregnant. Liliwen, their daughter, was now four months old.

He smiled. "There goes the great creativity of the Sayer-Hughes art team; nothing will emerge for your fans to buy owing to the distractions of screaming babies in a pottery. I will tell Liz."

"She already knows and is starting to beat us both up."

Driving back after the meal Catrin thought Keith was being a little pessimistic. Of course the art investigation units of the Met were under budget constraints and headcount pressures. All specialist units were. The Met had to cope with the changes he had mentioned and more. Everyone knew it. Open positions were frozen and operating pennies were being counted.

But art crime was up there in the higher levels of economic crime in the UK and across Europe. They were all busy. It was leaner times than they had previously experienced but it couldn't get much tighter, she thought. It would all work out. They couldn't handle cases of the sort they had dealt with recently with anything less than the current team strength.

Despite her confident assurances that she and Chris had it all worked out, she was also nervous about the big changes about to occur in her life. She was sure that she wanted to be a mother and have children but unsure how everything would fit together. Sometimes it got on top of her.

She had no idea then of the much bigger heartache and challenges coming her way.

2 NORWICH CASTLE MUSEUM

Three weeks later, PC Melissa Nunn was over the moon despite another row with her partner Barry last night. She had arrived at work this morning self-absorbed and despondent, thinking about 'Bas'; that their relationship was going nowhere and she was in turmoil about what to do. The shift briefing was focused on the issues around the looming Halloween. Like any holiday, it had its own challenges for police officers.

At the end of the briefing she had been called in to see Inspector Golding. Melissa had passed her sergeant's exam; well done, Golding said. Now it was an issue of finding the right position. Golding said it would take a little time, but it would happen soon.

The Norfolk Constabulary is a county operation covering the northern half of East Anglia, responsible for policing an area of about two thousand square miles. Melissa knew that a new position with her promotion may not be based at her current location near Norwich, the police headquarters in Wymondham. Her assignments so far had been in community policing. Work in that field could base her at a number of police stations across the county. Thrilled with her result, she also realised it may be the answer to her relationship with Barry. They would need to face up to whether they wanted separate lives or to make sacrifices to be together.

On her return to her unit her own sergeant, an older man, gave her a smile and told her that they had heard the news that they were going to get rid of her at last. In the meantime would she deign to pop along to the Castle Museum? She was to see a Nicholas Taunton there, the director, regarding a report just in about a painting mix-up of some sort.

"See if it's worth bothering 'The Suits' about."

It was his nickname for any of the plain-clothes services across the county.

Melissa parried back. "A painting? Just up my street. I will call in JMIT and tell them you were ordering them to drop everything and head over to the castle."

The Joint Major Investigation Team, shared between Norfolk and the Suffolk Police, dealt with all major crimes in East Anglia; but a stolen or vandalized painting would probably fall below their radar.

His parting shot was, "Ever since that robbery at Halsting Hall you have had your eyes on art crime, so you may as well do this one. And a painting isn't going to interest JMIT unless its first name is Mona and its last is Lisa."

The Norwich Castle Museum and Art Gallery sits atop a central hill in the city. Built by William the Conqueror as a major fortification, these days it functioned as a museum and art gallery. The Norwich Registry Office was also located there, so as Melissa entered through the main visitor doorway there was a momentary hush in a small group in the foyer area. They were dressed to the nines and were in the midst of celebrating the initial aftermath of a wedding ceremony.

The appearance of police uniforms did that, she knew, so she smiled and said 'congratulations' to the couple being photographed as she passed. By the time she reached the reception desk the noise from the party had returned.

Melissa was led straight over to an inner office. Waiting there was Taunton, the young museum director. Melissa knew of him vaguely; he had been on Anglia Television a couple of times. Sitting across from him was a casually-dressed, slim woman in her forties, Melissa judged, with her backpack-style purse firmly placed on her lap.

"This is Miss Cartwright; she is an artist, I understand," he said. "We have a painting here she says is hers."

His tone of voice showed his disbelief at the woman's claim.

"We are waiting on Mrs. Cole to arrive, our curator of art; she is on her way in from Spixworth but Miss Cartwright insisted that it was a police matter. I invited her in for coffee so that other visitors weren't disturbed."

Melissa saw two coffee cups on the desk. The one in front of Cartwright had hardly been touched. The expression on the artist's face was somewhere between annoyance and controlled anger so coffee and a chitchat wasn't quite the order of the day, Melissa concluded.

So all she said was, "Miss Cartwright, what's this about?"

Cartwright responded tersely. "I am a professional copyist of paintings. And an art teacher. I live in Aldeburgh and I came back to Norwich today to see various works, including the original of one I copied some years ago for a client. Now I find my painting on the wall and the original is where, I asked? They won't tell me and insist that mine is the original. It isn't, so I wanted the police involved right away. I don't want any trouble regarding my art."

Melissa took a moment to work out the meaning of Cartwright's last sentence. If the painting on the wall was her work and the original was missing, Cartwright didn't want to be accused of involvement or collusion in a theft.

But in the last few years Melissa had met people who were absolutely sure of things that were untrue, some of whom were found to be in need of psychiatric help. Cartwright could be another one of them.

"Do you have a business card, Miss Cartwright?" she asked. It was a start.

Ten minutes later, after seeing the painting in the gallery

and asking them to wait, she went outside to her car. Spix-worth was a village a little north of Norwich and the curator had called saying she wasn't far away now. Having her there would be the next step but Melissa was intrigued by a comment Cartwright had made as they talked.

"If you want to check my *bona fide* call the Art and Antiques Unit at the Metropolitan Police in London. They will vouch for me."

Melissa knew that Catrin Sayer was now a detective inspector there. She had met the art detective during the Halsting Hall case that her sergeant had referred to earlier. Melissa was just out of training at the time but it was a day or two of relative excitement for her, assisting with an investigation of a theft of several paintings from the stately home. She looked up the contact number and gave the Art and Antiques Unit a call, asking for DI Sayer. She wasn't put through directly but after a short wait, a woman answered.

"DC Howlett, Art and Antiques. How can I help?"

Melissa told her who she was and explained that she wanted to know about a Sophie Cartwright, a copyist from Suffolk; was she genuine? Howlett told her to 'hold on' and a minute later a deep male voice came on the line.

"DC John Obi here. Why are you asking about Sophie Cartwright?"

Melissa explained briefly again, not wanting to give too much away; it wasn't her place to do so. But she described the woman to him.

He said, "Cartwright is the genuine article, as you describe her to me."

Melissa replied, "We are waiting for the art curator to appear, to sort it out. The museum director thinks she will convince Cartwright that it is all a mistake."

Obi's voice came back with his amusement undisguised. "That will be interesting for you to watch. Sophie isn't easily persuaded. Hang on, it's coming back. Nunn, weren't you the 'probie' with Catrin on the Halsting Hall investigation?"

Melissa beamed at the reference. "Yes, I was a probationer

then. That was partly why I called. I thought I could ask to speak to DI Sayer and catch up a bit. It's been a long time."

Her cheerful voice was a contrast to his guarded response. "Unfortunately, you can't - she's not here, she's on leave at present. There's a lot going on today."

Melissa said, "I'd better let you go then, thanks for the help."

It was only as she put the phone down she though that Obi wasn't clear about the sense of 'a lot going on'; she just assumed that they were busy.

Back inside the museum, she joined Taunton and Cartwright as a middle-aged, bouncy woman, Mrs. Roberta Cole, joined them. She was full of bonhomie and clearly keen to resolve the problem. Cole talked non-stop. They had a number of paintings by George Vincent, she said.

She explained, "Vincent was a nineteenth century landscape artist originally from Norwich. One item of our Vincent collection is currently undergoing restoration but this one, 'The Wherry on the Yare at Dusk' has been in place for a long while. I like it, as do many visitors."

She kept talking, pointing out the detail on the painting of the square-rigged sailing boat on the river as Cartwright appeared to change from frustrated annoyance to complete calm.

Cutting across the monologue, Melissa asked Cartwright if she knew DI Catrin Sayer, by any chance; another step in assessing this Suffolk woman.

"Oh, yes. She's very good. Do you know her?"

Melissa replied, "I worked with her once on a case, that's all."

Cartwright nodded then said, "Dr. Cole, if I could just point out one or two things."

Three minutes later, all geniality now evaporated and Taunton calling another staff member to move visitors out of this gallery, Cole was looking upset. Cartwright had finished her exposition on her ownership of the painting with a flourish. She handed the woman a magnifier taken from her purse, pointed to a particular spot, a section of a broken tree trunk on the river bank, and asked her to view it from the right hand side.

"What do you see; very small, in a paler brown, in this tree texture?"

"An 's'," Cole replied.

"S for Sophie. I still do that somewhere on every painting even though my copies are microchipped these days to stop their fraudulent use. So where is the original?"

Cole looked at the director and at Melissa.

"I wish I knew."

Melissa moved away to report in and have her unit call 'The Suits', as her sergeant put it. She hoped they would keep her involved as she would love to work on this one.

3 CAREERS

Earlier, in the funereal atmosphere of the room in New Scotland Yard, John Obi had put down the phone and said, "Looks like a painting has gone missing in Norwich; Sophie Cartwright visited the museum and spotted it."

None of the others present said anything.

Isabelle Howlett looked at Obi. Until that morning it would be a routine matter for the ACU to take note of; it would probably have crossed Obi's desk. Howlett knew the man had worked with Sophie Cartwright directly on a case previously.

But the Art Crime Unit no longer existed.

The team members of both the Art Crime Unit and the Art and Antiques Unit were waiting to hear their own future assignments. That, in itself, would be a major thing but not a complete disaster; roles changed regularly in the Met. The team leader of the ACU, DCI Worsley, had been transferred back to the Diplomatic Protection Branch first thing that morning, they had just heard. She was now in further meetings and hadn't appeared yet.

Around the same time the head of the Art and Antiques Unit, DCI Neville Coltrane, had also been called to a meeting and shortly afterwards he left the building. He was 'let go' according to the rumour now circulating the floors. Isabelle, for one, didn't believe it. She fully expected him to come in and sort out this fiasco.

Neither were Neville's two team leaders around. DI 'Kip' Madder, head of the Antiques team, was currently in a similar meeting telling him his future role and DI Catrin Sayer was in hospital. They all knew that the night before last she had been taken into the emergency unit at the Royal London, a hospital near her home. She had suffered a miscarriage and had lost her baby.

Isabelle looked at the clock; it was 11.40 a.m. They had just been told that a DCI Timothy Wetherby would be briefing them at noon. The only topic of conversation now was this man Wetherby; they were trying to find out more about him other than he was a borough copper from Camden.

No one wanted to talk about a painting that had gone missing.

Isabelle gave a big sigh. "I should have stayed in Paris," she opined to herself.

Obi looked questioningly as Detective Sergeant Mark Harper said to him, "She's going out with an FBI guy, Morley Kerswell, who she met there. They fell down the stairs together."

Isabelle retorted, "We were pushed down, you stirrer. Here in London, in a restaurant, not in Paris."

She looked at John Obi. "I met Morley at an Art Crime Task Force meeting in Paris. We are seeing each other. We went back to Paris last week."

She wasn't going to say more, all thought of their blossoming romance had been overtaken by the events of the day. Once she knew what was happening to her, though, she needed to talk to Morley.

Mark was about to comment further, a mischievous look on his face, when a door opened and the woman from Personnel popped her head in and smiled at them.

How can she smile, thought Isabelle?

"Could we see you now, please, DS Harper?"

Thoughts of more jibes about Paris left Mark's mind.

~~

On her return from the museum to the Norfolk Constabulary headquarters, Melissa Nunn was contemplating her own career change. Golding had called her back into her office.

"Great Yarmouth, That's what I think will work, Nunn, for you. For now or the longer term, if you take to it and it takes to you. It will get you out of headquarters and into a posting which is not in a backwater. It's busy as hell there with tourist issues and the Broadlands boating thefts; you won't be idle."

Inspector Golding had a gleam in her eye, pleased with the find for this personable young officer.

"It's Danny Johnson's old job but it has a young team now, mind. We put a temporary in to cover until Danny's retirement comes through; it's about timing, showing some respect."

Nunn nodded but said nothing. In her mind was the fact that Great Yarmouth was only a drive of forty minutes or so away. That may be easy stuff for commuters in the big cities but for her, she would talk to Barry; it was time.

The additional comment about the temp in place caught her attention. Dan Johnson had fallen from a ladder that he shouldn't have been on while doing DIY stuff at home. He wouldn't be coming back to active duty but the man was finding it hard to accept; he had been a copper all his life.

"I was wondering, ma'am, in the interim, if I could help out on this theft from the Castle Museum? I mean, I really like the idea of the posting and appreciate it. But I feel a little at a loose end at present in my current role now the news is out; not that I haven't got work to do."

Golding pursed her lips. "I don't think so. It's been assigned to JMIT, I just heard, to DI Needham and his team; and that includes DS Hollis. You don't want to be working with Ray Hollis I think, not after the Liddle issue."

The arrest two years earlier of a thief called Thomas Liddle had backfired in the media on the Norfolk Police; it had been a rough arrest during which children present were traumatised. Hollis had been part of the JMIT contingent and Nunn, a community officer, had been there during the aftermath. Nunn had formally complained to Golding at the time.

Melissa responded quickly. "But I can't tip-toe around people and be picky, ma'am. Part of this has to be taking the rough with the smooth. DI Needham is a good team leader, I think, from what I heard."

Golding's eyebrows rose at the response. She expected acquiescence, not a counterpoint. But as she thought about it, she realised it made some sense. At worst, it was not for long.

"A fair point. I'll think on it. No, I've thought. I will give DI Needham a call; if he agrees, you can play 'gofer' for his team for few weeks. But don't complain if you get cross-threaded with Hollis or that you find yourself in muck up to your elbows while they dig out someone found dead in a ditch."

~~

In the large room in New Scotland Yard, Isabelle had walked away to find a quiet spot to call her *beau* and let him know about the bombshell of the reorganisation. He was an early riser and would be pottering about at home in Washington DC.

"It's a right mess, Morley. After our decisions last week it has thrown me into a real spin. Part of me wants to walk out the door right now, tell Personnel to sort out my package and go home."

In Paris they had been planning their future. They had met there, as Mark Harper said, and for over a year and a half it had been a long-distance romance between London and Washington, punctuated by a holiday in the UK together and a visit by her to Washington DC; her first trip to the USA.

Isabelle had a lot of baggage from the break-up of her first marriage still to let go of; she was feisty and in her mid-forties but her personal life was sealed off from her work colleagues.

Morley Kerswell was in his early fifties. He had been in a heavy-duty role at the FBI before a breakdown from stress. The transfer to the FBI Art Crime Unit turned out to be the environment he needed. Their relationship had developed solidly, but not with any rush of impetuous decision-making.

On hearing the news and how upset she was, he said, "Let's see how it all unfolds first; there is no rush to do anything. With Catrin away now, the dust needs to settle a little, don't you think?"

Isabelle replied, "I care about Catrin, but don't know whether I care about the job any more. We've just been told we are to be lumped in with two other units; Stolen Vehicle Recovery and the Met Film Unit. Next thing you know I will be put in charge of a car pound or given the job of preening some Hollywood crew's security requirements while they are filming at King's Cross Station."

"And Mark?"

"Clearing his desk now. He is assigned to a task force on knife crime. And I am worried to death about Catrin. We had planned to go see her if we could sometime today. She doesn't even know, I suppose."

Morley's previous life had been an FBI investigator of contract killers. He had seen the blood and the heartache; too often it turned out, spending too much time with families at hospitals. Sayer didn't need the worry of this now, he knew.

"The most important thing for her is to get well; that's what counts," he said quietly but firmly.

"You are right, but I had better go; I'll call again later. This new guy DCI Wetherby has just arrived, I gather. We are going to get a briefing."

4 THE ROYAL LONDON

The women were handling it better than the men, overall; not that they all weren't devastated. Catrin's dad had left the hospital room shortly after her parents' arrival from Wales. He had walked around for fifteen minutes outside the Royal London Hospital, getting his emotions back under control after seeing his daughter looking so drawn and pale, overwhelmed that his dreams for his first grandchild were in tatters.

Catrin's husband, Chris Treneer, was silent and lost in his own thoughts when not focused on his wife's needs. Catrin's mother was fussing over her daughter unnecessarily, trying her best to help by keeping busy.

Catrin and her friend Jean had just called Melanie. Jean and Melanie would take Catrin's parents to their flat soon for a meal before they went back to their hotel to rest. They would visit again in the evening. Her parents lived in Pontypridd in South Wales and, although they had visited London quite a few times now, this wasn't the time to leave them on their own. They had arrived late yesterday after hearing the news that morning but hadn't slept very much last night.

Melanie was happy to help but had some misgivings, wondering whether her own new baby girl would be a comfort or a burden for them, a reminder of their loss.

All of them had held such high hopes for the future; for young families developing together.

Catrin was improving physically quite quickly despite an overwhelming sense of loss and fatigue. She had haemorrhaged badly during the miscarriage. Transfusions, rest and her general good health had been restorative but the efforts in the ambulance and the time in the ER unit had taken its toll. She had slept a lot during the first day in hospital and actually had a good night's sleep last night. Her doctor had said that if she improved she could be discharged tomorrow or the day after; good news before the bad, really.

She also told Catrin and Chris that she would refer her case to Dr. Toth, a specialist obstetrician at the Royal.

"Two miscarriages without a clear basis for the loss is the point where I think you need to see a specialist, Catrin. We have to do what's best for you and that is what I recommend."

Neither Chris nor Catrin had mentioned to anyone other than her doctor that this was her second miscarriage. The first one occurred shortly after she had first become pregnant; within no time at all, it seemed, after first trying for a baby. Her doctor had told her that such an early miscarriage was a more frequent occurrence than people really recognized but women often had successful pregnancies shortly afterwards, so they tried again. They had kept that first loss to themselves.

But, after a second 'miss' now, later in her pregnancy, they had told their family and friends. The sense that the problem was possibly more serious overshadowed everyone.

For a short time in the early afternoon Chris and Catrin were alone and glad for the quiet so they could rest. Then Chris took a call from the office while Catrin was dozing and he walked outside to the corridor to talk. When he came back Catrin roused, looking at him questioningly, reading his expression.

"It was my boss. I have just been promoted, I gather. I have my own team. We didn't talk long; he just sent his sympathies and best wishes, telling me to take all the time we need."

Normally he would be overjoyed with such news, Catrin thought, but Chris looked somewhere between baffled and upset. It was just all too much, she concluded. She smiled supportively and then the smile left her face as he spoke again.

"Big changes at the Met have been announced today; it's a major reorganization. CTC is beefed up considerably, Trident has more people and so has the violent crimes lot, but the specialist crimes areas have taken some significant hits, he said. So I asked about your area."

Trident was the organized crime section of the Met. CTC was Counter Terrorism Command. Catrin could see he didn't know how to handle it.

"My area?"

"The Art Crime Unit in Serious Crimes is disbanded. Specialist Crimes Command is changing, too. The Art and Antiques Unit has been restructured and mixed in with others under one DCI, a man called Wetherby. And Neville is out, is the rumour, but no one knows exactly the circumstances yet. It's not been verified."

She was stunned to silence in disbelief but the news brought her fully awake. A few seconds later she pulled out her own phone and dialed a number. After holding for a minute and being transferred she talked to someone, Chris heard, asking what had happened. At the end all Catrin said was, "Thanks, I appreciate it. I was just getting some energy back but this... Could you ask Isabelle or Mark to give me a call when they can?"

Then she put the phone down. "They are all in a briefing and meetings, Vicky said. It's a real mess. Vicky can't tell me anything other than there is a message from Bob Matheson for me, to be passed on when I returned home or whenever I called. I am OK in the reorganization and I shouldn't worry or try to return earlier than I need to, it says. Chief Superintendent Matheson is changing too, now taking over Hendon and all the Met training oversight."

She paused, absorbing her own words, "Vicky is at her wit's end; there is so much change going on."

Victoria Camberwell had been the administrative assistant to DCI Coltrane; until today. She had told Catrin that she had already been transferred.

She looked at Chris. "We just have to wait, to see what happens; I'll try to find out more from Isabelle or Mark when one of them calls me. Or, you could phone your people. I'll try to reach Neville on his personal mobile or home number."

Chris had been looking out into the corridor.

"Perhaps you don't have to. There is a giant bunch of flowers advancing down the hallway with what I think is Neville Coltrane behind and a woman with him; it's Sylvia McNair by the description you gave me some time ago."

McNair was Coltrane's partner.

Chris's voice was leaden; it really was all too overwhelming.

It was indeed Neville Coltrane. The couple came in and after introduction of Chris and Sylvia to each other there was a moment's silence. Coltrane was as well-dressed as ever but his face looked like he had been at an all-night party. It has hit him hard, Catrin realised. Then she saw reflected in his expression the fact he was thinking the same thing about her own ordeal.

McNair broke the silence by pointing to the flowers now resting on the bed saying, "Neville ordered them by phone for us to pick up and he got carried away, I think. But we had to come. We are so sorry for your loss."

Both Catrin and Chris said, 'thank you'. It wasn't the first time today they had acknowledged such sympathy but they still didn't know how to handle it easily. However, Catrin wasn't having any small talk. She asked softly, "What happened, Neville?"

He smiled, more a grimace than a smile, "I wanted to come earlier, I was worried about you and - it has been a day of problems - ."

He stopped.

Chris said, "I had a call. I've been promoted. I didn't know what to say and probably sounded ungrateful, but we are start-ing to hear that there have been big changes."

McNair was a 'take charge' sort of person. She was the director of The Fens Trust, a Wetlands protection charity. She said to Chris, "I am surprised you can talk at all. I couldn't put two words together in a situation similar to yours."

McNair had been widowed some years before she met Neville.

He's lost a baby and is worried to death about his wife, she thought, looking at Chris. She saw him glance at Catrin and Neville, not knowing where to begin. So she took his hand in both of hers, to focus him. "Let's leave them a minute to talk; we can go and have tea or something, shall we?"

Chris nodded and she led him out of the room, talking all the time.

Coltrane said, "The only good news on this dark day, Catrin, is you are looked after, I promise you. Hunt fixed it, Matheson told me. She left, too; she was only weeks off retirement, as you know. You are marked as 'fast track' and have everything going for you in your career. I know it's not the time with your own loss and it seems so *gauche* to talk about it now but... you are OK career-wise. The fit they have for you is in Trident, a lateral move into organized crime and six months from now you will be a DCI. Whoever talks to you won't say it as more than a possibility but it's solid, I know. It will all sort itself out."

He made it sound upbeat and even smiled at her; not his normal smile, she saw, but he was making a big effort.

Catrin said nothing for a moment then looked down at the bed, at the bouquet, taking in the different flowers in the arrangement before she spoke.

"'But', Neville. There's a 'but' in there."

"It's the best possible career progression -"

She looked at him and smiled. "But? Come on, spit it out."

"Well, in a few days, when you are up and around, we should have lunch or dinner and -"

Catrin lost it. "For God's sake, Neville, you are worse than my Aunt Eira about hiding what you want to say - outside an interview room, I should add. I have worked with you for years. What?!"

She lay back heavily into the pillows. The energy needed to register her annoyance had worn her out. Coltrane relented, speaking quickly.

"If you choose to stay in Art and Antiques it will mean no promotion for sure in the current climate. A backwater; a limited budget, no more of - what I did. It will be 'coordinate, liaise, be an expert resource'; no funds or mandate for your own separate investigations. But you have the job if you insist on it; to be head of Art and Antiques. It will all be said as an obviously less attractive option. They know you'll jump at the Trident opportunity and part of me hopes you do."

He paused, "And part of me hopes that you don't. Lousy advice from me I didn't mean to give. But, Catrin, you are - ."

He stopped himself for a moment.

"From the time we talked about the Garin painting on the first day we met I had my eye on you; you have it. David, Gerhardt, Vittorio; we talk about you being one of us, a top league art crime detective. People in our line of work… it's a truly small group. It sounds arrogant and elitist, I know, but it's the way it is - or was for me until today. Selfishly, selfishly, I am hoping you will stick it out, weather the storm of change and keep Art and Antiques… meaningful."

David Klintz; head of the FBI Art Crime Unit. Gerhardt Amsel with the German counterpart agency and Vittorio Cuoco in Rome, who had, years ago, introduced her to the Borghese Museum there. These were men, like Coltrane, with international reputations as detectives in the world of art crime; people she had only known by those reputations previously. And they talked about her this way, she had just been told.

Catrin replied, "I lost my baby, Neville; not my senses. I wondered why you were blathering on about me moving to Trident. My turn, what did they do to make you leave?"

He seemed relieved by Catrin's reply and then his face fell.

"They offered me a promotion to superintendent, with fair

options, actually. 'Number Two' in Kingston-on-Thames. 'Back in uniform, big team management, a nice borough'; quote. Or similar in Greenwich as an alternative. But it had to be mainstream community policing; I had been away too long from anything like it, they felt, and if I was to rise further in the Met I needed that front-line experience. My current post was gone; there is no DCI level in the new structure for Art and Antiques, as I said. It's smaller; 'compact' was the word used. It will liaise with operating units only.

"I said 'no, thank you' immediately, which didn't go down well at all. And so that was it; severance after seventeen years. But it was my choice, in the end."

He paused. "It's not like I needed to worry about the income, so it's not the same as for others."

Coltrane came from wealth; large enough to spawn a family-owned charitable art institution, the Coltrane Foundation.

He looked at Catrin, blinking back something. "It's why you need to make the right decision for you; why I shouldn't have told you what I did. Chris is promoted, I just heard; it could be good for you, too. I know what you said, but please don't do the loyalty trick in the heat of the moment; I'm gone. Don't let me bias that decision. I was just being honest, which is what you were asking me to be."

Catrin responded, "I won't. I spent two years as Sandra Hunt's aide, remember? I was seeing Met policing from the level of an Assistant Commissioner, so I have more insight than most. I'm sure what they are thinking about will be a good challenge, well thought out. But it's not about the good jobs out there; it's about what I want to do."

He nodded, seeing that she was working it through. "Fair enough. But get yourself back on your feet first before you decide. Take your time and think it through - you are on medical leave, remember?"

Catrin said firmly, "I don't want to work in Trident, with DCS Moore. Or Commander Barlow."

Neville smiled. "You wouldn't be - exactly. It's Commander

Moore now. And Barlow is moving - developing a brand new area embracing all digital and electronic crime across the Met. In his new role, Chris will be part of Barlow's group now."

5 KOWLOON

On this rare occasion, taking a complete weekday afternoon away from his shop, Daniel Yeung had grabbed a taxi to travel from Connaught Road in Hong Kong across to Kowloon to his church rather than drive himself. It was cold for Hong Kong and raining; the roads would be slow with dense traffic. The tops of the taller buildings on either side of Victoria Harbour had disappeared into the thick grey cloud. Taxis always seemed to negotiate such traffic better than he did on days like this.

Daniel co-owned Coulter & Yarrow, a tailoring business. He had a silent partner, the offspring of one of the original owners, but Daniel had managed the enterprise for many years. His business, his family and his church were his life experience.

Today, he was meeting with Reverend Kwan. No church was without its problems and, even allowing for the current set of stewards, Kwan appreciated the advice of church elders. So it was a surprise as he entered the building to catch sight of his daughter Jian Li in the worship space, sitting on a chair in a row near the back and appearing to be praying; he hadn't expected her to be there. Although she had grown up in this Methodist community and had more recently married there, she was no longer a regular churchgoer.

She was a busy lawyer, a specialist in maritime law working for a large mercantile fleet operation based in Hong Kong, so he knew his daughter should be at work today. Only last night, at the regular Wednesday evening dinner she and her husband had with her parents, she had said how busy the remainder of the week was for her.

There were several other people seated further forward also praying. Conscious of the peace of the worship space yet intrigued by his daughter's presence, Daniel walked slowly up the centre aisle then waited until she sensed his presence. She looked up and he saw the tears, so he beckoned her out to the foyer to find out what was wrong.

"I was in a business meeting on Austin Road. An email came in from Chris, Catrin's husband. She is in hospital; she had a miscarriage. It was such a shock, so I phoned James and came here. But why aren't you at work?"

James Hoi was her husband.

Her father replied, "I have a meeting here with Reverend Kwan then I have my regular time at Shep Kip Mei Street with Enlai and Michael. But that is such sad news. I am so sorry for them - and for you, such a sudden blow."

Jian Li went on, "Chris's email said Catrin lost a lot of blood and is in hospital; she went in yesterday. It is best if he lets me know when I could call, he said; they are both in shock, of course. I have spoken to Jean, though; she is over there now at the hospital. I feel so far away, but she will keep me informed."

Jian Li and Catrin had been friends for a decade, having met at the time of another tragedy, the disappearance of Li's older brother, Han, in Wales. He had been a cruise ship officer and, while in the port of Holyhead for the day, he had gone for a bicycle ride from which he never returned. Catrin had been part of the investigative team that led to the arrest of the people responsible for Han's death; it was her first assignment as a detective constable.

Daniel knew that his daughter and son-in-law were

contemplating having a baby themselves. Catrin Sayer's pregnancy had seemed such a happy development between the two women, a precursor to Jian Li's own expectations. The realities of life at times came out of nowhere to hurt the young, he thought. And not so young, he then realised, thinking of Han.

His mind suddenly moved to the fact that his daughter chose to come to the church at this time and somehow it seemed a brighter facet of dark news, that she sought solace here. It was at that moment Reverend Kwan came into the building and, after being apprised of the situation, said to both of them, "Why don't we go into my office and I will make some tea?"

On seeing the expression on Daniel's face, he added, "I think we can leave our meeting to another time, Daniel."

He was a priest; pastoral care was a greater priority than church administration plans.

~~

It was later the same afternoon after Jian Li had returned to work that Daniel met with his two friends at their regular, some would say ritual, location; the Shep Kip Mei Street bathhouse. In a well-appointed private room there they had been meeting weekly for many years; 'to talk just as men, but not about business matters'. Daniel had been told this when invited to join these two very different men. By now, of course, it was a meeting of old friends.

Daniel always enjoyed the first moments in the hot water of the communal bath; his leg damaged years ago when he worked as a fireman always seemed to benefit from this weekly treat. They talked of families and life so it was no surprise to the other two when Daniel said, "I just came from an unexpected meeting with Li; she was at church, upset; she had just had news that her friend in London, the police officer, had a miscarriage."

At times like this as each man shared their thoughts there was little polite solicitous response. After a moment, Enlai Lin, now retired from LinTan Shipping, the business where Jian Li worked, said, "Did you call Eu-Meh and tell her?"

Daniel's wife was as devout as him or, in a sense, moreso. It irritated Enlai a little that Eu-Meh would talk incessantly about 'God's hand in everything'.

Daniel nodded. "She is praying for Catrin and Chris, and Jian Li - and is also thankful that Li went to church in her moment of need."

Enlai thought, why am I not surprised?

The third person present, Michael Yau, said nothing. His mind was on the fact that, although he had only met this woman Sayer twice briefly, their lives had also intertwined during the years of the friendship between the two women.

Sayer had been instrumental in saving Li from injury or death in Wales. That situation had arisen unexpectedly from Yau's effort to clear Han Yeung's name in a crime associated with his disappearance. Some years later, Michael had intervened at Li's request during a reprisal threat to Sayer from a Triad member in Malaysia. That they were linked in a sense of *guanxi*, the invisible networks of people supporting each other, still surprised him. After all, she was a Metropolitan Police officer in London and he had retired from the role of White Paper Fan, the administrative mastermind of a Hong Kong-based triad called Four Square. Organized crime bosses in Hong Kong and British police officers didn't exactly have a lot in common.

He suddenly felt for the woman, the blow of losing a child. *Guanxi* has a strange effect on people, he thought.

Enlai suddenly said, "You are very quiet, Michael; even for you."

Yau sat forward in the bath disturbing the flow of the bubbling water.

"Hai is changing the name of this place to something with the word 'spa' in it, he decided. To get more of the younger clientele in."

Hai Lei was officially the owner of the Shep Kip Mei Street Bathhouse; he had been there ever since Daniel first attended and had seemed a fixture. It took a long time for him to clue in that it was owned mainly by Michael and one of his triad partners.

Michael paused. "And Jei-Jei retired last week. She gave the best foot massage of all of them."

This was news but not a new claim. Daniel and Enlai had sat in robes on many occasions after the bath listening to the woman perched on a low stool working away at Yau's feet, all the time beating up on her boss's boss to look after his feet more carefully. She was the same age as him, they knew, but she treated him like an errant son.

Then Michael added, "I saw my doctor; he is doing tests but it is not good news, I think. He and I have known each other for many years."

"You are ill?" asked Daniel, automatically. Enlai was looking hard at Michael, sensing the truth. He had noticed that the small man had been losing weight in the last few months.

"I am old; at least this body is, Daniel."

As Daniel realised and his expression changed Michael Yau reached over and touched his arm.

"It's what your God is for, right? We all have to face our destiny."

Enlai said more positively, "Perhaps the tests will be better news; they can do so much these days. How is your family coping?"

Yau said, "They don't know yet; I just came directly from the clinic to here and had my regular lunch in the White Moon before our meeting. I am hoping you two will help me find the right words."

He looked at Enlai's concerned face and his friend Daniel, eyes closed and now praying, seeking input from his god.

Enlai though that today was focused too much on death.

6 REORGANISATION

The following morning before being discharged from the hospital, Catrin called Isabelle Howlett at home early. "Tell me the best first. Brighten my morning."

"Well, I'm still here, ma'am. How are you? We were waiting to see when we could come and see you; that's why I didn't call back. But you have heard, I gather."

"I'm radiant about that; that you are still there, I mean. The rest, it's getting used to the loss... and now this lot, while I am away. The sods. I am a mess, to be honest."

"You should be, it's natural. We are all thinking about you, though. People keep asking me."

"So any other bright spots in this reorganization?"

"We got Aina. At least she knows the work. She thinks the world of you, you know that."

Aina Jinnah had been the Administration and File Officer with the Art Crime Unit. Catrin knew her well and liked her.

"So the Art Crime Unit has gone?"

"Gone completely, Catrin; the work is rolled in with us in part, but mainly devolved to the boroughs. Any support for other policing areas in the UK is to be resolved after current commitments are met. We have Aina and John Obi transferred to us. Jane Worsley is back in Diplomatic Protection. The boss has gone. Vicky is transferred to another DCI."

Catrin butted in, "You haven't mentioned Mark yet."

"Mark is a lateral to Territorial; some cross-borough team dealing with knife crime issues, a bit rougher than his past experience, he said. He wants to talk to you when you are well, to close out properly. But it's a good opportunity for him, he thinks. He starts there this morning.

"Most of the Antiques section has been split among other areas, also spread across the boroughs, like I said. Kip Madder has moved to Fraud. A DCI Tim Wetherby, a long-time borough man, briefed us yesterday afternoon. He is our new boss.

She added sarcastically, "Apparently antiques are just 'old stuff' and boroughs deal with theft of 'stuff' every day. Art, though, is a bit more complicated; there needs to be a small expert unit to advise the front-line coppers. And antiquities, we have that also, I think. He wasn't too clear on that point, to be honest. Liaise and coordinate, he said."

"So is there a name change, if Antiques is out?"

"Catrin, we are still the same name, apparently; if we can't get clarification on what the 'muckety mucks' consider to be antiques and antiquities, we just keep our current name, I gather; Aina asked the same question."

Catrin was taking it all in, seeing the new scenario unfold. Isabelle rushed on, wanting to get it all out.

"Laura was let go, as well as DCI Coltrane, although hers was a retirement push. But that one was funny."

Laura Bainbridge had been in Art and Antiques as a civilian support staffer for years. She was an expert philatelist, well regarded in the circles involving rare and valuable stamps and related collectables.

"How?"

"She showed me an email from Frank Connor at Stanley Gibbons offering her a job there right away, if she was free. They contacted her the minute the news about Art and Antiques broke. She starts a week on Monday at a salary a good bit bigger than she is getting here. Apparently the woman from Personnel was very solicitous with her, talking on about Laura's need to enjoy retirement. Laura strung her along mercilessly, she said."

"And the leader of this new, compact Art and Antiques Unit?"

"A DI rank, they said, unannounced. But you must be lined up for something else that's good, I am sure."

"Why?"

"When DCI Wetherby briefed me personally, as he did everyone after the announcement, he said the new boss would need to rely heavily on my considerable expertise."

Catrin said, "Well, I do already, don't I?"

"The impression I got was the new DI would be pig ignorant about art crime but well in with the powers-that-be. On the second count, I think you are in good shape but on the first you fail miserably. But how's the boss? Have you talked to him? We are all worried."

"Neville came to see me yesterday afternoon. Yes, we talked. He is knocked sideways, I would say, although he didn't say that. But he will come through, as will we all. You keep your nose clean until I get back."

"Back?" There was a note of surprise and pleasure in the one word.

"Wait and see how I survive my first conversation with... whomever. We'll see."

~~

Four days later Catrin reported herself fit for restricted duty. She was sent to a different floor where she had two meetings before Tim Wetherby showed her into the new office area on Floor Seven allocated to Art and Antiques. He called the small team together; it was still sorting itself out after the move.

"I am pleased to say that DI Sayer has been appointed to the position of head of the reorganized Art and Antiques Unit. We could not announce it, of course, until she had returned to work. I am sure you will give her your full support."

He didn't sound too convincing, or even make the effort to do so, Isabelle thought. We will give her more support than the one lined up for the job, she said to herself quietly.

When he finally left and Catrin had closed the door she began with, "We all know each other; at least I have worked with you all at different times. So the truth is, before you each ask me separately and delicately, I am a mess; still struggling. But work will help me, so that's the main reason I am back so early. I may not be on an even keel for a while, so bear with me. We have a job to do and we'll do it well, despite all the upheaval. No moaning and groaning about what just happened; we just get on with it. Right?"

It was John Obi who said, "Bite our heads off, boss; we are just happy to see you back."

Catrin felt numb still; not from her loss; her emotions there were so overwhelming it was an issue of keeping control. Rather, it was from the experience this morning. It brought home her first reaction; how could they do this? We had good teams doing useful, necessary work. How could they?

She saw a similar numbness in the eyes of her team remnants, hidden by the need to try to be positive. And she was their team leader, who needed to get them out of their despondency.

"So take me through what we have on our plate right now. I will be meeting later with DCI Wetherby and his other DI's to see what lies within our new scope. As far as we can, let's sort through this and set our own priorities."

They set to work. Doing that was normal, therapeutic - and not only for Catrin.

~~

Once they had been through the work assignments Catrin retreated to her office and called her husband.

"Well, I'm through the first round, back in Art and

Antiques. It was as Neville said, they assumed the Trident post would pull me; I just had to sit it out. They weren't too pushy and were trying to be considerate. I don't exactly look as if I am one hundred percent; they saw that. But I'm through and I have Aina, Isabelle and John as my team; they are getting into the work now."

Chris said, "Well, that's sorted; it's been on your mind. We'll meet at lunch; see how you are then. You can always take off early, I'm sure, if you get too tired."

She responded, "There's a raft of stuff for me, too. We'll see how it goes."

"So this DCI Wetherby?"

"He seems OK; I see him for a session with his other two team leads this afternoon. He reports to Patterson, who reports to Moore. She's out today, they said, breathing fire on people at the Home Office apparently, doing her Smaug act. I'd better get to it. See you later."

She called Mark Harper first. He had been on her team for over two years but part of the Arts and Antiques Unit for longer.

"How's it going?"

"Different. How are you, though, ma'am? I heard you were back today and I was planning to call when I got a minute free."

"Struggling, as I told the team. But focusing on work helps. I think it's the same for Chris, a sense of getting back to normal things. And how about your new role?"

"I've quite a bit to learn. Remember our discussion at my last performance review? About needing to broaden my experience? Well, it happened, whether I wanted to do so now or not. I am staying positive. It's not about art; it's about the culture of young gangs and knives. Some of them have quite ornate Japanese knives and swords. It's more like Kurosawa's 'Seven Samurai' in this new job."

It sounds as if he was trying to convince himself as much as her, she thought.

"It's the only way, Mark. Although I would talk more about Mutant Ninja Turtles than art films with your new lot, if I were you. Look, we should get together sometime with Isabelle; go the pub, reminisce and get you two merry."

He laughed. "But not you, ma'am?"

"I'm the perennial designated driver; you know that. I'll eat, build up my strength."

Catrin didn't drink alcohol. Her mother was a recovered alcoholic. The worst times of that experience were in Catrin's teens. She thought she was too like her mother and didn't want to go through that experience herself.

She didn't get the chance to call Jane Worsley; her first boss as a detective turned up at her door, entered and shut it firmly behind her.

"You are here; I just heard. What the hell are you doing coming back off medical leave so soon, to this mess?"

Catrin gave her a weak smile. "Work takes my mind off... Thank you for the flowers and the note. It was really good - and helpful - to read it. You know, I still remember you taking me to lunch in Bangor after I did my first autopsy attendance. You have a way of brightening my day. How's the new job?

"Familiar, like I am back where I was before SIS screwed up my life. Some of the same people, lots of new ones, too much to do, remembering things I thought I had forgotten. At least I don't have to worry about art any more. Anyway, we are going to lunch to talk; that's why I am here."

Catrin replied quickly, "I can't; it's only - ." She looked at the clock. "11.44. I have a meeting with DCI Wetherby at 1.30."

Worsley blinked, thrown, it seemed. But she opened the door and called, "Aina!"

The administrative assistant came running, all smiles to see her former boss.

"Hi Jane. You need something?"

"DI Sayer is coming with me on an important and urgent liaison meeting with Diplomatic Protection Branch, right now.

Sort it; we'll be back before two."

Aina smiled. "Diplomatic, boss; you call that diplomatic, on her first day back?"

"I have every confidence in you. Catrin, get your coat. We have a lot talk about."

Catrin said, as she stood, "Aina, call my husband first, will you? Tell him I've been kidnapped. The only bright spot is I expect to have better food than he is going to have in the cafeteria."

They had lunch in a small restaurant inside a hotel near Lennox Gardens. Catrin hadn't been there before. At one point Worsley said, "Now, about your new boss."

She stopped and stared at Sayer waiting for a comment or a question.

Catrin thought about it. "You know him? I only met him this morning. A Camden Borough man, I was told, brought in to manage the 'odds and sods' department; Arts and Antiques, Stolen Vehicle Recovery and the Met Film Unit. They have nothing in common with each other except nobody wants them. And you are threatening to make me late for my first proper meeting with him."

Jane laughed. "He knows we were having lunch. He is from the Camden lot; born and bred there; joined up and worked two other boroughs before he went back. Along the way he became a DS, then DI and finally DCI a year ago. He didn't ask for this, either, so give him a break.

"He's a cautious man; not like Neville or me. Remember coming into the Yard to join ACU? How different that was for you? You think it is because you were young. Partly true; but not totally. He has to settle in, find his feet."

Catrin smiled. "You seem to know a bit about him; how come?"

"I would point out to you, a Welsh stranger who knows a little of Brixton and Lambeth and nothing else of the great city of London other than a potter's shop in Spitalfields, that Camden Town is across Regent's Park from my DP stomping ground. We ran across each other from time to time in the past. Just work.

"After the debacle which threw me out of DP the first time, while I was waiting at home to find out my future, only five people called me. Three were my team members; another, bless his silk socks, was Neville after he heard I had been shunted off to the Art Crime Unit. He wanted to let me know he would work with me, a bit like the king talking to the cat, I thought. But he was gracious about it.

"But the fifth was Tim Wetherby, sorry to hear that we wouldn't be 'overlapping' on our beats and wishing me the best. He wasn't critical of the Met, just polite and considerate. It wasn't much, but in the sea of people I knew, he was one who didn't treat me like a leper. So give him some time."

~~

Across London, Lyall and Seb were at the Centurions' clubhouse, talking. It seemed weeks ago now since Seb had turned up at his first meeting after the rib incident, looking apprehensive. Chas had treated him just like always, as had the others. The message was, 'you screwed up but you took you punishment without bleating about it. Move on.'

Since then it had been OK. But Lyall wasn't convinced that Seb had learned his lesson. His friend's next comment just validated his concern.

"What was it like? Doing the deal at Brands Hatch?" Seb asked, out of the blue.

If Lyall had learnt anything, it was not to gossip about his patches or the club business.

"It went down fine. Leo is really cool under these situations."

He said no more, despite the expectant look on Seb's face. Then the tall 'hangaround' caught on. He wasn't getting any more.

Lyall smiled. "If you don't want the other rib taped up you will need to remember; mouth shut."

"They weren't taped; I was just on painkillers."

But Lyall wasn't listening closely. His eyes were on Leo, talking with several patches. He caught the words, "Renée heard it. Hadn't heard from him in a while. Cancer they say, but somehow Norfolk's finest are on to him. We need to watch out."

It was something to do with 'The man from Norfolk' then. Therefore, it had to do with paintings and deals. Whatever it was, Lyall wasn't going to ask and if he was told, he wouldn't be passing anything on to Seb.

7 CORMORANT WELLMAN

It was the following day when Catrin found time to return the call to Melissa Nunn in Norwich; her message was way down the priority list. John said that he had already answered Nunn's question. When Catrin got to it she still wanted to touch base with the woman, at least. They had worked together years ago for only a couple of days but had got along well. She wondered how the former probationer had fared now she had some time under her belt.

By now the Norwich painting issue may well have resolved itself, Catrin thought. It would probably be one of those 'the left hand not knowing what the right hand had been doing' mix-ups.

After catching up on their respective career changes and turning to the reason for the call, Nunn said, "I am in transition, as I said, so I am working temporarily with the JMIT team this week and next. It's funny that you called now; DS Hollis is currently heading over to Swaffham to visit the person who commissioned the copy from Sophie Cartwright. It's been days since the report was filed with them and, apart from verifying what I had already established, nothing has been done, I gather. They have been busy with more important cases.

"But that artist Sophie Cartwright knows her stuff and she is very assertive. It was clear that she knows you."

Cartwright had been engaged by Art and Antiques some years earlier to make a copy of a painting stolen in a bank robbery.

Catrin replied, "Oh, we know Sophie; she is very competent but a bit of a bear with people."

Melissa continued, "They have to interview her further, of course. But DI Needham wants to leave that until after they have talked to this man Brian Sleaman. He commissioned the copy, so he may be involved somehow even if he isn't the perpetrator of the theft."

"What do you know about him?"

"Nothing much. He's a retired engineer; has no criminal record, never brought any complaints to us that we are aware of and he has no on-line presence. Older people often don't, do they? I am just pulling it back up… He retired early, sometime last year, I see, and he is now fifty-nine. He used to work for a company called Cormorant Wellman Technologies Ltd. No doubt DS Hollis will find out more."

Melissa expected that would close out the call; DI Sayer was a busy person, she could tell.

What she got was a moment of silence then Sayer said, "Melissa, give your DS Hollis a call if he isn't there yet. Cormorant Wellman is not an easy company to find out much about. It's an engineering firm, that's true. One of its lesser known divisions is as a principal supplier of specialized security equipment to art galleries and museums. It may not be flagged as that in your files but we have had contact with them in the past. Not any flags of criminal concern, but they have been brought in after thefts to put in new security systems. They are top notch."

The significance of Sayer's information hit Melissa. "This could be a lot bigger than one painting in Norwich, from what you say. I will call him right now."

After they closed the call Catrin thought she should brief

DCI Wetherby; it would help her assess how much the world of Art and Antiques had changed.

Her new boss said, "It may just be a one-off, Sayer. Even if this man had access to the security system at Norwich Castle museum, that may be the scope of it. It's premature to get involved further. Besides, aren't we in 'workload elimination' mode? You and I spent an hour yesterday agreeing what would be dropped and what would be continued, given the limited resources. That is the expectation, surely?"

He sounded reasonable, she thought; avuncular. She sensed beneath his pleasant, persuasive manner there was a rigor; it was his way or the highway. Arts and Antiques was one of three diverse support units he had responsibilities for now. Wetherby had no specific feel for the work of the Art and Antiques specialists at all.

"We will wait to hear further then, sir."

Neville would have been all over this one, she thought.

Later wasn't much later, it turned out. And it wasn't a DS Hollis that called Catrin; it was a Superintendent Edward Lubbock, the Norfolk lead in the East Anglia JMIT.

"This Castle Museum theft has taken on a much larger significance, DI Sayer, beyond the borders of our operation for sure. Let me brief you and see whether you can help us further with this, if possible."

Catrin smiled to herself. "Certainly, sir; but could I bring in my boss DCI Wetherby, if he is free? It may expedite things."

"Given your restructuring, I take it you mean? You have my sympathies. Call me back at this number, if you would, but within the half-hour. Before the media make a meal of it."

"Media?"

"This one could be a case similar to your friend Green-halgh, only different. Shaun Greenhalgh forged art in his home that fooled the major experts before he was arrested by Art and Antiques, if I got it right. It made all these experts look stupid, right?"

She replied, "It was before my time here, but he certainly

fooled a lot of people, sir; he even wrote a book about it."

Lubbock continued, "Well, if I am sensing this correctly, Brian Sleaman has done something along the same lines. Not made the forgeries himself, I think, but I suspect that there may be paintings all over the place which the experts are proudly showing off as originals when they aren't. I hope I am wrong but…"

"I will be right back, sir, I promise."

Catrin had to overcome the desire to run down the corridor to Wetherby's office; she was physically in no shape to run yet, anyway, she had been told.

For some reason she was happy, if not with the news of what would probably be a lot of extra work, but with the idea of a big case. Let's see what the boys and girls upstairs want us to do with this one, now they have pruned our capabilities right back and we are exiting support for other police services in the UK.

They called Norwich back within ten minutes.

Lubbock said, "Sleaman is dead; he died not long ago from cancer, we understand. Someone missed the death record first time on the data search. We are looking into that, to make sure it's true and he hasn't simply changed identities, but his divorced sister inherited his house in Swaffham. She was living in a small rental flat after the split-up with her husband a year ago and she moved into Sleaman's former home only last month. Fortunately, she had only just started her 'renovations', as it was put to my people there.

"There are seven paintings hanging on the walls in the house, including the one from the museum by this artist George Vincent. I had Dr. Cole, the curator at the Castle museum accompany DS Hollis and myself on the second visit to the home. The SOCOs are still there as we speak.

"Dr. Cole is now sure that the painting by George Vincent in Swaffham is the original, but looking at the others in the house just made her unwell; she became heady and had to sit for a while. If they are originals, they are significant. I am sending photos to you as we speak, with Dr. Cole's preliminary identifications.

"Mrs. Cannon, Sleaman's sister, had given one work she didn't like to a charity shop. They sold it; DI Needham and PC Nunn are out now trying to chase that down. And Cannon thinks her brother must have sold a few works over the years; there were different paintings on the walls at times when she visited. Her brother had told her that they were good copies he had bought 'on the cheap', with him being in the business he was in. She had no reason to doubt him, she said."

The email popped into Catrin's browser. One by one she opened the images and the list provided, which she printed, giving a copy to DCI Wetherby, who was saying nothing.

Superintendent Lubbock asked, "Any thoughts, at this point?"

She looked to see if her boss would take the lead, but it was obvious he was looking to her to do so.

She replied, "From a first glance, they all look to be good paintings; how good, I don't know. The Degas 'Woman in a tub II', number six on the list, is definitely not his work; I know pretty well all the Degas paintings on that theme. The original is a pastel drawing, not done in oils.

"Number three looks to be by Gabriel Griffon, a minor impressionist, if that signature is right and it could be genuine; if so, it's worth about twenty thousand these days. If he collected, to use the term loosely, on that scale there are some sizeable numbers starting to add up. If there are more like that and the Vincent, Sleaman is staying away from the big names and the million dollar prices. However, if he was more on the track of trying to pass off Degas copies as genuine, he is getting into really big money."

Wetherby looked at her; it was his first experience of her artistic knowledge. In turn, Catrin was thinking how the discussion would have gone if Neville was still here, with his input. It was a different world.

Lubbock added, "And, at this stage, we have no idea about

how many are out there."

Wetherby asked, "Were there any records found?"

Lubbock sounded disappointed. "Nothing useful to us, so far, but it is early in the investigation. He had no computer at the house, his phone account had been closed, of course, and if he had a personal mobile, we haven't found it yet. He had a work one, we found out, but he returned it to the company when he retired, they say. The files about the house are just his gas and electric bills and bank statements. We will be going through those in detail. We are still checking. His sister said she hadn't thrown any paperwork out yet; she hadn't got as far as upstairs, where he used a spare bedroom as an office."

Catrin asked, "Sophie Cartwright? How many did she paint?"

"Just the one, the George Vincent, she claims, and she has a copy of the sales receipt. We are not sure about her."

Catrin said, "You will need to interview her, no doubt. But don't be surprised if she is telling the truth. She has done work for us and other police services in the past, including the FBI, making copies needed for cases. She's not stupid."

Lubbock replied, "She talked about you; in fact, we are hoping you can participate in the next interview with her. And someone from your team can go with DS Hollis to Cormorant Wellman, to talk about the work that Sleaman did."

Here DCI Wetherby spoke up. "We will need to seek more senior approval at this stage, I think. Given that, we would be happy to cooperate to some extent. We have limited capacity, as you can well imagine, given our recent changes."

There was a moment of silence on the other end then Superintendent Lubbock said, "We will make a formal request; that should help, shouldn't it? We had the word you are cutting back."

He sounded a little exasperated.

"Indeed," said Wetherby happily.

Always pass the buck up the chain, thought Catrin.

She spoke up. "If you get better quality images to me; high magnification, professional copies, we will do all we can to help with the preliminary identification of those works and pin down the current locations of the supposed originals. I have someone here who is good at that and it won't take much effort, at least, for an initial run at it."

She was thinking that this was right up Isabelle's street: she loved this sort of work. It would pick her up a bit, something new to look into.

~~

The following morning's BBC East Anglia news contained an article entitled 'Castle Museum fooled by art forgery' giving the bare facts. 'Police had been called in after a forgery was spotted by a visitor from Suffolk, a painting supposedly by a local artist, George Vincent'.

Catrin noted that the work was mentioned but not Sophie Cartwright by name. The museum had been asked for their input and the director had said that the matter was under investigation. At this time, he couldn't say anything further.

Anglia TV reported the same thing plus the fact that police had also been to a home in Swaffham which may be connected with the fraud. A neighbour had seen a number of paintings being removed from the house, but the police would not comment further.

They are getting closer, Catrin thought.

Around 11.00 a.m. Wetherby called Catrin into his office. "Apparently an Assistant Chief Constable from the Norfolk police has been on to Assistant Commissioner Hall. We are to offer our support to the Norwich investigation as a top priority. We get no additional manpower, though. I suggest you call Superintendent Lubbock and see what they want."

"Yes, sir."

She turned to go.

"And Sayer, I want everything itemized. Hours by each officer; related expenses here and if you or your team go up there I want travel expenditures and mileages on the vehicles. I am not having this come out of our budget; I agreed that with Superintendent Patterson. He has Commander Moore's agreement on that."

Catrin was still adjusting to the new hierarchy and Karen Moore's new empire including her little team. With DCI Wetherby reporting through Patterson to Moore, she didn't expect to cross the path of the pushy Mancunian too often.

Catrin thought Wetherby sounded far more zealous about budget protection than about the investigation of a crime, but she was just happy to have authorisation to proceed. She went back to the Art and Antiques area and told them. She would be contacting Norwich, after which she would assign roles; who would go to Cormorant Wellman and who would go to see first-hand the work of the copyist.

"Aina, you will guard the fort; keep the current mix on hold for a day or so. It's not like there is any great pressure on us there."

"Some fort," said John.

His tone of voice suggested it was more like the last outpost.

8 THE SAINSBURY CENTRE

"Aren't you going to test her, Sophie?" John Obi called out mischievously, after the artist had invited them into her home to have coffee. She was in a good mood, he thought.

Isabelle and John had arrived at Cartwright's home, a bungalow in Aldeburgh, Suffolk, initially driving through rain, then sleet and, in the final half-hour, in snow along slippery roads. He was scraping some of the accumulated ice from the bottom of the windshield when he called out the question, just as Howlett scurried through the front door of the home.

His jibe about a test was a question whether Sophie would ensure Isabelle was knowledgeable about art. On his first visit to see Cartwright with Catrin some years ago, she had done exactly that with him, seeking his assessments of some of her own paintings before deigning to work with them. Neville Coltrane and Sophie Cartwright had known each other for a long time and Coltrane had warned them that she was prickly about not working with 'art fools'.

As he followed the two women inside and closed the front door, Cartwright ignored his question. She addressed Isabelle with, "We've not met but I know of you; as I recall, you did the conservator course at the Courtauld Institute."

"Yes, but I didn't finish it; I went back to the Met," she

replied. It had been years ago; Howlett's marriage had broken up at the time, but she wasn't going to say that.

John tried not to show his surprise. He knew his new colleague had a degree in Fine Arts from the University of London. He had a similar degree from the University of Birmingham where his own particular interest had been Islamic art.

"So," said Sophie, glancing between them, "Am I, as you people say, 'in the frame' or not now?"

Isabelle said shortly, "We wouldn't be taking you with us if you were a suspect. Your interview satisfied the Norfolk police. They also had someone from the Sainsbury Centre look at your copy and the two others found; they were very different, he said."

Cartwright's eyes sparkled. "I can't wait to see the work of this copyist close up. I am good, but this one must be special."

It had been Catrin's suggestion to Superintendent Lubbock. "What we need is copyist expertise, not more experts on the original art works. As I said, I think Cartwright wouldn't knowingly be involved in a fraud of this nature, so she would be a good candidate. But if you agree, I have been instructed to say it is on your account, not ours."

Snow was forecast. Sophie told them she didn't want to drive to Norwich in this weather so the solution was to have John and Isabelle collect her from her home in Suffolk on the way north to Norwich.

Cartwright caught Isabelle looking around the room at the paintings present. "Like any?" she asked.

Isabelle took a sip of coffee. "Catrin told me to look out for your painting in the window in Paris, the last original you did."

Cartwright said, "It's in the studio, next door. That Welsh woman is good. Thank God she is still there after the debacle about Neville. The bunch of imbeciles!"

John Obi revised his opinion about Cartwright's mood. She had always been testy. He said firmly, "We can't talk about that, Sophie, by policy - and frankly we don't want to. The truth is it's a lot of heartache for us at present, I tell you."

You don't know the half of it, his eyes said. The news had leaked, as it always does, that Sayer had turned down a plum post in Trident to stay with the Art and Antiques Unit. He was grateful for that.

"Fair enough," replied the artist. She could see when wounds were raw; she had had a few of her own over the years. The painting in Paris that Isabelle had referred to was of her former partner, Andrew Helmsley, an art teacher who died there. Catrin had focused in on it almost immediately on her first visit as being an original, not a copy. It was the last original work she painted. The sudden loss of her partner had destroyed her creativity, Sophie knew.

Now she only painted copies and she lived alone.

"We'd better head out soon," Isabelle said firmly. "This weather; it's going to take more than an hour to get to Norwich."

The paintings from the Swaffham home and the copy from the Castle Museum were now in the care of the Sainsbury Centre for Visual Arts at the University of East Anglia, in the outskirts of Norwich. The forensic work for fingerprints or other traces of the perpetrators had been completed at Wymondham and the Centre was now assessing the condition and artistic aspects of each work.

As one of the paintings found in Swaffham was a work supposedly located at a college in Cambridge University, the Fitzwilliam Museum there had offered to provide a similar service. But senior officers had insisted that, for now, the items must stay within the Norfolk Constabulary jurisdiction. Hence the use of the modern art gallery at the University of East Anglia nearby. That was their destination this morning.

"I'm sure Jacobi at the Fitzwilliam will be miffed at the snub," said Cartwright. "It warms my heart on a cold day like today."

~~

The Sainsbury Centre, a large rectangular modern building set in the campus of the University of East Anglia, had been built in the nineteen seventies. Designed by the architects Norman Foster and Wendy Cheesman, it housed the world art collection of Sir Robert and Lady Lisa Sainsbury. An open plan exhibit space, it still held in its basement a number of private areas for conservation and related work. One of these had been assigned temporarily to the Swaffham case.

A DI Lawrence Needham and PC Melissa Nunn were there, awaiting their arrival. They met up outside the work room and Catrin's name was bandied about yet again.

"I had hoped she would come up," said Melissa, "now that I am assigned to support this; it makes a change for me."

"From what role?" Howlett asked, wanting to get inside to see the art.

"Community policing," replied Nunn, "but I am sort of in transition now, as I just passed my sergeant exams."

"They wanted me to do that once; community stuff," was the London detective's response.

"And?" said Obi, recognizing that a punch line was coming from his colleague.

"They found out I had no heart at all, so I didn't qualify."

Obi smiled. "Really? Not what I hear. You are dating an FBI copper; soirées in Paris, Mark Harper said, as I recall."

Melissa smiled; Isabelle Howlett didn't. She replied, "It's 'agent' not 'copper', John; get it right. And yes, I have mellowed a little of late; it's why I am so nice to you. There are some people here already, I think? Someone has been assigned from the Centre and there is an expert from the Fitzwilliam Gallery. Which one is here?"

"Yes," responded Needham. It was evident that this wasn't his field or experience. "But the man from Cambridge is from the college, not the gallery, we found out. He didn't bring the copy of the Klinkenburg painting with him, either. College politics he said. Nunn and I were just talking whether or not they are put out about us turning down their offer to do… this."

He pointed at the paintings laid out on tables across the room. Already there were three people inside including, Howlett assumed, the Cambridge man.

"Let's join in," she said.

Cartwright needed no second invitation; she was at the table in an instant.

They got to work examining the paintings, the lightheartedness gone. Melissa was reminded of Sayer's visit years ago during the Halsting Hall investigation; the comments passed between her and the curator there. They saw things she didn't and didn't even understand. After about half an hour, Melissa saw DC Howlett say something *sotto voce* to Obi and she left the room.

Melissa moved round the table closer to him. He said, "Isabelle's gone to phone our boss; she's meeting up with your DS Hollis about now, I think."

~~

Catrin was driving carefully through snow on her way to Cormorant Wellman Technologies Ltd. DS Ray Hollis, the Norwich investigator, had just called her with information on his current location and ETA. They were there to interview employees of Sleaman's former company at premises located in an industrial estate near St. Albans. As she closed that call the phone rang again.

Isabelle said, "Sophie and the others here are getting really worked up over this set. I can confirm that the work on the two other copies is clearly not Sophie's. Both are good but, as she said when she saw them, "the copyist is extraordinary. He or she must have some training in art but... more.""

"More?" said Catrin, talking into the speaker phone as she exited the A1 on to the smaller roads, concentrating on getting through a double roundabout.

"She meant not just copying the painting carefully but copying the brush strokes accurately. The proper base and colour build have been used and meticulous care taken in the drafting, but it is the accuracy of the paint loading and placement that stands out.

"The really obvious giveaway if anyone had looked properly is the back of each copy. Fairly rudimentary work there, to give the canvas a sense of aging over time, but nothing that would stand up to scrutiny. Whoever did that used different diluted teas for the staining, it turns out. Weird; the backs are much more amateurish."

Catrin saw the sign she was looking for and turned into Balmoral Drive. "I am just arriving," she said. "What about the canvases used for the copies?"

"Just one source, we think and thoroughly modern; the weave and the fibres. Top quality; better than the original artists had, in reality. Why would someone who took so much care on a forgery be so sloppy about the back or the selection of canvas? Or not use an old painting from the right period as the base?"

Isabelle paused, a silence while both of them thought about it. She suddenly heard the sounds indicating that the engine had been switched off.

Catrin said, "My first thought is this may be a large-scale fraud, but the artist or artists involved don't know about the end use of their paintings. Talk to Sophie - she rang the alarm. There's someone there, I think, from the Fitzwilliam, if I recall right?"

Isabelle replied, "Yes, a Dr. Howard Toller, but he's from the college itself, though. He hasn't said much other than to confirm the Klinkenburg and to ask DI Needham twice when they were getting their painting back."

Catrin said, "I bet he didn't bring the copy along with him, did he? He should have done, to help. I don't know if anyone in the Norfolk mob has asked Toller more about that theft yet - can you check?"

Howlett saw where Catrin was leading. "You think they are covering up?"

"I don't know; but it's worth asking. From what you just

said, they have the expertise to spot the forgery as soon as they see the back of the work. Why don't you and John talk it through with DI Needham and haul the Cambridge guy away for a little talk, if it is merited. But I had better go. DS Hollis is here now; he has just got out of his car."

9 KLINKENBURG

"Dr. Toller, or is it professor?"

DI Needham sounded disarming, pleasant.

"It's both, actually," smiled the Cambridge man. "This is quite some development, don't you think?"

Needham smiled back. "Yes it is. Could we have a quiet word please, in the office over there?"

He turned, pointing at the small empty office in the corner with a circular meeting table. As Toller walked with him Isabelle Howlett followed behind and after they all entered she closed the door.

Back in the viewing area Melissa smiled, a small confirmatory smile to John Obi. "It's to do with him not bringing the copy, isn't it?"

John nodded. "Yes. Isabelle is going to help DI Needham break a knuckle or two, metaphorically speaking."

He flexed his hands unconsciously. Melissa thought that if it was an issue of breaking knuckles in reality John Obi was the man for the job. He was a big, powerful man.

"I'm embarrassed to say, it's approvals and politics, albeit petty politics," Dr. Toller replied, in response to the question about the location of the copy and why it wasn't possible to bring it today. "I'm being candid now, I must admit, seeing as you are asking again."

DI Needham had said that he was a little bemused by the earlier statement about the 'release of the copy still awaiting university approval, unfortunately'.

Toller pointed through the glass wall at the area where the paintings were laid out. "We did offer to do this at the Fitzwilliam, as you know and… it does have a certain reputation."

Isabelle thought that his glance around the modern environment of the Sainsbury Centre implied that this place wasn't old enough to have a 'certain reputation'.

Howlett had raised her eyebrows at Needham. When a person being interviewed says, 'I'm being candid now' it generally means there is a gold seam awaiting a police officer's pick and shovel.

Toller added, "Some of my colleagues are a little miffed at the rejection so there is a squabble at present."

Needham had been looking again at the man's business card he had provided previously.

"But I see you are a Fellow of Homsley College, rather than actually on the staff of the Fitzwilliam."

It was phrased as a statement. They were interested how he would explain that.

"We are all part of the university," he responded, "and my specialty is the Dutch nineteenth century, so…" He shrugged.

Needham glanced at Isabelle, passing over the lead and she said, "Dr. Toller?"

He turned to face her, seeing her warm smile as she stated the first of her questions designed to throw him over the cliff.

"This Amsterdam scene by Johannes Klinkenburg is typical of his work in the 1880's, is it not?"

He smiled; a fellow art expert to talk to.

"It is. I've seen quite a number of them, over the years, a wonderful - ."

"So you know what the back of a painting from 1885 should look like today, don't you?"

His smile froze. Isabelle bulldozed on.

"The painting was hung in your college somewhere, wasn't it? So when precisely did you or someone else spot the forgery?"

His face registered surprise then fear as he realised his cozy revelations weren't having any success. As an academic, he took a favorite line; he vacillated.

"Well, I rather think we are getting into semantics here about a university-owned work of art, DC Howlett. I came to assist today, not be interrogated in this manner."

He had turned sulky and annoyed in an instant.

Howlett said, "Do you want me to contact the Cambridge-shire Police and get a warrant to search the college records? My boss is quite prepared to do that, I expect. We know all about maintenance and cleaning programs for art on display in colleges; this is not the first painting that has gone missing from a university."

Then she added, "Of course, a search warrant is likely to draw attention not only to the theft but questions about when the theft was first spotted - and we know the media is all over this case; at least in a Norfolk perspective."

The Cambridge don was clearly annoyed but had reined in his initial outburst.

"I do believe I need to speak with people at my college - ."

The pleasant Norfolk detective inspector said gently, "Then you had better do that from Wymondham, from our head-quarters."

He pulled out his mobile phone and added, "I am calling Superintendent Lubbock as I think you are obstructing our legitimate enquiries."

"Look, it's not that." He let out a sigh.

They both heard the thump of his metaphorical body hitting the base of the cliff. It was in his tone of voice.

"We have known for nearly a year that the Klinkenburg hanging in the college was not the original. We just wanted to keep it quiet, you see. We never connected it to this man Sleaman you have discovered. Cormorant Wellman people were last into the college over a year earlier than our discovery, to upgrade the system. We thought the theft was by one of ours, a fellow of the college now on sabbatical. It had been in his rooms."

He paused, lost in thought. "In fact, the man concerned has been subject to a lot of pressure, the way colleges keep these things inside our own doors. I think we owe someone an apology."

Needham said, "You are saying a work of art went missing and you thought a college professor had substituted it with a copy, yet you didn't report it to the police?"

"Yes. We didn't report it, and he is a Fellow of the college. The Master would have none of it. We just needed to bring him to his senses and have him return the original, not involve outsiders. We have a lot of art at Homsley and the Klinkenburg wasn't exactly part of the cream. Best dealt with internally, we all agreed."

"And the professor, Fellow, whatever term you used?"

"He denied it strenuously. Talked about finishing his sabbatical and staying on teaching in the USA. He is reluctant to come back now."

"I can quite see why he may not," said Isabelle. "As may any future donors of art to your college. People don't like to see their gifts being treated in such a cavalier manner."

He responded acquiescently now, by his tone of voice. "I'd better call the college and talk with them. I should add that, other than my offer to come today which I talked to the people at the Fitzwilliam about, they knew nothing of this. They are busy checking their own works and anywhere Cormorant Wellman had worked within the university."

"That may be so," DI Needham said, "but I am sure, under the circumstances, that it is highly unlikely we will be availing ourselves of their kind offer of assistance. The only thing heading back to Cambridge, in due course, will be your original. Now, unless you want the Cambridgeshire Police involved, you had better call your 'Master' and get the copy brought over here right now, by car."

10 THE WHITE MOON

"Jian Li?"

Michael Yau's voice sounded the same as usual, not that she spoke to him very often. It was that she knew the man was dying and he had just called her that jolted Li. She wasn't sure of the right words of response.

"Mr. Yau. Good morning. I heard the news and am so sorry. How are you?"

There was a small laugh on the other end of the line and then Yau said, "Enjoying life - while my strength holds, at least. But I am calling because I have a request of you; two in fact, if I may ask them in person."

Li said, "Please; how can I help?"

"Are you free for lunch today? Could you come to the restaurant we met at before in Kowloon; the White Moon?"

"Yes, I can do that. What time?"

She knew that the restaurant on Shep Kip Mei Street was in the same building as the bathhouse her father went to. Knowing from him that Michel Yau was a part-owner of that business, she wouldn't be surprised to find he had the same arrangements with the restaurant. She had discovered over the years that the man liked to control things, but with invisible strings. As had Catrin.

"At 1.00 p.m. Alex will collect you, if convenient, at 12.30."
Another ride in one of Mr. Yau's Mercedes.

There was something in the smile and deportment of the
driver this time that showed a strain, but Li knew better than
to comment on it. The last time she had seen this man, she
recalled, was when she met Miele Yau for the first time; Mr.
Yau had called out to both chauffeurs present - one was Alex,
the other was Tak. So this man was Alex.

He was triad; she had first encountered him in such a
vehicle in Malta while she was on a training course there. Emily
Yang, Michael Yau's assistant of some sort, Li wasn't sure quite
what, had wanted to talk with Li in strict confidence using a
phone from within the triad control.

To make one video call to tell Li that the person who had
threatened to kill her friend Catrin was now dead, to show her
proof of that, Yau had sent this man from Hong Kong to
Malta and fixed him up with a limo to use to intercept her. It
was so nothing could be traced. The world of Four Square; its
wealth, its secrecy and its organizational capabilities had hit her
back then. A world she stayed away from.

She took in the competency of the driver; his choice of
routes and short cuts; his skill in less capable traffic; profess-
ionalism in a sea of amateurs. They travelled in silence until she
suddenly said, "Alex; will Miss Yang be at lunch, do you
know?"

The driver seemed caught out for a moment. "No; not that
I am aware of. Miss Yang, no; I believe you are meeting Mr.
Yau and Miss Miele."

Michael's granddaughter had now finished her degree in
Fine Arts at the University of Hong Kong. She knew Miele was
setting up a studio of her own in a re-purposed industrial and
commercial building with another artist; paralleling, Li thought,
the way in which Jean and Melanie had started up in London.

Michael hadn't mentioned that she would be there, Li
thought; and wondered why.

They arrived at the building exactly five minutes before 1.00

p.m. Michael Yau's world remained well ordered and on time, as usual.

The lunch was in a private dining room; the same one, Li recalled, as the meeting some years ago with Emily Yang and Michael. But it was, as the chauffeur said, Yau and Miele this time.

After the small talk, the ordering of food and the departure of the waiter, they seated themselves at the table. Li hadn't noticed any difference in the man; just a sense of attentiveness to him from Miele. The young woman was quieter, less effusive than in past meetings.

Yau said, "My first request, Li, is that as a lawyer with corporate law experience, you take on Miele as a client; to look after her legal matters regarding her new business; her studio."

Li looked first at him then at Miele. "Well, I think that should really be a question from Miele, Michael, should it not?"

Miele smiled. The same thought must have been on her mind or had been previously discussed with her grandfather, but clearly it was an important issue for him.

Li added, "And I am not sure whether my current obligations allow it. In fact, I think they don't without LinTan Shipping's knowledge and their prior agreement. In principle, it is allowed for legal staff to have private clients, but only if I have direct approval of the company and it is never in conflict."

She was torn. In part, she had no need of such a small project but had no desire to disappoint this man.

He didn't argue or explain; he just waited.

Li looked at Miele and said, "What do you want?"

Miele Yau said, "Not to spoil our relationship. I spend more time in communication with Jean and Melanie than I do with either you or Catrin, but I don't want to spoil that either."

"And the scope of this work; as foreseen currently?"

Miele replied, "Incorporation of the pottery business. Transactional legalities of the purchase of a studio in Quarry

Bay that we have found. We have had preliminary discussions but nothing further. On an ongoing basis, probably annual corporate filings and oversight of any main purchase contracts for materials or, if we are as successful as we hope, the sales contracts for our art."

Li nodded. All well within her scope and experience and less complicated than the world of merchant shipping that now occupied her time.

Miele added, "My business solely. But set up with my grandfather's gift to me. His parting gift, he calls it."

She looked at her grandfather and smiled.

How the world mellows people, Li thought. Years ago in this very room she had asked for this man's help to deal with the threat against Catrin. She was a lawyer; she should have no dealings at all with a member of an organized crime group. His granddaughter had always wanted to 'go it alone' as an artist; now she was taking her grandfather's money as capital for her business. But how could she refuse, really? His parting gift, indeed.

Li smiled. "Knowing you, Michael, you have already dealt with my second point, I'm sure. With Enlai."

He nodded. "If you agree to the proposal, there will be a letter from Mr. Cho Bai to confirm its acceptability to your company, including flexibility around time needed. They will help make it work."

Stephen Cho Bai was the CEO of LinTan Shipping; he had replaced Enlai Lin on his retirement.

Michael held all the cards, she thought; except one.

"I would be happy to work with Miele in this capacity. Directly with Miele, on market terms."

His face clouded momentarily as Miele said, "You mean, your terms of payment, or what?"

Li nodded. "That's right. There are industry standards and reference data for legal services for small companies such as yours. I hope it grows in profits, if not in size but the fee scale will be on those terms, payment to be made by your company on a service contract, by invoice."

Miele clearly liked what she heard. "So how do I proceed with you?"

Li said, "Why don't we meet separately, deal with this another time, but soon? I would first want to secure the letter from LinTan to proceed. But in principle, Miele, your business now has a corporate lawyer to call on."

The women smiled at each other as Michael Yau said, "Well done, Li. Thank you."

It wasn't quite what he wanted, she thought, but he was happy with it anyway. She suspected he had a fat 'retainer' in mind for her.

Suddenly the old man rose from his seat and stood formally, one hand lightly touching the table. Li thought he might need help with something but seeing Miele's face she realised he didn't; it was expected by his granddaughter.

"My second reason for the meeting, Li. I ask your forgiveness for placing your life at risk all those years ago. It was not planned but it was my oversight. I am deeply sorry."

Li saw the seriousness in the man and the sincerity. She stood herself, not as formal a stance but just to be on the same level as him when she responded. She realized this was important to him and could not easily be dismissed.

She said, "What you did, you did for my father and for Han, to ensure my brother was not held to blame for the theft of those paintings. I never held you responsible for the incident in Bangor; only that woman. I say now, though, that I fully and freely forgive you any errors or omissions or miscalculations that happened then."

She smiled warmly. "And I thank you. For all you did then, and later; for me, for Catrin Sayer, for all my friends in London, I should add."

She reached across and took his hand. "You must give it no further thought - ever again - except pleasant ones about the friendships that have grown and developed since that day."

She stopped, looking at him closely. "Is that OK?"

He nodded wordlessly then said, "Thank you. And you will

still come and see me later, I hope?"

She smiled back. "Whenever you want, I would be delighted to. And if my professional work is in the way, I will simply call Enlai Lin and he will have a word with Mr. Cho Bai."

The old man smiled then gave a small sigh; business reasons for the lunch were concluded, Li read. He sat down again.

"Now," he said, "The pair of you should tell me more about your friends in London. You should visit them together sometime and have fun."

Sometime after he had died, he seemed to infer.

11 HUSQVARNA

The Art Security Division of Cormorant Wellman Technologies Ltd. was located in Hertsmere Industrial Park near St. Albans, in an anonymous set of three-storey office units. The various businesses located in the park all had matching green security fences. If anything distinguished Cormorant Wellman, it was that their fence gate was closed, with a passkey security access. A sharp eye would notice that the security cameras were a different brand to the others in place across the industrial complex, indicating a separate monitoring system.

Headley Smith, the division manager, was waiting for them; DS Hollis had phoned ahead and set up the meeting. As Catrin and Ray Hollis were escorted to his office it was obvious from the looks of other employees that the word of a visit from the police had spread. Given that some people would have known that the thefts reported in the media were all at sites that the company serviced, it was to be expected. People were nervous.

Smith was an older man with a brush-cut hairstyle and a Lancashire accent. Dressed in a suit, he gave Catrin the impression that he had risen through the organisation, not been dropped in at management level. It was intuitive but later he confirmed that.

With him was a young, red-headed solicitor, a Jessica

Hagers. During the introductions she made it clear that she had been asked to attend by the corporate head office in Birmingham. From her comments, it was evident to Catrin the woman was a corporate lawyer, not an expert in criminal law. For a moment it made her think of Jian Li and her job.

They started with the subject of Brian Sleaman's work history.

Smith said, "To be honest, since we had the call from you, DS Hollis, we are in shock. Brian was an exemplary employee. He was one of those rare events these days; a person who joined us as an apprentice and, other than one year when he left and we re-hired him, he worked at Cormorant Wellman until his early retirement.

"A number of our staff who worked closely with him kept in touch right to the end. His retirement was on medical grounds, as you may know. I wasn't close to him personally but I went to the funeral. I still can't believe it's not a mix-up somehow."

Hollis said, "He died of cancer, I gather."

"Yes, he had bad luck in that sense. Some years earlier he had a road accident but came through that. Then this. Otherwise he was a model of attendance and reliability."

Sayer asked, "Can you explain his work for us? DS Hollis has little background here. I have some, but not the detail."

Smith nodded. "Most aspects of gallery security or home art protection are standardized. For example, in almost all galleries with valuable paintings there is a marked or roped-off area about two feet from the wall with signs not to cross or to reach over. Most people realise that there is some sort of monitoring beam crossing the area, sending off an alarm if it is broken. But they know nothing of the nature of that coverage, the complexity of the sensor systems or the hidden and visible cameras that are all part of the security system installed in the walls or ceiling areas.

"For some art works motion sensors on studs fixed to the frames are in place. Move the item and an alarm is activated.

On others, there are location trackers added to the stretchers, the inner frame of the work. Their location can be monitored centrally if they are moved. It varies in complexity largely linked to the rarity or value of the art and what the gallery can afford to install - and operate.

"Brian didn't design these; we have other employees who do that; he was part of a section that installed the equipment and set up the control room monitoring units."

Hollis asked, "What about door locks, mechanical security? To get in and out of the building."

"We may or may not do that for the client, depending on their needs. Another group within the division deals with those, if we do; it's just four people, actually. But in the past, it was a job Brian did before promotion to the role I described. We haven't checked yet to see if he accessed that section at all in recent years. We can -"

Hollis interrupted him. "It's best if that is done in conjunction with our forensic staff, sir. They will also want someone on your team to take them through this in detail. We will try to interfere as little as possible in your day-to-day activity but some of our people will be coming in later today; how many will relate to the scope of work we see from this interview.

"The bottom line is this, I hear; if Brian Sleaman had a good copy of a painting and the gallery was not manually patrolled at night, he could make a switch without detection?"

Smith agreed. "Technically; if he had the replacement work? Yes, as could six or seven of the staff here."

He smiled at Catrin. "I know of you, though; obviously we follow the art crime scene in detail, so it's a pleasure to meet you. DI Sayer will have to inform you about the issue of removing the painting from its frame and mounting the forgery. Technically it's straightforward but it may show up in your examination."

Catrin responded, "My people are checking exactly that aspect right now, I hope. It was going to be one of my questions. If any tagging of the works directly was involved, I assume the museum curatorial staff would do it, not your employees?"

Hagers spoke up. "We don't touch the art works at all. It's a policy and an insurance issue."

Smith nodded in agreement with the lawyer. He continued. "The rest, with careful planning would be no problem at all with the right codes and key sets. But it makes me wonder if you are on the right track, or is Brian being set up because he is dead? Have you considered that? I worked with him here; not close personally, as I said. But he appeared to me to be a considerate, generous man."

The police officers expressions remained neutral. Catrin thought, how many exemplary testimonials over the years have I heard about people who turned out to have committed an offence?

Smith had, on request, passed over Sleaman's personnel file to Hollis to peruse as they talked. He was leading the questions and, after a brief glance through, he passed it to Sayer. He knew they would be taking it with them for detailed analysis.

Catrin began scanning it more closely.

Hollis moved on to the issue of work and home location. "We were surprised that he lived so far away from his work. Any thoughts?"

Smith was not put out by the question. "A number of the employees live elsewhere or have big commutes. We used to be based in Corby, further north, before the relocation here. We made arrangements for discount rates with a local Best Western if they need to visit for a period and we gave people the option of a one-time relocation sum or two years of travel expenses. Some relocated, some stayed put. Remember, a lot of these people are regularly all over the country for installation work, including Brian.

"He stayed put in Swaffham; it was his parent's home before his, I think. And he liked his own vehicles, driving them. Always took the option of the mileage allowance rather than a company vehicle and always had a nice one, too."

Catrin looked up from the file. "He went to work for

Husqvarna Sweden locally, I see, that year he was away," she said.

"Yes, I gather he liked motorbikes as well; always had one for recreational use until near the end."

DS Hollis said, "We found his motorbike gear at the house; he kept that. He sold his bike - it was the same make - when he lost his driving license for medical reasons. And he sold his car also - a high end one, a Range Rover."

The tone of voice made it a question.

Smith said, "We currently give people Skoda Octavia Estate vehicles for work travel purposes, unless they opt for the mileage allowance. Brian used his own car, as I said. He was particular about his bikes and his cars, I always thought. His last one was a Range Rover.

"He changed them every two years; always had a new-looking one. Mind you, there was just him, no family to support. Even so, it was always an expensive vehicle."

That takes some money, thought Catrin.

Hollis moved on.

"Were there any discipline problems; issues that were not recorded in the file that you or others would be aware of? And I would like a list of names of those who stayed in touch with him near the end, please, or others who may be close to him."

Smith was shaking his head. "I can give you the list - it's is probably most of the longer-serving people here - but as I said, his performance was exemplary. No problems that I know of."

Catrin said, "The road accident five years ago. He was away for an extended period, about six weeks, I see. There are notes about the next two months being office- or home-based duties. But there is a small side note here by his security rating entry at that time. 'Rounds spoke to him'. What was that about?"

Smith looked perplexed. "I don't know. But Mr. Rounds is here; you can ask him. He is the section supervisor. It was before my time in this position."

Jason Rounds appeared a similar age to Sleaman. Hollis explained the reason for the visit.

Rounds just said, "I came in two years after Brian; I am the longest serving employee now."

DS Hollis asked, "Could Brian have done this?"

Rounds nodded. "Yes, with planning. In fact a number of us could if we put our minds to it, truth be told. I'm not sure what I would do with the stolen art if I did or have the gall to do it in the first place. If he did it, it seems a stupid move by Brian; not like him at all."

Catrin smiled. "Selling stolen art is as complicated as stealing it. Can you tell us about the issue of his extended absence with a back injury? In the file by the security rating, it says, 'You spoke to him about it'. It sounded disciplinary, in a sense."

Rounds looked surprised. "God! That was a few years ago. It was nothing really. Not disciplinary, just good advice.

"Brian was involved with a bike charity thing, a club. I am not into bikes myself, so bear with me, I might get it wrong. Each year he would go to some big get-together of bike riders; something with bush or bash in the name?"

"The Bulldog Bash; that's the big one, near Stratford-on-Avon," prompted DS Hollis.

"Yes; that one. He was hurt on the way back. He told me he was passed by a group of bike riders and someone cut him off badly; intentionally he said, forcing him off the road. He came off his bike and that's when he did his back in. Brian thought that the guy who did it disliked Swedish bikes, he told me later. I got the impression it was one of the troublemaker sets of bikers.

"They rode off as he went down and another rider stopped to help him; called an ambulance and knew what to do, it seemed. He stopped Brian trying to get up and looked after him. Brian said that if he hadn't done that the injury could have been a lot worse."

Hollis asked, "And what you said? How does this tie in?"

"The man who helped him was a Hells Angel, Brian mentioned later. He wasn't interested in them, I know, but it impressed him that the man stopped. The biker went to visit him in hospital after his surgery too, I gather, and Brian was grateful. He had always stayed clear of people in clubs like that, I know. I just told him he was getting on dangerous ground if he kept that contact going.

"In this business the company has security checks on people regularly; we are told that. I had a duty to report what I heard and Brian accepted that. Mr. Smith's predecessor said we should make the note to his file in general, but nothing to get Brian into trouble. He hadn't done anything wrong."

DS Hollis said smoothly, "Did he mention the name of this man at all?"

Rounds thought about it. "Jim somebody, but I don't remember his surname or whether he even mentioned it."

He paused.

"No much help. I know. But the man had a 'get well' card for him when he went to the hospital; a humorous one with a photo of a Harley bike, I recall; I saw it there. Brian pointed it out to me. He would have kept all his cards, whether to do with that or birthdays and so on, I am sure; he was that sort of person. It will probably be somewhere at his house."

Outside Cormorant Wellman as they left, DS Hollis asked, "Tell me, ma'am; this issue of using new canvas rather than period stuff. Could there be a pair of the people from here doing this, Sleaman and the artist, both being techies, perhaps? I don't even know whether oil paintings can be prepared by computer systems these days."

Catrin replied, "They can; well, some can. There are such systems. Equally, there are places on-line you can buy copies painted by hand - good ones and not so good ones. But those are not in the same league as the works we are seeing here, from what DC Howlett told me. No, it's a puzzle, but Slea-man's partner in this is first rate. There is no automation in these copies; it is hand and eye work entirely.

"From what we learned in there, you may want someone to do a financial reconciliation on Sleaman; check the vehicle and home costs versus his salary and bonuses. The art fraud could be supplementing his lifestyle, it seems to me."

Hollis said, "I'll talk to DI Needham. We will do that and probably also run this Hells Angel link through Trident; they have a biker specialist group, don't they?"

"Yes," said Catrin, "It's quite a big team. 'One percenters' have a fair slice of the organized crime around the Met."

The name 'one percenter' arose from a media comment that 99% of motorcyclists were law-abiding. Hells Angels and other 'outlaw' motorcycle clubs then adopted the 'one percent' identification as their own descriptor.

Hollis said, "Tough policing, that; tougher than you and I handle most days, I think."

Catrin looked at the snow accumulating on her car. "Anyway, you have a longer drive than me and the snow isn't getting any better, is it? We had best be off."

~~

Less than an hour later the people going through Sleaman's home found a 'get well' card with a Harley motorcycle from a Jim Hughes. It was in a shoebox with other cards, as Smith had predicted. It took no time to establish that Hughes was a full patch member of Hells Angels, living in London. Other than that tidbit, they found nothing else at Sleaman's workplace to give them a lead.

Back at New Scotland Yard, Aina caught Catrin as she was getting settled. "I knew you were nearly back so thought I would wait, not call. Commander Moore wants you in her office when you get in."

Catrin asked, "With DCI Wetherby?"

Aina said neutrally, "That's what he assumed. She made it expressly clear that she wanted to see you alone as soon as you were settled. I think it was this biker issue that caught her attention."

Moore's ability to make things 'expressly clear' was well known in the Met. Some considered her a tyrant. Catrin had worked with her a year or so ago when Moore was a detective chief superintendent and they had got along well, it seemed.

Until now. A high-flying opportunity in Trident for Catrin's career development during the reorganization had been Moore's suggestion to Assistant Commissioner Hunt, she had found out. Moore had wanted her to head up the 'tough policing' area of biker crime that Hollis had unwittingly alluded to.

Catrin had turned it down.

12 MOORE

On entering Moore's office she was pointed to a chair at the small conference table as Moore rose from her desk and went to her door.

"No calls, unless - ."

Catrin heard 'the world is coming to -' from Moore's administrative assistant as the door closed. She braced herself.

Moore began, "We are here to talk about the issue of Mr. James Hughes, whom DCI Wetherby has brought to our attention. But first I want to know how you are doing now you are back?"

Her voice was soft, the Mancunian accent more moderated than Catrin recalled.

"Fine, ma'am. Busy - ."

"Catrin, I can't even get pregnant, I tried. In the end my husband and I got divorced; it broke us. How are you coping?"

It took Catrin totally by surprise. She had hardly seen Moore after the case that finished for her with the death of Nirupa Ranjani. Catrin had Moore marked as an 'all work and no social niceties' copper. Perhaps the promotion to commander rank had brought out different aspects of her personality.

She replied, "Struggling; we both are. I'm glad to be back to occupy my mind and so is Chris. But there are times when it overwhelms me, thinking about... my baby, what could have been. My team is supportive. And the work has changed so much... with Neville gone. Nothing seems the same. But it is early days.

"My husband is about the same. We just told others that it is more complicated for us now because it was my second miscarriage. We had kept quiet about the first one; when we decided try for a baby I got pregnant very quickly and then I lost it almost as fast. So we tried again and... it was going well until the eleventh week. Now I have to see a new doctor, an obstetrician who specializes in difficult pregnancy issues like this. But Chris and I want to try again."

Moore looked at her, assessing what to say next.

"You thought you were coming in for a bollocking, didn't you, because you turned down my offer; pushed back against our smooth road to you becoming a DCI?"

Catrin nodded, working at holding herself in check as Moore pulled a box of Kleenex closer to her.

Moore went on, "Before she left, Sandra Hunt told me one day you would be in that chair."

She pointed at her desk.

"I told her I had already seen that myself. So no recrimination. You chose to stay with your team; and it is your team, small as it is. I don't think you are afraid of the big world. I want to reassure you that you haven't spoiled anything for your career development in the future."

She paused again. "You are in a bit of a backwater now. DCI Wetherby is a different man - he manages a wider area of support activity, which is what the Art and Antiques Unit is now part of, effectively. You may see him as a paperclip manager, lost in detail - and he is, to some degree. But he has his marching orders, too and he is a steady leader. It may be good for a while for you, for ground we have just covered. There should be less travel and late nights. You need time to... recover; to re-group. So use it well. I won't forget what Sandra and I talked about, I assure you."

Catrin smiled, her eyes filling at the concern shown from unexpected quarters.

Moore sighed.

"Neville Coltrane. It was wrong to let him go and also necessary. The man drives a Bentley and would never drive a little Fiat; which, in a sense, you will need to do. But he was a good copper, even if he was a pretentious snob."

Catrin swallowed hard. "Not pretentious; a snob, yes. He just didn't hide his wealth or lifestyle. Didn't try to be 'one of the boys'. Remember the security director at the Kelvingrove Museum? She said it right, from her limited contact with him; he was very loyal to the Met."

She left the corollary accusation lie there, not sorry to have aired it.

Moore responded, "Do I try to be one of the boys?"

"No, ma'am; you are in a league of your own."

Moore smiled. "I just told you; not on my own. Sandra, you, a few others here. Get used to it. And heal. Now -"

Her voice took on a different, less personal tone.

"James Hughes. A one percenter and a full patch Hells Angel. We know him. Stay totally away, hear me? And from his gang. I don't want anyone outside the Trident team dealing with bikers near him. The Norfolk team has to follow up as they see fit with whomever, but no attendance by your team at interviews if it involves the Hells Angels; no follow up on leads here about them, despite working with Superintendent Lubbock on this one. The Bolan gang and the Ranjani issues we worked on together pale in comparison. The Ranjanis killed people, but not like the bikers do when they get the urge; they have a big sense of vengeance. Understood?"

Catrin nodded. "Yes ma'am, and thank you for your understanding. I really appreciate it. The Norfolk team is looking for any links between Sleaman and Hughes; we'll see what transpires. But you have given me clear direction."

She sensed the meeting was drawing to a close, so she pulled another tissue out of the box and dabbed at her eyes carefully then stood as Commander Moore did likewise.

Moore added, "I heard that Hughes stopped to help after Sleaman's accident. Do you know whether Sleaman was in a motorcycle club?"

Catrin replied, "Norfolk said yes; The 'Anglia Huskies'; not an outlaw group just a Husqvarna riders group, we heard. They are big on charity work."

Moore nodded, thinking. "As are Hells Angels. We see it as a PR cover for their real criminal work. They don't; they believe in their 'good cause' stuff; makes them feel good. They live in a different world. It may simply be that Hughes helped out of respect for a fellow biker; that's all."

She plonked herself behind her desk as Catrin reached the door and added, "Respect is everything to biker gangs; you can't buy or ask for it. Disrespect a patch and you pay for it."

Catrin left and walked down the corridor, thinking that she had previously admired Moore's tenacity as a career officer. The meeting had certainly raised the woman in her esteem.

"No direct involvement in anything to do with biker gangs, if it develops that way. If so, we brief DI Coombs in Trident. It is his area."

"Fine by me," said John, quickly.

DCI Wetherby seemed relieved. After the meeting broke up he said to Catrin, "Was there anything else she raised?"

No sir, she just asked after me, given the miscarriage."

"Right, glad she did that," he said quickly. His face showed his discomfort. He had been solicitous on her return but hadn't raised the subject since. Their relationship was still distant; strangers who worked together.

~~

At home later, she received a personal text from Jian Li. Thinking she was following up again on her own condition, as she read it she found that it did cover that but was mainly on an entirely different subject.

'I met with Miele and her grandfather today. We hadn't had

much contact of late; she mainly talks with Jean and Melanie, I think, about ceramics. As you know, after her mother's early death her grandparents and other family members were very involved in her upbringing.

'I didn't say earlier but Michael Yau is terminally ill. I don't know much else other than he is still active, not in hospital and he seemed the same when I saw him. But Enlai and my dad know, too, so I thought you should be informed.

'I am also going to become a little more interested in pottery businesses; Miele's to be precise. She has asked me to become her corporate lawyer. Knowing how Jean and Melanie started up and developed, I can say that Miele is following very much in their tracks.

"Glad to hear you are back at work despite the upheavals. Keep looking after yourself and we need to talk. Love from James and me'.

Catrin thought about it, saddened by the news about Michael Yau and a little surprised how it hit her; after all, the man was in organized crime.

'I thought you should know' Jian Li had written. They both knew why that was, even though others did not. Her tenuous links to Yau stretched over most of her career in the Met and some difficult times in her life. For a man she should have no contact with, a triad member half a world away, it hit her harder than she expected.

PART 2: BIKER

13 TARRANT

They heard no more from Norwich about Sleaman or his link to bikers in the next few days, which wasn't a surprise. The Norfolk JMIT members would have a lot to assess and follow up on now.

The silence turned into a week. Then two weeks. For Catrin's team, the sense of 'being a resource' rather than 'owning cases' was starting to set in, partly because the nature of this case interested them.

As they settled into their new roles they were busy enough with other matters but the silence couldn't help but remind them of the 'way it used to be'.

Obi and Howlett came from two different areas of recent work experience. One aspect was that a number of international cases that Catrin and Isabelle, with Mark Harper in the past, had worked on were now relegated to a 'monitor and advise' status. Catrin's first attendance as the head of the Art and Antiques Unit at the standing International Art Crime Task Force was welcomed; people made all the right noises. In the past she or Neville, or sometimes both, would attend this meeting in person, once or twice a year. This time she joined alone by videoconference link.

For John Obi, other than the mandate that they had to

'keep Norfolk happy', he was busy working with Catrin passing case files of the former Art Crime Unit over to the relevant boroughs or other police services. As a result, a number of these cases were going to be mothballed, that was obvious.

The backdrop to the changes was the growing holiday season; the inescapable advertisements grinding in the 'happiness through shopping' message and the increase in 'Holiday Madness', an annual blip for the Met in break-ins, shoplifting crimes, vehicle accidents from drunk-driving and arrests for disorderly behaviour. The most significant involvement of Art and Antiques in that mix was a request for confirmation of the identity of a small sixteenth century statuette of a hind, a female deer, originating in Qatar. It had been stolen during a break-in of a home in Shepherd's Bush and found in the possession of a suspect arrested. The owner had been badly beaten. John handled that; Islamic art was his specialty.

Ironically, one of the ACU 'transfers out' was a joint case with the Greater Manchester Police. Catrin talked with Keith Marshall there, even though it wasn't his assignment, after she had talked with his colleague; it seemed churlish not to call him while he was in her thoughts.

He referred back to their discussion at lunch at the Queens Larder. "Sorry to see that my rune-reading turned out to be so miserably accurate. I talked with Neville a bit. He's got something going on he said, but he wasn't specific. And it must be hard on you, with everything else."

"I've got John and Isabelle and Aina. It's a good little team. But you did the right thing, Keith. It's different now."

It was after the call she actually felt good about her team; people she worked with and trusted. But the ongoing silence from Norwich made her acutely aware that the Norfolk Constabulary was holding to the agreement with the Met to limit her unit's involvement to expertise support.

~~

The call from Neville Coltrane was during working hours on her mobile.

"Are you in your office, Catrin?"

She laughed. "I don't go very far these days, Neville; how are you?"

He replied, "I'll tell you, but only after you tell me how you are doing. Not the work; you. Are you free to talk now?"

She closed her office door as she said, "Yes, of course."

In a few minutes she turned the tables on him. "Your turn; that was the deal. How are you?"

"Busy. Better, in a sense. I've found something to occupy me usefully and want you to be aware of it, with a request - not for information; I wouldn't do that to you. Just - well - Sylvia and I had dinner with Sir Nigel Fielding and his wife Ivy. She's a Tarrant."

It struck her again about Neville; he would talk to people as if they, too, knew Debrett's Peerage by heart.

"I'm going after the Tarrant bodice piece. If you hear anything through contacts that I am doing that, I would like to know. It will tell me how it is feeding back on the grapevine."

Catrin didn't know quite what to say; it was such a surprise. So she temporized, "It's a lot of diamonds… and emeralds. Very…"

"Gargantuan," said Neville, "a big ostentatious brooch for a nineteenth century ball gown. Ivy said her ancestor must have worn a corset made of steel to support it."

He added, as a postscript, "It's not about the art, obviously; it's not my thing at all."

Catrin let out a big laugh. "Glad to hear it; they have items like that in the V&A but they don't inspire me."

The Victoria & Albert Museum, the V&A, had a large collection of designer jewellery.

Neville's voice smiled at her down the phone. "If I get it, you will find out why; if not, and the rumours circulate, you can nod when people say I went batty after leaving the Met."

She asked, "Can I tell others? Isabelle perhaps? She has her ear to what's going on."

"Just her, then. And I want to hear, tell her, if the rumour comes to you two, not for it to be spread."

"Well, I talked with Keith yesterday; he said that you and he talked recently and 'you are into something'. How's that for starters?"

"Is he going to buy a trench coat and get an SIA licence, do you think?" asked Isabelle. "The boss; meeting informers in dark alleys in Lisbon."

Private investigators in the UK needed a licence from the Security Industry Authority.

She added, "Didn't the Tarrant jewellery disappear there?"

Catrin replied, "You have a memory like a… I don't know what. I had to look it up; you are right. 'Made in 1843, a floral bouquet of diamonds, some rose-cut, some old mine cut, and emeralds, set on white and yellow gold in the shape of a large floral sprig, with sections on 'tremblers' to catch the light and attract attention. Big enough that one flower spray can be removed for use as a smaller brooch on 'less formal occasions'. Nicked at a Royal Ball in Lisbon in 1902, shortly before the dissolution of the Portuguese monarchy."

Isabelle shook her head and asked, "What's got into him?"

"It's some rich friend of Neville's, his wife is a Tarrant. It belongs in her family. She would like it back, if you please."

Isabelle was nodding, visualizing the piece. "The closest I've seen to one like that is in the V&A."

"That's what I said to him!"

Isabelle said, "There was a rumour that it went to Russia, but your predecessor always insisted it eventually went to someone in Africa. Neville agreed with DI Caldwell. But the Portuguese had primary case responsibility, then and now; it was stolen there, even if its owners were British. Nothing really happened."

"Well, something is happening now. Neville obviously has some lead on it. I just hope he stays out of trouble."

~~

A gallery in Lincolnshire reported that its Henrietta Berk landscape, donated by a Lincoln man who had lived his later years in California, was now suspect. They were comparing it with the Swaffham find. Being a contemporary work, it was harder to use the canvas quality as the obvious giveaway. But it didn't take long to confirm that Sleaman had worked his vanishing trick there, too.

A country house in Cambridgeshire, owned by a company which used it as a training centre, made an enquiry to Art and Antiques. They had followed the news items and rechecked the paperwork for the name of the security person who installed their system; it was Sleaman. Catrin phoned DI Needham who wasn't there, but spoke to DS Hollis, just to get an update.

He said, "We are dreading this; we are still working through the list of private installations in which Sleaman was the lead security installer. It could be a long list."

Ironically, a new turn to the case came not from within the UK or through the East Anglia JMIT but from the Germans through Catrin. Gerhardt Amsel, the head of their Art Crime Unit, called her.

"We have a Klinkenburg Amsterdam scene here that may fit your new case, based on the information circulated. It's in our storage now but it is exactly like the one in the photo you circulated, the one from Cambridge University."

Catrin replied, "Well, we definitely have the original and the copy in the UK; both are in Norwich. Where did this one turn up?"

"It came up in a raid on a drug supplier near Berlin not long ago. That group got it from an Italian gang. The Italians in turn, according to an informant, took it as a part-payment from a gang that is local in Munich. This painting has seen more of the Alps in the last months than I have."

"I suppose we have no way of finding the link back to Sleaman from your end, from this Munich lot, if that is the first link in this chain?"

"No; they are a biker gang; you don't get a word out of

those people."

He paused.

"I don't suppose you want to have someone fly over with the copy you have and compare the two paintings, perhaps?"

"Gerhardt, it's not the old days. I couldn't justify a trip like that at present. It's not even our case; we are just the expert resource."

"You have my sympathies; but we know what it's like. But you may want to reconsider. Heidi went to look at it and she is convinced that it is a copy. The back gives it away."

Catrin mused, "It doesn't seem right. We definitely have the copy in Norwich now; my people have seen it and the people at Cambridge said it disappeared from the college over a year ago. The original was in Sleaman's home."

Gerhardt responded, "As I said, it needs a review from your end. In fact it sounds very much like there are two copies and the original in play in this case. In any event I will have the one here checked thoroughly and I will pick up the forensic costs to validate our observations and send them to you."

Catrin said, "We will send you this copyist's fingerprints. Norfolk found them on all the copies so far, other than the one painted by Cartwright; they are the only consistent set of prints we found, but we can't trace them."

"No doubt you have run them through Interpol, but we will double-check here."

He paused.

"On a different note I had dinner with Neville last night. He seems to be holding his own. He is heavily into this brooch thing; he said you know about it. I think it is therapeutic - or obsessive - or both! He is following up with a man in Cologne. Then he talked about going to Latvia."

"Why?"

"He knows someone there who, he believes, knows where the Tarrant is."

Catrin said, "He told me about it, yes, but not that he was on some sort of epic trip. But going back for a moment to the Klinkenburg copy; has anyone told those biker people it's not the original?"

Gerhardt paused. "I blush to say, Catrin; and please don't let Neville know ever; although I know you won't talk about cases with him now, but no; they don't. In fact, we thought it was an original at first and stored it labelled as such. It is a big error for my team, to be honest."

He stopped and the line went quiet.

"Catrin?" he asked.

Her voice came back rich and warm, her Welsh accent more prominent. "Oh Gerhardt, you have made my day! But it has to come out sometime."

"I know; but please allow us to do that bit our way directly with the people in Norfolk."

Catrin briefed Wetherby on the finding then had the job of calling Superintendent Lubbock.

He said, "So it looks like Sleaman may have had dealings with bikers in Munich perhaps, if a copy ends up in Germany with a group there. He had a motorbike but wasn't a one per-center, though; but he must have contacts."

Catrin said, "The only motorcycle gang link we know about is this incident after the biker gathering, this Bash thing, when he was injured."

Lubbock sounded as if she had been the bearer of bad news. "And the copyist isn't sticking at one copy. It makes our life even more complicated, doesn't it? I think we had better talk with your Trident specialists on biker gangs; see if they can work out the biker link. This issue of multiple copies; does this happen a lot?"

Catrin responded, "A forger selling multiple copies of the same work; yes, fraud's like that aren't uncommon. Yes, now it broadens the case, potentially."

14 TONYPANDY

It was the following day, a Friday, in a videoconference between Art and Antiques and Trident biker gang specialists at one end with the Norwich JMIT team at the other.

Catrin and John were in the room at New Scotland Yard representing Art and Antiques, with a DI Gregory Coombs and an older woman, DS Hilary Eaton; they were representing the Trident Biker Gang Unit. In Norwich were Superintendent Lubbock, DI Needham and DS Hollis. It was Eaton, the experienced member of the biker team, who spoke to the issue. Coombs had recently been appointed; in effect, filling the role that Catrin had turned down.

Eaton said, "I don't see the link to Germany, somehow, even if Hughes and Sleaman became friends after he came off his bike. The biker gang that the Germans identified in Munich, the Demons, is affiliated with the Outlaws, not the Hells Angels. Hughes is a long-time Angel."

She mused, "The Demons and a club in North London, the Centurions, go back a bit. Their top people know each other. Could be…" She trailed off, then added, "Outlaws and Angels are probably the biggest one-percenter affiliations worldwide but are like oil and water, like competing mafia families. The best relationships they ever achieve are peaceful co-existence, ignoring each other and often not even that. Generally they are in conflict over territory or business."

DI Needham asked, "So could the people who knocked Sleaman down be tied to the Outlaws somehow? Or to this club you mentioned; the Centurions? Did he somehow sell it to them? The Munich gang will be livid to find out that not only did the German police seize their asset but they had forked out money for a fake. It could be a poke in the eye from Sleaman to the people who hurt him."

DS Eaton said, "It could be; there are so many unknowns. The only person who may know who knocked Sleaman down would be Jim Hughes, if he saw them or if Sleaman mentioned it to him. And Hughes is more likely to tell DI Sayer than me."

Her boss looked as surprised as Catrin herself.

Eaton explained. "He's Welsh; from north of Cardiff. He sounds a bit like you; that's what I meant. His bottom rocker is 'Wales' even if he lives in London."

The bottom part of a 'one percenter's patches, emblems on their vests or jackets, was an arc of letters; a 'bottom rocker'. It showed their area affiliation, the territory they claimed - and sometimes fought over.

Catrin said, "Well, I'm from Pontypridd, which is north of Cardiff."

Hilary Eaton pulled a face slightly. "Not there; something like 'panda' not 'ponty'; I need to look it up."

Catrin said quickly, "Tonypandy, a town about five miles from where I grew up."

She suddenly looked as if a light had switched on. "Does he have a younger brother, Euan?"

Eaton shook her head. "I have no idea, but I could check the file. Why, do you know him?"

"If it's Euan Hughes older brother, then I know of him. Euan's brother, I thought, was called John but it could be James. Euan Hughes from Tonypandy went out with my friend Jean Hughes for a couple of dates. She's the person I do my art with."

"It didn't last, then? Were they related somehow?"

Catrin smiled. "No, it didn't last. There are a lot of families called Hughes in South Wales, so no, they weren't related."

It didn't last when Jean finally accepted that she was gay and tried to hide it, Catrin recalled. She paused. "Well, they say it's a small world, but who would have thought?"

DI Coombs said more seriously, "But I doubt Commander Moore will let you anywhere near him."

Catrin stared at him. "Let's see what she thinks. As I recall from past experience working with DCS Moore, as she was then, she likes to 'stir the pot' with villains."

He responded quickly, "Well, I can't agree with this approach without Commander Moore's approval. She was very clear on that to me; and to you, she said."

Superintendent Lubbock said, "Well, I like it, so perhaps we should ask her?"

Coombs said, "OK. But it will have to be next week. She is not around today."

~~

On Saturday at the Cwmbran Kiln as she was working on a vase at her bench next to Jean's, Catrin asked her friend casually, "Do you stay in touch with Euan Hughes, by any chance?"

Jean looked surprised. "Now what dark recess did that thought come out of? No, not for years. But I ran into him in the Taft Street shopping area a couple of years ago when I was home. He's doing well, I think."

"Who's that?" asked Melanie, sitting breastfeeding Lili before the next nap. 'For both of us' she had said earlier.

Catrin smiled mischievously. "Her first boyfriend. I was just checking she wasn't keeping him on a string…"

"Tell me more," said Melanie, conspiratorially.

Jean said, "Careful, Catrin. Tit for tat. I can tell your husband a thing or two."

Melanie looked at her partner. "Tell me more about that, too. I am just a bored housewife stuck at home with a baby…"

97

Catrin laughed. "Troublemaker. No way. Jean did you ever hear anything about Euan's older brother?"

Her friend scrunched up her nose, thinking. "Jim? No. Last thing I heard he had moved away. He was big on bikes, Euan said. He's probably a mechanic somewhere, fixing up these race bikes that you see on TV. He goes home a lot, though; more than we do. He went home for Pauline's funeral."

Catrin looked blank.

Jean said, "Pauline Myers was his cousin. She fell downstairs after getting back from the pub; they say she had too much. Must be four or five years ago now."

Catrin nodded as something came back to her. She changed the subject.

~~

When Chris and Catrin kept busy, they could cope. The work during the week; Chris's five-a-side team on Saturdays, Catrin's art at the Kiln. But there were moments when they were together alone when one look from the other would have them hugging for support.

At one of these, Catrin said, "Penny for them?"

Chris took a second. "I'm scared for us to start again. You did ask."

Catrin responded, "I'm scared of not starting again, what it means."

Chris sighed. "And neither of us like being in this limbo. If only this new specialist could say something clearer, give us more… guidance."

Catrin had gone to a first consultation with Dr. Toth, an obstetrician in her early forties. She seemed competent but, like any new set of medical activities, she started with the preliminaries; repeats of examinations and tests, plus some new ones. Catrin's own GP spoke very highly of her and thought that the referral had been quite appropriate, under the circumstances.

But they were treading water about what to do next.

15 THE WHEATSHEAF

The following Monday, later in the morning, she was asked to join a videoconference call with the Norfolk team.

"We have had a breakthrough of our own over the weekend," Superintendent Lubbock began. "A small notebook was found in Sleaman's possessions. He used a basic code to disguise names, but dates and money numbers were clear. We now have the names of five people. He sold paintings to each one of them; we think they are all copies. There are two in Cambridgeshire, one in Norfolk, two in London. We will send the details over now. We haven't got it fully clear yet but we hope that, with the others we already know about, the end may be in sight.

"Three names on the list have neutral 'smiley face' symbols against them. One of the Cambridgeshire entries has a sad face - the country house entry, not the university college - and one of the London pair has a happy face. We are wondering if you could do the London locations; we'll do the rest. I would rather have a picture of the whole thing before the media go at us again, if possible. We plan to release Sleaman's identity and his photo on Thursday, to tie it into the existing news coverage in the hope that more information on his partner, the forger, will surface. We need these visits completed by then."

Catrin exchanged glances with DCI Wetherby; it was his call. Her boss said, "Yes, a little extra effort; I believe we can do that, superintendent. And I think we have a little break-through of our own. DI Sayer?"

Catrin said, "The man who helped Sleaman after the biker bash incident, Jim Hughes; the 'small world' coincidence. It is the man I mentioned last week. Commander Moore has approved my contact with him simply to see if he can tell us who knocked Sleaman off his bike."

Lubbock said, "That could help, too. Thank you."

Catrin added, "If so, we should do that before Thursday, too."

"Why?" asked DI Needham.

"It will appear to him as privileged information, a trading point with the biker; which may make him more amenable."

~~

It was the following day at lunchtime when Catrin and DS Hilary Eaton walked into the Wheatsheaf pub near Tooting Bec in South London. Jim Hughes was a creature of habit, Eaton said - most of the time.

"It's when he disappears for a while and I check with the South Wales lot; if they haven't seen him around home we know he is up to something."

Moore had seen no problem, despite DI Coombs earlier comments. "But I want Hilary with you. She has experience and is known to Jim Hughes and many others in that world. Keep it on the issue; in and out and that's the only focus. Got it? Not his shenanigans."

"Yes, ma'am."

James Hughes was well-dressed, wearing pressed pants and a suede bomber jacket; not one from Marks & Spencer either. Catrin had bought one like it in a different colour for Chris from M&S, a birthday present. It was not cheap and was good quality but Hughes' jacket was private label, fashion-house stuff. He was a long way from the borough of Rhondda Cynon Taf now. His income, according to Hilary and the tax people, was ostensibly derived from being a co-owner of a carpet-cleaning business in Cardiff with his older brother, Colin. Hilary said it must be very successful to pay Hughes and his family to live the way they lived. They hadn't yet pinned anything else on him but it was certain that money from criminal activity was part of his income.

Hughes was tall and solid with dark hair and a more weather-beaten than tanned complexion. He worked out, Catrin concluded, but liked his food; he was starting to thicken at the waist. The Welsh biker recognized DS Eaton as she approached but he didn't seem perturbed. Nor was he surrounded by other bikers; it was just his local pub, Eaton had said. He didn't speak, just raised an eyebrow slightly; the obvious question; what now?

Hilary said quietly, "We'd like a word, in private, if we could?"

She pointed to an empty table in the far end of the room. With the murmur of the lunchtime crowd it would be suitable enough.

"Unless you would like to go somewhere more private again. We can find a room at the Tooting Manor, for example. But it's nothing you need a solicitor for. Not this time."

The Tooting police station was about one mile away.

He didn't answer, just stood there looking as if an irritant had disturbed his day; bad news, like a fly in his beer or something similar. Catrin thought he might turn his back and ignore them. So she spoke in Welsh, deliberately.

"I'm Catrin Sayer, Jean Hughes friend; she used to go out with Euan. I'm a detective inspector now with the Met Art and Antiques Unit."

He nodded but with no sense of recognition or warmth in his face. He replied in English. "Small world."

Just what I said too, thought Catrin.

He sighed and took a decision, pointing to the same table and picked up his glass. "I'll be over there, Liam," he said to the barman, "when it's ready."

His food, he meant.

Then, after walking over and sitting down, he asked Eaton, "What do you want?"

Hilary nodded at Catrin. "Answers to her questions."

Catrin said, "We are investigating a number of art frauds in conjunction with another police service - ."

Hughes interrupted, "Is this the Norfolk thing I have been hearing about? Fooling the experts?"

Catrin said, "I can't say, even if it is patently obvious. Rules."

He smiled briefly to himself.

She pressed on. "As part of our enquiries we are looking into a man called Brian Sleaman, who was also a motorcyclist. He's dead now. You helped him once. Do you recall him?"

Jim Hughes nodded then stuck out his lower lip, thinking. "Yes, I remember Brian. He's dead, you say?"

Catrin replied, "Yes, some months ago, from natural causes, we gather."

Hughes considered his words. "I met him after the Bash in 2009 or 2010, I think, not quite sure which one. He had come a cropper on the A14. But I had seen him on the site in earlier years. He is - was - a member of an East Anglia bike club; Huskies; Swedish bikes. He used to be a scrambler in his younger days, he said."

Then seeing the expression on Catrin's face, he added, "dirt-bikes; up and down muddy hills?"

"Got it," she replied. "As you can tell, I don't know much about them."

"Husky bikes are mainly race bikes, not big road bikes. But his club came to the Bash and they are good fundraisers for charity. I had no trouble with him. He came off his bike, had been run off the road and I stopped and helped. That's all."

"Right. Do you know who ran him off?"

"If he's dead and it was way back, why does it matter?"

Catrin replied, "It's complicated. I can't say, but we need to know."

He looked at her, his face neutral. He said, "I can't help you. Nothing to do with me or mine."

Eaton said, "So it wasn't Angels then?"

Hughes looked at her. "No, it wasn't; I'll give you that."

Catrin asked him, "Do you know what Sleaman did for a living?"

"No," he replied.

"It will come out in a day or so. He was in art gallery security."

Hughes looked bemused for a moment then he smiled. "Brian was involved in this theft and fraud thing, I take it? Who would have thought?"

Catrin asked, "The extent of your involvement with him was what?"

Jim Hughes held up both hands in denial, suddenly looking hostile. "Hey, I just helped him after the accident. He sent me a 'thank you' letter later. I had gone to see him in hospital and gave him a 'get well' card. I saw him a couple of times at the Bash in later years, just to say hello to; no more than that."

He glared at Eaton. "I thought you said I didn't need representation."

Catrin said, "You don't. I am simply asking how often you had contact with him; you just told me."

Then the biker's interest got the better of him and he asked, "Are you saying a club is involved in this, too?"

Catrin said, "I have no idea, at present. But I will tell you something else, if you give me a straight answer to my earlier question. I do know there was a motorcycle club in Berlin raided a month or so ago."

Hughes said nothing, but his face showed he was aware of it.

"They had in their goods seized what they thought was a valuable painting by an artist called Johannes Klinkenburg. It turns out to be a fake which traces back to another club, the Munich Dämon, the Demons."

He sat thinking then smiled. He turned to Hilary Eaton. "You'll work it out, but yes, I can see it, somehow."

Eaton took a guess, watching his response. "The riders who ran him off were Centurions, I take it?"

Hughes didn't answer her question, just gave her a neutral look. Catrin thought, he doesn't want to confirm it, in words or expression. But she was looking at his eyes, seeing the pleasure still held there. That was as much as they were going to get. Silence can speak volumes.

Instead, he asked Catrin, "How much do you think Brian would have been paid for the painting? A lot?"

She replied, "I have no information, really. A good Klinkenburg of that size is worth about a hundred thousand euros - legal pricing, that is; illegally, how much less, I don't know offhand."

Hughes suddenly stood up; he was done with them. "Then I think Brian had more 'go' about him than I gave him credit for. He could have got some financial satisfaction from the people who ran him off. Possibly."

He nodded, sure of himself. Then he focused again on Catrin.

"Do you go back much?"

To South Wales, to the Rhondda, he meant.

Still sitting, she looked up at him. "Not as often as I would like, no. And you?"

"Yes; regularly. My club is there. Your mother is the salt of the earth, our Donna said. She's my aunt; same fellowship. She helped Donna after Pauline, you know?"

Catrin said, "No, I didn't, but as you mention it, I am not surprised; and you have my condolences. I didn't know Pauline, but Jean did. Jean and I work together on art; ceramics and pottery."

He smiled at the mention of Jean Hughes. "Our Euan had a candle lit for her for a long time; his first girlfriend. She's around here, is she? If you do art together."

"She has a pottery shop in the Spitalfields Market."

He looked at Eaton, obviously not wanting to say more. Catrin's mother was a long-time Alcoholics Anonymous member, as was Hughes's Aunt Donna, the mother of the young woman who fell down the stairs.

He turned and, seeing the barman just appearing with a plate, he signaled that he wanted it back where he had been previously. He walked away without another word.

Catrin and Hilary left the premises and as they walked over to Catrin's car Hilary said, "Well, it paid off, the 'small world' thing. The link to the painting in Germany is probably through the Centurions, the way I read him."

She added, "The bit at the end; I take it your mother is in AA?"

Catrin looked at her. "How do you get that, though?"

"He had a relative who died falling down stairs drunk; it's in his file. And of the fellowship; of which I know a little more myself. I gave up fifteen years ago."

She too was in Alcoholics Anonymous, she was intimating.

"I just don't drink," said Catrin. "Too much like my mum in personality and it was my teens when she hit the worst part. Put me off. Still, nice to hear a compliment for my mum, even from the mouth of a Hells Angel."

Hughes comment about his 'Aunt Donna' brought back a memory from a few years earlier of a trip home when her dad was badly ill with pneumonia. He had been taken into hospital and she had gone back to Pontypridd to see him and her mother. He had turned the corner by the time she arrived and was starting to recover, so Catrin said she would help out at home, make the bedrooms ready, cleaning up before he was released. Her mother was going to sleep in the spare room, she said.

Catrin told them she would come back later and drive them home once he had been released.

"I think one or more of my girls may be doing that, cleaning up. Donna said she would come round with them; she has a key."

Catrin arrived at her family home, a terraced house, to find two women making it spotless and doing laundry. One was

Donna Myers; the other was a young woman she didn't know.

"You are doing what I came round to do, but a better job of it than me, I see. They say my dad can come home after the evening rounds, if the doctor agrees."

They had a cup of tea together and chatted. Then as she was leaving to return to the hospital, she told them how much she appreciated the help.

The young woman said matter-of-factly, "Your mother saved my life. There's nothing I wouldn't do for her."

Donna said, "Sponsees. She has four more like this one; not all as together as you, Carol, eh?"

Catrin had asked, "And you, Donna?"

The older woman just smiled. "Your mum and I went into AA around the same time. We are soulmates in recovery."

Donna had always been part of the little gatherings to recognize her mother's continuing sobriety that Catrin had been able to attend over the years.

For years before she left for university, her mother had been busy with people like Carol; calling them or having anxious women call their home asking for her and giving only a first name. Then, often as not, her mother would disappear for a couple of hours, whether it was day or night.

It was good to hear the perspective Jim Hughes had shared and be reminded. As she drove away from the Wheatsheaf, Catrin had a small smile on her face.

16 POTTERS BAR

Catrin and John's plan was to collect the paintings that Norfolk wanted the following day, the Wednesday, starting mid-morning. Isabelle hoped to leave early that day.

"Potters Bar and Noak Hill are the locations so choose your first poison; I'm easy," said Catrin. She had asked John to drive. She didn't say why but she still had some soreness from the hospital procedures which were more problematic whenever she drove for any length of time.

John thought for a moment.

"At least they are both on the north side of London. Potters Bar first. Then we can we spin round the M25 to Noak Hill. Depending how long these take, you can drop me off on the way back."

He smiled at his boss. John lived in Tower Hamlets, where he used to be a borough copper. Catrin also lived on the east side of London, near Spitalfields, near the Cwmbran Kiln.

She smiled back, amused. "See how it goes."

Meaning that if they finished sooner rather than later, she would want to go back to the office, not call it an early finish.

"Slave driver," John said.

She replied, "At least it's dry and sunny today, so the drive should be easier than we had to St. Albans or Norwich."

The house in Potters Bar was big and modern, with a small semi-circular drive in front and nothing parked in it. The gates on both sides were open. Catrin decided they should leave the car outside on the road and together they walked up to the front door and rang the bell.

Beside the house was an adjoining garage, its doors on one side open, with a newish-looking white Vauxhall Insignia in view. In the shadow thrown from the other closed door, a motorbike was just visible. The bike was big and it had dark purple paintwork. Although she knew little about them, it gave her some unease, given the recent talk of biker gangs.

The purchaser of the painting was a forty-eight year old woman called Mrs. Renée Altman. According to Lubbock it was a work by a German artist called Franz-Xavier Winterhalter, a nineteenth century high society portrait painter.

Isabelle said during the briefing, "It will be an image of a frothy silk and lace princess or aristocrat and also a fake. Genuine Winterhalter works are up there in the quarter million region."

John had shaken his head. "Is there anything this woman doesn't know?"

Isabelle had just smiled questioningly.

"Did you run this Renée Altman through the database?" she asked as they approached the double front door.

"Yes; nothing," was Obi's short response.

The door was opened by a woman in her early twenties, well dressed casually but with heavy makeup. She was too young to be the owner of the painting.

They showed their warrant cards and gave their names. "Can we come in?" Catrin asked.

The woman moved back, signifying agreement, but was looking apprehensively at Obi.

In the hallway, Catrin asked, "Is Mrs. Renée Altman available? We are here about a painting."

"Mum's out in the laundry room; we were just starting doing it together. I'll go call her. Wait here."

She turned and headed into the house.

Obi was looking through the living room entrance and said quietly, "It's in there, I think," pointing at an ornately-framed 'princess-type' painting on the far wall.

But Catrin wasn't looking in that direction; suddenly she saw in the open hall closet a motorbike helmet and a pair of leather gloves on a shelf, side by side. Below it, among the coats, there was a leather jacket and part of its back was showing a corner of an emblem.

Suddenly she was on tenterhooks, thinking back to yesterday's discussion with Jim Hughes and putting two and two together. She didn't like where this was going. Two years as a security aide to Sandra Hunt had her fine-tuned. She glanced at Obi and whispered, "Call for back-up immediately if I nod to you; don't wait."

He looked surprised, just as two men entered across the open plan living room from the other direction than the route that Renée Altman's daughter had taken. The younger one was in jeans and a T-shirt, the older man in jeans and a black collared dress shirt. Catrin moved forward to introduce herself as the older man's face turned sour and the younger man looked irritated, angry. She wondered why, then realised it was focused on the presence of Obi.

"I'm Detective Inspector Sayer, this is Detective Constable Obi; we are with the Metropolitan Police. We are here about that painting, I believe," she said, pointing at it, trying to move things along.

"It's ours; it's my mum's," the younger man said.

She replied, "I know. There is a strong possibility that it's a copy, not an original. You may have seen the news about a series of - ."

The voice of the older woman who had walked through from the kitchen area was between a shout and a cry. "Get him out of my house. I don't want no black person in my house! Renata, why did you let him in? Out! She can stay, you - you are not welcome!"

The vehemence of the older woman's diatribe surprised

Catrin but she responded firmly, "DC Obi stays Mrs. Altman; it's procedure. And you need to be careful about what you say, if you would, please."

John had also been taken by surprise by the outburst. To his eyes, the woman looked unwell. She was panting and had breathing difficulties. But it wasn't the first time on the job he had met outright prejudice about the colour of his skin. He stayed calm and left it to his boss.

The older man said, "It's about the painting, Renée." He pronounced it 'Reenee'.

"She says it may be a copy, a fake. It's that thing on the news."

The older woman looked dumbfounded and sat in the chair.

The daughter, Renata apparently, said, "She's not well."

That's obvious, thought John.

Renée whispered, "How do you know?"

Catrin replied, "We just need to look at the back to tell, probably. Can we?"

The older man nodded and Catrin and John pulled out standard forensic gloves and put them on, then took the painting down, resting its edge on a chair seat. It only took a moment to examine, but it was obvious; it had the same familiar newish canvas poorly stained in darker irregular patches to give it the semblance of age and it showed the same weave as others they had seen.

Catrin looked at John first, seeing him nod, before she turned to face Renée.

 "We are sorry, but it does appear to be a copy. There have been a number of paintings discovered, some in galleries where the originals have disappeared and others have been found in the home of a person under investigation, a man called Brian Sleaman."

The older man looked dumbfounded.

His wife said to him, "He sold me a fake? He was so friendly, but - ."

The man snapped, "Don't - ." Then he stopped himself.

Catrin spoke up, cutting through a potential argument, "We are going to have to take this away for examination, I am afraid, and we will need to see any documentation of sale and take a statement of how you acquired it. I will be giving you a written confirmation of our seizure of the painting, as evidence in the investigation and will explain what happens next. It will, in all probability, be returned in due course if it has no other rightful owner."

She turned towards the older man as Obi lifted the painting to lean it against a nearby table leg. They had brought two transport cases with them in the car and he was about to go out and get one.

The woman raised her voice again, angry and on the verge of tears as she stood up. "I don't want him touching my - ."

She stopped suddenly, looking shocked, falling back on to the floor beside the chair, her head and one elbow hitting with thumps that made Catrin wince. In the ensuing reaction and confusion she said firmly to John, "Call an ambulance. And back up."

She went over to take charge; at least she knew First Aid. The family members were still in shock other than the husband, who was now down on his knees by his wife's side calling to her. But he wasn't doing anything else to assist.

Catrin knelt down the other side of the woman and checked the carotid artery for a pulse, finding none.

She said to him, "No pulse; she's not breathing; I have to do CPR. If you could give me room to - ."

The man moved back slightly and Catrin started the chest compressions and mouth-to-mouth resuscitation, focusing entirely on this new development.

She had no idea how long that went on for before the amb-ulance team arrived and took over. Later, it turned out to be seven and a half minutes between the time Obi's call was received and the crew called in their arrival at the house.

As the ambulance sped away Catrin had no doubt that the woman was dead - a stroke or aneurism, perhaps. Renée

Altman had shown no response before the ambulance team arrived, nor did she respond to the portable defibrillator they had used upon arrival.

In the shock and confusion only one more issue arose. Alerted by the 999 call a police car had also arrived, for which Catrin was grateful. She talked to one of the officers as the other talked with the older man, who had asked for help in the identification of the hospital his wife was being taken to. Obi packed the painting in the case and quickly wrote out an official record of seizure, not wanting to leave empty-handed or make a fuss about it.

The young man who hadn't said a word after the opening comment about the painting being bought by his father came up and said stonily, "If you hadn't come here, my mum would still be alive."

He wasn't threatening, John thought. But he was unshakably certain, resolute. John didn't respond and just looked away. He didn't want it to escalate and cause more trouble for the family or the Met.

Of course, they had to wait and give statements to the local officers; that was routine. It was after doing so that one of them said quietly to Catrin, "You did know, I take it? The husband, Leo Altman, is a biker. He is with the Centurions, the president of the local chapter."

Catrin said, "I didn't. Somehow we missed it when we did the background check."

He nodded. "He and his wife are on the radar; I don't know the details. The son isn't; he is into bikes but the Centurions won't take him, we heard."

Catrin wondered about the link with the German find. Was this the starting point?

She shook her head. She didn't want to say anything, unclear why they had missed the link in the records search.

The local officer didn't ask her; he was a uniform constable, she was a more senior officer, but his expression was clear.

What were you doing walking into a known biker gang family living in our borough without knowing that fact?

Catrin said after a moment, "We just came here to see a painting."

~~

It was Aina Jinnah who provided a possible answer. She and Isabelle had looked into it as soon Catrin had called in, reporting to DCI Wetherby. Catrin had called him as soon as they cleared the home, reaching his voicemail. So she called Aina and filled her in. Wetherby was in a meeting offsite with one of his other teams, she said; she would interrupt it.

Catrin and John had found a café next to a betting shop about a mile away when her boss called her back. She had just wanted tea but, despite the events, John turned out to be hungry, so in the end she ordered some soup. Before it arrived her mobile rang.

"Wetherby," she said as she answered.

He was disturbed, initially wanting to make sure they had gone 'by the book' during the visit.

He added, "I didn't understand how the woman wasn't flagged, if DC Obi had checked as he said, but Aina has an idea; I am linking her in now."

Aina spoke up. "Hi. There was a 'page jump', I think, in the database. Both Isabelle and I just tried it on our computers, with the same result. There are three entries for people called Renée Altman listed. Two were complainants; the third had her home broken into. They appear at the bottom of that screen page of people with surnames beginning with A when you enter the search name. It's only a second or so, but the screen jumps and another Renée Altman from the next page listing moves up, showing four names in total, the new one at the bottom. This last one is actually recorded as related to a watch list name - a Leonard K. Altman. The link code is to Trident, so it is to organized crime."

John looked stupefied when Catrin explained quickly and

quietly to him across the table. In reality, every officer struggled with the databases in this way at times. It was a fault supposedly corrected again and again by the systems people.

She said into the mobile, "John is a bit shocked, sir."

DCI Wetherby turned out to be a practical man under pressure. "Tell him not to fret on it. You have given statements. I will get on to Hertfordshire Police to get copies and follow up, to monitor the situation. I see no basis for any complaint or criticism and you did render the appropriate emergency assistance, Sayer. I would like you to document more completely your observations of the woman, her behaviour and her comments for the record on your return. Just in case.

"Now, are you two up to completing the Norfolk request? If not, you may want to come back here or take time off. DC Howlett and I could go out to the Noak Hill location."

It was the first time he had offered to do anything operational, Catrin noted. But it was appreciated. She thought of Howlett's plan to leave early and looked at John.

"OK for Noak Hill?" she asked him. He nodded.

"We are having a break, sorting ourselves out. It was a bit of a shock, that's all. We are fine for completing the collection of number two. Hopefully it will be less eventful."

Then she added quietly, "Sir, it's not the time and we need to work out when to do it, but we have nothing on how this man got the painting from Sleaman. We didn't follow up on the paperwork aspect, obviously. But it was clear from Mrs. Altman's outburst that her husband bought it from a 'person' rather than a gallery or a shop. I think that DI Needham was right."

She paused.

"Inadvertently we walked in on a biker from the club that gave Sleaman the injury after the Bash years ago, I suspect. It may be that Sleaman deliberately sold Altman a fake for revenge, hence the smiley symbol in his notebook against this entry."

It dawned on Catrin and Wetherby at the same time, it

appeared. He said, "I think we have already disobeyed Commander Moore's earlier instruction."

Catrin agreed. "I think she and DI Coombs should be briefed straight away, sir. Should I come back?"

He thought about it.

"No, I'll do that. You didn't disobey at all is my position. It was just an unfortunate oversight."

They closed the call.

"Bloody computer," said Obi, "I shouldn't have rushed; should have seen it."

17 NOAK HILL

Fortunately, the Noak Hill visit went smoothly. They left nothing behind this time other than a bewildered accountant living in a thatched roof house worth several million pounds. He had bought the painting from Sleaman directly as a result of a conversation while new security protection for another work he owned was being installed in the home.

The owner said, "He said it was the finest copy of Turner's 'Petworth House from the Lake' he had ever seen, and he had seen a few. It would be worth a lot in the long term, he believed. So I thought, why not?"

"Did he say who the copyist was?"

The man smiled conspiratorially. "He just said that he was a great artist and, when it was known who he was, the value would jump through the roof."

Catrin glanced at John. The man had paid £15,000 for an unsigned, unknown copy of a frequently copied work by an artist with no provenance.

"Can we see the paperwork?"

As they were leaving the man asked, "You wouldn't by any chance have any idea how much a copy like this, a good copy that is, would actually cost, do you? Bit late to ask, I suppose?"

He looked embarrassed.

Obi looked at him, his expression clear. "A commissioned copy with a reputable copyist, done from the original; a bit variable. About half the price you paid, perhaps. The original work by Turner is in Petworth House, I think. But this copy is top quality, as he said, he wasn't lying about that. So you weren't taken to the cleaners too badly."

As they walked out Catrin said quietly, "You were nice at the end, there, ramping it up like that."

On the drive back, she mused, "So, we think the copyist is likely a man, an existing artist, perhaps, if Sleaman's spin is to be believed. We now have evidence that Sleaman sold copies as fakes both to fool people maliciously and also reasonably fairly; he could have taken the Noak Hill guy for more, I think, if he had spun the story better. It will be really interesting to find out how much Leo Altman paid for his Winterhalter; if we ever can."

She dropped him at a tube station as she headed back to the Yard. She wanted to transfer the paintings collected to forensic custody before any other mishap occurred. She wasn't looking forward to tomorrow at all.

~~

Several days after the meeting in the White Moon restaurant Li and Miele met for a business lunch in Kowloon. For the first half of the meeting they discussed the outline of working together as client and legal representative. Li gave Miele some sense of the processes that would need to be followed and a timeline she had prepared. She concluded with, "But from now on business is not an issue for lunches; I will come to your studio, we will meet there by appointment and I will work and bill accordingly."

Miele nodded. They then talked about the issue of ownership and decision-making. Although Miele owned the business outright, her artistic partner, a graduate of the same class as Miele, needed clarity.

Li had said, "You and Jonathon are sharing artistic input, for which there is always intrinsic emotional ownership. It is not a standard employer/employee situation. The rights and expectations of each person need to be crystal clear and under-stood and agreed to by the other. So it's best that, as you enter into this asset purchase, you also formalize your working relationship contractually."

Miele responded, "I had thought about that a bit based on our last discussion, but was focusing more on the studio first. You are right; they go hand-in-hand."

She paused. "I'm looking forward to working with you. And thank you again for accommodating my grandfather's ways and particularly heading off further financial involvement by him."

Li asked, "How is he doing now?"

Michael Yau became the next topic of conversation. It would help Li prepare for her own visit to see him.

During the discussion, Li mentioned her father's reaction to the last meeting with Michael.

"I thought he would be even more subdued when he came home but he wasn't. Somehow, it seemed to resolve things for him; he seems happier, though I am not sure why."

Miele smiled. "My grandad said the same, really; it was a good farewell. He asked neither of his bathhouse friends to come in his final days. They are to continue to meet weekly as usual and find a new third participant; someone who is not from their businesses or their worlds, he suggested. He wants the bathhouse ritual to go on for them. It's their gift from him; the use of the spa room there for the rest of their lives. He's getting good at these finales; yesterday was his last visit to his enterprise. I went with him, at his request, with my aunt and grandmother."

Li gave her a deliberate astonished blink. "I thought you were steering clear of triad life?"

"I am, it's what I planned. I have too much to do with my art and my studio. But it brought home what it truly meant to my grandad."

She went on. "It's a ritual, the last visit; very respectful. The old one gets to see the people he helped to put in place and to mentor, the ones he now leaves in charge. The young ones, the newest members, are also given some time with him alone to hear what a life with Four Square means; what they get from it, what they have to give to it - and give up for it.

"He was happy there but he was also worn out on the ride home. And he has a question I am to pass on, to give you time to think of the answer before you see him. To do with Bangor."

Li said, "Go on."

"The earrings you wore. Would you like them as a gift, as a memory of him, or not? And he quite understands if the answer is no. I don't, they are beautiful. He showed them to me; he has them stored away."

Li was surprised. "He has them; he bought them? When? They were - no, they were never rented, then, after all."

The image of the expensive white gold hoops each with their row of diamonds flooded back; a distant memory from that unbearable day.

The young woman smiled. "No they weren't. He had someone buy them. My grandfather was adamant about it at the time, my aunt said."

Li nodded. "Emily Chang bought them, then."

Miele looked questioning for a second then said, "You know Emily?"

"I have met her, yes."

She wasn't going to elaborate. She added, "Emily was at the enterprise, no doubt, when your grandfather visited?"

"No, she was away on business, unfortunately. She will visit my grandfather at home. She is… the last of his protégés in Four Square, he said. And I am his last protégé outside. The meeting at the university where we first met, for example."

Li laughed, "Yes, he maneuvered that one well, didn't he?"

She turned serious. "The earrings. No, I don't want them. They bring back a memory of the time I wore them - did he tell you the story?"

"No."

"Then its time you knew. And understood what it is about. I wore them for less than half an hour to impress and disconcert the woman who was responsible for my brother's death. It was during her police interview in Wales after her arrest. She had asked to see me as a condition of saying more to them. The police thought she was looking for comments from me that would help her legal case. She didn't get those."

Li's mind went back to the day of the interview, of being with Catrin.

"The woman liked jewellery, I knew. I wanted to make her realise that there was more to me than just being a student; in fact, to fool her into believing I had power within the triad world, would you believe? Students don't wear earrings costing many thousands of pounds. I asked Mr. Lin if an expensive pair could be borrowed or rented. He and your grandfather were together on the effort to clear Han's name, I know. So no, that interview is not a memory I would like regularly re-awakened, I think, beautiful as they are. They should be yours."

Miele shook her head. "I'm glad you made the suggestion, because he wants you to choose their fate if you don't accept them yourself, but I am the only person you can't pick, he said. Anyone else, even your mother; but not me. Take your time. Think about it.

"Now, let's talk about Catrin; how is she doing?"

"Having a rough time. Not just the loss of the baby, which is bad enough. She went recently to investigate a fraudulent painting and the owner, a woman in ill-health, died suddenly. She'd made a fuss about Catrin's sergeant being black and had some sort of stroke. It was stressful. She doesn't need it."

Miele asked, "Will she try again, her and Chris, do you think?"

I don't know, I didn't ask last time I spoke to her; it wasn't appropriate. She is seeing some specialist obstetrician now. I wish she'd just give up being a police officer, do her art and take it easy."

"As do I," said Miele. It always brought a sense of unease for her, even though Miele was not a member of Four Square.

18 DEMONS

Sayer, Obi and Wetherby, with Wetherby's own boss Superintendent Patterson, had been called into a conference room later on during the afternoon of the day following the incident. Present were several people from the Trident Biker Gang team - and Karen Moore.

Commander Moore was not known to mince words. "Give me the current status."

It was clear that she expected that from DCI Wetherby, who did a reasonable job, Catrin thought, for someone who hadn't been directly involved.

Then Moore looked at Catrin and John Obi. Catrin braced herself but Moore just said, "Accidents happen. I talked with the systems people this morning; told them one of the worst-case scenarios we envisioned for the 'screen jump' problem had actually happened. Both I and Commander Barlow are holding their feet to the fire to get this permanently fixed."

She turned to look at the other side of the table. "DI Coombs, update us on the Altman family and the Centurions."

Coombs did so, efficiently and neutrally. "Here's what's come back so far. The Centurions are into drug shipment, not distribution, as we know. They have links with the 'Demons' gang in Munich, where this other painting popped up. Now it's out there that the painting is a forgery, Leo Altman is in some trouble with his Munich friends. Coupled with his wife's untimely death, he will no doubt be under a lot of stress.

"If Sleaman were alive or the identity of the forger involved is known to the Centurions, it could mean that some form of retribution could be in the works. Currently we are waiting to see how it plays between the German and British biker clubs."

Moore nodded and turned back to the Arts and Antiques Team.

"You will stay away from Altman. And I want Norfolk to do the same now; I spoke to them before this meeting. Given that the family may well try to make an issue of police harassment contributing to Renée Altman's death - which has no basis and won't stick - we will give them no further basis for complaint.

"I know you want the paperwork on the painting, but we will leave it be, at least until after the funeral is over and the dust has settled. If they were normal, they would see it as a sad coincidence. But I never regard a 'one percenter' biker to be predictable. DI Coombs, please keep the club and particularly Altman in your sights if you think some vengeance attack is in the works."

Coombs replied, "We are, ma'am; we saw it the same way. I have five people on this; it's a focal area for us at present. That and the Hammersmith club aftermath."

Moore nodded. Everyone was aware that a brawl at a nightclub a week ago had put a biker in intensive care and resulted in three arrests.

Moore continued, "I understand that the coroner has already issued a temporary death certificate to allow Renée Altman's funeral to take place. In time, not until the Assistant Chief Constable in Norwich and I say, the Norfolk JMIT can go in and follow up on their case with Leo Altman. Sayer, what do they need?"

Catrin replied, "A receipt; which they probably won't get if it was a cash deal between Sleaman and Altman. And they want to ask for the provenance documents; the supposed history of the painting - who had it when, tracing back to when it was painted."

John Obi added, "If nothing else, when did he buy it? It was for his wife; if so, what occasion was it? A birthday, whatever. Get a year, even."

DI Coombs said, nodding, "Because it's big money. Then we can go back through his finances."

Moore said, "Exactly."

She took the lead again.

"Based on the autopsy and the woman's medical history, the Coroner doesn't see the need for an open inquest but, given the circumstances, she wants her own reports. So interviews with the Coroner's Officer will be set up for all people present at the time of death, probably sometime in the next two weeks."

Obi was looking apprehensive.

Moore looked at him. "DC Obi, your boss was quite right to insist you stay and I am sorry you were subjected to such treatment. DS Eaton told me that the Altman family is known to be vocally racist in the biker community. If they sue us, I will take issue with your treatment in their home; we will see how Leo Altman wants his dead wife's name dragged through the courts. We will also make sure that interviews with family members at the Coroner's office are well separated from those of the police and ambulance personnel; I don't want you two running into them.

"That's it for that fiasco. On the Sleaman case, what are the next steps?"

Catrin said, "We will touch base with the Norfolk team on a call tomorrow morning, to review the result of all five visits and reassess the scope of the frauds. We are looking for leads to the artist. Ma'am, the painting in Germany needs to be confirmed formally as arising from the same artist, particularly if it later features as evidence in some sort of drug transaction prosecution."

Moore nodded, agreeing with the actions.

"The visit to Germany for someone: DCI Wetherby, I'll put

it on my budget. The rest sounds fine. I think that's it."

As they all stood she said, "Sayer, can you spare me a minute?"

Catrin thought, she wants to ream me out in private, at least.

When they were alone, Moore said, "Send Obi to Germany, if you would? He needs support and reinforcing, I can see it in his face. He is feeling it badly. And you, you need more rest; not travel."

Catrin smiled. "Thank you; I thought you were going to tear a strip off, to be honest, ma'am."

Moore looked surprised. "If I have a bone to pick with one of my teams over their conduct, they know it. If not, they get my support. That's my job. And it's yours, with your team, too."

She paused then asked quietly, "Coombs. Have you talked to him at all?"

Catrin said, "No. This is the first case we have worked on together, actually."

Moore responded, "He's good, but... I sense he knew that he was the person appointed after you turned the position down. It was in his eyes."

She looked at Sayer. "I don't want you two getting cross-threaded."

"No, ma'am; I take your point."

She, too, had seen some elements of competitiveness in the man's communication.

Catrin returned to her area with a lighter step than she had on the way upstairs. She had no axe to grind with DI Coombs and hadn't been hauled over the coals by the unpredictable Mancunian.

~~

It was the following Sunday that Neville rang Catrin on her personal phone. She hadn't heard much other than a couple of emails since the last call so she was pleased to hear his voice. They talked for a few minutes, catching up as much as they could; both were aware of the limitations of confidentiality surrounding police work.

"Where are you, by the way?" asked Catrin.

"Dessau, following up with someone. I had dinner again last night with Gerhardt in Berlin. He paid because he said I did a good job of keeping you in Art and Antiques, despite better opportunities being offered."

"Gerhardt wouldn't say that!"

"No he wouldn't; I lie. He is just happy to have you there. He will give all the support he can, I think, on any international matters that come up."

She said, "I talked with him recently."

She didn't say what about.

He said suddenly, "I have something delicate to suggest, but I don't want to offend."

She laughed. "More delicate than bludgeoning me to stay in Art and Antiques? No, you didn't; I retract that. It was always my decision, I know."

But he didn't quip back. "Yes, so tell me straight off if I am off-base, but I wonder would you be open to seeing my cousin, Louis Cameron. He is a consultant obstetrician in Harley Street. And he is rather good; actually Louis is top of the line but I never give him compliments if he is remotely near. But after visiting you in hospital it's been on my mind and… would you be open to it?"

Catrin replied, "I have a new specialist, Neville. I had my first appointment and am waiting on the results and my next appointment. Chris and I were saying how it is like starting afresh, building new trust. I don't really see how - ."

She stopped.

"But I do appreciate that you care and take the trouble to raise it with me. In fact, that makes me feel very good indeed, you know."

Her voice had softened.

Neville said, "Then do me a favour, please; see him just

once. First check with your own person whether he or she - ."

"It's a female - ."

"- she thinks it is worth a shot. She will probably know of Louis, being in the field."

Catrin was swaying in her resolve. "Is he expensive? We have BUPA but... Harley Street."

"He's my cousin, Catrin. Seeing him will cost you nothing. Thank you for being open to it."

She took the moment to strike.

"And how are you doing, honestly now?"

He paused. The picture of his restlessness came together for Catrin in a mix of sentences.

"It's a big transition, obviously. Unsettling. I'm traveling a lot. I was given a private tour of the Bauhaus facility today. It is quite astonishing to see the original design school and remember it was happening in the nineteen twenties. I was just filling in time before my meeting, which will take place any minute, I hope.

"The search for the Tarrant is occupying me. Sylvia calls it my quest, which makes the family talk, of course. But... it's not the item as much as the sort of investigation I would have daydreamed about if I had *carte blanche* while at the Met; which I never had, of course.

"So I am enjoying it for now but also I am no further forward in what I want to do, to be honest. Look, I see my guest coming in, so I had better go. Someone at Louis's clinic will be in touch. Take care and say hello to Chris."

As Catrin said, "Goodbye, Neville," the line closed. She wasn't sure whether he was avoiding talking further about himself or he really had someone to see at that precise moment.

The opportunity might be a good one, to see this cousin, if he is that good, she thought, now that things seem to be settling down after the problem with the Altman family. She was glad that had gone quiet. They only had the coroner's officer to speak with, and they could put that unwelcome incident behind them.

Catrin thought back to the comment forced out of Neville

in the hospital and the troubled days and nights after the all the changes, personal and professional. Somehow, she felt she had arrived; that she had made the right job decision, at least. Hopefully it would get better from hereon in.

19 MUTTON LANE

Two days after her funeral, Renée Altman's ashes were interred in Mutton Lane Cemetery in Potters Bar, according to her wishes. Not that she had put it in her will, but she had occasionally voiced it. St. Margaret's Cemetery, as it was officially known, had closed to new burials in the nineteen seventies but interment of ashes was still allowed. And price and social barriers to access the cemetery was no deterrent to Leo. People fixed it for him.

Renée had no family there or connection to the church; she was born in Leytonstone. The cemetery, not far from their home, was picturesque and had a memorial garden for prisoners of war. Renée's step-dad had been a POW; she was as sentimental about that as she was about Princess Di. Ironically, although her dislike of government and authority in all its forms had led her to the biker world and to Leo, she never saw the Royal family as a bulwark of these institutions; only as glamorous people.

The funeral had been small, by Leo's wish; families on both sides and a few closer friends from their world. In contrast, the turnout for the interment was large. Despite the cold, damp day and the threat of rain, they were mainly there on bikes; gleaming and clean other than the ride dirt getting there today.

129

That the Centurions turned out *en masse* was a given; indeed, they formed the vanguard and lined the road to the old cemetery. It was their right; she was Leo's wife and one of them. But there were others, from near and far; people who had known Renée, bikers and their women, in leathers with patches on show.

And in the corner of the cemetery providing a good view of the entrance were two cars, visible to all. It was also a given that the police would observe from a distance. Who turned up, who was known; who was unknown, who talked to who; all to be recorded and analysed - in this case by DC Long and two others, under the eagle eye of DS Hilary Eaton.

Hilary turned her gaze from the main gathering near the interment plot to two people, a man and a woman, a little distance away. The man was in a sharp, dark grey suit, the woman similarly attired; funeral clothes.

"Who's he?" asked Hilary.

Keith Long swung his glasses round. "Lyall Beddows; a hangaround, may be a prospect, now. Close to Leo, became his 'gofer' a while ago."

Hilary adjusted her binoculars. "Now that is Gerda Lentz with him, if I am right. Wife of the president of the Munich Demons. She's come over. Keith, phone back; get a photo sent over; I want to be doubly sure."

Gerda was being motherly. "It is alright to be upset, Lyall. Do not be embarrassed. Oskar says real men can show their feelings. I am the same. Renée was a good person."

The short sentences delivered sincerely seemed to register with Lyall. He had held it together since the news came in, a thunderbolt of tragedy, he thought; even through the funeral, trying to be strong for Leo, Steve and Renata. Leo had been the same, until the funeral. Renata had fallen apart and Steve seemed stunned, lost in himself.

Seeing Leo now at the plot in tears and thinking back to how his mentor was the pillar of strength only days ago had overwhelmed him; he had to break away and Gerda had accompanied him.

Lyall said, "She was good to me, she really was. Like a second mother, one who…" he ran out of words. He had become very close to the older woman in the time he had been running around fetching and carrying for Leo.

As he pulled himself together, Gerda turned to face him, her head now directly in front of him; close.

"Now listen. No, keep still. You see and hear me and I you, but no one else will, even the police over there watching everyone. You have a message to pass on to Leo alone, from Oskar; not today but within the next few days. Ready?"

Realising this was business, that the Dämon president's wife trusted him to deliver it brought Lyall out of his focus on himself. He nodded.

"The Klinkenburg painting fraud is bouncing around our entire network in Germany and Italy. Not as bad as it could be, seeing as the police had already seized it, but we have to sort it out. We bought it and our expert is very embarrassed that it got past her. You saw how borderline it was when we discussed it in Brands Hatch, right? You speak German, I think?"

Caught unawares, Lyall blushed as Gerda gave him a small smile.

"We expect the Centurions to re-pay half the price and we will absorb the rest; to share the burden equally. That is not what we will be saying on the street; we will be making a lot of noise about it to feed the police. But Oskar is tight with Leo and we have no resentments. Even before the news of Renée but moreso now.

"You will tell him; him alone?"

Lyall replied, "As soon as I can, under the circumstances."

She continued, "This man who is dead, from Norfolk, the one who cheated Leo; he sold other stuff to the family, we heard?"

Lyall was torn; he couldn't talk about Leo or the club but…

"I shouldn't say anything, Frau Lentz; it was what I was told. But this man misled Renée also, I know."

Gerda looked serious. "He had a partner, the forger. We want him, as will Leo. Just remind Leo of that. Outlaws don't forgive such people. Ever. Tell him Eric will help."

"Eric?"

"That's enough. And Lyall, do not ever let Leo down. Got me?"

Lyall nodded vigorously as Gerda looked over his shoulder. "Photo time."

Lyall turned round to see a patch member of the Centurions with a Nikon camera and telephoto lens approach the two cars parked in the corner, carefully and boldly taking photographs of the people inside. A car door opened and closed again; a man was about to get out but the woman in the front passenger seat stopped him, from her head movement and her mouth moving. He was trying to remember the name; he had seen her before, a Met Police officer specializing in bikers, Leo said; a Helen or Hilary, he couldn't quite be sure.

"It's definitely Gerda Lentz," said DC Long after looking at his phone, at the image received.

Hilary commented, "She's representing the Demons, then. Oskar Lentz doesn't leave Germany, I was told. He runs his clubhouse with an iron rod - literally, I suspect."

She paused, thinking. "This Lyall Beddows must be Leo's prospect, not a hangaround; the Demons president's wife wouldn't waste time with a hangaround. I suspect it means that Beddows has met her before. Leo may have involved him in the painting deal back when. Keith, make a note of it; the man is on the rise, perhaps."

A bleat came over the radio from a new transfer into the Biker Gang Unit during the re-organisation; a young female DC in the second car.

"Can't we stop this guy photographing us so blatantly, sarge?"

"Not without risking escalation, Iris. We take their pics; they take ours; it's the way. Don't let it intimidate you. Ignore it unless I say different. If it becomes a threat we will call in the cars outside and disturb the whole shebang. But I don't want to do that, if I can avoid it."

She looked across at Keith Long as she closed the switch on the microphone.

He nodded. "Right. It's a burial, after all."

20 THE BELL COMMON TUNNEL

The interviews with the Coroner's Officer, a Hertfordshire Constabulary employee with specialist duties to support the coroner, took place at The Old Court House, Welwyn Garden City. The notice had gone out arranging for the family members to be interviewed on the Tuesday morning, with the police officers and ambulance responders being scheduled for interview the following day.

It was clearly a routine issue; no one had a slot of more than forty-five minutes. The proforma cover note pointed out that it was not a police investigation; rather, it was to gain the facts around the causes and circumstances of the death to assist the coroner to finalize the death certificate.

In the wake of the meeting with Moore, the days running up to the visit to Welwyn had been largely in the office. John had taken a day trip to Berlin where he saw the second copy of the Klinkenburg painting stolen from Cambridge. The German police had provided professional quality images previously and it was little more than a formality for him to confirm that the work appeared to be from the same copyist.

John was given lunch by Heidi Schmidt, the second-in-command on Gerhardt Amstel's team. Later, at the airport, waiting for his return flight home, he called Catrin.

"The copy is virtually identical to the one I saw in Norwich. But looking at the images of the two of them, there are small differences; you can see them in the overlays with the software that they have here. Amstel's group is really well equipped."

"Don't rub it in," responded Catrin.

John finished with, "What I can say is that they are by the same artist and not produced by any computer-based layout technique. He or she does this entirely by eye, with very little variation."

~~

The Old Courthouse in Hatfield turned out to be a redbrick building with two wings, primarily serving now as a centre for citizenship ceremonies and a location for the registrar of births, deaths and marriages. It also housed the coroner assigned to Renée Altman's death. The Coroner's Officer was a silver-haired, fit woman in her fifties, as far as John could assess, in civilian attire. She was formal rather than friendly and John got the impression that whether he was a constable or a chief superintendent, she would act in exactly the same way.

At one point she said to John Obi, "Mrs. Altman has been reported by several witnesses to have become agitated because you were present and that she was uneasy around anyone who wasn't Caucasian. Did you talk to her at all?"

A delicate way to put it, thought John, but he responded. "I didn't speak. I have had similar racist comments in the past, of course, but this one was a surprise. DI Sayer dealt with it firmly but without fuss."

"So you did nothing provocative?"

"No, I stayed in the background. Even when she collapsed, it was DI Sayer who went forward to give CPR. I immediately called for the ambulance. I thought of it - CPR - obviously; it's part of the training. But it was also obvious that it was better for a woman, a white person as well, to administer first aid."

"Mrs. Altman was shocked by the visit, though?"

John thought a moment. "She didn't want me in the house. But she was shocked as well by the news that her painting was a possible forgery, yes. I saw that clearly. She started to talk to her husband about the purchase but he didn't have time to answer before she collapsed. That's all I recall."

John was through in twenty minutes. He went outside to where Catrin was waiting; she had already been interviewed. As he approached, she said, "I was just talking to Isabelle. She has some additional questions for the guy in Noak Hill about the relationship between him and Sleaman that built up to the sale and the timings of their contacts.

"We should have caught them at the time. I guess, after the experience at the Altman home, we didn't focus too hard in our interview. We can, what was the term you used, 'spin round the M25' to Noak Hill and get it over with. I called; he is home today. I'll tell you what Isabelle and I discussed in the car."

They were on the motorway crossing the Crown Hill overpass when John said, out of the blue and obviously thinking back to the interview, "The Coroner's Officer was pretty good, but a bit formal."

Catrin replied, "Yes, she knew her job. She was a bit more open with me, I felt. She asked about Wales - her own family history is there. Apparently the interviews yesterday were more difficult, of course. Altman and his daughter were very emotional and the son didn't even turn up. One of the ambulance team sprained his ankle on the steps coming into the Court House this morning, as well."

Catrin, partly lost in her own thoughts, was concentrating on her driving. They had passed signs warning of road maintenance between junctions 24 and 28 and she could see the traffic slowing and the flashing lights of the maintenance vehicles stationary on the left side. For about two hundred metres they were queued in the reduced lane congestion, the line of traffic moving steadily but slowly.

She was thinking it wouldn't delay them enough to be late for the Noak Hill follow-up when the glint of colour on a motorbike four vehicles behind her changed her focus entirely.

The reason that Catrin Sayer had spent two years as a security aide to a senior executive officer of the Metropolitan Police arose from one second like this. On a PR tourist junket tagged on to an official visit to Malaysia, supposedly to see Kuala Lumpur in the slipstream of an assertive Foreign Office bureaucrat, the expression on the face of the local police officer accompanying them changed from relaxed and easy-going to tense and panicky. In seconds, she went from sight-seeing to armed combat, using that injured officer's weapon to shoot their assailant. It was that fast.

It was Assistant Commissioner Sandra Hunt who later transferred Sayer to be her own security aide for two years, but she didn't do that blindly. Officers whose personal make-up enables them to handle a crisis fast, whose reaction times are far better than the average, are rare. And for the next two years Sayer received specialized training as she lived the life of a security officer whose primary job was to protect her boss.

The glint of colour had been the same deep purple as the motorbike she had seen in the Altman garage. That had triggered her alarm response. She monitored it as they all moved forward, passing the maintenance vehicles at the point where the motorway opened up and traffic sped forward, the constraint removed.

The bike stayed behind, moving up the line of vehicles as the opportunity arose so that soon there was only one vehicle between it and Catrin's Audi. The motion of other traffic overtaking or changing lanes interrupted her view. In the glimpses she had, she couldn't identify the rider; he was helmeted and the visor was tinted and closed. She was struggling to recall the image of the motorbike helmet in the closet at the Altman home as she told herself that there were lots of bikes in London with the same paint job.

It was seconds later, as they entered the three lane east-bound underpass of the Bell Common tunnel that the bike sped up cutting inside to the middle lane; then she knew it was no coincidence.

Sayer was in the fast lane, on the outside. Belatedly the car behind her, also wanting to get back into a slower lane, honked in protest as the bike overtook illegally on the inside, but by then it was moving up on her fast. In her side mirror Catrin saw the right arm reach into the jacket and when it emerged there was a reflection from something in the gloved hand. She couldn't identify it clearly but intuitively she knew what it was.

She shouted, 'gun; down!' to a shocked John Obi as, sensing and assessing the speeding vehicles all around her, she swerved violently to her left, crashing the rear end of her Audi into the bike as it tried to come along inside her. It sent both vehicles heading directly for the tunnel wall.

She braced herself for the impact and the bang of airbags.

Her training had kicked in. Don't think; act. You haven't time to think; just do instinctively the things that intuition and training tell you to do.

Obi's hand shot out and grabbed the side of the steering wheel. Instinctively, seeing the wall approaching he used his strength to force the wheel to the right as the tyres squealed and the car swung. The back nearside corner, already damaged from contact with the bike, slid along the wall first and the front end turned out again. The bike went down, disappearing from Catrin's view.

She shouted, "I've got it!" as the Audi slowed a little from the contact. She braked hard, forcing the front of the car to the left again, first into the curbside lane parallel to the wall then finally pulling over to the left, on to the hard shoulder, stopping abruptly a yard from the guard rail and the tunnel wall. Something fell off the car's rear quarter panel as she came to a complete halt; the indicator light bracket of the motorbike, torn away in the crash.

They were about sixty metres from the point of the crash as vehicles in the other lanes shot past them with horns blaring. Catrin could hear the noise of another vehicle screeching to a halt behind her on the shoulder, stopping just inches from her own. Sayer braced for the impact that never came. She could see the white faces of the older couple in the Passat behind her. The Audi's airbags, ironically, front, side or back, had not gone off, despite the bang on the rear corner with the bike and then the tunnel wall. But it was Obi on the inside who was out of the vehicle first, heading back.

Catrin called 'John!' and looked at her driver-side mirror, then thought better of the idea of opening the door. She could be killed, drawn into the slipstream of the vehicles going past. She swung her legs over the centre console and shuffled her way out of same door as her team member.

Catrin moved back to the vehicle now stopped behind them where the occupants were sitting unharmed but shocked. John was further back still. The bike was on its side, straddling the inside lane and hard shoulder as John's wide running steps crossed the narrow gap between the front wheel and the tunnel wall. She could see part of the bike rider lying prone, one leg struggling for purchase. She turned to the people in the car sitting transfixed and yelled through the glass, "Don't move. Help is coming."

She knew that by now the traffic camera monitoring system would have emergency vehicles mobilized. It was only a second or so delay as she went after John, seeing his leg go up and then stamp down, landing on the gloved hand of the rider. As she closed on them she saw the gun. A Beretta M9, she registered unconsciously, now a couple of feet away from the biker's hand. Obi had moved back a step, panting, assessing what to do next.

The biker was screaming in pain. Obi moved to push the gun further away with his foot.

Catrin shouted, "Don't touch it. Leave it."

She shouted again as she arrived next to her sergeant. "Just keep him from getting it and don't touch him otherwise."

She could see the back of the biker jacket and realised that it was the one from the closet in the Altman home. She was reacting now, she knew; feeling waves of relief on seeing the gun, ironically; that the man she had hit had been bringing out a weapon from his jacket, after all.

Some twenty metres further back was the front end of a large lorry hissing to a stop as the air brakes took hold. The glare of the headlights, closer now, illuminated the scene. She recalled that it had been moving slowly up the inside lane, gathering speed after passing the roadworks. There had been nothing in front of it at the time and she was glad of that.

It came to a halt stopping hard and the final hiss of airbrakes was suddenly unnaturally loud in the tunnel confines. The big emergency flashers on the lorry started up, making the light level in the tunnel vary in colour and intensity.

The prospect of a vehicle pile-up caused by her actions washed over her. As she moved towards the truck, the driver slid across to open the nearside door; he, too, understood the risk of getting out on the driver's side in traffic. He had a plastic first aid case in his hand. Catrin stopped him, waving her warrant card, saying she was a police officer.

"Does he need help, though?"

She ignored the question.

Did you see what happened, sir?"

"Some of it, yes. I have a dash-cam, too. But - ."

"If you could move down the inside, sir, past this man as near to the wall as possible, if you will. See to the couple in the car behind mine, please. I would really appreciate it. I think they are alright but a bit shocked. It would help."

"Not this man - ."

No, sir; you can't go near him. My colleague and I have first aid training and I can already hear the emergency vehicles coming."

She looked back. John's foot was firmly between the gun and the biker and her team member had the man's visor up, talking to him. From the angle of his foot, she could tell that one of his legs was damaged. There was also blood flowing from under his left arm; the roadside limb, not the one he had stretched out towards the gun.

Then there were more lights flashing as a police car stopped, blocking the middle lane just in front of the truck, forming a diversion bulwark around the mess on the inside lane and hard shoulder. The driver was talking animatedly, presumably to his control. She held up her warrant card as the traffic officer got out and quickly summarized the incident.

Within five minutes, there was a sea of flashing lights surrounding them.

She pulled out her mobile and called Wetherby. Aina answered; Wetherby was in yet another meeting.

"We are in the M25 tunnel near Epping; Leo Altman's son tried to kill us, shoot John or me from a motorbike. It's a real mess but we are both uninjured. Let people know and get on to traffic, as well. I've got to go."

21 COLLAR

As she spoke with the traffic officers arriving on the scene, Catrin felt OK, in control. She saw that John had moved away nearer to the tunnel wall and had sat down on the low curb there, back against the guard rail, his head bowed. Another traffic officer was leaning over him, checking on whether he needed medical assistance.

He was shaking his head.

Something in her started to build; an anger and resentment to the mess they found themselves in. I should be grateful I am alive, she told herself, seeing another officer with the lorry driver now, and a third talking with the couple in the car behind her Audi. But what I want to do is kick the hell out of that biker. She started shaking, in her shoulders to begin with and then moving to shivers up the small of her back.

As she walked back closer to her colleague, she heard his reply to the traffic cop. "I'm just a bit shaken. Give me a minute."

He looked up at Catrin, his face showing puzzlement.

"Geez, boss. How did you see it all so fast? I mean, by the time you shouted you had started the turn. It gave me the fright of my life, the wall coming up. I was still thinking you had hit someone in your blind spot. I looked in the side mirror

142

and saw the gun and then that frightened the hell out of me more. It was so close. How?"

Catrin put her hand on Obi's shoulder; whether to reassure him or steady herself she wasn't sure.

"I called out 'gun'; didn't you hear me?"

He shook his head, more bewildered.

She went on, "I didn't see it all. Only bits, but together, it was as I thought. I reacted the way I had been trained. Security work is stressful that way. I came back to art crime work for an easy life."

He looked at her. "Not too easy these days, for either of us. I thought back then your move to work for Hunt was a fix, to be honest, but no; it's not just training. You have something, I don't know what; but thank God you do."

Then he noticed that she was shaking too. Two other uniformed officers came forward from another traffic vehicle that had just pulled up.

One said, "If you could come over to the vehicle over there, please, one of you; the driver who just closed the M25."

The officer was acting 'no nonsense' but being a little smart-mouthed as he pulled out his notebook.

Catrin realised that they were being separated before being checked by the arriving ambulance crews and already she was being asked to make a statement. It surprised her. But the man's comment got to her and she was in no mood to be tolerant. She looked at him sharply.

She snapped out, "It's Detective Inspector Sayer; I was the driver. What's your name and collar?"

Obi heard the tone. His boss was demanding the 'collar number', now more usually known as the shoulder ident-ification number, of the officer. She could read it if she wanted to but was clearly making the point aggressively to the officer. It was a preliminary to making a complaint.

Obi stood up as the constable, surprised, replied, "PC Jackson, ma'am, I didn't - ."

Obi interjected, "I can see a resemblance. Are you related to Sergeant Walter Jackson at Bethnal Green?"

The young officer seemed even more surprised.

"He's my Uncle Wally; and you are?"

"John Obi. DC John Obi. I used to work in the borough. Now, go and get us some blankets; it's cold in here and we are both shivering. Or I will get your Uncle Wally to kick your arse around the M25 all the way to the Southend Arterial."

John turned and put his arm around his boss's shoulder. "It's OK; you are in shock, ma'am."

Catrin said firmly, "No I'm not; I've been in shock. This isn't it. I am just so bloody angry, that's why I am shaking. This piece of biker shit was sent to kill us. You let our friend in Traffic off lightly."

John's eyes widened a bit and he smiled. Sayer wasn't noted for swearing at all and certainly not like this. She really was steamed up.

"Did you see who it was?" he asked gently.

Catrin said tersely, "Leo Altman's son; I recognized the jacket; it was in the house in Potters Bar, in the hall closet. We just stay clear; leave it to them to deal with."

Jackson was hurrying back from his vehicle with two blankets.

John added, "Actually, it's survival instinct, that's why I intervened. Wally Jackson would kick my rear end around the other side of the M25 if I let his nephew be put on report."

He felt the tension go out of her and he let her go; his arm dropped to his side.

Catrin said, "OK, they need to separate us, John; be nice. Not like me."

She looked at the manifest unease in the young constable as he offered the blankets and said, 'thank you' as she took hers and wrapped it round her shoulders. As she walked ahead to the vehicle, John Obi heard his boss say, "You can have your collar back; thanks to John."

Sayer and Obi were checked over medically at the nearby Princess Alexandra hospital. Both of them were physically fine and, surprisingly, appeared mentally and emotionally in balance with respect to the incident. John had recovered quickly; he had experienced his share of rough stuff on the streets of East London. Catrin had her own prior traumas. They were shaken initially by it, but the ER staff found no signs of shock or other trauma.

The older couple had also been taken there. The two police officers were just leaving, being taken home in a police vehicle, when John saw them and pointed. They went over to talk and found them also in good shape.

Catrin said, "We are sorry you were involved but glad you didn't get hurt. And your car is OK?"

The woman replied, "Yes. They want us to wait for a while here, just to be sure while some blood test results come back, because of his heart history. Someone is bringing our car to us, but we have called our daughter and her husband; they will get it and also take us two home. It wasn't like you see on television, at all. We saw them putting your car on a transporter."

Catrin knew it was being taken away for forensic examination before being repaired.

The man said, "One of the officers said it wasn't an accident, it was an incident; that the rider had tried to shoot one of you. We aren't supposed to know, he said, it's hush-hush; but we are all lucky, really."

~~

The eastbound section of the M25 was closed between junction 26 and the M11 interchange for four hours over the late afternoon and evening rush hour. Throughout the night, as the SOCOs worked under floodlights, eastbound traffic was reduced to two lanes through the tunnel. By the morning it was fully opened as if nothing had happened there. But the traffic problems were a big news item, with the fact that a police car and a bike rider were involved.

But also by the morning there was a clip on YouTube, freely referenced in the morning news sites that showed a powerful-built black man in a suit stamping on the hand of a motorcyclist sprawled on the ground. From the angle it was taken, the back seat of a car passing as the incident unfolded, the gun wasn't visible.

What should have been a story about a massive traffic jam caused by a thwarted attempt to kill two police officers was transformed into an accident in which a black plain-clothed policeman made a vicious attack on person being arrested. The speed of reporting outstripped the Met's capabilities to respond in a timely fashion and, when they did, the image of John Obi stamping on Stevie Altman's hand was still dominant.

22 JUICE

On Thursday morning, as the media coverage worsened, Catrin and John were in New Scotland Yard being interviewed separately by a homicide team from Serious Crime Command now assigned to the attempted murder case. Catrin was questioned particularly about the actions she took on seeing the motorcycle.

But the two officers found the growing media coverage far worse than being in the interviews themselves.

"Just plough through," Catrin said to John when they were finally allowed back to the Art and Antiques Unit.

They did so until two-thirty p.m. when DCI Wetherby and Superintendent Patterson called them into Patterson's office. A Police Federation representative was with them there so, on arrival, John and Catrin saw the writing on the wall. Superintendent Patterson apologized for what he was about to do right up front.

"DI Sayer, the initial assessment exonerates you for your actions leading up to the vehicle accident and you are to be congratulated on your quick-thinking to stop the attack. DC Obi, I wish I could say similar words to you, but I can't. That you quickly followed up to ensure that Stephen Altman could not get to his weapon was both brave and highly commendable. But I regret I have to place you on suspension from duty."

Catrin sat there, taking it all in; her being lauded and, in contrast, John being advised of an impending disciplinary investigation. She listened mutely as Obi was suspended on full pay indefinitely until the assessment of his action outside the vehicle had been fully reviewed; not the arrest of Stevie Altman but the manner of the arrest.

Patterson continued in the same monotone, his heart not in it, clearly.

"We had to act fast, given the broad media attention. The Commissioner wanted the news brief at 4.00 p.m. to show responsive behaviour by the Met. DC Obi, I have every wish and hope that you come through this smoothly; I see no reason why you should not do so, personally. However, from the initial assessment report your actions at the incident are being referred to OPS."

He paused, letting it sink in. A review by the Met's 'internal police', the Office of Professional Standards, was a serious issue.

Then he added, "So we are clear, procedure requires me to also inform you that we cannot rule out the possibility of a further referral to IOPC. With your representative here, I must mention that; it's protocol."

The Independent Office of Police Conduct. The most serious place a police officer never wishes to be - other than the dock of a courtroom, on trial.

Catrin sat still, blinking. Obi looked deflated. She was thinking back to how she felt years ago when the news about the Scottish equivalent to IOPC, the Police Investigation and Review Commissioner, PIRC, launched an investigation against her. She had been blown away by the news. On hearing John Obi faced with the same issue, something broke within her.

She focused on John and interrupted the formal flow of the meeting, saying thickly, intensely, "Hey, I'm with you on this

John, no matter what."

He looked at her and nodded. Obi could see that the anger in her was building in the same way as he had seen yesterday in the tunnel.

Catrin turned to face Superintendent Patterson. "Is that it?" she said icily. She didn't bother with 'sir'.

The senior officer was clearly feeling badly about the whole thing but she ignored that, waiting on his response.

"With DC Obi, yes; he is to go home. But you are to go up to see Commander Moore when she gets back. She left the meeting she was in up north and will be in soon. She wants to see you."

Obi gave Catrin a weak smile. "Just plough through, boss."

He stood up. "I am going home," he said to his rep. "Let's meet tomorrow. With yesterday, now the interviews today and this; I'm bushed."

The rep said, "Of course. I'll drive you home, if you'll let me, John. It's been a shock, I know."

He felt as angry as Sayer was visibly reflecting, but in his job it didn't do to show it. It wasn't the first time rank and file police officers had been thrown under the bus for political expediency around a media issue.

~~

On leaving the meeting room, Catrin started to head back to her area then stopped suddenly and went into the nearest women's washroom - to escape more than anything else. She splashed her face with cold water, fully aware she would need to redo her make-up. In the mirror, she could see the outline of the scar on her cheek more clearly; sudden cold or heat always made it more visible.

She was finishing her lipstick when a younger woman, a constable in uniform came in. Catrin couldn't recall her name but she was on the same floor as the relocated Art and Antiques Unit and she had seen her around. And it was clear that the younger officer recognized her.

The woman smiled at her then said sympathetically, "Sorry to hear about the mess yesterday, ma'am. It must be awful for you and your - what's his name?"

"Obi. DC John Obi. It is and it's getting worse; he's just been suspended."

Her short comment to the well-meaning colleague and the officer's expression of shock at the news sent Catrin over the top. She threw the lipstick in her bag and walked out, the door banging shut behind her.

She headed along the corridor up a flight of stairs and turned left into the Trident area. In the various operation rooms and work areas that she passed through people who knew her either nodded or stopped talking for a moment; others seemed surprised at her appearance. Her expression was uncontained anger.

When she reached the Biker Gang Unit operations area DI Coombs was standing with two of his team members near a whiteboard loaded with images and writing. Several members of his team, including DS Hilary Eaton, were working at desks, on computers or phones. Coombs had a small bottle of tomato juice in one hand, partly consumed, the bent straw wobbling around as he talked and unconsciously gesticulated.

Coombs saw her and said, "Hi, it's a real mess, I gather."

His tone was neutral. She couldn't tell where he stood on it.

"What happened?" she asked.

He frowned, looking surprised. "Well, you were there, we are just preparing to observe the interview with Leo Altman, he was brought in -.

Sayer's voice was a yell that ended high-pitched, almost a scream.

"What happened with the monitoring of the Altmans and the Centurions, I meant? How the hell did he send his son Stevie to kill John and probably me and none of you picked up on it? That's what I want to know. You have five officers full-time on this single operation. Art and Antiques and a dozen other teams round here have been reduced to nothing so that

Trident and Counter Terrorism had sufficient resources and you - you, stand here sipping at that!"

She pulled the bottle from his hand and threw it at the operations board. By chance, a gob of tomato juice flew out and partly covered the eye and nose of Leo, the photo at the centre of the web lines, as the bottle banged on the board and the remaining juice went everywhere.

As she did so she realised that she had lost it completely, gulped and started to cry. Eaton jumped out of her seat, heading over to her as DI Coombs, taking the path of righteousness, said, "Now look here, you can't come in here doing that sort of thing, DI Sayer. What the hell - ."

"She's right," said a soft voice, as another voice immediately said, "Keep your mouth f- ."

"Sayer!"

It was loud, a single voice, male, authoritative.

"I can hear you halfway across the building. My office. DI Coombs, my office; right now. Not another word, either of you. Out!"

Superintendent Howard Thurman of Counter Terrorism was standing in the doorway.

As Catrin turned and headed out, sensing rather than seeing Coombs follow behind her, she heard Thurman say in more normal tones, "DC Long; you want your colleague to keep his mouth shut about what?"

They didn't speak to each other before Thurman entered his office. He glared at both of them and sat down, but pointedly invited neither of them to do likewise.

"Your spat interrupted my conversation with Commander Moore, of all people. I have to call her back now. She had already left the meeting she was attending early because of the M25 media situation.

"It appears that DC Long told DC Fellows to shut up because Fellows had made the point that Stevie Altman was unstable, DI Coombs. You excluded Stevie from the focus because he wasn't even a Centurion club member; he hadn't been accepted and had no priors. He was with some half-baked 'hangaround' club. Well, it seems like he was trying to prove something yesterday, don't you think?"

Coombs looked at him and then Catrin, his face turning defensive, looking for the right words but Superintendent Thurman pre-empted him.

"Perhaps you could inform the lead officer of the investigation that you were not monitoring this man? Now, you go back to work and focus on the job. Like, right now, if you please."

Coombs said, "Yes, sir." He briefly looked at Catrin and left the room. Thurman looked at her a moment then pointed at one of the chairs on the other side of his desk. She sat down wondering what was next.

He waited half a minute before saying softly, "Sayer, I understand you have been through a lot in the last while but your behaviour was totally unacceptable, primarily because you are a team leader. You know how this sort of venting upsets teams. You are to go up to Moore's office and wait. She should be here within thirty minutes."

~~

Moore swept into her outer office, put down her briefcase and removed her coat.

"Go on in, Sayer. I'll be there in a minute."

Catrin went into the inner office and, unsure what to do, decided to stand again. Take it on the chin standing up, she thought, contemplating the possible consequences. Since her miscarriage life had just gone downhill. It had to stop doing so; it needed to sort itself out, probably without the Met.

"Take a seat, please."

Commander Moore had entered and shut the door. She pointed to the visitor's chair at the desk and positioned herself in her own desk chair, keeping the desk between them this time.

"You were nearly killed; your team member is suspended and so I understand the basis of your outrage. It's the talk of the Yard at present, it seems. Normally I would give both you and DI Coombs some appropriate disciplinary action - with you, a suspension pending confirmation by the psychologist of your suitability for duty. Which one of ours did you see previously?"

"Dr. Herrington, ma'am."

Moore swung her chair round, facing the window, lost in thought for twenty seconds or so, saying nothing. It seemed an age to Catrin. Then the senior detective said softly, "Take off; go for a run, I know you run for exercise. Or go to a spa, or tell your husband to leave work early and meet him, whatever. Try and relax, destress. But be back here at six thirty p.m."

"In here, ma'am?"

Moore shook her head. "No, in Trident, in the operations area that is currently the scene of your tomato juice crime. Then we will see."

She paused, leaving Catrin waiting for the next words but after a moment Moore said, "Off you go."

She turned and picked up the phone. She was done; she needed to get on.

Catrin stood up and turned, thinking she knew what 'we will see' meant. It would be a repeat of the meeting with John or worse.

If that was the outcome, so be it.

She met Chris in the cafeteria.

"I heard, should we go home?" were his first words as they sat down. He was looking anxious.

"I have to come back tonight to face the music, whatever that is. Moore told me to take off, go for a run or something; which I can't do yet, anyway. But by the time we get back I would need to head over here again."

He asked, "Shall we go somewhere and get away for a couple of hours?"

She shook her head. "No, I'm not good company until I

sort this out. And, given my record over the past week, if I go for a walk rather than a run I will probably fall in a sewer that has its manhole cover off."

She forced a smile at him. "No, you go back to work. I will meet up with you directly after the 6.30 thing and we can go to eat somewhere. I am going see Aina and give Jane a call."

"Worsley? Will she be free?"

"I don't know until I ask. Besides, I want to talk to Jian Li, take my mind off all this for a while, if I can. The good thing about her is that she is half a world away. And she is going to see Michael Yau tomorrow, she said in her last email."

He said nothing, but his eyes were asking, 'why?'

"I want her to give an old gangster my best wishes and say that he is in my thoughts."

He sipped his tea. "That's probably a good idea, focus on other things. I'll be right outside Trident when you are finished tonight and yes, we are going for a good dinner, no matter what. People are really annoyed about the news of John's suspension; it's going around the place."

23 STAIN

John Obi's wife, already distraught from the information he had shared with her after he got home yesterday, had been cautious that morning about switching on the news on television or checking her phone. She waited until their two girls were in school and her husband was off to work. When she did, she saw the clips and the headlines and cried; it was selective, judgmental and wrong.

But by mid-afternoon her husband was home. He had been suspended pending an enquiry into his actions during the arrest. Some in the media were calling it 'police brutality'. Four of the twenty-seven bones in Stephen Altman's right hand were fractured; someone had leaked the news to a Daily Mirror reporter.

John said, "I'm to meet with the guy from the Federation tomorrow and I have access to stress counselling, that sort of thing. Everyone on the team was very supportive including Wetherby, but Superintendent Patterson said they had no choice really; it was the visibility of the issue. We aren't to talk to the press if they turn up."

She looked lost; how their life had changed so suddenly. Last night was bad enough when John got home. Then she suddenly thought and asked, "And Catrin?"

"I don't know now. She got sent up to Moore. As I was leaving, I heard she had lost it with someone in Trident, but I was already in the car with my rep. DCI Wetherby told us that Stevie Altman has just been charged in hospital with attempted murder and other charges related to causing the traffic accidents. They will be part of the same news brief later, to try to counter this lot."

"Why did Catrin get sent to Moore?" she asked.

John said gently, "Aina told me she thought it was about seeing her psychologist, Dr. Herrington, for all the stress and the blow-up. With the loss of her baby, then the Renée Altman thing and now this, I think they are worried about her. She looked really angry when I got suspended."

Kaila said, "Good for her; someone should be; I am, too. He was the psychologist she saw after her injury to her cheek. Didn't she see one of those after that death threat thing?"

"The same man."

Kaila shook her head, trying to get it around the changes.

"And the man who caused all this, the biker?"

"Leg badly broken, lost skin and flesh from his arm and knee, I gather, where the leathers wore through. And the broken bones in his hand that I gave him. He's in hospital under arrest but conscious. I don't know any more than that."

His wife just stared. "You went to a home to look at a painting and were treated like shit. And they have the gall to say these things about you. The Commissioner should be ashamed of himself."

John looked surprised at his wife's anger. He was working out what to say when his mobile rang. He glanced at it then answered.

"Catrin?"

Kaila watch him listen, his eyes going moist then he said, "OK boss; thanks, yes, 'I'll keep the faith'. Thanks, I will look out for them."

He closed the call.

"She's really upset, doesn't want to talk. Now she has something she has to do this evening at the Met. She called to say Aina and Jane Worsley are heading over."

Aina and Kaila were friends; had been ever since John joined the Art Crime Unit. Their families came from the same part of Pakistan. Kaila could understand why she was coming, in support; but DCI Worsley? She had been John's boss for a number of years but... that had all changed.

John, seeing the changes in expression on his wife's face, said, "Moral support, I gather, both of them. Worsley is absolutely livid with the decision and, you know Jane; she supports her team."

He took a deep breath, a sigh. "With Jane and Catrin pulling for me, I feel better. Not good, but better." He moved over, hugging his wife. "I think I will head over to the school and collect the kids; give them a surprise, if that's OK."

"Let's both of us go. I need to walk, I am angry, too."

Half-way there Kaila's phone rang. It was Aina. "We are getting supper and will stop at Tayyabs; Jane's on the other line phoning in an order. Anything special you want?"

"Tayyabs?" she repeated and John's face broke into a smile, realizing what was happening. It was a favorite restaurant of both of their families, serving Punjabi cuisine.

Kaila's immediate reaction was, "We are not hungry, I suspect; well I'm not, but John is nodding and the kids will eat just about anything. But - what's the noise?"

John had reached across and pressed the 'speaker' button on Kaila's phone as Aina's answer came out loud and clear. "It's Jane arguing with Chittnaam at the restaurant. She told him she was buying and he said he has been following the news, seeing John on television clips. He is insisting it's all on him. And he sends his best wishes. Go for it, have a feast."

~~

Just before six thirty p.m. Catrin found Coombs with his entire team waiting. He said, evenly, "We were instructed to be here; that's all I know."

157

She stood there, silent and uncomfortable. Hilary Eaton came up to her and smiled, standing beside her in a room of people waiting; some reading emails, others just looking bored or put out by the wait. No one wanted any small talk.

Catrin saw that the mess around the whiteboard had been cleaned up other than the photo of Leo Altman still with its tomato stain, now brown and dried. It looked as if he had been shot in the eye. Surely they had other copies, she thought.

Commander Moore, Superintendent Patterson and DCI Wetherby came in together promptly at 6.30 p.m., standing as a trio in the centre of the room.

Moore spoke firmly. "We are very busy, all of us, under the trying times of a major reorganization and a number of unfortunate circumstances beyond our control. A page jump on a computer. A sick woman dying suddenly. An unstable son trying to prove himself to someone.

"The weight is heavy but we can't buckle under it. Sayer, Coombs; you get one chance each, now, in front of everyone. A meaningful apology from each of you. And if I hear 'I'm sorry, but -' from either of you, I'm done trying it this way. We will go by the book. DI Coombs, you first."

The room went very still as the people gathered realised what Moore was trying to do.

Coombs looked surprised and took a deep breath. For a moment it looked as if he would tell his bosses to stuff it, but he said nothing. Instead he looked at Catrin.

"I couldn't get used to the fact you turned down the job I got - this one. No one said openly that had happened but it was on the rumour mill and the team all heard it. To me, this is a great job; I was so pleased to get it and wanted to do the best by my team. I don't think I really showed you the respect I should have and for that I am sorry.

"I made a really bad call on Stevie and didn't take into account sufficiently DC Fellow's comments about his instability. But - ."

Moore interrupted immediately. "What did I say?"

Coombs shook his head. "Not an excuse, ma'am - a new piece of information. Leo didn't set his son on you, it appears. He had no knowledge of it, he said. Stevie is taking it all on himself.

"I was focused on the Centurions and I... missed it. I screwed up and as a result, two officers were nearly killed. And I am ripped up about that, I honestly am."

He stopped, looking at Moore wondering if he needed to say more. She simply said, "Sayer?"

Catrin eyes were already moist hearing Coombs's apology and she had absorbed the effort Moore was making.

"It just got on top of me and I didn't deal with things either professionally or properly. I really feel the absence of my old boss and, frankly, haven't made the effort to build a relationship with my new one, so I felt unsupported. Rightly or wrongly, that's the way I felt. I should have gone and talked to DCI Wetherby after John was suspended, not let it steam up inside me."

She glanced at Wetherby then back at Coombs.

"Only weeks ago I had a miscarriage. I hurried back to work to fill the void, fill my time, to stop thinking about the loss. When I crashed in here, I blamed myself and your team. Between us, I thought, we were responsible for just about everything that had gone wrong today. That was way off and absolutely wrong. Life happens and with Renée Altman's death and her son's crazy attempt at revenge, it was beyond our control or reasonable expectation."

She wiped her eyes.

"And the person I feel worst about is DC Obi. He's a good officer. It's not right he is under review. But I apologize to all of you for my outburst; none of you needed that; none of you deserved it, you have enough to do."

She sniffed and took a deep breath then looked at Moore, her expression saying she was done.

Moore said, "It my job to build teams, not wreck them, suspending people. Obi will get treated fairly, I assure you and

Greg, I offered a number of people alternative opportunities as part of the reorganization, but every post I filled I did so with people I felt capable of doing it. Move on, both of you."

Her voice lightened, "Now, a question. Catrin, do you think that they can wipe the tomato juice off the whiteboard? I wouldn't let them, you see."

The stain, literal and figurative, she meant.

Catrin walked forward, "I'll do it myself, ma'am."

As she passed, she said to her, "Thank you."

The tension broke and people started talking.

Moore looked around. It's going to be alright in here she thought; it's just the world outside we have to deal with. She was now heading over to the Media Communications area to review the next news release on the Bell Common Tunnel incident. The afternoon briefing already had the main media changing their tune; now they wanted to hammer it home.

Catrin returned to the Art and Antiques area a little later with Chris to get her coat and found DCI Wetherby waiting - for her, it appeared. No one else was there.

She looked at Chris. "I'll just be a minute."

She went into Wetherby's office and closed the door.

"I'm sorry," she said.

He said, "Thank you for what you said earlier. We didn't get off to a good start, I know. I will try to do better, be more supportive and give clearer direction. This job is as new to me as Art and Antiques is familiar ground to you. I have to rely on you a great deal. I know so little about each of the three specialist teams that I now manage. So, let's begin again, can we? I will never be a Neville Coltrane."

She smiled. "You don't have a Bentley then?"

"No. At home we have a Fiesta that my wife drives and I take what I am given from the car pool."

She nodded.

"It's going to mean a lot to me for us to support John, sir."

"He's part of my team, too, Catrin. We aren't going to let him down."

Despite the upheaval and emotions of the day, Catrin headed out to dinner with her husband feeling a lot better than she had for quite some time.

~~

Later, at John Obi's home, after the family was alone and girls were asleep, Kaila came downstairs and sat on the sofa, pulling the arm of her big husband around her so that as he adjusted she settled back, leaning on his chest.

"The meal was good; I appreciated Aina and Jane coming round, making the effort. You work with some very good people, you know? They think a lot about you."

"I know. It's the media and politics. But they can kill you as well. I was just watching; the tone of the coverage is changing now that the news of the gun is out and Stevie Altman has been charged."

"Pity Catrin didn't come tonight, being tied up. What did she mean when she called earlier, 'keep the faith'?"

He thought about it. "When we were put together as a team, she told us that she was staying to get Art and Antiques back on its feet, to do its job well. 'Keep the faith,' she said. It came out of her discussion with Neville. I took it to be that.

"But Jane said she had told Catrin to focus on the work now, the rest was in the hands of others. Catrin told her that her primary job now was to get me out of this, free and clear. So I am not too sure, to be honest, what the term, 'keep the faith' means now."

24 EVELYN

The Metropolitan Police Federation, the staff association for serving officers up to the rank of chief inspector, is based in Bromley, South London, in an anonymous office block next to an Asda grocery store. However, its legal services for members were provided by a firm with a far more upscale address in Central London; Slater & Gordon UK of Chancery Lane; 'within spitting distance' of the Old Bailey, as Keith Marshall once described it.

An Australian-owned mega-practice of lawyers, it had representation rights for a large portion of the Metropolitan Police staff and for other officers in the Police Federation of England and Wales.

There was no Asda in sight as Catrin drove around the corner of Serle Street, WC2, near Chancery Lane, and saw the 'permit reserved' parking spot just being vacated by a lunging Peugeot, departing as if the driver was having a tantrum. Then she saw the parking warden writing in her book.

As she parallel parked into the space the woman looked at her in disbelief, turning the page of her ticket book to a new form. As Catrin lowered the curbside window the warden started talking about restricted parking rights. Catrin flashed her warrant card and told her to move on.

"I don't want any uniform here for the next half-hour, if you don't mind."

The warden listened to the Welsh melody of the request and nodded and walked off.

Catrin had phoned John the following day, in part to check how he was doing, in part to ask a question.

"Do you have someone in the Federation you would like to use for the meeting with OPS?"

"No, the guy who sat in with me back in Tower Hamlets once wasn't top notch, really. He was overworked and it was trivial, a claim that I thumped someone. It will come up, I suppose."

"Leave it to me, I will get someone organized."

John Obi sensed what was happening. "You are going after the one who represented you, aren't you? Evelyn what's-her-name? The holy terror. She won't do this, Catrin; she is in court most of the time; she's one of their senior people."

"Carter, yes. Leave it to me, I said. I told you; I am with you on this, and I mean it."

She closed the call. Her mind was on how to get Evelyn Carter to agree.

Colin Murray was nowhere in sight. She texted him again. He appeared as the text obviously reached him, crossing the street to her car.

"Morning, ma'am; rain's keeping off."

He pronounced it 'mum'. She recalled that he used to call Neville Coltrane 'guv'. A year in the police cadets before he changed course and went to work in law chambers with his dad had the man acting like an old-fashioned London copper. She noticed that the well-cut suit was looking a little tired. Someone in his chambers would take him to task on it. Chancery Lane was no place for a barrister's clerk to look less than smart.

She gave him a suspicious look. "Optimistic today, I see,

Colin. You in charge of the weather?"

He smiled, "No, just the comings and goings of a bunch of briefs. What's up?"

"I want some of Evelyn Carter's time."

He laughed. "She's tied up on the City case today. And I have her booked up solid."

"I thought so."

He glanced at her. "This is the tunnel thing. I bet. The man accused has Toomey for the defense, I heard this morning. He's wasted no time, or someone has pull."

He pursed his lips. "You on suspension for closing the M25, or something?"

"No, John Obi on my team is suspended; he was the one who prevented the guy from reaching his gun. He's been referred to OPS for stamping on the sod's hand."

Colin wrinkled his nose. "Evelyn won't touch the prelims; you know that. She works on the finals, prepping the barristers, generally with a blowtorch tickling their rear ends."

"She is still bloodthirsty then, not tiring?" Catrin said.

Colin looked at her. "You could say that. Keen to win, she would say. She is on the go all the time. Jane Worsley wangled her for you to do your interview years ago, my dad said, but Evelyn only did it because she was interested in the fact it was the Scots going after you. Willy Dennison is probably the one who will get Obi, the way it sits now."

Colin's dad used to be the head clerk of chambers.

Catrin asked, "If I get Evelyn to agree, you will sort it, right?"

She meant timing, calendars, priorities; the clerks had more control on that than the lawyers.

He nodded reluctantly. "If she agrees, I'll do it for you. Mr. Coltrane said I had to look after you like gold dust when he called me after he left. But I doubt that she will. She's at the Central today, the sentencing hearing of Cassidy and Lee."

He was referring to two City of London police officers who had let women off petty charges in turn for sexual favours. It had turned nasty when one woman had made a complaint. The

Magistrates' Court had found them guilty but then deferred sentencing to the Central Crown Court; they held police officers to a higher standard of accountability.

Catrin nodded. "We've been in touch; she said no to me already but agreed to meet at the lunch break. I head there next, to her 'outside office'."

Colin smiled. He knew she was referring to a bench on the street along from the courthouse. Evelyn sat there smoking and drinking her coffee.

He glanced at her. "She likes Starbucks - ."

"Grande Latte; no sugar, no fancy stuff. I know."

He looked at her. "Well, good luck with that one."

Colin didn't sound as if luck would matter much.

Catrin smiled, "So my turn. What you got?"

Colin Murray was one of the strangest CIs - confidential informants - she had come across; principally because he didn't want any money. He and his dad before him, then head clerk of chambers, were formerly Coltrane's informants and Neville was not the sort to be handing out envelopes of greasy bank-notes to people. He had fixed it with yet another cousin of his for Colin's dad to be invited annually into the Member's Pavilion at Lord's Cricket Ground for some games; the man was an avid cricketer and it meant a lot. The waiting list for new members was decades, Catrin had heard.

At Catrin's first meeting with Colin she said, "I don't have any clout with cricket clubs."

"Doesn't matter; the pleasure it gives my dad; you couldn't buy that, ma'am."

He'd been true to his word.

This time he said, "A Swiss work, I gather, a painting I heard about, in the White Hart…"

After Colin left, she called Isabelle Howlett.

"It sounds like the Alice Bailly painting from the Lucerne robbery last year may now be in the country; it came through Hull, I heard, about a week ago. Let Werner in Geneva know and Interpol."

"Nothing for us to follow up on, then?" Howlett asked.

"We aren't exactly going to start trotting up to Hull to follow up ourselves."

Isabelle sighed. "Liaise and coordinate. And until John gets back, it's just us doing that."

Catrin brightened up. "There is one more thing; Neville. The Tarrant."

Isabelle laughed. "And?"

"Colin had heard a rumour. 'How was Mr. Coltrane these days? Was he really on a case? Some people thought he was. He had been seen at Biggin Hill getting out of a corporate jet with Sir Nigel Fielding. Someone suggested that the Fielding family wanted to get some stolen jewellery back. Was Neville involved?"

"What did you say?"

"I told him that whatever Mr. Coltrane was doing other than being busy with the Coltrane Foundation, it was nothing to do with the Met - or him or me. And he would not be held in favour for spreading wild rumours. Can you give Neville a call on your personal mobile; pass it on. I have my appointment with Evelyn."

"I'll do that. Good luck, Catrin."

~~

Evelyn Carter came out of the front entrance of the law courts, head moving in an arc until she saw Catrin sitting on the bench further down the road holding two Starbucks Grande cups in a cardboard tray. She automatically reached into her purse for her cigarettes and lighter and starting smoking as she walked over.

Evelyn was in her fifties, overweight with a taste for bling jewellery, Catrin recalled. She had worked for the Federation legal group for years, building up a reputation as a 'no holds barred' defender that irritated the top brass of the Met and other police services. Today she was in a formal dark grey suit with an eye-catching necklace that was far from 'bling', Catrin thought. Evelyn was going up in the world.

The lawyer's opening volley was, "Sitting upwind, I see; prepared. That a Grande Latte? And the answer is still no."

"Hello Evelyn. Nice to see you after all this time. You are looking on top of the world."

That comment made Carter laugh. "I feel about one hundred and fifty and you... look tired. Not the bright young thing you were, even if the cheek has healed."

Catrin held out the cup. "Touché."

The first round over, they settled for a drink of their respective coffees.

Catrin asked, "Cassidy and Lee?"

"Eighteen months each. I'm not doing their dismissal hearing when it comes up now; I've had enough of them."

Evelyn didn't sound happy or sad, just matter-of-fact. She added, "Now I'm up to my eyes starting with the aftermath of the Commissioner's last feeding frenzy, the 'unfair dismissals' claims. You were OK though. Other than closing down the motorway. Not sure you are still as popular as sliced bread."

She blew a stream of smoke.

"Catrin, you have a habit of getting into trouble. Scotland; then I heard about Malaysia. Now this; bikers. Is this still about Obi or are you in trouble yourself again?"

Catrin looked at her for a moment before responding.

"It's John. I know it could work out to be simply a reprimand. Unless that went off-track, for some reason. Willy Dennison could handle that. But I want him off free and clear. You can do that, if anyone can."

She paused.

"You've had a lot like Cassidy and Lee in the last while, I know. I keep track of you. You are a professional and will give every client your best but... John is clean. This is one you will want to win, I tell you."

"I want to win them all, Catrin. You know that; it's my nature," Evelyn retorted. Then she said, "But why do you want him unsullied. Has he got anything already?"

Catrin nodded. "One in Tower Hamlets, an 'excessive use of force' in an arrest. It was dropped."

Evelyn nodded, "A nice start for the opposition; a similar act. But this one was on the news. Dropping it isn't on the cards."

So Catrin told her really why she wanted Obi free and clear before she gave Carter her final plea. "Just the prelim, Evelyn. If that goes south, then I will live with the Federation lottery on the assignment. But give me a chance, please."

The lawyer relented. "A day, perhaps a day and a half total, max for the prep and I assume a half day in the interview. No more, understand. You hear; are we agreed?"

Catrin smiled. "Agreed."

Evelyn shook her head. "I don't know how, though; with what I've got lined…"

She stopped, looking at Sayer's face.

"You've already fixed it with Colin, haven't you? I can see it."

"We did have a word or two."

"He's not Welsh, is he? He doesn't sound like it."

Catrin laughed. "Not that I am aware of. Not that I would use that sort of leverage, of course."

She looked innocent. Evelyn gave her a black look.

25 GUANXI

Li had steeled herself for this meeting, but it turned out to be one to treasure. Hearing updates from Miele on her grandfather's deteriorating health, she was a little uneasy when the familiar face of Alex appeared driving the white Mercedes to collect her for this final visit.

At the home, a discrete but expensive house tucked away off Chui Shin Road, Li found Michael Yau dressed, seated in a comfortable chair in the patio garden with family members and other people in the home making sure he was comfortable and cared for.

Yau smiled. "Thank you for coming."

She replied, "How could I not? I just don't know what to say other than to thank you."

He smiled but asked, "For what particularly?"

"For being my dad's friend principally. Through that action everything else came about, did it not? And I know you feel you owed him too, for his efforts to save your son. This is no time for false niceties, is it? But my dad was doing his job and yet... you and Enlai took him on board. Made him a friend and in doing so, rounded him out."

Yau momentarily looked surprised then chuckled; it hadn't occurred to him.

Li pressed on with what she wanted to say; what she had prepared for this visit. "Han was the first to comment on it to me in our teens. 'Dad has a mellower perspective than Mom. They are both church crazy but I can talk to him more easily', he said. As could I. We loved both our parents - I still do - but in the transition to adulthood, it made a difference for us both."

She gave him a knowing smile. "And that was long before any events in Wales."

Yau said after a moment, "You surprise me. I hadn't thought back that far, to be honest. I thought we would talk of Wales… and after."

We'll cover that too, she thought.

It was after they had talked about 'things today' Li could see that Michael was tiring. He said suddenly, "I am so glad you came. I think others can't; it's too awkward, the thought of death. They will come to the funeral, no doubt and speak there to my family. For me to see the friendship you have with Miele and your friends in England has been a real pleasure in these last few years. And now you will guide her business issues legally. It is a great gift to me."

Li said, "She's doing well as an artist; she and Jean, particularly, are very close. They text or email almost daily about ceramics, I think."

"Not Catrin Sayer, then, about design? She and Jean Hughes split the work, I know."

Li thought about it. "I think Miele is a little more reserved around Catrin. She was during the year in London, I know. But Catrin was busy more with her police work. There are times, like in Bangor, when I am glad she does that and others when I wish she just gave it up. If she concentrated on her art, she could make a lot more money than she does."

Yau said nothing in direct response, but Li's tone of voice had alerted him. "How is she doing? It's a big thing to lose a baby."

Li said, "Trudging along, adjusting to it. She is seeing a

specialist now. They want to see if there is any clinical issue that has been missed before they try again. But she has other problems now. She had a run-in with a biker on some case just days ago; he tried to kill her or her colleague; I'm not sure of the details though. She's OK, she says but I wish she would just do art …"

She didn't finish the sentence.

"But she called me specifically, knowing I was coming to see you. She asked me to pass on her best wishes to you and to thank you. She doesn't know any of the detail of course, about your intervention regarding Nam Wu, but she worked it out and wants you to know you are in her thoughts."

He nodded, saying nothing. His own challenges had preoccupied him.

He said suddenly, "I meant to ask earlier, about the earrings. I quite understand your own decision. But have you thought who they should go to?"

She saw how tired he was and steeled herself for the worst part; saying goodbye. It had too much finality to it now.

She smiled. "To Catrin. I suspect you would like her to have them if I don't accept them, given their original purpose; but when and how, you will need to leave to me and Miele. But I promise you we will give them to her at the right time."

His face broke into a big smile. "You are learning to read me too well! Yes, if they are not for you then I would like the woman who saved you to have them more than anything else. Tell me, at the time you wore them, did she like them? She was with you, I recall you said."

"I believe so. I remember her being open-mouthed in astonishment for a moment when I put them on. So yes; she said they were beautiful. It is just the issue of your different worlds and her police rules on receiving presents. But we will find a way. Not for the monetary value, but to have something to remind her of you. We all have *guanxi*, do we not?"

On impulse, seeing the look on the old man's face, she reached out and put her hand on his, holding it. The fingers felt cool; his circulation was not doing too well she thought.

He was no longer the triad boss, just a frail old man.

He said firmly, "We are connected; yes. I feel that."

She thought he might say more but his eyes looked into the distance; whether into the past or around the world to her friend in London, she could not say.

~~

It was the following day that Miele popped into see her grandfather and found him picking at the keys of his small laptop with two fingers. He had never been a techie. As she gave him a smile and chatted he placed the open computer on the side table by the bed.

Years of growing up in a family that called itself triad had taught her when not to comment on things. So she never mentioned to him or anyone else the fact the Google search term "M25 tunnel crash" was on his computer and a number of tabs were open which referenced motorbikes, she thought. But, knowing Catrin's recent problem, she was intrigued.

~~

Catrin, however, was busy still with the Norfolk case, in a call between Art and Antiques and JMIT.

"The revenge theory seems solid," said Superintendent Lubbock. "For two of the paintings found in Sleaman's home, there are two copies of each. One copy has replaced the original in the gallery, the other has been found in organized crime gangs affiliated with the Outlaws. There is the one found in Germany and now another in Finland. Both clubs have links to the Centurions, DI Coombs says. There may well be others, channeled through Altman's club."

"More retribution against Leo's people," said Catrin. "It's a different twist to an old theme. Some forgers have sold or given their copies of the same work to different galleries for exactly that reason."

"Given?" asked DS Hollis, a little incredulously.

She nodded. "Mark Landis in the USA donated works he painted to galleries around the USA. The gallery staff happily concluded that they had found originals. It was deceptive, but not illegal as he didn't sell them. Like this forger and Sleaman, he embarrassed a lot of experts."

Hollis said, "This wasn't a donation, though. It's clear now that Sleaman was far wealthier than his employment income can account for. He didn't do this simply to embarrass art experts. He did it for a nicer life and for revenge. And we found how he made the link with Altman; through Renée."

DI Needham took over.

"It was in his office upstairs, a file with clippings, buried among other things. Renée was a Princess Diana and Royalty fan; it was known in club circles, so Sleaman must have picked up on it. At one of the Bulldog Bash events he sold her a supposed 'unofficial' copy of a formal photograph of Princess Diana that he picked up in his work 'from a friend in a gallery'. There is a printout of follow-up emails from her asking what else he could get in that line. He came up with a supposedly 'rare' photograph of a painting of Queen Elizabeth as a child. I don't recall the painter, but he said the photograph had been taken by Lord Snowdon. There's no basis for that, apparently."

Isabelle tried to keep her voice even; it was too funny. "The Philip De Lazo painting of the Queen, age seven? A photograph of it by Lord Snowdon? Sleaman really was quite a con artist."

Needham replied, "De Lazlo; that's right; that's the name. But it meant he had a real fixation on revenge and planned it carefully, getting into contact with Leo to pitch art to them bit by bit. We don't have the paperwork, but a painting of British monarchy and this frou-frou one of some German blue-blood are in the same vein, it seems. What's the painter's name again?"

Isabelle said, "Winterhalter."

Catrin added, "And Sleaman would have picked up a lot about stolen art uses. It wouldn't take much to move Leo and Renée's interests in paintings obtained illegally on to their commercial value as an underground currency."

Needham moved on.

"And from the forensics, if we ever find the forger, we will have no problem linking the person to the paintings. All of the copies have a set of prints in common, besides Sleaman's. They are not in any record database we have checked so far but once we have a suspect, we will know very quickly."

"I take it you've checked here and overseas; the artist could be international?" asked Sayer.

Superintendent Lubbock confirmed it.

DI Needham added, "And we are hearing that the German and Finnish gangs are a little put out with the Centurions. It hurt their pride - probably lethally for someone, if they get him - or her. They can't get at Sleaman now."

DCI Wetherby, ever one for process and accountability, asked, "Superintendent Lubbock, I am not sure what further support you need from us?"

The Norfolk detective replied, "Well, I was coming to that. I think, in fact, it is more that we should be supporting you, given the recent events. Technically we have all we need at present. It's with us now to try to pin down this forger. If we do, we would want to share that with you but until then, I think our liaison should be on an 'as needs', rather than a regular basis, don't you? And regarding our support, our Chief Constable has already reached out to yours. We are all pulling here for DC Obi, hoping that he comes through this review."

After the call, DCI Wetherby said to his team, "Well, that was a successful conclusion to our involvement. You all did well. Now we wait on the OPS review and hopefully put a successful end to that matter, too."

He looked at Sayer. "I heard just before we took the call that Evelyn Carter with the Federation is assigned to Obi. Unusual that. Someone brought influence to bear on it, Superintendent Patterson said rather pointedly to me. I told him that I didn't have that sort of influence, unfortunately. And if I did, I would use it."

His voice hadn't changed, he was still soft-spoken but his face showed his resolve. Isabelle looked surprised. Wetherby looked intently at Catrin, who just looked innocent.

Later, Howlett said to her, "You know, he's mellowing. There's hope yet."

"There's always hope, Isabelle. And a lot of on-going work backed up we need to clear."

PART 3: FORGER

26 HARLEY STREET

Catrin had been sitting in the waiting area for fifteen minutes mulling over her decision to see the man. Why did I agree to do this? She had asked herself the same question before her examination and assessment last week by Neville's cousin, the Harley Street obstetrician. Now she was getting nervous, seeing him again for the results.

It was the second week of January and the holidays seemed to be fading. Catrin and Chris had gone down to her parents for Christmas Eve and then on to Cornwall after Christmas. They had returned to London in time to spend New Year with Jean and Melanie; the least strained time of the holiday, it turned out, enjoying playing with Lili and being relaxed with friends.

At one point in Pontypridd with her mother, Catrin said, "I'm seeing another specialist when I get back."

"You've seen this Dr. Toth already, I thought."

"Not her. A cousin of Neville Coltrane's; a Harley Street doctor, a bigwig in the field. Neville arranged it. I don't even have to pay. So we are really doing everything we can, you see."

But it was a shadow over the holidays, despite everyone's efforts for it not to be.

She was about to approach the medical receptionist, a grey-haired woman who looked very much like a trainer she once knew at Hendon, a 'no bloody nonsense' sort, to ask how long it would be just as a light flashed on the telephone on the woman's desk.

"You may go in to see Mr. Cameron, Mrs. Treneer," the woman said, standing up to lead her back to the office.

Mr. Cameron, please; not Dr. Cameron even though he was one, Catrin knew. Some obscure British thing about surgeons always being called 'Mr.', one-upping other physicians.

"Tricky things, implantation loss and placental abruption, Mrs. Treneer. So many direct and indirect factors contribute, you see. It takes some sorting out."

It was almost his opening comment after the preliminaries. A week ago at the Harley Street clinic he had examined her and had her run through a series of tests, but was all business then, not very talkative at all. Today he was positively verbose.

No, she didn't smoke, drink or use drugs. There didn't appear to be physiological risk factors nor had she had recent trauma of any sort that brought it on. She wasn't chronically hypertensive.

He paused in his spiel as Catrin thought there must be a Latin term for 'tricky thing'. No one pays good money for that sort of answer from Harley Street. Her grandad, a former union rep for the miners in the Rhondda valley, was probably turning in his grave at the thought of a Sayer seeking out private medical care here.

Ten minutes later she had changed her mind. The man had obviously done his homework on her medical record and he had spoken to Toth. His summary of her experiences and clinical condition were precise and accurate.

"Your first miscarriage was after a flight, it says; how long after?"

She told him. A sudden call to interview a former art thief

from London in terminal care in Florida; a wild goose chase, it turned out to be. It had never occurred to her that flying would be a problem. Her worry was more about developing nausea. But she had no symptoms like that the first time.

They went through her experience during the second pregnancy. In concluding that part he noted, "It was just before what we refer to in the family as, 'Neville's fall from grace', I see."

He was right, of course, but she couldn't comment. She gave him a stony look.

He looked down at his notes. "Dr. Toth is doing all the right things technically, I must say. I can't suggest anything further clinically, I am afraid. Nothing missed that I can see."

He paused.

"You didn't discuss with her, I think, your history of trauma therapy with Dr. Herrington. Or did you?"

Neville must have told his cousin about the psychologist, she realised.

"No, I didn't see the relevance, to be honest. It was years ago. It's in the past."

"You had a bout with him after an injury in Scotland, the scar to your face."

"Well, I did mention to Dr. Toth the cause of my injury, obviously; and also told my first gynecologist. She suspected that the fall then may have caused some womb displacement but - ."

"No, that's not an issue; I checked that carefully, too. Then you killed a gunman in Malaysia, defending yourself and others. That sent you back to Dr Herrington."

Neville, you have been talking very freely, I must say, she thought.

"Well, yes. It was hard, very stressful at the time, but it was years ago. It's past."

He said nothing. From his expression, she saw that he too recognized the denial in her voice.

"Mrs. Treneer, I have patients who look fragile and incapable of handling the whole pressure and process of pregnancy and childbirth yet they seem to carry on through; some of them could get pregnant and carry through to term in a war zone. Let's face it; many women do just that.

"I have others who look like they could cope quite well during pregnancy on the front line of that battlefield, or on the battleground of party politics at the Palace of Westminster, but they can't. They have careers and work problems to worry about and the baby just has to fit in. And some of them run into problems similar to yours.

"I have no clinical basis to say this; just case experience. These days many doctors are a little leery of giving advice that could be seen as 'old-fashioned' but I am not one of them. My goal is simply to help people in your situation carry their child through to full term and deliver safely a healthy baby and mother."

He paused, giving her his full stare. "I have a suspicion that the internalized stress of being a police officer, despite your apparent ability to handle it well, is far more significant than you are giving it credit for. If so, you and your husband may need to decide; either you are going to be a pregnant woman and hopefully a mother or are you are going to be a detective inspector, but perhaps not both during the course of your early pregnancy. And I haven't even touched on your art career that Neville mentioned to me; that has to be taken into account also, although I don't see any evidence that working on your art sent you to seek out a psychologist.

"I don't suppose in the current climate that you can take an extended leave of absence for the early part of the pregnancy, could you? Or would you, if you could? It may come down to that simple choice rather than alternative clinical approaches, you see?"

He looked at her, waiting for a response.

She replied, "In practice it would be difficult at present but not impossible; the Met does has structures in place for such circumstances."

It does sound old-fashioned, thought Catrin. But she had to concentrate as he pressed on.

"I suggest you talk to Dr. Toth about these aspects and if she asks you to, go back to talk further with this psychologist, Herrington. You have seen him several times and seem to trust him, so he would be the best person to approach."

He was searching her face, studying the reaction and, it was in the stare she could see a family resemblance to Neville, in the mannerism rather than the man's features.

She had thought he would be coming up with some new wonder pill for her, not old-fashioned commonsense.

27 FINER DETAILS

It was the following Friday when Isabelle knocked and entered Catrin's office.

"I traced the canvas used in Sleaman's forgeries. It was bought in three lots, from the same supplier," she announced, adding the caveats, "in my spare moments, when I wasn't liaising and coordinating. Or covering John's stuff. Or my own."

Norwich hadn't asked her to do it, Catrin knew.

Isabelle seemed quite proud of herself. Catrin smiled. "Well done. A wholesaler?"

Isabelle shook her head. "Surprisingly, Sleaman bought it from Atlantis Art Supply, right on our doorstep. He got a discount on the quantity; it's Medium Fine Grain Linen, Unprimed."

Catrin looked surprised. The art supply shop was in East London - she had an account there herself as it was the closest serious art shop to her home.

Catrin responded, "Well, that's a turn up. I thought it might have come from Europe. It still bothers me that the forger didn't use appropriately-aged canvas and stretchers; it's sort of '101' in art forgery, as we know."

"Well the forger didn't even buy it. Sleaman did, as I said."

"So you did. Even stranger, He was no artist, Smith said."

Isabelle said, "I will give DI Needham a call, let him know."

"You are making me feel guilty; I haven't thought about it," called out Catrin to the retreating figure.

Later that afternoon, Catrin called Isabelle into her office. On her screen were sections of the various photographic images that they had received from Norfolk of works by Sleaman's forger. Isabelle saw that she had chosen the same type of detail in each one and alongside each was a matching photo strip of the original painting.

She pointed. "I sorted the copies as best as I could by date, given what we know about them. You found the canvas, I found this - look at them in sequence, fast; then repeat. What do you see?"

Isabelle looked, her eyes moving around the screen again and again. Twice she said, "I don't quite -," then she stopped and looked at Catrin.

"He or she is changing over time; the detail is getting finer, as if - what?"

Catrin responded, "You are right. That's what I saw, too. This artist is not in a steady state when deciding on the level of detail. I have come to the conclusion that the person isn't trying simply to be consistent with the original. It's as if they have a mental viewing lens - but one that is changing focus with time."

Isabelle said, "We talked about that - the artist must be using a visor or lens to paint, to get this type of detail."

Catrin shook her head. "Even so, it would be constant; particularly as the magnification of the lens is set. No, this person is different and... do you know why? Did you ever do borough policing, schools and so on? No you didn't, I knew that, didn't I?"

Howlett waited for the punch line.

"I think this person has some physical or mental condition which is still developing, an Asperger's type thing, perhaps. It's the attention to detail, the ability to produce almost exact copies. That's my theory, anyway."

She sighed. "But that's enough of my time on that; I'll let Norwich know; they can follow up and we can call it a day."

She picked up her phone and called DI Needham again, but got no answer; it transferred to DS Hollis's line and was answered by a familiar voice.

"Melissa, hi; it's Catrin. You still with JMIT then?"

Nunn laughed. "A little longer than I planned for, yes. But it's my own fault, I asked for it."

Catrin responded, "Well, I think we have another thing for your lot that may help."

"I heard about the canvas earlier, ma'am."

"No, it's not that. Hang on while I put you on the speaker phone so that Isabelle can join in."

At the end of the explanation, Melissa said, "I am the only one here at present. It has been a long week for the team and Superintendent Lubbock told them last night to make today a short one, wrap up early and take the weekend off. Should I call them, do you think? This is significant."

Catrin said, "No. It could help focus the search, but it's not urgent. Tell them about it next week. On Monday and Tuesday I will be out, but Isabelle can take them through it in detail; she'll be here."

They wrapped up the call.

After they finished, Isabelle said, "Changing the subject…"

She paused, checking Catrin out, who just raised one eyebrow.

"Morley and I are planning to get married, but he is going to live in Paris, get an apartment. He really likes it, as you know, and it's not a bad distance for me for long weekends and holidays until I can retire. We worked it all out."

It came out in a rush.

Catrin said, "Well, congratulations to you both; is he still over? We should - ."

Morley Kerswell had flown over for the holidays.

"He went back to Washington, back to work. He needs to

talk to David, sort out his early retirement package. But it's not like it is going to happen right now."

Isabelle paused, finding the right words. "I'm just giving you early warning so you know... I'll still be around. I may want more long weekends than I have had in the past - I tended to be the one to cover here. But I'll be around."

I got the message, thought Catrin; including the one you didn't want to give me. I will have a quiet word with David Klintz, I think.

Then Howlett added, "Given where we are now, weekend coverage isn't a big need anyway, is it?"

Catrin responded, "Nevertheless, we should do something to celebrate. When's Morley coming back over?"

"In about six weeks. I'm going over there a month or so later and after that, I hope we will have things squared away regarding Paris. But I'm going to pack up; get out of here tonight. A big day on Monday for you."

"For us; for the team. But thank you for letting me know."

Isabelle smiled. "It was actually good to tell someone here; I've been bursting with it. I'll tell Aina on Monday."

She turned and went back to her desk.

Monday was John Obi's formal meeting with the internal review team, the OPS. A DCI Courtney would give a decision regarding the Tunnel incident. DCI Wetherby had insisted that Catrin and he would be present as observers, to show support. She was pleased her own boss had done this, stepping up to the plate.

Thinking of John made her decide to give him a call, check on how he was doing.

Obi said, "I had a call today, boss, on the QT from DS Dodds. They had to give their recommendation to Courtney yesterday, he said. He couldn't talk about it but he felt it was only right to have me well-prepared. Courtney's reputation is that he is a tough one. Dodds gave me some tips for making sure I got my full rights from the Federation but he doesn't know that I've got Evelyn, clearly. He's a good bloke."

"How are you coping?"

"Not easily; I am restless, as you can imagine. I am enjoying the time with the family, though, which is a plus.

"If the Met wants to let me go, I will fight it all the way. If they want to short circuit to some sort of lesser thing, like a reprimand and putting me back in uniform, I'll go along with it. I just don't want it to drag on. An IOPC review could take months, you know that."

"John, don't give up. Courtney is as you said; I know him by reputation. He's good, but he is no pushover. That's my read of him from the time I was working with Hunt."

John sounded morose. "I hope you are right. See you on Monday and… thanks for coming and standing up for me."

28 PULLS FERRY

After the call from the Met on the Friday, Melissa had sent an email with the details to DI Needham then left the Wymondham headquarters. Barry had been happy enough on Friday night but by late Saturday morning it had taken just a couple of remarks between them to rekindle how precarious their relationship was. By lunchtime, the combination of that and the issues now playing through her mind after the call from Catrin Sayer made her change her plans; to get some space away from him, in fact.

She said brightly, "I'm off to work; some things I need to catch up on."

She expected an outburst, but it didn't happen. He just looked up then stood, uncertain.

"It's not working, is it? We are both struggling."

Well, that's different, she thought.

She nodded. "Yes, I feel the same way. It's too forced. It's taking too much effort… but I don't want to fight over it again, about whose fault that is. It's getting us nowhere."

He nodded, looking glum.

She really wanted to escape now it was out there, between them.

"I really do need to go." She didn't, but the alternative was a well-worn path, she thought.

Instead, he said, "Would you keep this flat if I moved out? Find someone else - another renter, I meant - to share the costs. I don't want to leave you in the lurch financially, but I have been thinking about moving out. The strain is too much."

She kept her voice steady. "I was thinking about that, too. With my promotion, I could end up being relocated anywhere in the county."

"I wondered about that also; you hadn't said. I suppose if you did, you would have put the same question to me - about finding someone to share with?"

She nodded.

Ten minutes later, when she finally left the flat, she felt it was all on the table now, visible at least - and there hadn't been another scene. That aspect, at least, felt better.

"Mr. Jenks, this is PC Nunn at Norfolk Police. You spoke with one of my colleagues a little while ago."

Jenks was one of the Post Office staff who had been interviewed. He had been the postman delivering the mail most regularly to Sleaman's home over the last two years. Nunn had been assigned about a dozen minor follow-up items for the following week, but it was clear that the investigation was winding down; team strength had been reduced as people were reassigned to new cases. Inspector Golding had told her that she wanted to see her next Thursday about the Great Yarmouth post.

Jenks said, "Yes, I did."

She continued, "I am looking at the notes of your interview. You mentioned that Mr. Sleaman regularly received letters, a number from the same place, it says here, but you couldn't remember the return address. With so many items to deliver, I quite understand. But what was it that made you say they were from the same place? I don't see the reason mentioned here."

"Well, the other officer never asked, to be honest, as I recall. And we get a lot less personal letters these days; it's mainly bills and printed matter. Personal letters stand out more."

"So was it the handwriting, or what?"

He thought a moment. "No, now I think of it; it was the stamps, not the writing. They were from a Titchwell Marsh bird set issued some years ago, I recall. I am a bit of a 'twitcher' myself."

"Twitcher is a bird watcher, isn't it?"

"Yes, but more of a bird counter - how many different bird species one gets to see. I think the sender was either a bird watcher who especially asked for them or a person living in the Titchwell area. You see, the local area for each new stamp issue gets flooded with sets of the special covers."

Having explained it, he paused. "I now worry that I am adding two and two and making five."

"Well, thank you, anyway; that new piece of information may prove helpful. If you recall anything else you have DC Williams' number there, so please give him a call."

She closed the line and moved on to the second 'worry bead' playing in her mind from last night.

"Anne; how are you? It's Melissa."

"Well, well; long time no hear from! How are you and Barry?"

Anne Thorold and Melissa had been friends for years; regular but not close on a daily basis. She was a social worker who had been really supportive of Melissa during the Liddle aftermath.

"A bit ropey at present; actually very ropey, I am not sure where it's going. But look, I have a question. I am looking for an artist around here, probably a person with some sort of developmental challenge, perhaps autism-related: a really good artist but with that sort of diagnosis."

She outlined the observations made by Sayer and Howlett.

Thorold was quiet when she finished, then said, "It could well be that sort of behaviour, a focus on increasingly smaller detail. But I take it this is the case I saw in the paper? I don't think I can help. You can understand."

Melissa got the impression that Anne possibly could, but wouldn't. So she said, "I am hoping that if we can pin it down, it can be handled sensitively. Not like the Liddle debacle."

"I can't break client confidentiality or talk about anyone really, in my role; you know that."

"I know. My thinking is this, but I don't have the time or resource to slog it through. I shouldn't even be working today or if I was, I would be told what to do, not necessarily be given this to follow up. But the person who painted these is good enough perhaps to have exhibitions or news coverage locally, so that would be public domain stuff we could find eventually, you see. Or sooner, if I had a pointer. And if I don't, someone else in JMIT will follow up in the same way come Monday, I know."

She left the implication of that to settle and waited.

Anne said, "Two art exhibitions come to mind recently; like in the past few years. A woman in Ormesby St Margaret. She is doing well. You can find out a lot about her, I would think, on-line."

"And the other?"

"A young man in Thornham. He used to paint birds, beautiful things, really. Then he stopped. He had an exhibition some years ago at All Saints in Thornham and there was some media coverage; it got moved for a week to Norwich Cathedral for a special display. They have a lot of local art exhibitions at the cathedral, you know. It's where I met the artist."

She paused.

"Melissa, if I find either of these people goes through what the Liddle family went through, I will be totally shattered. I trust you on this one. From what you said, I take it you want that too. That's the only reason I am even giving this to you."

Melissa replied, "I do, Anne. I'll do my level best, I promise you. And thanks."

She thought she was done; time to wrap up. But Thorold asked, "Do you know Reverend Innes? He is a canon at Norwich Cathedral."

"No. I don't go to church. I visited there a few times, once on a call."

Clearly something had clicked with the social worker. "Go talk to him; I'll call him now; tell him that for a copper you are almost human. But do that first, please, before anything else. Promise me!"

"Ok, I promise, I promise. If he's around."

~~

The Reverend Canon Peter Innes was in his fifties, Melissa thought. She had checked the cathedral website and given him a call before heading over to the cathedral in the old Tombland area.

After meeting up in the entrance there, the combination of her uniform and his clerical attire had the attention of a party of visitors, so he suggested that they walk outside.

"First, though, note this area, it is where we have exhibitions on different themes; art, local history; that sort of thing. We have one on now."

Outside, he said candidly, "Anne called me. She says she is worried that an artist who exhibited here may be in trouble with the police. Or someone else with a similar challenge."

Melissa rushed in. "I don't know that exactly. What I do know is that an investigation into a major crime, a series of forgeries substituted for original art works, is linked to a man in Swaffham who was not an artist. He was working with a painter who made the forgeries. As of Friday, art experts in the Metropolitan Police are now suggesting that this artist may have developmental challenges; they see something in the detail which leads them to that conclusion. I have to report on this on Monday; in fact, the call is logged, already reported. It's just that the investigation team has the weekend off; it has been going full tilt."

He looked ahead, into the distance, before he responded.

"I had heard of the investigation, of course. An interesting development. You are working on it today, though, your own decision, Anne said. Why?"

It was a question she hadn't expected but if Anne Thorold had suggested that she talk to him there was an ulterior reason.

"Reverend Innes, next week I'll be gone; I am only assigned temporarily to this investigation team. Soon I'll be off elsewhere in Norfolk with a promotion. I am a community officer. But I am also the woman who held Sean Liddle's son in my arms after the man's arrest. It was a rough time and I was with the mother and the kids in the aftermath. His son's expression still haunts me; absolute serenity and absolute fear interchangeable by the second."

He looked at her but said nothing, waiting for her to continue. She pointed ahead to the archway and Ferry House framing the view of the waters of the River Wensum beyond, thinking it best to change the subject; in hindsight she had spoken too personally, she thought.

"The only time I came to Pulls Ferry for work was on a call about kids loitering, possibly doing drugs, the caller said. They weren't; it was just boys meeting girls, the social dance around each other away from adults. Nothing to it, really."

He said, "The ferry was the gateway for the stone for the cathedral."

Still he waited.

Melissa said, at last, "I'm in a real dilemma; not professionally; inside me. If a person in some way like the little boy I held is involved, I want it handled with kid gloves, not the heavy stuff; and if he isn't, I don't want the person bothered at all."

For some reason, Innes smiled gently to himself. He asked, "Do you know Chief Superintendent Kane?"

Melissa looked surprised. "Well, she's the big boss of community policing so, in a sense, yes. I have heard her speak at times and met her briefly. She has spoken to me on a few occasions, but no… I don't know her, really."

He paused for a moment, thinking, then stopped walking and faced her.

"I'll tell you about an exhibition held here about four years ago with a young artist called Brendan Atkin from Thornham.

And then, I hope, you will have the sense to call Janet Kane and talk to her directly."

Melissa replied, "I don't know I can - ."

He looked at her intently. "You are working on your day off and meeting me on the word of a social worker. Somehow I think you will, for Brendan. And his parents, perhaps. He is a talented young man who will smile and relate to you instantly or cover his head in terror; and you will have done nothing to stimulate either response. And it's not perceptions of beauty or ugliness that drives that; it is within him. He sees people he can trust implicitly and others… he fears instantly.

"Like me. I came in to see his work, a series of bird paintings from Titchwell Marsh and he shrieked. His parents were calming him down - they had said he might not last long at the opening, I understood. Whether it was me, or my clerical collar, who knows?

"Then a man came out through the nave to see what the problem was and Brendan just smiled at him. In fact, the man stayed with him for a while during the opening event then went back to work."

Melissa picked up on it. "This man works here, does he?"

Innes looked at her intently. "No, he was a contractor. He had something to do with installing a security alarm for the altar screen in St. Saviour's Chapel. It's very valuable."

She could see he was already there; that the news media had reported a person working in art security had perpetrated the frauds and someone in that field had met a talented artist in this very spot.

It was as they walked back and parted and she headed to her car that Melissa thought to ask.

"Chief Superintendent Kane is known here, I gather; is she involved in the cathedral?"

He called back.

"A little. Not enough. But my sister is a busy woman."

Just as her phone rang. It was Barry. As she looked at the screen, Innes smiled and walked away. She opened the call.

"I've moved my stuff into the other bedroom, for the time being. Let's just try to be flatmates, at least; see if that helps?"

She said warmly, "Thanks for that. It does, for me, I have been feeling so stifled and… guilty, to be honest; trying too hard."

"I know. It irritated me because I couldn't do that; I just pulled away. Hid in my shell. Let's give this a try. I'll look for somewhere but not make any serious decision until you know what you plan to do; okay?"

Somehow it picked her up. She took the plunge and phoned Kane's office. The senior officer held community safety responsibilities for the entire county. In her role prior to promotion, Kane had been directly involved in the aftermath of the Liddle affair, so she had that background, at least.

Melissa would leave her a voicemail, seek her advice then head back home to talk further with Barry.

The desk line was answered immediately, which threw Melissa for a moment. She responded to the terse 'Kane' with, "PC Nunn, ma'am; I am working on the forgery case with Superintendent Lubbock's team. I need advice. I think one of the possible perpetrators is from Norfolk and may be developmentally challenged, so with the Liddle experience, it worries me."

"Where are you, Nunn?"

"At the cathedral. In fact, I just finished talking with your brother. He said I should call you, but I wasn't sure it was the right thing, given the chain of command…."

She petered off then added lamely, "I was following up; I came in today to check on some things and the possible identification of the forger came out of that, but…"

She left it hanging. She didn't want to repeat herself.

Kane said, "Come back here to my office - I was just wrapping up, but I will wait."

"Yes ma'am."

Melissa hoped she had done the right thing; my promotion could turn into a demotion before I put the stripes on my sleeve, she thought as she closed the call.

29 COURTNEY

The weather on Monday in London was unexpected, a day of sunshine and warmth; a welcome change after a long period of cloudy skies and rain. As he travelled in by Underground, John Obi hoped it boded well but he had no illusions. It seemed to be strange to be back, in a sense, but on arrival people were coming up to him saying the right things in support. But the time dragged.

Evelyn Carter came along half an hour before ten; the time he was to be there. She concentrated on settling his nerves. About 9.45 he said, "You must have nerves of steel, doing this sort of thing day in and day out."

"Really?" she replied. "I'm going out for a quick smoke, warm up the steel a bit."

The meeting room door opened and John and Evelyn were invited in. As John entered, he saw Wetherby and Catrin sitting on chairs at one side of the room.

Superintendent Courtney said, "Please be seated both of you. Miss Carter, I must say I am a little surprised to see you here."

"DC Obi is my client, Superintendent, and a possibility of a recommendation to IOPC for one of my clients always gets my attention."

Her voice was wheezy from smoking then coming inside. Courtney flashed a look at Sayer and Wetherby. Catrin just stared back. Yes, she thought, we brought in the big guns.

Inspector Morton led off, sitting with DS Dodds on one side of the table across from John and Evelyn. He ran back through the statements by Obi and Sayer, the statement by the truck driver and a list of evidence. It took about half an hour.

At each stage Courtney asked for John's perspective on the points raised.

Catrin thought that, factually, what was unfolding was accurate but it dealt too much with the damage to the hand of Stevie Altman, as if he was a victim. But a core issue was the allegation of 'excessive use of force', so it was to be expected.

Courtney had just asked John, "You don't, I see, dispute that the injury to his hand was caused by your foot?"

Obi said, "No sir, there was no abrasion consistent with damage arising from road impact or friction. I accept that."

Courtney nodded but said nothing.

At the end, it was simply a summary that Obi had other opportunities, means and training to remove the weapon from the proximity of Altman without inflicting the injury sustained. Inspector Morton didn't look too happy about it, but he did his job thoroughly.

"Do you have anything else to add to the statement already made, DC Obi?"

Courtney was clearly at the end of the process.

"Yes sir, I do." John paused, getting it clear in his head. He and Evelyn had worked on this intensively.

"My earlier statement is correct factually, sir. My additional comments are to my state of mind at the time. I received no questions in that area, you will note.

"My boss had just saved my life by her quick response; faster than mine, really. I only saw what Altman was trying to do in the door mirror after DI Sayer braked. I jumped out and ran back with the sole intention of preventing him reaching the gun."

He paused again.

"I was in shock, to be honest, it just got to me. My eyes were watering with the emotions welling up; fear, relief and, I admit, anger. Then the headlights of the truck in the lane were closing in, partially blinding me as he jammed on his brakes. I knew I had virtually no time, so I went in hard. If Stephen Altman had got the gun he could have shot me, shot DI Sayer or even, if he shot wild, the man who made the complaint or someone else in a passing car. I had one chance and, despite being here now, I didn't want to screw up. No matter what it looked like to others, or on the video, that was what was in my head. Not retribution or hurting him, just stopping his hand from reaching the gun."

His eyes were moist now, his suppressed anger showing a little, but he was containing it. He stopped, but kept his gaze on Courtney, as Evelyn had instructed him.

"I don't care if you are impassive or blubbering by then; look at him, open up; tell him the full truth," she had said.

"Is that all, DC Obi?"

Evelyn spoke up. "Not quite, Superintendent; just one more item of evidence. I submit this still image magnified from the recording on the dashboard camera of the lorry that stopped behind the incident."

Inspector Morton interjected, "We have the video, so we have it already."

His tone was terse. Evelyn gave him a look that would fry eggs and held up the image.

She said, "The expression on Altman's face is pain and rage; it's clear. What's the expression on DC Obi's face?"

Morton said quickly, "You can't see his exp- ."

"Quite," said Courtney, getting the point faster than his lead investigating officer.

There was a long silence in the room as Catrin absorbed the impact of Evelyn's tactic. You couldn't see John's expression because it was a dark tunnel and his face was dark-skinned, not clearly standing out in the reflected headlight beam as did Stephen Altman's angry and pained expression. And Altman's hand was clearly reaching in the direction of the gun he had just dropped.

It meant that there was no physical evidence to counter what John had just said to Courtney and there was a solid image to support it.

All Evelyn added was, "DC Obi was subject to racial abuse at the home of this man and his family. Unfortunate as Renée Altman's death was, Stephen Altman's targeting of my client, by his own admission, was racially motivated, too. We will be seeking access to the transcript of his interview if this complaint goes forward."

She left the last bit unsaid. Let's not add to that abuse by our actions today, her look said, because if this case gets referred to IOPC then the photo is in evidence now, too, and Courtney, I will haul OPS and the Met over the coals on that one.

Superintendent Courtney said, "I see. And is there anything else?"

"Not evidence, no; at this stage. But I flag this…"

She pulled out a list of some sort and passed it over. Catrin hadn't heard of this aspect of her tactic and, looking at his expression, neither had John.

Evelyn said, "I didn't ask any of these people at this stage to be present, as this is an internal assessment. But I will if it gets referred. They will all attest to the DC Obi's action being correct, given the circumstances. One has already been recognized for his bravery, another is a platoon commander in the Royal - ."

Courtney interrupted her and handed back the list. "I recognize a couple of the names. And I understand the intent, Miss Carter. Thank you. Now, DC Obi, if you and Miss Carter could wait outside."

Catrin and Wetherby stood also, to leave with them.

"If you could stay, please, DI Sayer and DCI Wetherby."

Courtney took a moment after the door closed and gave Wetherby and Catrin his full gaze.

"We are off the record now. If I recall rightly, DI Sayer, Miss Carter was your rep in that Scottish thing, was she not? The PIRC issue, years ago?"

Catrin said neutrally, "Yes, sir."

He nodded and smiled briefly. "You and she must get along quite well; she has bigger fish to fry than this meeting."

His smile vanished as he spoke to the room.

"OPS's job is to investigate police officers who break the rules. That is our primary role. The people who are bent, those who corrupt others and those that get in the way of honest coppers protecting the public. These are the investigations that go beyond our doors into IOPC or to the courts. We are busy people."

He looked down briefly at the table, weighing his next words carefully.

"Considering an IOPC review for DC Obi, just because it was a big media issue sticks in my craw, I tell you."

He looked at DCI Wetherby. "I said as much to Assistant Commissioner Hall. I expected support for the man right down to Obi's own team. It's what I would expect in his place and that is what I got from you, DCI Wetherby, and your team."

He paused, the silence dragging on, emphasizing the implied compliment. Catrin let out a breath she hadn't realised was being held. She could see where it was going now.

Courtney continued, "Now, I am going to bring that officer back in with Miss Hell Hath No Fury. And I am going to tell him the case is dismissed not on the basis of absence of evidence but on ample evidence to show he was doing his job and doing it well. Yes, it is a big public issue. Yes, the Commissioner and his team will be in the limelight again. Some in the public will scream about police protecting their own, no doubt and Communications will be running about dealing with press enquiries - but that's not my concern. This one is over with.

"DS Dobbs, call them back in then we go back on the record."

Later, outside the Yard entrance, Evelyn's parting words were, "Catrin, I forgive you this time for the sudden upheaval in my life but next time, it had better be when you've shot some sod again. John, you keep this one; you won't find many bosses like her, even if she does talk funny."

"How many were on your list, Evelyn?" asked Catrin, smiling.

"Six. All people who would have embarrassed the Met, one way or another and everyone agreed to appear, if needed. You see, you two and the bigwigs sweating about the public image of the Met saw the video as a liability. I saw it as an asset to get people to stand up for you, John."

She smiled. "That's my job."

With that she was off, walking down to St. James's Park underground, pulling out another cigarette.

Catrin shook her head. "She'll pop a blood vessel like Renée did."

John didn't respond directly. He just looked at Catrin and said, "Thanks boss. I really mean it. I - ."

She smiled. "Go home John, let Kaila know; play with the kids after school. You've earned the rest of the day off, I think. Tomorrow, get in early; you will find your desk a foot high with case files I haven't got around to in the last while. I'm taking the day off; you can get back to work."

Back in the office, Aina was beaming at her when she entered. "I heard - in fact, it's going the rounds."

Then Isabelle walked in and saw them, eyeing up the situation. "Some days," she said loudly, "the Art and Antiques Unit is the best place in the entire Met to work, you know?"

30 REQUEST

Ever since his medical diagnosis was made known Michael Yau had insisted that his family not mope around him, but get on with their lives. He told Miele particularly that she needed to focus on her career. She was not easy to reason with on that point and the tradeoff was that each week while he had the strength, he would visit her pottery for an hour or so to watch her and her partner work, talking about life in general.

His mainstays helping him cope were Alex and Tak, his drivers, who now brought in other triad people as needed to do their work; they focused entirely on Michael. One or other of his little team were always at his elbow, ready to do anything he required.

It was in the visit to the studio following the final meeting with Jian Li that he was struck by a decision he hadn't known he needed to make and, somehow, it energized him. Miele had been talking as usual about her work and project plans when she incidentally brought in a conversation with Jean Hughes in London; some advice she had sought from her friend.

She then added, "Jean says Catrin is not working on art at present; she doesn't know when they will start again. It's so sad."

She hit an artistic block, I suppose?" he said, showing he was listening.

"She nearly hit something far more tangible; a wall of a tunnel near London, a run-in with a biker trying to kill her colleague."

"I read about it; Li mentioned something similar when she visited."

Miele went on, "But it sounded as if Catrin's security training saved them. I don't think I would have just driven into a bike like that. I would just freeze, particularly if the biker had a gun."

She stopped, concentrating on her work then she smiled at her grandfather. "I am prattling on, aren't I?"

"No, it's very interesting, actually."

Miele looked at him carefully then continued. "After losing her baby and her job changes, Jean says it has all got on top of her. All she is interested in is getting her colleague off an internal review charge. He stomped on the hand of the man who tried to shoot them and was accused of improper conduct."

Yau thought that, under similar circumstances, he would do far more than stomp on the man's hand. But that was the old days. Now he couldn't stomp on anything. He made some appropriately solicitous remark and left it there. But he knew a decision within him had just been made. He had become too lost in himself, was the issue, he knew. Now he would look into this.

After he got back into the car with Tak's help, the driver said, "Home, boss?"

"Yes, but please call Emily; ask her to meet me there, if she is available."

Emily Yang, who Michael had mentored through her time with Four Square, was at Michael's home within an hour. Normally stoic and imperturbable, she seemed tense, holding in her emotions as the housekeeper served tea.

Yau said, "Emily, I will transition soon from appearing

unwell to being a person who is obviously dying. Psychologically that will make an impact. People will see me as failing, weak; whatever, but different."

She opened her mouth to protest but his raised finger silenced her.

"In a business sense, of course, I am retired, it is irrelevant. I am well regarded; honoured even, I know. But I no longer influence the business, nor should I.

"I asked you to come today because I have a request of you, one in which I want you to see my strength, my resolute commitment. You and I have *guanxi*; it underpins everything, does it not? The oaths? The loyalty to the enterprise and to our members. But *guanxi* is strange. At some time you will find it has a life of its own, not limited to those who you would choose; or who would choose you. It extends to others. And I must bore you again with a story you have heard already no doubt, from me or others, in part or in whole. But you should hear it from my current perspective."

Finally Emily got to speak. She smiled, relaxed a little. "Michael, not boring, ever. You must at least accept that rejection."

He smiled back but instantly became serious again.

"Many years ago, my son Shing went to a party. We know what happened after Shing and Enlai Lin's son Simon died there together in that fire. First Enlai came into my life, then, in sequence, a religious fireman called Daniel Yeung, his daughter and, in turn, her friends in England. Who would have thought it? My life is here, with you, with my family and my people.

"And now I see some of that spiraling around again. Look at Miele; her life is so happy with her art business and part of that is to do with this strange mix of people; with the *guanxi* between them - with Jian Li and her friends in England. They are now Miele's friends. And of them all, only Jian Li and Catrin Sayer know about me and our ways."

"When Sayer lost her baby recently they were all there for her, in different ways but, in a sense, in the ways we recognize ourselves, do we not? I would like to die knowing I have taken steps to protect that group and to do so, protect this woman Sayer. She saved Jian Li in Wales; we saved her in Malaysia. Now I suspect she may be in more trouble. I hope I am wrong, but if I am not, I hope that you will put it right."

Precisely, he gave a summary of the information he had picked up from Li and Miele and his own research.

"I think that this biker club could do something to Sayer and the other policeman, or may at least be considering it. I want you to deal with it. If it's running, stop it if you can. If it's not, prevent it happening permanently. It will help me to know this is being addressed."

Emily said slowly, "Permanently could be significant, Michael."

He nodded. "I will be explicit. If need be, eliminate this man and his son in prison. If it turns out it is a motorcycle club issue, deal with them. If you see fit, make the club blow away in the wind, if need be. I will cover every cost personally."

"A whirlwind?"

"If necessary. But you are very capable of making that wind blow gently and achieve the same end. I know that. I hope that will happen first, if any action is needed."

To Emily this was suddenly the Michael Yau of years ago. His eyes had a life to them which belied his precarious state of health and he had the intensity she had seen in him before; analytical, resolute and demanding of those around him to do whatever was necessary to achieve the vision and objectives of Four Square.

"Check it, but unless urgent action is needed, simply make plans. However, first we have the New Year ahead; my last, I know. I hope, unless you have other commitments, you will spend it with me and my family? It will not be a sad time, I assure you."

He knew that Emily was a loner and often went away for the Chinese New Year. This year, the year of the sheep, it was quite late in February. From the time he had first come across her in Four Square he had steered her career but not her personal life, where she would allow No one, it seemed, to get close to her.

She whispered, "I would be honored to do so. Thank you."

This task had nothing to do with her triad, yet she knew she would try to fulfill his request as if it was the most important job of her life. The problem that she faced, which she would not share with Mr. Yau in his current state of health, was that it was virtually impossible to assure success. If a biker organisation wanted someone dead, they had many means and resources available to achieve their goal. And a secretive triad could hardly mount a security protection operation around this woman Sayer.

She had accepted the task, but was a little lost as to how to achieve the goal at this stage.

31 HUNSTANTON

Catrin had booked the Tuesday off to finish a piece at the Kiln that Liz had been pressing her for and she also planned to get her hair cut. If Monday went well, she had rationalised, it would be a needed mini-break; if it went wrong and John came out of the review badly, she would need the time to get herself prepared for whatever was then needed going forward. These days, management of even a small team was a weight on her shoulders.

Heading home that Monday evening she was happy with the outcome of John's review. Her mind moved on the art that she and Jean had put on one side.

The call later in the evening turned her plan on its head, particularly as it came from Commander Moore.

"Sayer, I have DCI Wetherby on the line; he tells me you have the day off tomorrow. I'm sorry; I am going to have to cancel it. Where are you?"

"At home, Ma'am."

"You know this officer in Norwich, PC Nunn, I gather? You spoke to her last Friday. With the events today, I quite understand, but DCI Wetherby is not current on the outcome of that conversation. Can you summarize it briefly, please?"

Catrin knew that something serious was amiss. She took a moment and then said, "We called the Norfolk team twice on Friday; once with the information Howlett found regarding the source of the canvas used for the copies. Later we gave them the observation that DC Howlett and I made in the afternoon, reviewing again the large magnification prints of the copies. We suggested that there was a steady change in the level of minute detail. It could be consistent with a trait in the artist that the person wasn't aware of. I thought it may be something akin to Asperger's or a related autism-type condition. It was only a suggestion. Nunn was the only person there at the time and noted it. She said she would brief the team."

She stopped. It was up to Moore now.

"Over the weekend Nunn went off playing Sherlock Holmes. She located the alleged forger then did something she may come to regret; she informed the Chief Superintendent of Community Policing, outside her own line of command on the case. Chief Superintendent Kane called Lubbock and the two senior officers sorted it out, of course, but it didn't sit well.

"The outcome was that two team members went up to Hunstanton on Sunday; that's the closest police station to the location of this alleged copyist, and did some background checks. JMIT has concluded today that it is highly likely that Nunn is on the ball regarding the identity of the forger.

"There are some tensions in the Norfolk group now, as you can imagine. So to do this properly, they have to cover all the bases. The location of the alleged forger is a farmhouse and farmhouses can have guns, as we know; in fact, a person there had a licence for shotguns once. But they can't hammer in with a tactical team. Supposedly, there are two elderly parents and their adult son, the painter, living there. He is developmentally challenged. All he does is paint, they heard."

"So what do they want to do?" Catrin asked, meaning more, what did Moore want her to do. But she couldn't say that with Moore in the middle of her soliloquy.

"It seems normal at the house from a distance but... they are giving Nunn a chance to follow through herself. She will go in tomorrow morning with an experienced female tactical officer, firearms trained and armed. A tactical team will be close, ready to follow, if needed and they want you."

"Me? Why me?"

"If the forger is as isolated in his behaviour as they have heard, they want someone who can talk art with him, to keep him calm while they do whatever is necessary. You were to go in immediately after the scene was contained."

"Was?"

Moore's voice became more enthusiastic.

"If this is some sort of weird recluse who could be violent and pose a risk to others, they need people there who understand tactical unit entry, particularly as it will be the cart before the horse, so to speak. So I said you could go in with Nunn, too; you know what to do. You are a security officer; trained. Just the right person for both jobs, I said to Neil Lubbock. Duck and run if you see a shotgun at all. And you are to keep Nunn from getting in the way or getting hurt, if needed."

You don't run from a shotgun, thought Catrin; not easily.

Moore added, with a sense of satisfaction in her voice, "I'll be getting some value from the AFO maintenance costs for you after all, even if you aren't in the job I first wanted you in."

Catrin was still an Authorised Firearms Officer. The quarterly maintenance costs of range training had been left on Moore's budget.

She paused. "Three women dropping by the house, to begin with. It will either quieten down or a cavalry unit will trample through."

Catrin looked at her watch.

"How do I get there and when do they want me?"

"A car will collect you at 5.00 a.m. You will be in Hunstanton by 7.30. They will brief you then."

"I don't need to be armed, I take it?"

"No. That's not your role, nor our jurisdiction. Just take your tactical vest and a coat big enough to cover it. Weapons are the job of the locals, so just keep your eyes and ears open and use your experience. I don't want anyone hurt but I particularly don't want you hurt; there would be a lot of paper-work to fill in and that would be irritating."

"Thank you, ma'am; I think."

Moore said, her voice warming, "And by the way, both of you, well done with DC Obi. I like to see teams pull together and the word came up that you had done that. Nice job."

Wetherby's and Catrin's replies were followed by the phone line closing. Within seconds, hers rang again; it was Wetherby.

"Well, I am surprised by that. She was very wound up, Sayer. I wondered, given the time of night… Are you OK with this?"

Catrin smiled to herself. Had Karen Moore been drinking, he was alluding to. She replied, "Well, I am sure that the Norfolk tactical team will have it sorted out with no in-appropriate risks. Actually, this is more the Karen Moore I remember from working on the Ranjani case with Trident. She must be settling into her new job, sir."

He paused, mulling it over then replied, "It is different, I must admit. But good luck tomorrow. Call me once it's done or if you need anything. I will check in on DC Obi, see if he is settling back properly. There is a lot to do and this sort of thing doesn't help, does it?"

"No sir, not with our current files, I must say."

He sounded reflective, as if he had just realised for the first time that there was only Superintendent Patterson protecting him from the regular onslaughts of Commander Moore, who could create chaos in his well-ordered life.

For Catrin's part, she was quite pleased with the call, she decided; she would get to see the forger first hand.

~~

The following morning at 5.00 a.m. Catrin was collected in an unmarked black BMW5 by a driver in uniform called Stan. It was nice inside. Hopefully this isn't on DCI Wetherby's budget, she thought, as they drove through the reasonably empty roads around Wanstead, heading for the M11.

Stan said, "You may want to tip the headrest back, ma'am and get some more sleep when we are on the motorway. They told me you were in for a busy morning."

It seemed good advice. She dozed intermittently until Saffron Walden and they stopped at a service area for a coffee and a quick breakfast.

After that her mind was on the day ahead.

32 FARMHOUSE

They bypassed Kings Lynn skirting the Sandringham Royal Estate, still heading north. The night had first turned to a bleak grey dawn over the East Anglian countryside. Then a fresh morning light from a low sun promised to make the world a little warmer. But it was winter; the wind would continue to break that promise, according to the outside temperature reading on the car dashboard.

Stan hadn't been to these parts before. "Big skies," he said more than once.

They were soon near their destination, approaching the section of Lynn Road with the fire station and the local police station. It was a smaller building, but this was the briefing and assembly point for the morning operation to take place ten minutes away.

As they parked and walked forward, it was Stan's Metropolitan Police uniform that got the looks, not the blonde woman in the dark casual pants and short topcoat beside him.

In the meeting room, they introduced themselves. Melissa and Ray Hollis were the only people Catrin could recognize at first as they made the rounds, but they had no time then to talk.

A dark-haired, fit woman in her forties approached Catrin to introduce herself; Sergeant Christine Thomas, the lead of the five-person tactical team. In plain clothes and wearing a cropped leather jacket that did nothing to conceal the holstered sidearm, she got straight down to business. "Superintendent Lubbock said you are trained; a security officer, ma'am."

Catrin replied, "It's Catrin and yes; I was a security aide to an assistant commissioner at the Met for two years. I am still current AFO. Not that I am armed."

Thomas responded, "I'm Chrissie, then. Current, as in 'Take Nunn down' if I call?"

Catrin replied, "Flat on the floor before she realises it, if she doesn't respond to your call. The worst that can happen, I hope, is that we get trampled with boots when your team enters."

Sergeant Thomas smiled. They understood each other.

Then something came to mind, showing on the Norfolk officer's face. "The scar; you're the one who took out the Malaysian a few years ago. We heard about it."

Tactical units around the country had their own cliques and contacts; their own world of war stories.

Catrin nodded. Normally she would say nothing on that score but suddenly she said, "He was a big kid with a gun, really."

Thomas's lips pursed. "It's the reality, these days. Mine was a twenty-two year old waving a Glock wildly, then he stopped, focused on one person. It was through a scope but it stays with you, despite the counselling."

She took a breath. "Let's do this one safely."

In the briefing session it was evident to Catrin that there were tensions between the people gathered, particularly notice-able between Nunn and DS Hollis. Tactical were outside it all, other than securing safe access. Catrin was a visitor who reminded herself she had two very specific duties; look after Nunn if needed then, hopefully, look at this forger's art with the man.

But an Inspector Moyers from Community Policing clearly wanted an approach without the weapons aspect surfacing. Needham and Hollis re-emphasized that this was a higher-risk approach for the officers involved. Lubbock was steering a middle path. It was obvious that he had already reached an accommodation with some other senior officer.

Afterwards, they had thirty minutes before the sequence began. The start would be when Mrs. Atkin arrived at Thornham Church for some event there; she was scheduled to do that and it meant that one person would be out of the way.

As they spread out from the briefing table Melissa came up to Catrin and smiled.

"Thanks for saying yes, ma'am, and coming up all this way. It just got a bit out of hand."

Catrin said, "Do you want a coffee and to tell me about it?"

Melissa was holding the cup of coffee in both hands. "The bottom line is me and DS Hollis, I think. He is a good detective, but - ."

"He's keen, I'll give him that," said Catrin.

"I'm torn, to be honest. There are aspects of community policing that I love and others I hate. And I like the investigations I have been on peripherally, like this one. I left a note for them for Monday about calling Isabelle. Did they?"

Catrin nodded. "They did. She said they seemed less enthused than we were when we called you, she thought. But why all this?"

The stress; the visit.

Melissa put her cup down and said, "Two years ago I was assigned to an arrest team of a thief with a violent streak, a miserable man called Sean Liddle who couldn't be located at first. Then someone's informer said he was at his ex-wife's overnight. His ex has two small kids and didn't want anything to do with him but she was co-dependent, unable to resist. He'd done it before, we found out later.

"We went in at 6.30 a.m. They broke the door, handcuffed

him, pulling him off the sofa where he had been sleeping. The ex was in the bedroom asleep; she had been up half the night with the younger child. I wasn't inside the home then, I was on duty outside, but I heard it got rough; he resisted, head-butted and kicked someone and they took him down hard."

"Then they went thought the house looking for his things, anything that would be evidence. Fifteen minutes later DC Hollis, as he was then, had brought the wife from anger to tears by implying she would be arrested for harboring a known fugitive. They all went off leaving me and another constable there holding the fort until the social services people came. We were left with a sobbing woman and the two kids and a front door that would need replacing.

"I'd done it before, of course."

She looked at Catrin enquiringly.

Catrin said, "Two years assisting the drug squad in Brixton and a probationer in Lambeth before that. I told you that when we first met."

"So you did, now you mention it. So you have been there. Aftermath time; the stuff they miss out covering on the police shows on television, like puke smells in the back seat of cars abandoned in laybys.

"The older kid, a girl, was a mess, an absolute mess; frightened, crying. Nothing could calm her. She thought her dad was wonderful and all these people manhandling him sent her off the wall. But the younger one was totally calm, couldn't be moved from a cot toy he was playing with. When I went to pick him up, he wouldn't be distracted from it. Then he threw a fit as I tried to help the mother give them some breakfast to calm them down. But, right from when I picked him up, his eyes were wide with fright, I thought.

"The mother said, 'don't bother; he won't eat or drink for a while, he's autistic; it's the way he copes with everything, really. It's lucky they didn't hurt him'. Then I realised that the child must have been in the front room with his dad. But he appeared calm, other than the eyes; it was weird."

She took a sip of her coffee. Catrin was getting the picture but waited on Nunn to finish her story.

"She got some help and is a cashier in Norwich now. I see her from time to time when I shop, ask how she's doing and how the kids are. I saw her last time about two months ago; she was on a shift break and told me things were going well. Then she showed me a drawing that the younger child did. The accuracy and detail was astonishing; and he is so young. So when you called it brought it back.

"On Saturday I followed up on a lead I was to do on Monday, with a postman; it led me to this area. Then I couldn't put it down, for some reason. I called a woman I know and she gave me some pointers on autistic artists in the area, one of which was here. I talked with someone else she knew then I told Chief Superintendent Kane. She had to deal with the Liddle complaint and I knew she wouldn't want a repeat with another person who had development issues."

Catrin smiled. "It sounds like you did some good work there, Melissa."

Just as DI Needham called out, "She's in the car, leaving the farm. Let's get going."

~~

It didn't take long for the convoy of vehicles led by Sergeant Thomas to arrive at the farm near Thornham. The whitewashed walls of the two-story building caught the sun and made the tile roof seem deeper orange-red than it really was. Catrin swiftly took in the layout; the farmhouse with its four small-paned windows upstairs, all closed against the chill air; the cottage further back and the work sheds over to the south side. Automatically she was scanning for weapons, lines of sight and cover opportunities from the planned arrival point. It surprised her how swiftly she dropped back into the security role she had occupied for two years as Sandra Hunt's aide.

The car with the three women turned into the farmyard entrance and parked as close to the front door as possible as a plain white panel van slowed to a halt, the rear end partly blocking the farm gate. The doors on the rear of the van opened but no one got out. Behind it, several yards away, half-hidden by the hedge, two white, yellow and blue Ford Mondeo standard patrol units came to a halt but, again, no one got out. People on the passenger side of each vehicle trained binoculars on the building and the windows.

Catrin knew they were all waiting on the word from Sergeant Thomas, who now had an earpiece in place and a microphone at her collar. She was in charge until she said otherwise.

They exited the vehicle and Catrin stood by Melissa, who pressed the doorbell, partly concealing Thomas, whose hand was on her weapon. The wind was blowing in gusts and was quite chilly still. Catrin moved her hair away from her face as they waited, suddenly reminded that as a security aide her hair had been shorter. Most women on such duties wore their hair either longer and tied back or very short. I should be at home, getting mine cut, not be here, she thought.

The older man who opened the door just said, "Yes?"

Melissa said, "We are police officers, Mr. Atkin, making some enquiries. We understand your son Brendan is an artist. Is he here?"

The youngest woman there was to ask the first questions; it would be the least alarming approach, they had decided. Look pleasant and friendly, Lubbock had told Nunn, tersely.

Hubert Atkin stood still for a moment, not responding, his face showing he was absorbing the message. 'The game was over' was written on it; that was the impression that Catrin got.

Then he said, "You'd better come in. I will tell you all about it. But be quiet, please. Brendan is finishing getting dressed. It's his medication; he sleeps late. He needs to wake up fully by himself or he gets in a state. He'll be down in a minute."

He looked like he had taken a body blow, for the police to arrive now; not angry, Catrin thought, just stopped in his tracks, sensing his imminent defeat. But she knew reactions like that could produce sudden changes in behaviour and a violent response, so like Thomas, she was intently focused on the man.

He moved back a pace or two before turning to lead them through the house, apparently into the comfortable, large kitchen at the back that they could see down the hallway. Chrissie Thomas took over the lead moving close to Atkin, her eyes and head focused on the doorways of two rooms as they passed. Catrin was watching his hands as he entered the kitchen. He didn't reach for anything, just turned and pointed, offering them seats at the kitchen table.

But there was no way they were going to sit down.

Catrin looked at Thomas. If Brendan was upstairs, then the Norfolk officer needed to monitor the staircase, Catrin knew. She pointed at Hubert Atkin as Thomas nodded and pointed back to the hall; they understood each other. Nunn was focused entirely on the old man, making conversational noises about 'needing a quiet talk to clarify a few things'; that was her job, to calm things. Catrin moved alongside her as the tactical officer moved back to the door.

Atkin said quietly, "We had hoped that we had longer, you see. Keeping Brendan here. Once I saw the news, I knew we would be arrested. It is all a matter of time, isn't it; for all of us, really?"

Catrin said, "Hold on, Mr. Atkin. Let's take this step by step, if you don't mind."

She walked over a couple of paces to a painting on the wall: a waterfowl, some sort of duck. She examined it very quickly before her attention returned to the man.

"Brendan is a wonderful artist, isn't he?"

The older man nodded. "It's his great love now and his best therapy. Too far along, too many problems."

Thomas looked back from the base of the stairwell and called out, "Being a farm, are there any guns on the premises, Mr. Atkin?"

He looked surprised then shook his head. "No, all we do is look after Brendan now. The Bowerman family owns the land;

they lease it to others, so I have no need of any guns. We got rid of my shotguns - legally, I might add - when he was a boy. Even locked up, I didn't want to take the risk, you know?"

The tactical officer moved back into the kitchen closer to Catrin and said quietly, "I doubt we'll need my team; we'll wait to get him down, then he's yours, I believe."

It was spoken as much for her team outside and the people in Hunstanton following the operation remotely, Catrin knew.

Melissa Nunn said, "Mr. Atkin, we are going to have to get Brendan down here and talk to him. Once he's here, Sergeant Thomas will leave and other officers will join us to ask you some questions."

The man looked puzzled, then relieved. "I have a number to call that Brian arranged; a solicitor, a Mr. Olson. Brian said I should call him when you arrested us and say, 'I invoke my right to a solicitor for me, my wife and Brendan'. There; is that OK?"

Melissa looked bemused. "OK or not, sir, it is your right and you've just exercised it."

They heard a noise on the landing upstairs as a door closed and Catrin and Chrissie Thomas immediately moved back closer to the stairwell. Catrin pointed; she would take the lead now; it had been agreed that she should have the first contact with the artist, if possible. Thomas moved behind her, her arm at her side, close to but obscuring the holstered weapon.

Down the stairs came a tousle-headed man in his late-twenties suddenly looking surprised and then upset. Catrin said softly, "Brendan, I'm Catrin. I've come to see your art, if you will show it to me?"

His face changed into a smile. "Did Brian send you?"

"Well, we are here because of him so, yes, in a sense. But I have seen some of your work already and it is very impressive; your Klinkenburg copy, for instance."

"Are you an artist?"

"I'm a police officer and an artist, yes."

Catrin could hear behind her Chrissie Thomas reporting

quietly into her microphone.

Brendan smiled. "It's being an artist that counts. Yes, my art is in my studio; do you want to come over?"

But by then DS Hollis and DI Needham were coming through the front door.

Catrin said to Brendan, "Yes, let's go and see."

She looked at Thomas, who nodded. She said quietly, "I'll be right behind."

As they moved forward through the hallway to the kitchen, Brendan said to his dad, "This is Catrin, she's an artist. Brian sent her. I'll show her my art then come back for my breakfast."

He didn't wait for a response or notice the subdued look on his father's face with the group of people present. Nor did he seem bothered by the appearance of a lot of people. He had someone to talk to about art.

33 STUDIO

Crossing the farmyard to the old cottage Brendan was focused, walking ahead as if he was unaccompanied. Physically he appeared and moved as a healthy young man, but in the short space of a minute or so, Catrin had felt the difference; Brendan lived entirely in a world of his own, it appeared.

He opened the vestibule door and went in first, saying, "Shoes off, slippers on," to himself; and to her. He ignored Chrissie Thomas.

In the small vestibule area were several sets of slippers. Not wanting to disturb the man any more than necessary she unzipped her boots as he said, "You can use mum's."

The slippers looked well-worn; Catrin said nothing but elected to stay in her socks instead.

With that he opened the inner door into a different world.

Inside the old building was a spotless modern-looking art studio. Renovated walls, floors and ceiling were the most obvious features, along with a good easel and, from Catrin's first glance around, an abundant supply of artist materials. Many appeared to be from Atlantic Art Supplies and Cornelissen's in London.

And it was pleasantly warm, warmer than the farmhouse.

The two officers looked around from the vestibule entrance, assessing the studio for weapons of any sort and seeing nothing of concern. Catrin nodded and Thomas said, "It's all yours, I think."

She backed out of the vestibule, gave Catrin a smile and headed out, still talking into her microphone. Catrin closed the door and entered a world of art.

She first took off her coat and opened the Velcro on the tactical vest. It was too warm in the room to keep them on. Brendan looked across at the noise as the fastening parted then deliberately looked away. She realised that the word 'police' on it had disturbed him.

The most startling element initially for her was the large North-facing window, something added to replace the smaller originals, no doubt, with a view across the field. Brendan looked at it first before moving to the canvas on his easel and then back to Catrin.

She smiled and said, "Wonderful light. Just what an artist needs."

He smiled back conspiratorially, artist to artist, "It's the best part, really. Dad paid Mr. Bramley to come and do it; it took ages. But Brian wanted the best for me."

He went across the room to a Bose sound system and switched it on. Out of it came the opening notes of Arvo Pärt's Speigel im Speigel. Brendan followed his routine, putting on an apron and tying it at the back before returning to the swivel stool by the easel.

Catrin could see he was ready; he was in his world.

It was the rack in the corner that caught Catrin's eye next, not the easel with its current work or the large, wall-mounted monitor behind it. From inside the doorway she could see about twenty unframed oil paintings of various dimensions neatly stacked in rows, with separators between each one.

But she focused on the one that Brendan was pointing to on the easel, his work in progress.

It was a Joan Miro painting, one from the Spanish painter's Fauvist period, Catrin recognized.

"It's coming along very well."

The man didn't react to the compliment, just said, "I love this one. I did it twice already but it is really hard. People copy it wrong, you know? They think it is easy because it looks coarse, childish, but it isn't. I forgot what you said earlier; do you paint, too?"

"I'm a ceramic artist. I'll show you some of my work on my iPhone. In fact, later, I could show you some on the internet, on your screen."

She pointed at the wall monitor.

But he wasn't interested or polite about it. "No thanks, I can't do them, they are too difficult. Paintings ceramics has complicated surfaces to work on; too complicated for me."

Not that way, then, thought Catrin.

She said, "My brother-in-law is Mason Carrington, the watercolourist. Do you know his work?"

Brother-in-law was a relationship stretch, she thought, but she needed to keep it simple.

He brightened. "Yes, I've seen him on television; he's good. But I can't do watercolour. It's too difficult; all those glazes and flows. Too dynamic. I wish I could. Turner could. But I can only copy Turner oils, really. Not full size, his big ones. I would like to do one full size but... I can't concentrate for very long anymore."

"Joan Miro," she said, pointing at the work on the easel. He nodded.

"He could do ceramics," she said.

Brendan smiled. "And sculptures. A great man."

A few seconds later he said, "The other two copies are over there."

He pointed to the storage rack.

She asked, "Can I look, Brendan?"

He didn't look at her but said, "Yes, but be careful."

She replied, "The paint hasn't hardened, you mean?"

"Yes. You know. Brian knew too but I have to remind

mum. They are on the top on the right."

Catrin moved over to the shelves. She slid out one of the two copies of the work by the Spanish artist and examined it carefully, thinking what to say next.

"How do you know when to stop copying one painting and start a different one?"

He stopped his preparations and replied, "You are the first person to ask that question quite like that. People usually ask me why I copy the same painting more than once."

He smiled at her, an almost impudent smile. "Why do I?"

Catrin replied, "It takes a long time to get into the head of an artist. That's what you are doing, I think. Trying to experience the creation of - ."

She pointed. "This; the way that Joan painted it. What it must have been like the first time."

She moved over to a large bookshelf, seeing a range of classic works on artists; all provided by Brian Sleaman, no doubt.

"It's why you have the books; to understand the artists."

He smiled again. "I like you. You know why I paint. Brian understood, too. He came to see me last time and said he wouldn't be coming for a long while now but I would see him again."

Catrin nodded. "When did you meet Mr. Sleaman?"

His face went from happiness to pain. "I don't want to talk about that."

"You don't have to. How do you copy, can I ask that?"

His face brightened. "I'll show you."

He crossed the room to the walls and pressed a button on a controller. The large TV monitor lit up and he pulled a computer tablet in a sleeve from a drawer. He took it out and switched it on. Catrin got the impression that, as serene as the room appeared, everything in it had a place and use in this man's world.

On the large wall screen a section of the Miro painting was

shown in painstaking detail. She was working out the possible magnification and the size of the image - it was no ordinary image. It came to her as Brendan said, "Brian takes the pictures with a special camera and gives them to me. I give him some of my paintings because he is very good to me. Dad says he paid the money for my studio."

The door opened and Melissa came into the vestibule area carrying a tray. On it was a bowl of cereal, two triangles of buttered toast with the crusts cut off and a teapot, milk, sugar and two mugs.

"Shoes off," said Brendan, automatically, not looking up from his painting.

"I'll get that," said Catrin, moving forward.

Melissa stood there after transferring the tray. She said clearly, "Your dad sent your breakfast over, Brendan. He is busy talking with people. He told me you will say that you always have it in the kitchen but he wants you to have it with Catrin, here, and she can have tea with you. It's special."

Brendan looked at her, said nothing, but nodded.

She looked at Catrin and said more quietly. "So far, so good. Hollis is itching to get over here and get the SOCOs in but we are waiting on this solicitor Olson coming in from King's Lynn. And they have gone to get Mrs. Atkin from the church.

Brendan must have overhead, at least that last part. He said sharply, "Mum's at church. She's busy. It's the Altar Guild planning."

Melissa looked at him and smiled then focused again on Catrin. "What do you think?"

"So far, so good. It's a treasure trove in here."

"That's what Hollis thinks. But not quite from your viewpoint, I think."

He means evidence, Catrin knew; she meant art.

34 OLSON

Catrin looked at Melissa. She thought about the impact of the SOCOs working away in the studio when they were sent over.

She moved closer to Nunn and said quietly, "Did they find anything at the house?"

Nunn whispered, "Money - quite a lot of cash. And letters from Brian, in a box. It was their regular means of communication, apparently; at his insistence. The solicitor is from Kings Lynn; he should be here in half an hour. You good here until then?"

Catrin nodded. "Fine. Time for a tea break, by the looks of it."

She raised her voice slightly. "Brendan, it's time for your breakfast, your dad said."

The two women watched Brendan leave his easel, sit at the table and begin eating as if he didn't have a care in the world.

After a couple of minutes, Catrin said quietly to Nunn, "Brian Sleaman chose Olson, placed him on retainer before his last visit here for this eventuality. Why this man? Because he is local?"

Melissa smiled. "No. His own daughter is autistic, Atkin said; she is in her teens, younger than Brendan. Sleaman had carefully worked out what to do it seems, preparing for this outcome. By the way, a Mrs. Chalmers, a social worker, is coming over."

She raised her voice. "Brendan, you know Mrs. Chalmers, don't you?"

He nodded, lost in his breakfast for a moment. "Then he looked at her. "Yes. I see Mrs. Chalmers regularly. She helps mum and dad with me."

Melissa said, "I'd better get back. I'll leave you to it."

Catrin smiled. "Brendan is just showing me how he gets such fine detail."

She pointed at the monitor. Nunn looked and her first impression was that it was an abstract image. Then she realised that it was a large magnification of the image half-finished on the easel.

"Brian photographed the works in advance of the copy being made. Let DI Needham know."

Melissa nodded.

~~

In the house, the SOCOs were moving through systematically. DS Hollis and another team member were also looking around. DI Needham was sitting with Hubert; not interviewing him but talking with him conversationally.

He told the older man, "Mr. Olson just called back; he is about five minutes away. We will brief him about why we are here when he arrives then he will spend some time with you. We will then take you for a formal interview at the police station in Hunstanton. But we won't go there until your wife and Mrs. Chalmers arrive. We want to make this as smooth as possible for Brendan but we do have duties and obligations under the law; we have to follow certain procedures."

The older man nodded. "I appreciate that; in fact, you don't know how much. You see these things on the TV, all the shouting and so on. It was part of my nightmare."

And part of Melissa Nunn's, thought Needham. You don't

know the half of what we had prepared.

Instead, he said, "It appears that Brian Sleaman took a lot of trouble preparing for this eventuality."

Hubert Atkin nodded, "He told us everything on his final visit. Yes he did. To us, he was a good man and we will always be grateful for his help."

Then DI Needham went silent. He didn't want a run-in with the solicitor about interviewing his client in his absence and without cautioning him.

Olson was a rotund, balding man in his early fifties, in a suit and tie, which appeared incongruous in a farm context. He was polite to the officers but direct.

"I would like some time with my client first. Then I will hear your preliminary disclosure, if I may, not the other way round. Has he been charged or cautioned yet?"

DI Needham said, "No sir, in fact no one has been yet. Mr. Atkin invoked his rights to a solicitor immediately and we simply had him call you."

Olson asked, "Will you be taking him to Hunstanton or another location?"

"Superintendent Lubbock is at the Hunstanton police station now, sir. Initially, it will be there. We have Mrs. Atkin here also now; she returned a couple of minutes ago from the church and is with one of my female officers in a bedroom upstairs. And a Detective Inspector Sayer from London is with Brendan in his studio. She is an art expert and is talking with him about his art. PC Nunn says everything is quiet there. A Mrs. Chalmers, a social worker, is on her way but will be delayed a little, I gather."

"I know Harriet Chalmers," Olson said.

He seemed to calm a little, to be less agitated, Needham thought, but the police officer said nothing, just waited for Olson's next comment or question.

"I will meet first with Mr. Atkin now," the lawyer said.

Then they heard the loud cry, a male voice, from the cottage in the rear and the kitchen door burst open as Hubert

Atkin ran out. Needham looked at Olson and they both ran after him.

~~

DS Hollis had walked over and peered in the door of the studio, eyes taking in the array of canvases he had been told about. As he entered, Sayer and the artist were at the easel talking about eyes shapes, he heard.

He smiled at them. Catrin gave him a sharp look but then spoke gently to Brendan about the highlight he had been working on.

Bolstered by the silence of his reception, Hollis walked further in, surveying the art on the shelves. He said warmly, "Brendan, you have some nice painting here, don't you? Some you kept and some you gave to Brian."

Brendan came out of the reverie of his focus on the current work, looked at Hollis then screamed, his arms moving up, elbows out and his wrists pressed to the sides of his head.

"Go!" instructed Catrin, in a hiss, who had been caught by the brush still in Brendan's hand as he reacted. The point of the handle had jabbed her in the soft tissue below her cheekbone near the corner of her mouth. It was lucky it missed my eye, she thought.

Then Hubert Atkin was there, arms around his son, talking to him as the younger man looked up and started crying. Hubert didn't try to stop him; just took in the scene and glared at Hollis and then the two other men now arriving outside.

"He is so sensitive, you see," he said, unnecessarily now.

Needham and Olson didn't enter. The senior officer looked at Hollis and gave a nod, his meaning clear; back to the house. Olson said, "I'll stay a minute, then see Mr. Atkin."

Needham nodded and he too left as the solicitor entered slowly.

Hubert waited twenty seconds or so. "Brendan, you know Jessica Olson, don't you? From the class."

Through his sniffles, he said, "Yes, she's nice."

"This is Jessica's dad, Mr. Olson. He's come to help us. He will talk to you for a while. I have to go and talk with those people."

Brendan looked at Olson. "You have Jessica's eyes."

Well, it was a sort of 'hello', Catrin thought.

Olson smiled at him. "I do; not many people mention that, you know."

"And her smile. That too."

He turned and looked at Catrin, his face showing his upset again. "I've hurt you. I'm sorry," he said.

She touched the spot on her face where she thought she was getting a bruise but found a small amount of blood; he must have broken the skin.

"That's OK; it was an accident."

"Hubert," said John Olson, "it is probably best if Brendan gets back to his work, don't you think?" He knew he needed to separate his clients at this stage, before the police did so. He turned to Catrin.

"You are getting on well together, I see. You are from London, I gather; but not by that voice."

Catrin smiled. "DI Sayer, with the Met, yes. The Art and Antiques Unit. And I am from Pontypridd. I have been seeing some of Brendan's paintings in the last few weeks and came to see him."

She hoped he would get it from that. He nodded.

"Then if I could leave you and Brendan together. I take it…"

"We are just talking about art technique, Mr. Olson, that's all."

"Then I think that's fine; Brendan will enjoy that, I'm sure. I will consider you more as an AA at present, if I may, until Mrs. Chalmers gets here. Under the circumstances?"

His voice made it a question. An AA; an appropriate adult, to look after Brendan's interests in the interim. Under the circumstances of other nosy policemen coming in and upsetting him, he meant.

"That would be fine sir. But I will be leaving in a while, you understand?"

Olson nodded, indicating he understood. "I do. And thank you. It seems that someone has gone to considerable trouble; I will speak to Superintendent Lubbock and say so."

Catrin said candidly, "It was PC Nunn, back at the house, Melissa Nunn."

He nodded, understanding the context. "Hubert, we can go back to the house now, leave Brendan and DI Sayer?"

Brendan smiled and looked at him. "It's Catrin. She's an artist."

~~

Sometime later Melissa came back in carrying a tray with more tea and biscuits.

Brendan asked, "Where's mum? Is she back?"

"Yes," said Melissa. "She is. She sent these. She and your dad are talking with someone, Brendan."

"There is something wrong, isn't there?"

Melissa said gently, "Yes there is, but nothing you have done and nothing that can't be fixed. And your mum will start making lunch soon. And Mrs. Chalmers has just arrived, I think."

A couple of minutes later the door opened and John Olson came in with an older woman. Brendan clearly knew her and they started talking.

John Olson joined them and he spoke to Brendan. "Now you and I need to talk but would you like to say goodbye to Detective Inspector Sayer, before she goes?"

Brendan looked at Catrin afresh, "You are a police officer, too. I forgot. Thank you for coming, I really enjoyed our talk."

Catrin smiled at him and he held out his arm for a formal handshake.

"As did I, Brendan. A lot. You are very talented. But I would like a minute with Mr. Olson too, first, it I could. Everything is going to work out fine. But I have to go now."

In the vestibule, as she put on her boots, Olson said, "Thank you for filling in. I appreciate it."

Catrin smiled briefly, but replied, "PC Nunn asked for me to come up. She was concerned."

He nodded. "I got that impression from your earlier comment. But you wanted a word?"

They stepped outside.

"Yes. His art. I'll speak with the head of the SOCOs but I think it will prove to be quite valuable; monies he may need in the future. A lot of it is quite separate from the case, I think; or Brian Sleaman hadn't used it yet. I got the impression that Brendan didn't paint only what Sleaman asked for, he had his own reasons, his own drivers on selection of works. Similarly, I haven't seen his originals - bird paintings - other than a quick glimpse at one, but they too may become valuable, if only for the associated notoriety over time, in a sense. So they should be carefully handled.

"As some of the works are very recent, they are easy to damage. My suggestion would be to insist on people from UEA to be engaged to do an inventory and storage; don't leave them unprotected. But watch out for these aspects."

The solicitor was nodding, seeing the issue. "Thank you. Tell me, if you can. Why did Brendan make these copies, in your opinion?"

Catrin smiled at him. "Oh, he will tell you himself, if the questions are framed right. He wants to understand how the artist painted the original; that's at the core of it. He has convinced himself that he couldn't focus on his own original art, rightly or wrongly, but I am conscious that he doesn't have an art tutor. It may be worth exploring."

He nodded.

"My turn," she said. "I'm not part of the arrest team, as you know. What does it look like?"

He looked into the distance, measuring what to say.

"Mr. Atkin says that Brian Sleaman only told them the full implications of his actions on the last visit. They were in a dilemma then. We shall see what charges your colleagues are

considering for the parents but there are extenuating circumstances if it comes to sentencing. They were tenant farmers;
had been here since their marriage and when the family that
owns the land didn't want to continue the tenancy they faced
possible eviction, if nothing else turned up. Without Sleaman
they could have been out on their ear; not with their home and
a purpose-made studio for Brendan to use.

"So for Brendan; there can't be charges, I think, given his
situation. It's the parents I am concerned about. But Superintendent Lubbock has said they aren't looking at remand; they
can have police bail and the first interviews are being timed
separately so one parent or the other is at home. I am quite
pleased about the consideration being shown."

Catrin replied, "Thank you. I hope it turns out well for
them. By the sound of it, we now have a basis for knowing
what was copied and transferred to Sleaman, so we can scope
out the full scale of this case, from an art perspective, at least."

Olson said, "Well, I wish you well on that but my focus, of
course, must be the Atkin family."

She nodded then as she started to leave she leaned back and
said more as a whisper, "If it were me, I'd sentence Mrs. Atkin
to two years community service on the altar guild and her husband to something similar. What they did, they did out of love.
Look at this cottage, for example; that's where the money was
spent, not on modernising the house or fancy things for
them."

She took a last look at Brendan. He was already working at
the easel, focused intently on the painting. Mrs. Chalmers,
seated at the table, had pulled out her mobile phone. She, more
than anyone other than the family, would realise he just needed
to be left alone to continue his journey through the mind of his
current artist.

Catrin walked away from the building and pulled out her
phone, returning it to 'sound' from 'vibrate'. She called her
driver. "Stan, I'm finished here. Can you come and get me?
Give me twenty minutes. And we need to have lunch on the

way back somewhere."

She headed across to the main farmhouse to close out with DI Needham and hopefully see some of Brendan's original bird paintings.

Later, as she was walking over to the BMW, Melissa came with her.

"Thanks again, ma'am. I really appreciated it, even if DS Hollis didn't. I'm pleased how it went down."

Catrin climbed in the passenger seat and held the door open. "So far, Melissa. Remember what I said on leaving you the first time we met. Be careful in there."

She closed the door and grinned at her. Nunn laughed out loud. "I will. Bye now."

Stan pulled forward, heading back on to the road to Kings Lynn. She caught his quizzical expression.

"We worked together once before, Stan, when she was a probationer. I told her then not to put her foot through a valuable painting. I have told them to be careful with all the paintings in that place; I think they could be worth a bit, too."

35 TOOTING BEC

They were near London when Catrin took another call. She had been on the phone a bit; to her team, to Wetherby and to Chris. As she answered she saw it was from DI Coombs.

"Catrin, I thought you should know. Jim Hughes was badly beaten at lunchtime. He is now in St. George's Hospital in intensive care. Two men took him down outside the Wheatsheaf, the pub you met at. It looks to be premeditated, not a fight between people over something in the pub. Eaton is at the hospital now."

Catrin was suddenly struck by the fact that Hughes had been attacked where she and Hilary had tracked him down.

"Any arrest or suspects?"

"No arrests yet. But we think that it's the Centurions and it's going to escalate. People here think that Leo set it up in revenge, thinking Hughes was involved with Sleaman somehow. Word had leaked out from someone at that pub, we suspect, about you and Hilary meeting with him there."

"Also, we hear that a bunch of Hells Angels are setting out from South Wales, some as we speak. They are in full gear; patches on display. You know what that means."

"It won't take much for open warfare to begin."

They lapsed into silence, thinking. Then Catrin said, "Who

is with him at the hospital now? Family, I mean, not any bikers getting in the way."

"His wife Toni. Her mother is looking after the kids, Eaton says; it is too distressing to have them there. He is now in an induced coma after surgery; they had to deal with swelling to the brain. It's still touch and go. And his aunt and mother are coming in from Wales. As you know them, Hilary says, I was wondering if you could help out in some way? That was the real purpose in calling you, to be honest."

Catrin said, "We'll head straight there, see if I can find out more. Who from the Met is with Eaton at the hospital?"

"In the room; no one. We put tight security around. Hilary didn't want someone there who was new and my other people are all dealing with the Angel's influx and watching the Centurions. I have some extra manpower allocated later for any shift extensions but it would be appreciated if you could try to do something to calm this a little, if possible."

She closed the call and said, "Stan, a change in plans; Tooting, not home. St. George's Hospital. A biker has been beaten up and more are on the way."

The driver said, "Farmyards to bikers, ma'am; the joy of the job." He sighed.

It was true. Days could go by routinely then, like today, it was one thing after another.

She said, "It's the way it is. I once found myself dealing with an old lady who had just lost her grandson to an overdose and two hours later being prepped for undercover work in Wales. And my big plan for the day had been to catch up on laundry after my shift."

He laughed.

~~

Despite her warrant card, it took another call to Eaton directly to enable Catrin to get to the room with Hughes; security was that tight. The two detectives left to talk after a quick glance at the biker and a brief introduction to his wife, who was too distressed to say much. Another police officer appearing didn't really register with her. She was a local; Hughes had met her in London, Eaton told her.

Catrin asked, "What's the latest?"

"It's 'wait and see', the doctor said an hour ago. Won't say more than that. Hughes was muttering in Welsh every now and again before they induced him. But we know who did this; I don't need Welsh for that."

Catrin just looked, waiting.

"Twice, according to DC Long, who was first on scene from our team, Hughes said 'Skelly' clearly but angrily. That's a Centurion called Doug Skelton, I think. And if 'Skelly', as he likes to be known, did this, his pal was probably a man called Tim Furneaux; they pair up for this sort of thing, or at least they have done so in the past."

Catrin said, "It's not evidence, but did his wife hear also? Will the Angels know by now?"

"I don't know; she may have. There was a time they were alone; he could have mumbled it then, too. In any event, it won't matter. His club is coming in and they won't care who did it; they will go after the lot of them. The Centurions clubhouse is probably turning into a fortress about now."

"They'll fight it out there?"

"No. That's not the way. They will pick a place away from us, if they can. There will be some preliminaries, arguing the justification - the 'righteousness' - of the attack on Hughes."

She looked intently at Sayer. "These are one percenters, ma'am. It's not going to be a pub brawl. Not scrapes and bruises. When the Outlaws and the Angels had their battle in Birmingham Airport some years ago, there were knives, clubs, hammers and a meat cleaver used. And that was improvisation at short notice."

Catrin said, "I recall; it was like a riot at the airport, they said. Who's in charge of the Welsh bikers, do we know?"

Eaton looked a little pensive. "Not sure. Our opposite numbers in the South Wales Police say their president and vice-president are on holiday together at present, with their families in Spain. Their road captain will be organizing the troops and their sergeant-at-arms will be doing likewise with their response. He is probably the key person present."

"Do we know him?"

"Not us; South Wales do; a man called Keith Parry."

Catrin nodded, taking the point. "Sergeant-at-arms, as in 'enforcer'?"

Eaton just nodded.

Catrin thought suddenly of Colin Cheney, the drug gang enforcer who had given her the facial scar in Scotland. Every gang needs its hard cases and they all have different titles.

"I need the loo and then some tea; where's the café?"

Catrin and Hilary were sitting silently at a table in the coffee shop with Stan, who had refused to go back to the Met. "It's a long day for both of us, ma'am; but until I get you delivered home or back to the Yard, I am still on this one."

Catrin suddenly said to Hilary, "Let's talk to your boss. I need Howlett to run some numbers, but I have an idea."

"What, just now?"

"Funnily enough, no. This morning in an art studio, thinking about a man who I thought could need protection from people like Leo Altman and not sure how to do that. Now I do, but it will need your team and mine to work together and convince Commander Moore that we should be proactive on this."

Eaton looked surprised. "I can't wait to hear about it. I'll check in with DI Coombs right now."

Catrin said, "And find out where this man Parry is."

Eaton looked over Catrin's shoulder. "More arrivals. Family I think."

Catrin turned round. A uniformed officer was escorting two women to see Hilary, the only one with the authority for security clearance. One woman started walking purposefully across the café.

"Catrin Sayer. I thought it looked like you from the back.

You've come to see Jim, too, then? Terrible, terrible thing."

Then she saw Stan, in his uniform and clued in. "Of course, you are here for work."

Eaton was surprised to see this woman, now saying something in Welsh, move forward and hug Detective Inspector Sayer. Coppers didn't normally get hugs from the family of 'one percenter' bikers.

Catrin said, "This is Detective Sergeant Eaton; she responded when the call came in. This is Jim's Aunt Donna; a friend of my mother's. A good friend of my mum's I might add. Donna, this is a right mess."

Donna introduced Jim's mother, who looked quite stressed. She sounded down-to-earth Valley Welsh and made no bones about the situation.

"A mess, so it is. The life our Jim lives. I think there will be more trouble, to be honest."

Donna looked anxious. "Tit-for-tat sort of violence; it never does any good."

Catrin said, "Do you think Jim's wife could spare us a minute; you as well, Donna? But let's get you both in to be with him first."

They were walking now down the corridor to the lift.

Donna said, "I'll ask. Hang on, though; I want to see Jim myself, too; although he is out for the count at present, they say."

As the two older women went into the hospital room, Sayer and Eaton hung around outside.

"You were saying, Catrin?"

"Let's see Toni Hughes' reaction when Donna talks to her."

They were back in the café, at a different table.

Toni Hughes said tersely, "So you are that Catrin; I didn't catch it earlier; I thought you were with DS Eaton. Jim mentioned you. I wondered whether Jim talking to a copper was part of the problem, to be honest."

Catrin replied, "It could be, I don't know. But I think it is because Jim helped a man some years ago; a person who is now dead."

The woman looked at her suspiciously. "They say it was the Centurions. Some of Jim's people are coming. They will find out."

She sounded certain, emphatic.

Catrin said, "And then something else will happen, right? And someone get hurt or caught and put away. Not solve the problem, just make it worse."

Toni replied dismissively, "I want to get back. What do you really want?"

Catrin replied, "I have a proposal. Talk to Jim's people, the person in charge here. See if he will talk just with me; no one else. I'll give you my number. No promises, but I think we can deal with this and get the people responsible without further bloodshed or any of yours getting arrested."

She passed over her business card and could see she had the woman's attention.

"Who do you want to talk to?"

Eaton said, "Keith Parry; the sergeant-at-arms."

"I'll see. I'll call him. No promises though. My Jim… like that. No, no promises."

She stood up suddenly and went back to the lift.

Catrin saw Stan loitering. She called him over as she said to Hilary, "Stick to her like glue until we get an answer. And call your boss; say he needs to set up a meeting for us with Moore as soon as possible, in person or by phone. Stan, we are going back to the Yard."

36 RAID

Catrin's discussion with Keith Parry had been tense but productive; it had bought them a day. But Parry wanted action. "We look after our own and have no truck with the police; you know that. It's only that Toni says you are from Wales and she asked us to be open to listen that I am talking to you at all."

All Catrin said was, based on the guidance from DI Coombs and Commander Moore, "Give us a day, that's all, to bring in whoever did it. You will hear from us through Mrs. Hughes before midnight tomorrow, I promise. I will call her."

"And if you get lost in your red tape and lawyers…"

"I will call one way or the other, not leave it open. Give us a chance."

Moore had said, "Don't, under any circumstances, point out to this man that any threats he makes or any consequent actions the club takes that break the law will bring us down on them. They are impervious to that and it will kill any opportunity. They will cut you off mid-sentence and walk away."

She hadn't - and the call hadn't been cut off. They now had a day before a biker war started up somewhere in North London.

~~

The Centurions clubhouse was formerly a launderette that went out of business in Edmonton, just south of the North Circular Road. The raid by the Metropolitan Police on it was timed for 7.30 p.m. the following day, in part to maximize attendance of the club members with minimum drunkenness and associated stupidity to complicate an already chancy operation. It was a combined operation of SCO19, the armed tactical unit, with the drug squad, the Trident biker team and Art and Antiques.

In the teams assigned, the most incongruous person there, Catrin felt, was her own boss in a black and yellow road jacket with reflective chevrons, worn over a tactical vest. She wasn't sure why he had put that coat on, though; he looked like he should be directing traffic.

The previous day, in reviewing Catrin's proposal, DCI Wetherby had insisted to Karen Moore that he should be there with his team.

Moore had just nodded. She just said, "Well, my job is to call one of the gods of CPS and be persuasive."

The Crown Prosecution Service. Catrin would have loved to be sitting in on that one, to hear Moore in action.

Then Moore had focused on DI Coombs.

"Greg, it may be Catrin's idea, but it's your plan to finalise and execute; you own it. Sort out the logistics and you lead. With bikers like these, this operational exposure will either make or break you in one shot, so don't screw up. You aren't after their love and understanding, hear me?"

With those heart-warming words she picked up her phone as people trooped out of her office.

The control of the premises and the people in it was SCO19's job. They were fast and there were no niceties. The rest of the teams waited outside.

But from the moment the Tactical Unit commander announced it was secure, the operation was led by DI Coombs. He, his team and the drug squad went it first. Catrin said to her own team, "And still we wait; I wonder what it's like inside."

Isabelle was interested too, mainly to see the biker women; her career hadn't involved that side of things previously.

Ten minutes later, Hilary Eaton came out. "Three arrested for weapons possession, one of them serious, a firearm; four with drugs on them, a stack of other drugs around and - guess what - a painting. You were right; someone must have returned it under a money-back guarantee or a threat of serious damage if they didn't get repaid."

Once Catrin's team entered, she focused on Leo Altman and saw him stiffen on seeing her and John Obi. He spoke quietly to another man.

Clubs and nightclubs of any sort didn't look good in strong light; it shows off the wear and tear. The Centurions clubhouse was no exception. It had a lot of biker paraphernalia, a bar, and odd array of furnishings which seemed to reflect a mix of tastes or tastelessness, depending on one's viewpoint, and two antique pinball machines.

Isabelle whispered to her, "Those machines could be the most valuable things in the place; other than the booze stocks. They don't plan to run short."

But Catrin was all work. "Go look at the painting, Isabelle; let me know the total when I ask."

John walked up with her to Leo. She said quietly to him, "This time it's me who has people with guns."

She didn't wait on an answer, just turned round and moved over to stand by Coombs. John Obi moved in uncomfortably close to Altman, as he had been instructed. He could see two of the tactical team ready close by just in case Leo turned on him; three big men almost surrounding the biker.

Coombs nodded at Catrin and she pulled out of her pocket a small black Bluetooth speaker and her mobile. The she dialed a preset number.

Over the speaker they heard the call answered by a female voice.

"Mrs. Hughes?" asked Catrin, speaking to the room but

with her eyes on Leo. "Can you hear me?"

She was at the hospital, Catrin knew. They had command-eered a meeting room of some sort for the call to take place, giving Toni Hughes an approximate time for the promised call to Parry and a place to take it.

On hearing the name, Leo looked at her as if he would kill her with his own eyes, if he could.

The woman's voice came back clearly over the speaker. "Yes I can. And so can Jim's friends."

"How many are with you?"

"Two here, but we have twelve more outside at present. They all wanted to know what's happening."

Catrin responded, "If you will give us a few more minutes, you will find out. DI Coombs is in charge and we are inside the Centurions clubhouse. He has something to say to everyone."

She could see that several of the men and women present were working it out and becoming less than comfortable with this development.

Leo said, "You can't do this!"

Coombs replied, "She can do what she wants, if I say so, at present."

He spoke up. "I'm going to tell you a story. A few years ago on the way back from the Bulldog Bash someone in your lot thought it was a good idea to take out a rider on a Husky and put him in hospital; a man called Brian Sleaman. Just for the fun of it."

His eyes were moving round the room eyeing people. He may be new to the biker team, Catrin thought, but he is setting his stamp on it. They will remember him here.

Coombs went on, "Well, perhaps he got the last laugh, didn't he, Leo? DI Sayer; how much in total did Sleaman get to laugh about?"

Catrin responded with a question of her own, "Howlett?"

From the back from the room Isabelle's voice rang out firm. "I am now up to about £350,000, with this one. Roughly speaking. And it all fits, ma'am."

Coombs went on. "So this man, for reasons we won't go

into, found a person who could make good copies he could use as forgeries. Then he worked you over. Currently to the tune of well over a third of a million that my colleague just said. Your money gone into thin air. Not just yours, Leo; the club's money."

He stared at Leo Altman. "Obi, cuff him; I don't like his expression."

As John Obi obeyed DI Coombs and put Leo in handcuffs, Leo looked repulsed by being touched by him; it was a reaction they had expected.

John just gave him a blank stare.

Coombs continued, "Then we come to our side of the fence, our discovery of the forgeries."

He nodded at Catrin who also stepped forward, surveying the main group. She spoke equally loudly for everyone to hear, in the room and on the phone. "So, in the course of looking into these paintings we inadvertently cross Leo's path. We missed how important he was, you see. We just went to see a painting; that was all. And Renée died, unfortunately. She was very ill, stressed by us being there and by the news that the painting on their wall was a fake. It was sad and regrettable, but not our fault. We were simply doing our job."

Coombs took up the tale again.

"From Sleaman's home and work colleagues we traced that it was Jim Hughes who helped him after you ran him off the road; Hughes had sent him a 'get well' card, so we followed that up. Simply, it was a biker helping a biker. He knew that Sleaman's club was just a regular club, not elite like his and yours, but he helped him anyway and later he sent him a get well card. That was the extent of it."

"Leo found out that Jim Hughes talked to DI Sayer in the Wheatsheaf. All he did was confirm he had helped the man and it wasn't any Hells Angel that took Sleaman down; he didn't rat on you. We put the rest together ourselves."

He moved closer to one biker.

"So there was no big conspiracy between Sleaman and Hughes to rob the Centurions, no matter what Leo or anyone else may claim. You are Skelly, right?"

The man looked at him but ignored him.

"Douglas Skelton. And your pal Tim Furneaux isn't here. No doubt the word will get back to him but tell me, why did Mr. Hughes mumble 'Skelly' a few times before he was put into an induced coma? I am sure that the people on the phone are wondering that, too."

Leo said angrily, "You can't do this; finger people; you are the law!"

Coombs said firmly, "I'm just stating facts, Mr. Altman and I'm going to give them one more; they may already know it. Skelly here and his sidekick did seven months in Scrubs a few years ago for beating up a Bandidos member. It seems to take two of them to handle a one percenter from any other club."

Skelly's eyes were looking wild. Careful, thought Catrin, you may be overplaying this; he's not handcuffed. She signaled to one of the tactical officers; but he nodded: he had noticed it, too and he visibly took a step closer to Skelton, prepared.

Coombs broke the eye contact and turned to face her.

"And you have more of the story to tell them; things they definitely don't know."

Catrin spoke up again. "Brian Sleaman is dead, died of natural causes. Art and Antiques, my unit, and the Norfolk Police were also looking for the forger who worked with him and did the copies. This painting here and the others that were used to take your money were all done by an artist who is truly talented.

"However, that person is also developmentally disabled, living in an environment that is carefully controlled. The person paints wonderfully but had no idea that these paintings were being used in this manner, then or now; that was all down to Sleaman. Who, we have discovered, also treated this person fairly, by his own lights. Brian got what he wanted; a lot of money and to get at you. Some of the money from these thefts and forgeries was provided to the artist and the caregivers; it enabled them to provide the home environment I mentioned.

"Notice I say neither he nor she. Because as of this morning the investigation file is sealed; with us and with the Norfolk Police looking into Sleaman's activities. No further charges will be laid.

'Sleaman had a number of originals and copies, his 'bank' of works to sell to continue this way of life, but those are now in our possession or returned to the galleries he stole them from originally. His monies are gone; spent or tied up. I can also assure you that the money the painter received has already been spent; you can't get that back. Nor would I try to find out more about that individual. We will be watching very carefully. Other people will be watching, too."

She spoke into the phone. "I don't think even Centurions will go after a developmentally disabled person. I hope not, anyway."

She looked slowly round the room, a look challenging anyone to take issue with her.

DI Coombs moved across to face Leo Altman.

"So; to the last bit. Stevie tried to kill DC Obi and DI Sayer in the Bell Common Tunnel and is now facing an array of charges, including attempted murder. We were told that he did this off his own bat; even he says so. Nothing to do with your club, right?"

He waved his hand at one of the officers, who came across with an evidence bag.

Coombs continued, "This makes it easier than I thought. An M9. The one Stevie used was the same Beretta model. Interpol tells us a number of these came in from Germany a year ago, stolen from a US military storage facility there. So how did Stephen Altman, not a one percenter, get his gun?"

It was a rhetorical question, posed to the room. He looked again at Skelton and then back to Altman.

"Why him do it, we asked, not one of you? Stevie won't talk further. He wanted to prove himself to his dad; and to the club, he said. But even Skelly here wouldn't try a hit in a tunnel, would you? It's dark, true, but motorway tunnels have more cameras than the motorway themselves. People know that.

"Did he really do it off his own bat, we ask? Just now, Leo almost recoiled when DC Obi cuffed him; he detests black people as much as his wife did; she was just more strident about it."

He was focused on Leo now.

"So who encouraged who; we ask? And if we trace the gun used against us to the same batch as this one - ."

He held up the evidence bag.

"- this Centurions chapter will be in for it. A biker club that specifically targets police officers is truly marked. We will get resources to sit on you 'til you scream. You think your club looks after its own? Try ours. The Met will come after you in a way you have had no experience of yet. We will go after each and every one of you; every operation you have. Pay your road tax a day late and we'll put your gleaming bikes sitting out there in our pound and by the time they are released your handlebars will be rusty.

"I think we have what we want now, so we'll leave. Obi, take the cuffs off Mr. Altman; he is looking less threatening now."

Catrin spoke into the phone in Welsh and a male voice spoke back, after which she switched it off and put the small box back in her pocket.

She said, "Did you catch that last bit? Some important Welsh words for you; 'pedair awr ar hugain'; twenty four hours. That's what he said. You can guess what that means. It will be like Custer's Last Stand in here. Good luck with that."

She moved back, away from the centre of the room to stand near two tactical officers as a woman said truculently, "You're police. You can't do that, side with them Angels on the phone and tell us we are going to be massacred in here. That's wrong!"

For the first time Catrin's boss spoke up, sharply. Wetherby said, "Do you speak Welsh? No? You have no idea what she said or didn't say to the people with Jim Hughes wife, do you? And anyone can predict what will happen when an outlaw club beats up a Hells Angel so badly he needs to be put into an induced coma. It's your lifestyle; you live it. We'll mop up afterwards."

Coombs pointed at the people in handcuffs arrested for weapons or drug possession, and said, "Take them out; they may actually appreciate being in the cells for a while. Mr. Skelton, we aren't arresting you - yet. But I doubt we will need a protective cordon around you in hospital, will we?"

As he started for the door he stopped and turned, suddenly remembering something.

"You know, I'm new to this team. My people tell me that the big thing with you lot is 'respect'; it's paramount. In this whole sorry mess the one I see who has shown that is Hughes, for another biker. The rest of you…"

He walked out, the rest unsaid and the other officers, with the people arrested, did the same. Only the tactical officers stood still, waiting to make their own exit in a disciplined manner.

Outside, as they went back to the array of vehicles drawing stares from people in the neighbourhood, Catrin said quietly to Coombs, "Well done; I think you made your mark; they will know who you are now."

His response was similarly quiet. "My heart was in my mouth; some of them look like they would eat me for breakfast. But thank you, too; for the idea and the support. It wasn't easy for you either, but no one saw that."

Catrin said, "Strangely enough, with John there and the tactical team, I was OK. My mind was on making sure no one went after Brendan, ever. I think that message got across, looking at their faces."

Coombs says, "Now we wait and see. But not long, I think, watching Skelly's face at the end."

Wetherby had been silent, standing with them. He added, "It went to plan and hopefully it will pay off. And if it doesn't, we will have a mess to clear up but they will have far more to worry about than what was said inside."

~~

At 3.30 a.m. the following morning Douglas Skelton and Tim Furneaux, dressed in new track suits rather than riding leathers or patch vests, walked into Wood Green Police Station and confessed to the assault on Jim Hughes. They were held in custody and told that the investigating officers would see them first thing in the morning.

"It was a business misunderstanding," was the core message.

They had no expectations of bail, nor did they get any.

PART 4: ANGEL

37 ROCKEFELLER PLAZA

It was, of course, a set piece; a game, but a serious, occasionally deadly one. Police kept an eye on the key people in 'one percenter clubs' in New York state and they, in turn, watched the police. It was debatable who kept the best information set on their front-line adversaries.

When Detective (third grade) Roderick Growski in the Fifth Precinct in lower Manhattan and his new partner Monica Kelly, in her first week out of uniform, got called in by their sergeant they were given a new assignment. Their focus in the last week had been on monitoring some Hells Angels. Now they were to head downtown to observe two bikers coming into the Big Apple from Buffalo. And they were Outlaws.

"I'm sending you their sheets now. Jerry Prowse looks normal; Giuseppe 'Joe' De Souza is a Technicolor tall guy, covered in ink. Both are 'patched' and proven, so take them very seriously. Hopefully these two won't get into a blood bath with any Angels or others. They are going to 30 Rockefeller but I don't think they are there for tourism."

The building, 30 Rockefeller Plaza, was a seventy storey Art Deco skyscraper, part of the complex dominating midtown Manhattan.

Monica asked, "How do we know they will go there?

Should we pick them up at the bridge instead? Just in case."

Growski didn't want to hack it across to the George Washington Bridge, the arrival point of much of the traffic from upstate if he could help it. But neither he nor their boss said anything in direct response.

"Just head over to where I told you," the sergeant said flatly, after a pause.

Growski said a few moments later, when it was just the two of them, "Monica, don't ask him questions like that. Particularly about how he knows things. Understand?"

Monica said nothing but blushed. She concentrated on the information coming up on the screen at their desk before they set out. The world of informants and people undercover was just opening up for her.

"This Joe guy has a lot of tattoos," she said unnecessarily, to ease the momentary tension.

They were inside 30 Rockefeller when Growski called the sergeant on his cell phone.

"We got them, no problem; they went straight into the parking. De Souza is a sight to see, dressed up," he said. "His tattoos peak out at you from his shirt collar and cuffs. Jerry, though, fits right in; looks like any other businessman in here."

"He is," was the terse response. "Just a different sort of rip-off business than the others. And?"

"There's snag. They have gone into Milotti's."

Milotti's restaurant was so exclusive it didn't take bookings. You knew the chef or maître d' personally or you were already a valued guest - otherwise you didn't get in. Two NYPD cops waving badges or quietly asking for a table would cause a scene; a small discrete scene, but nonetheless, a scene. Without a warrant or probable cause for entry, they would be firmly asked to leave.

"Then go - no, don't go in; not that place. Spell each other; grab a sandwich, but you are not eating there, not on my budget, even if you did get past the door. Mo didn't wave at the Buffalo boys, friendly-like?"

"Give her a break, Sarge; no. She was good. It's her first week."

Growski's supervisor said, "I'll send Yanni over to take shots of the people leaving afterwards. It may give some clues. You two stay on Prowse and De Souza when they leave; hopefully they will go straight home."

The upstate bikers left the restaurant together after lunch and did exactly that. Yanni was by then well set up; he photographed every guest leaving, but that gave no obvious link to anyone in the world of biker crime in New York, just a 'who's who' of people in good standing with the restauranteur - including an NYPD deputy commissioner's wife.

A week later, a report came in to a different NYPD investigative unit that a Ton Huan with the triad group Four Square had been spotted in 30 Rockefeller that day, but it wasn't given any weight or connection. Life was busy.

~~

The tables for four in Milotti's were placed with just enough separation to allow confidential conversations under the hum and bustle of customers and service. A Mr. Ton Huan, the head of the Four Square triad in New York accompanied by a Chinese woman were waiting for the two Buffalo bikers. Somehow Jerry Prowse knew instinctively that Huan's colleague wasn't local; it was something about her clothes and jewellery. It made him think that the respective number two's present made a great contrast. Joe was already uneasy in the place, he could tell; he was acting too self-assured.

They stood and shook hands as Mr. Huan said, "Thank you for making the time available to join us for lunch today. We very much appreciate it."

Jerry wasn't to be outdone in the niceties, Joe noted.

"Mr. Huan, thank you for the invitation. It's a pleasure to meet you again, although it has been quite some time."

They got into the small talk around introductions, ordering drinks and food, which was a relief for Joe De Souza as it was Italian cuisine. After the waiter had departed Prowse said, "Miss Yang, I take it you are not from New York?"

"No," Emily Yang replied with a smile. She chose not to elaborate. Ton Huan, sensing his moment, said, "Jerry, if I may be so bold as to move us to first name terms? We have a proposition for you. We haven't worked together before but I see an opportunity for us to do so, one you may particularly like because it doesn't involve you paying a dollar while you sample our wares, so to speak."

Jerry was warm but blunt in his response, Joe noted. "Ton, you deal in information and you choose your own clients; we know that. But we have our own sources. So I am not sure I need to either sample or buy. However, I am always open to suggestions. No commitments, but a fair hearing. You have my time and you are graciously buying us lunch. And Joe, you amazed me."

His last comment was to his partner, who had ordered in Italian and in doing so, wowed the waiter with his choices and serious questions. De Souza had chosen carefully and well while Jerry had staggered through the menu, irritating the waiter with a question as to whether the Steak Florentine would be 'prime grade'.

"We use nothing but the best in this restaurant, sir."

Huan continued his pitch. "Our services are somewhat specialized; take a certain Agent Morrison for example. As you now know, he is undercover for Alcohol and Tobacco. You are, we suspect, working out what to do with him; string him along or dump him on the steps on Main St."

The US Alcohol, Tobacco and Firearms office was on Main Street in Buffalo. Jerry's eyes fixed on Ton Huan impassively. Joe decided just to look lost in thought.

Jerry shrugged. "So you know a little…"

He wrinkled his forehead. Do better than that was the message.

Huan said, "You found out three weeks ago."

Jerry shot back, "And you, when did you find out?"

Huan simply said, "Earlier; quite a bit earlier, in fact. The question is, what would you do if you knew things as early as we do? That is the sort of service we provide to our clients."

Jerry considered the importance of the opportunity. He needed to play this carefully.

"I'm giving that some thought," he replied, as the waiter appeared with a colleague to present the drinks and a selection of antipasto dishes.

They focused on the food.

It was during the main course that Jerry suddenly returned to the reason for the visit and the triad's offer.

"And what is the cost for your services - and what does sample mean?"

Huan replied, "Six months at no cost for conducting a simple operation; you, Jerry, will deliver personally a message to a motorcycle club member in the UK, at your own time and expense."

Jerry shook his head, smiling. "The chapters are separate, you know that. We don't interfere with others; they don't interfere with us. Providing they observe the rules the AOA established worldwide, each call their own shots."

The legal incorporation of the Outlaws Motorcycle Club was named the American Outlaws Association and known as AOA. It was formed in McCook, Illinois in 1935.

Emily spoke up. "It's not club-to-club that I want; it's man to man; personal. If I wanted it sent to a chapter, I would have gone to Illinois. I want a message passed to Leo Altman in person, face-to-face; you know him from way back. And you know what went down recently, I hope."

The moments of silence after Emily Yang spoke made De Souza a little tense. Jerry and Leo had history together, he knew, though the Centurions weren't a member of AOA yet, he understood. Even knowing about that history wasn't a good idea to admit inside the Buffalo chapter. To break the growing tension, he decided to use his charm and said to the woman, "Your people like tattoos as well, I gather, Miss Yang?"

Ton Huan looked surprised at the digression and the reply by Emily, but she just smiled. "We do. You have quite a set, I think, from the edges."

Joe nodded. "'Some are top notch parlor work and some a little rough. And you? Any dragons?"

He was trying to be a bit of a lady's man.

"Just one tattoo I would show you."

He raised his eyebrows. None were visible on the woman. She flipped open her phone and pulled up an image.

"Not in the flesh, of course."

She held the phone out for them to see. It was a simple Chinese character set.

"I don't know those," said Joe.

Emily said, "In English, it reads 'as necessary' or, 'whatever it takes'. Both translations work."

She paused and refocused on Jerry. "To get the job done."

Jerry asked, "This message to Leo. What's it about?"

She told him the general thrust of it.

"You think I can have more powers of persuasion with Leo than people over there?"

She nodded. "Old friends have bonds, and you have also his respect."

Jerry thought about it. These people must have a good idea of what went down between him and Leo years ago - and probably who they did it to. The police only knew part of it, he was sure.

"Just a conversation?"

She shook her head. "And feedback to me directly; an assessment of how he takes the message; an honest one from you."

A flight, a chat and a telephone call in exchange for six months of information flow from this secretive triad, known for top quality information. The fact that they didn't seek business but chose their clients had been the reason he'd agreed to drive down to New York in the first place.

"I'll consider doing it," he said, "to see how it works out. And if it proves useful to us, what does it take to continue?"

Mr. Huan gave him the monthly base fee and the payment terms for any relevant information delivered in each period. Prowse looked impassive but Joe thought it was a hell of a lot of money.

Jerry said to Emily, "This message to Leo appears to be worth quite a lot to someone, I gather."

Emily responded, "So please make sure it is delivered right."

Jerry thought for a moment. "Let me say it more clearly, then. At the monthly rate you charge for your services, six months at no cost seems a lot of value for a simple flight over to the UK and a conversation. So I need to know the message in detail, before I decide."

Emily seemed to expect that response. "I'll give it to you then I want a yes or a no right now. And if it's no, you are to discuss it no further with anyone. He and his club are not to engage in any action against two police officers I will name, ever; or anyone they are linked to. If he does, I'll have him eliminated."

She sounded matter of fact.

"I want his reaction to that. And if, in the six months of your trial period he shows to you signs of ignoring that, you are going to call him again to remind him. That's part of the deal. Not that you have to monitor him and check, but if you hear, you are to try to stop it again. You of all people will know he will have had a fair warning if I act."

Jerry was surprised; he expected a bigger business issue than that to be the reason for all this.

"You've got it. I agree. And after the six months?"

Emilie stared at him. "It's between Mr. Huan for Four Square and you and your chapter; strictly business. Please let Leo Altman know that, as of your meeting with him, the grace period will be over. We will deal with him given any hint whatsoever that he is ignoring the message."

Joe De Souza sat there, waiting to see how Jerry would take

this. It was his friend Leo they were talking about. He was hoping Jerry didn't have them storm out; the food so far had been delicious; he wanted the cassata for dessert. It had dawned on him a lot earlier that his assumption that this woman was his opposite number was wrong; it was Huan who was there in support of her.

Jerry said, "We have a deal. I think it's time for a cappuccino."

Joe winced. Another thing to put the waiter's nose out of joint; they hadn't yet been offered the cheese or dessert menus and the complimentary digestivo of lemoncello in little cut crystal glasses that he had seen at other tables. There were rituals to follow. He planned to tell his mother all about this great food.

As Prowse and De Souza left the restaurant together later the maître d' pressed a small card into Joe's hand and said something softly in Italian.

Outside Jerry asked, "What was that about?"

"I can make reservations, bring people," Joe replied. He didn't say the last bit. Don't bring your buddy back, though, had been whispered at the end.

38 GALA

By late-February signs of an early spring were bursting through in the south of England although there was flooding in Derbyshire and heavy snows in Scotland. But the crocuses in Weavers Field, a park close to Catrin's home, were a sign of new life and spring promise; and a reminder of her personal plan going forward.

She had decided that she was going to listen to the advice of Neville's cousin and, once discussed with Chris, he was fully in support. .

Her new obstetrician, Dr. Toth, had been candid. "It can't hurt and possibly could be the solution, but we won't know without trying. But it's a significant disruption to your life plans, in a sense. Probably many of Mr. Cameron's patients don't have the work challenges you face and their lives are... more flexible."

She's putting it very delicately, thought Catrin; rich women without commitments, some of them.

Toth continued, "We will, in any case, be monitoring you very carefully once you become pregnant, whichever path you choose regarding work, but there aren't any 'sure-fire' treatments. You already have a list of things I don't want you to do, including running; and a list of foods and beverages I would rather you avoided. It is helpful already that you don't drink alcohol at all.

"In general, it has to be very much a symptomatic approach."

~~

DCI Wetherby was meeting with his three team leaders, a regular logistics and management meeting.

"I'm glad things have settled down in your unit, Sayer," said Wetherby, "after the initial upheavals and distractions."

"Yes, sir. Things are running smoothly."

"And we are well within budget, I am glad to see. In fact all units are, other than Stolen Vehicle Recovery personnel costs."

He looked at the DI running the unit, June Dearborn.

She responded, somewhat exasperated, in an explanation to the others. "Stress and civilian staff turnover. The things people say when you phone them to give the good news that their stolen car has been recovered; but they have to pay us £150 recovery fee to get it back. 'Blackmail' is the mildest used. Some of the reassigned people just can't take it. That and the commute in; I quite wish myself at times that I had stayed in Havering."

As they wrapped up he said to them all, "You may be feeling we are still in different and difficult times but we have to support the priorities given to us. Things will get better."

It was DI Pascal Thomas, with the Met Film Unit who, blank-faced, replied. "Did you see the news articles about us this morning, sir?"

He gave Catrin a surreptitious glance, then a full smile.

Wetherby replied, "The report on the banquet thing, the Garner Award. Yes I did. Have you seen it, Sayer? It's your area."

She looked blank-faced. "I've not read any newspapers this morning."

Wetherby said. "The award to Sir Nigel Fielding for his donation to charities, including ours, for the recovery of that diamond brooch. Neville Coltrane was involved privately, after his time here."

Catrin said, "Yes, I was aware of that, he told me earlier. And the recovery of the Tarrant jewellery was also commented on by our French colleagues last Friday on this year's first Art Crime conference call."

DCI Wetherby said studiously, "I see in the calendar that the next meeting of that task force is in March, in Brussels. I think, given our situation, you may want to attend in person this time. It doesn't do to go too long without face-to-face contact and, as I recall, the mid-year meeting is set for Greece, which would have higher travel costs, or course."

He has all the contact meetings of his teams with other police services memorized, Catrin thought, ranked by travel cost.

"I will make arrangements, sir; thank you. Just overnight, by Eurostar, of course."

He smiled. They understood each other.

After the meeting broke and they left, Catrin said with a grin, "Pascal, you are a right stirrer. You should sod off back to Southwark!"

The Film Unit was located in the borough. DI Thomas just laughed.

"I knew it," he said to Dearborn. "She was there, at the banquet. I should have bet on it."

June Dearborn looked at Catrin. "One day, perhaps. I would have loved to have been at some gala like that, if I had the right clothes and the invitation."

Pascal said, "It was a good thing that Neville did. I am not sure how the Commissioner could look him in the eye as he accepted the cheque."

The Times had reported that Fielding and his wife had donated £1 million, divided among the Metropolitan Police and City of London Police Benevolent Funds and the London operations of the John Howard and Elizabeth Fry Societies. It said that Ivy Fielding and Neville Coltrane had jointly agreed the selection.

Catrin smiled, remembering the speech. "It was indeed. And the Commissioner didn't look the slightest bit abashed or embarrassed. Nor did Neville; they had both moved on, I guess."

Catrin and Chris had been guests at a table sponsored by Neville Coltrane. Neville was looking splendid in his tuxedo, far more comfortable than Chris in his own new attire.

"I should rent again," Chris had said, once they knew they were going.

Catrin replied, "It's time to buy. Nothing too flashy, something conservative; one that will last; assuming your waist doesn't expand beyond the give they put into these things. With my art these days, we should go to more of them. Jean and I get asked, you know."

But Neville looked totally at ease. He had caught some sun, she noted. And he looked relaxed even when he was called up to the dais to join the couple receiving the award. Sir Nigel Fielding made it clear that they saw the success of the venture lay with Neville, not him or his wife.

His concluding remark had been, "So that's why we are humbled. We have gained far more than we have given; we did not do the work yet we are the ones being honored today. We thank you, all of you for coming tonight and adding to this fund-raising through your contributions at this gala."

It was later in the evening when Catrin and Neville Coltrane found themselves able to chat in private for a moment.

She asked, "What now, Neville?"

He looked into the distance before answering. "Not sure really. I needed to do something like this to validate... what could have been, if there had been no constraints of budget, or jurisdictions. And you? Apart from tunnels and bikers, I gather; how is it now?"

She looked at him and smiled. "Smaller, more constrained, quieter most of the time after the M25 fiasco; but I am glad you said what you did in the hospital. I wouldn't have wanted the biker team role, despite tripping over them in the Norfolk case."

"So it's OK; I didn't say the wrong thing at a difficult time for you?"

"No. Not at all. And for Dr. - mean - Mr. Cameron; it was only one visit but he made a lot of sense to me. I will be taking time off when we try again, I decided."

Coltrane seemed more pleased about that than about the job issue.

39 PROWSE

It was the week following the New York meeting with Four Square when Jerry Prowse visited the UK. He always flew American Airlines for two reasons. The planes used to look right; unpainted shiny metal like the ones his granddaddy flew in over Korea. That was one of the aspects he liked. They also had quality leather seats in First Class, like in a Caddy or a Lincoln.

But the last time he flew them the airline had gone down-hill, he thought, pandering to democrats and left wingers; the big bird was painted white and only the headrest was leather now, so it wasn't the same.

His ticket was issued by American, though; a small plane from Buffalo to Philadelphia where he changed to a British Airways 747 going to London, with a complimentary upgrade from Business to First through a 'brother' in ticketing. If American Airlines had a silver bird on the run, he would have taken it. Their loss.

Even before he changed planes in Philadelphia, Hilary Eaton was heading in to see her boss.

"One of the routine flags from Immigration. An Outlaw called Jerry Prowse from the US is visiting us; he's coming in overnight through Heathrow."

Coombs knew that the 'movements lists' of organized crime figures internationally had about ten to fifteen names of bikers on it daily, either arriving or leaving the UK. He replied, "And he is special; why?"

"He is high up in the New York state structure - and he and Leo go back a long time. In fact, he was the person who first talked to Leo about his Centurions chapter affiliating with the Outlaws in the UK."

Coombs mused on it. "To see Altman or the new chapter president, I wonder? Well, there is only one way to know. Keep an eye on him."

That turned out to be all too easy. Lyall Beddows met Jerry outside the Arrivals area at Terminal 5 and drove him at a sedate pace to Leo Altman's home in a restored 1972 Ford Cortina Mark II GT in racing green with white stripes. No one could lose that vehicle in traffic around London.

~~

"Lyall, why don't you go get yourself a coffee or something? Take Renata out for a drive, whatever; but mind the wheels."

Get lost, leave us two alone, put in nicer terms but equally understood by Altman's daughter and the 'prospect'.

When they were alone, Jerry chuckled. "Lyall drove very carefully; he is worried stiff about damaging that rebuild of yours."

Leo smiled. "But before we go to the club, get warm and fuzzy with the new man in charge, you had something specific for me, you said?"

Jerry nodded. His face turned serious. "It's the main reason I am over here. There is a Chinese triad interested in you, my friend. Very interested. They think you are going to go after the cops that led to your, shall we say, problem. Is that true; you are still thinking about payback?"

Leo didn't answer, just posed his own question. "What's it

got to do with them? Which one? We don't talk to the triads here. They have nothing to do with us."

"That's why they came to me, obviously. You and I do have things to do with each other; at least we did things together in the past. They knew that."

As it sunk in, Leo responded, his tone of voice somewhere between light mockery and annoyance, "Blackmail? You? You must be getting soft in your old age. How old? Forty-seven, I recall, a year younger than me."

Jerry gave a hearty laugh. "No. Simply a deal. I get some-thing from them in return for just passing on their message. I think you should take it formally as a warning. Leave those two cops well alone or they will eliminate you, they said. One of them, the female cop, is in this Triad's good books, I gather. That's all you or I need to know, I was told. Don't touch."

"She's in Jim Hughes' good books, too. She comes from the same place in Wales."

"And look where going after that Angel got you! Leave well alone, I just said, Leo; these people mean business in the same way as we do. Move on, is my advice."

He was watching Leo as the message was repeated, holding his gaze.

He added, "They are serious enough to take you out; explicitly stated. And the fact that you have your brothers in the club and the Centurions may join the Outlaws won't stop them; they made that clear. There's been enough trouble, Leo, don't you think?"

Leo said, "Duly noted. It's good advice, I know."

Jerry pressed on. "You've got Renata to look after; she's grown into a stunner, Leo. She needs to find the right 'next step' for her. You have Stevie in prison; he is going to need support, moral and practical - and the best lawyers for parole hearings. Keep busy with those things."

Leo looked out the window, contemplating for a moment. "Good advice, Jerry. Good advice, as I said. Thank you." He changed the subject. "Another Talisker?"

Jerry got the impression that he hadn't won the day but had

given his friend a lot to think about.

~~

"Pretty open, the pair of them," said Coombs two days later, listening to the feedback on Jerry Prowse.

"Whatever they are up to, they had plenty of time to discuss it - Leo's home and the club. This Lyall Beddows, what's he, other than a driver? It doesn't show any of his history."

DC Fellows said, "He has none, boss. He was upgraded from a hangaround to a prospect not that long ago. We are watching, though. A prospect in the Centurions wanting patches…"

He left the rest unsaid. To gain the trust of other patch members, a prospect needed to do whatever he was told, often something illegal.

Coombs shook his head slightly. "Not Sayer and Obi; or the artist. Leo doesn't have the backing of the club on that one now. Nor, given the experience with his son, would he leave it to an unproven amateur. How about this man Prowse? Would he do it?"

DS Eaton liked her boss's analysis; he was settling in to the job, she could see. Coombs pressed the point. "Would he be a candidate?"

Eaton said, "I doubt it. He is not a soldier anymore; still a tough guy, though. He would have the profile to do it but not the reason. The story goes that fifteen years ago Jerry was in the UK for work, with riding privileges with the Centurions. On a ride through France and Belgium some biker insulted Renée and it spiraled, turned into cowboy stuff. The man decided to use a knife during the fist fight with Leo. Jerry crowned him with his brain bucket - got that one yet, boss?"

Coombs said, "The small crash helmet, yes. And?"

"They took Leo away; had a local medic within their world deal with his wound. But when the other guy came to and was up and moving properly, several of them stood corner post while the fight continued - but with Jerry instead. He floored the guy eventually then deliberately broke his arm, the one he had put around Renée. So if anyone owes anyone - ."

Coombs interrupted, "It's Leo who owes Jerry, not the other way round. Got it."

He shook his head. "Don't you want a transfer from this stuff? You've been in this team for eight years, now."

Hilary look surprised. "My undergraduate degree was in behavioral psychology. I'd hate to be in traffic or something like that. Cult mentalities, that's me."

~~

The idea that Jerry Prowse was in the UK to do some damage was not borne out. He had been driven the following afternoon to Heathrow where CCTV showed that he looked a bit worse for wear from his visit to the clubhouse, but he was mobile. Nothing flagged as he went through security, other than he had a few words with a Chinese woman who briefly sat next to him in the British Airways lounge. She moved away almost as soon as she sat down.

"I hope he had a shower before he took that flight," said DC Fellows, reviewing the report and concluding why the woman had moved away so quickly.

Jerry had returned to Buffalo sleeping most of the way over the Atlantic.

In the lounge, Jerry had fixed himself a stiff vodka and tomato juice, with Worcester sauce, allowing Emily Chang the time to pack her laptop, move from the business area and sit at the adjoining seat around the low coffee table.

"Hard night?" she asked.

He smiled but didn't answer, just took a sip of the drink. Then another.

He said, "You will need to watch him like a hawk, is my honest assessment. I delivered the message and he made the right noises. That's all I will say and I don't feel good about even saying that part. I just hope he listened."

Chang said, "Thank you. We will do that. And not like a hawk, like a sparrow."

He raised an eyebrow.

She said, "Every prey watches out for the hawk, Mr. Prowse. No one pays much attention to sparrows."

Emily stood up and headed out of the lounge. Her flight to Vienna was on Four Square business; her stopover in London was not. There she had been organizing sparrows - and others, just in case.

40 CONFESSIONS

It was coincidence that Catrin planned the team meal at Osteria Dell' Angolo, an Italian restaurant near the Met head-quarters, on the very evening of the day that the news broke regarding the relocation of New Scotland Yard. The decision to move from the building by St. James's Park Tube station had been announced well over a year earlier. Now they had a date; it was only months before the headquarters group would be moving into the renovated Curtis Green building on the north side of the Victoria Embankment.

Isabelle said, "It's so the 'mukety-muks' on the top floor can have a nice view of the Thames before their afternoon nap."

She pulled a face at Catrin, a regular mock battle between them about the role and value of senior officers at the Met.

Catrin smiled. "I'm surprised the FBI is allowing you marry one of theirs; you should be on one of their lists as an anarchist agitator."

The implications of the move continued to be discussed throughout the day and into the evening get-together, held in a semi-private alcove table in the busy restaurant. That the dinner was special was understood; partners were invited. It was a meal in a quality restaurant, not a 'drink and a sandwich' in a bar. And they weren't paying individually. Catrin was hosting; she had said her art sales were doing well.

The other surprise was the appearance of a young borough copper, DC Derek Nkrumah, whom they hadn't seen for a long time before the demise of the old Art and Antiques Unit. Back then he had been seconded to Art and Antiques for six months and had hoped for a transfer into the specialist group. That was before the writing on the wall made it clear that that pruning, not growing, was the order of the day.

When the participants from the Met arrived direct from work, Kaila Obi and Morley Kerswell were already at the table talking with Derek and an attractive young woman, a PC Anisha Green, both casually dressed.

Isabelle was sure what this was about; her boss was going to announce that she was pregnant again.

She was wrong.

Catrin told them that, in the best traditions of all those formal dinners she had attended with Sandra Hunt, she would say a few words between the main course and dessert. Until then, it was to be 'just a good time'.

Isabelle and Kaila protested, wanting to hear the reason up front, to which Catrin said, "If you go on, I will tell you in Welsh, then you won't get any of it anyway."

"I would have to translate," announced Anisha, which surprised everyone except Nkrumah, who had a big grin on his face.

"You don't sound Welsh, if I may say so?" said Catrin.

Anisha had a neutral but cultured English accent, but when she responded to Catrin in Welsh, the other Anglophones could hear the fluency but not follow the content. She had been raised in Conwy, in North Wales, it turned out. Even Catrin was surprised.

So Catrin stuck it out until the main course plates were cleared away then stood up with her glass of mineral water in her hand. "It's time. Confession time, in a sense."

"Confession time?" asked Isabelle.

"Yes; and I am going to start with John."

That's surprised everyone, including John. He said, "Me - confess what?"

Catrin quipped, "You don't have to; I'll do it for you. John confesses that he gave up trying for his sergeant's exams back in the ACU when the girls were small."

Aina laughed. "We know that; Kaila kept on at him to get back to it, I recall."

"I didn't know!" responded Isabelle.

Catrin said, "And now he is confessing that he is going to start preparing for them again."

She had a mischievous expression on her face.

John looked at her. "Am I? Is this a sort of public performance review, boss?"

Catrin shook her head. "I need a sergeant. Isabelle is a conscientious objector when it comes to promotion; it's against her Trotskyist leanings. So you are it."

He looked at her, suddenly serious. "You would have me as a DS if I qualified?"

"In a heartbeat."

Kaila looked happy. Her husband just smiled and nodded his head a few times, thinking. "I'll have to get the coursework out. Start again then, won't I?"

"I hope so. The only reason Evelyn Carter came to bat for you was I told her your chance of promotion would be dead in the water unless you got through the OPS interview free and clear."

"Now my turn," said Catrin. She looked at Chris and smiled.

"I will be taking time off, a lot of time off, I hope, but not for a while. Chris and I plan to try again for a baby. And for me, it's not about getting pregnant, it's about staying so. And if I do get pregnant, when I get pregnant I should say, I am going on leave. Not maternity leave; not yet. That will come later, God willing. I'm going to take the advice of a leading

obstetrician and put the baby and my own body before anything else. He'll give me the paperwork so that the Met will
have no option but to give me an extended medical leave."

There were words of encouragement and applause from
Kaila but Catrin held up one hand.

"In part, having John become a sergeant is all part of the
plan to guard the fort. The Art and Antiques Unit needs to run
smoothly, so no one will even think of disturbing the boat. But
there's more."

She smiled and looked at Isabelle. "There is only one more
confession I have lined up; it's Isabelle's."

Now Howlett looked surprised. "And what are you
confessing to on my behalf?"

"I'm not. You are. I talked with David Klintz. Morley?"

Howlett's eyes went moist. "You shouldn't have."

Morley Kerswell just looked at his fiancée. "You'd better
tell them."

Isabelle took a breath. "Morley and I have been looking at
setting up in Paris, as you know. For him it's early retirement;
for me, weekends and holidays until I qualify for full retirement here."

"We know," said John.

"Well, the original plan was that I was going to leave; take
the early retirement package. Morley quite likes his FBI job and
some law firm in DC seemed keen to hire me as an art investigator. But then the world fell in and... Catrin stayed. I
couldn't go. Paris is the fallback plan - but we are both good
with it, honestly."

She looked at Catrin, "I couldn't leave, could I? After what
you did; stay with us. There; confession done. I need another
drink."

She reached for the wine bottle and glowered at Catrin who
just smiled back.

John said, "You have got to do what's right for you both,
Isabelle; but only you can say."

"Now I have a horrible suspicion I know why Derek is
here," Howlett replied, looking down the table.

Catrin said, "I talked to Derek last week. He was with us a while ago. Fits well. Still wants to join this strange team when commonsense would say the safest place for him now is in a borough. Right, Derek?"

"It was the best time I had since joining the Met," he replied.

Aina shook her head. "There is a risk. They could use any vacancy to freeze the post…"

"No they couldn't; not this one," said Catrin. "I talked to Jameson in the Federation on the quiet. They won't be able to do away with my job, the team will be short-handed and Derek has prior experience. If I can, and I have Wetherby's agreement on this, we will try to get Derek in the team anyway. It has a good chance, he thinks."

"You went through all this with him, too?"

Catrin nodded. She looked at Isabelle. "Other than Isabelle and Morley's situation; that's their business. Not that I am kicking you out, Isabelle; it would be great if you stay. But, as John says, you have a decision to make and I want it unfettered by your much-appreciated loyalty. Think about it. Take us all to dinner when you decide, either way."

She smiled, adding, "But not in an upstairs restaurant."

Morley and Isabelle's tumble down the stairs of a pub in the Strand shortly after they met had not been forgotten.

Catrin raised her glass. "So a toast. To Art and Antiques; as we said, keeping the faith."

As they repeated the toast Isabelle said facetiously, "To liaison and coordination."

Aina, never one to lead, didn't let it stop there. She added, "And another, to Catrin and Chris; good health, bright future and in making the really big decision we haven't talked about yet."

"What's that?" Catrin asked.

"Whether, when you look into your baby's eyes for the first time, Catrin, you may realise that you actually want to stay home as a mum - and an artist - and give all this up."

41 CUSTOM HOUSE QUAY

It was June and Wimbledon fortnight. A week after Catrin's departure on leave on medical grounds she was still feeling pangs of guilt about being away from her job, her mind thinking about the on-going work of the unit. The weather was perfect and life was good. She had planned carefully for her time on leave, her new regime and lifestyle.

But it troubled her, for some reason.

"I can't get my head out of the casework," she confided to Chris, "even when I am at the Kiln working on something."

"It takes time to let go," was his response. "It will come."

"I'm not sure when," she shot back.

"When you hear they have done something big without you, probably in the way you wouldn't have done it anyway."

She wasn't sure she liked that answer. They can't do without me completely, she thought. There is the rigmarole of the Stephen Altman trial to go through soon.

That, in fact, turned out to be the example Chris had talked about. He had taken a couple of days off to make a long week-end so that they could go to Cornwall, stay with his sister. The siblings owned a boutique handmade paper business in Falmouth and Catrin always enjoyed it down there.

Jenifer, Chris's sister, had a longtime relationship with the watercolour artist Catrin had mentioned to Brendan in his studio, Mason Carrington, and she enjoyed the occasional opportunity to paint with the man. Internationally recognized and a nomadic world traveler, he gave classes on watercolour painting in different countries. This visit was one of those times. Mason was on a trip to China, a country with a major interest in watercolour art.

Jenifer and Mason had never moved in together, just had separate small homes. "If I had him underfoot I would kill him," she often said, "him and his messy paints."

"Mason paints loosely," Chris would chime back, knowing that it would provoke his sister further.

The weather in Falmouth was holding, but rain was in the air as she painted *en plein air*, her easel set up on Custom House Quay but facing inland, across the small harbour, with the light reflecting off the boats and water. Mason had left a list of 'possibles; with the best time of day' on a sticky note attached to a copy of one of his books, 'New Watercolour Visions; Falmouth to Land's End'.

At the bottom he had written cryptically, 'Go for it!!'

Catrin was painting away, talking a little with the occasional passerby who took an interest. It was relaxing, moreso than her ceramic decoration at the Kiln. She was in conversation with an older amateur painter who was walking his dog on the quay about choices of blues when her mobile rang. She glanced at the screen and said to him, "I'm sorry, I have to take this call."

It was Wetherby. She walked away downwind as she answered, "Sir?"

"A complication, Sayer, unfortunately. We are well into the disclosure stage of the Altman case. CPS is being pressed by Altman's solicitor on your driver training expertise level."

She said, "Standard advanced, it's in the record."

He sounded exasperated. "I know. We have been through that once with them. The fact that you were a security officer is making them push the issue of whether you had training in anti-terrorist or related offensive driver techniques."

"I never drove as a security aide. AC Hunt had a driver with that training. I was armed; that was my role."

The wind was suddenly picking up, gusting. She saw the older man hold her easel steady, making his dog sit still; one of her brushes had rolled on to the floor and the dog was about to chew it.

You have all this on file, she thought. Then it struck her.

Wetherby said, confirming her thought, "We are concerned that it is a signal that Stephen Altman's defense is targeting you for some reason. We can think of several defense ploys they will introduce but my concern is that they will be pressing this all the way through to the trial itself."

That was what had hit Catrin too. Right through her pregnancy.

"Where are you, by the way?"

"Visiting relatives in Cornwall. I was out painting. It looks like a dog is about to chew one of my brushes that fell on the floor. I'll be back on Tuesday; Chris has Monday off."

"Catrin, we'll work on this; we will do what we can to alleviate it but if you could come on in and talk with us and CPS next Tuesday, that would be very helpful. You'd better go and get your brush."

He rang off and Catrin walked back, thanking the man for his help. He had spotted the dog's interest in time and picked up the brush.

"Rosemary & Co. A good one; we can't have Cindy here damaging this. This little squall could blow over in ten minutes. Will you be risking it?"

Catrin shook her head. "No, I think I will call it a day, but thank you for your help."

It wasn't the weather that put her off, she thought.

As she packed up and walked back to Jenifer's home it struck her that most people wouldn't even understand the problem; they thought the next thing that happened after someone was charged and remanded to prison was the court-room and the trial. They had no idea about the intermediate stages, slogging through the preliminaries of the evidence disclosure.

It had only been a little over ten days, but it still felt strange on the following Tuesday to be heading into New Scotland Yard. Catrin's assigned vehicle had been returned to the car pool the day she started her medical leave so she travelled in by Tube, as did Chris these days. It was like earlier times in her career, but somehow it didn't feel right.

In the office she spent some time catching up with people but there was no sign of DCI Wetherby until she arrived at the meeting room with John, who was also to attend. There she found Wetherby and Superintendent Patterson with a smartly-dressed CPS solicitor she had come across before, a Charles Cantrell, accompanied by a junior litigator, a young woman almost straight out of graduate school.

Cantrell got down to business straight away, starting with an update on the progress of the prosecution, the person he was dealing with 'from the opposition'; a Sean Toomey. He laid out the timelines expected and the probable series of witnesses for both sides.

Throughout it Wetherby sat stoically, taking notes in an A4 size notebook he always seemed to have with him.

Cantrell finished his report and said brightly, "Pretty much standard fare this one, despite the seriousness of the charge. Should be wrapped up by next Christmas at the latest. Fay and I will be assigned throughout; a good trial case experience for her to get her teeth into now she is with CPS."

He gave his assistant a brief smile.

Wetherby seemed to emerge from his note-taking and reached over to a file folder he had brought with him, centering it above his notebook as he opened it.

He said, "This issue of Mr. Toomey pressing for more information on DI Sayer's driving record and on DC Obi's personnel file information; what is it about, exactly? You commented earlier on him making difficulties, wanting to chip away at witness credibility. I understand that; it's not exactly a new tactic. But what specifically is this about?"

Cantrell replied, a little surprised, "Well, DI Sayer is a trained security officer, so her training is fair game. If she was trained to use a vehicle to attack a person, it would be relevant to Altman's injuries. DC Obi was subject to a preliminary review of his conduct. If there are past examples of violent behaviour, they will be brought out, too."

He looked at John, his expression saying that he expected something of this sort to be self-evident.

The junior, Fay, jumped in. "Of course, we will prepare you both appropriately prior to the trial."

Catrin wondered how this woman would fare with some of the cross-examination she had experienced in her times as a witness.

Cantrell added, "When the defense barrister places each of you in the witness box he will be looking for anything that can be used for sentence mitigation. That will be part of Toomey's brief to the barrister. The verdict is a 'given', short of a screw-up and Toomey knows it, but a sentence for attempted murder can be anything up to a life term. Up to. Stephen Altman is twenty-three, so Toomey will try to limit his term in prison accordingly. Standard stuff."

Wetherby nodded. It appeared that he just wanted CPS to confirm the facts.

He said carefully, "We do not wish DI Sayer to be involved further; she is on medical leave and has come in today especially for this meeting."

Cantrell smiled indulgently and gave his junior a conspiratorial glance before responding directly to Wetherby. "I understand that may be your wish but if the defense requests it, she has to; she would be subpoenaed at trial at the very least, even if she is excused from the preliminaries."

Wetherby said implacably, "Then the trial will be put off well beyond next Easter and Altman will stay in remand."

He opened the file, pulling out the first document.

"This is a duly sworn statement by former Assistant Commissioner Sandra Hunt on the training and experience of

DI Sayer during her preparation for her security role and the two years she was her aide. There is no reference to any specialized driver training. Miss Hunt is quite willing to appear as a witness, if needed, if Toomey presses this line - and we expect you to use her. I'm not sure Mr. Toomey wants someone with her capabilities tearing his gambit apart in a courtroom."

Cantrell raised his eyebrows, showing his surprise, but said nothing as Wetherby reached into the folder for another document.

"DC Obi is more than willing to appear as a witness. In fact, he and I will be the only witnesses to represent our unit. During the discovery phase he will be personally represented by Miss Evelyn Carter who will be contacting Mr. Toomey directly. We will oppose any release of prior information on DC Obi as irrelevant, given that the incident in question was examined in detail. They can have DCI Courtney's report; that's it. Do you think Mr. Toomey knows Miss Carter? I see their offices aren't far from each other?"

Cantrell said, "We all know Evelyn Carter, indeed. Well, this is a development I -"

Wetherby butted in. "Moreover, we will be providing a duly authorised medical certificate of exemption for DI Sayer from all preliminary hearings and from appearing as witness in court until after the birth of her child; the trial will have to be re-scheduled accordingly, if needed, as I said. We are quite immovable on this point if Mr. Toomey persists."

He glanced at Superintendent Patterson who said, in endorsement, "Totally immovable."

Fay was looking at her senior colleague a little askance, her worry evident. This didn't seem to be going along the lines of the routine update she thought they were supposed to be providing to the Met.

Wetherby pressed on. "As we are immovable on sentencing recommendations. The Met expects the CPS to press for a life term for this man. He tried to kill two police officers; not only that, but in a manner that would have created mayhem on the

M25, with possibly many more deaths and injuries. This - .''

He slapped a quarter-inch thick report on the table and slid it across to the lawyer.

"- is an analysis by our traffic experts of the possible consequences if he had been successful in incapacitating DI Sayer while she was driving."

Cantrell glanced at Wetherby's superior, his expression showing he was questioning whether this DCI truly had full support for this heavy-handed approach. Just as the door opened and Commander Moore walked in.

She said, interrupting, "I got delayed; my apologies. I'm not sure where you are but my job here is to read the riot act to you, Mr. Cantrell, as I have just done to your boss. We - ."

Superintendent Patterson said, "Ma'am, it's already been read."

She caught his glance and looked at Wetherby, now seeing his controlled annoyance. She smiled and turned to Catrin. "Well, that saves me time. Catrin, how are you doing, enjoying life?"

It was later, back in the Art and Antiques Unit, that Aina told Catrin, "John and the boss got together; decided that there was no way you were being brought back into this. Tim Wetherby is not Neville or Jane, but he's his own man, quiet but determined. He worked last week and over the weekend to get all this stuff together. Patterson and Moore were right on board, too."

'The boss', not 'sir' any more, Catrin noted. It was a good sign.

"I've got a lot more support than I realised," said Catrin, "I need to go and talk to him."

"He went straight into another meeting, to do with Stolen Vehicles budget planning. He is a busy man these days. Catrin, leave it be a while. He's settled into his stride, it seems."

Catrin went over to John. "Thank you; are you up to this?"

"I need to be. And I am happy with it. All being well I'll have my promotion through by the time I go through the hoops CPS have put in my way. Evelyn… once I called her, she was firing on all cylinders. I gather she and this Sean Toomey don't see eye to eye. I'm looking forward to that bit. I think Cantrell's junior is in for a rude awakening about the realities of trial preparation."

He smiled. "And I owe you. It's my bit of 'keeping the faith'. I want you have peace and quiet, to become a mum; that's worth any time I spend in the witness box."

As she headed home on the Tube Catrin felt really good. Something had clicked; she would enjoy her leave and nurture herself and her baby while doing so but she knew, deep down, she wanted to come back in due course. She wasn't a biker, but she had her club, her affiliation; the Met was it.

42 KIEL

"I don't like it, but don't have a solid reason why," said Hilary Eaton.

It was the weekly status review of the Trident biker gang team; a time when thematic issues were reviewed as well as planned assignments for the week ahead. They were working down the list of gangs and reviewing their movements. The subject of the Centurions annual bike ride to Belgium was being discussed.

Greg Coombs wasn't dismissive. He said, "What doesn't sit well?"

Eaton shook her head. "Something about the fact that they are separating, not travelling together; that Leo, particularly, is routing through Germany."

DC Fellows said, "The ones who are going with him are all Leo's friends but there is no sign of division or breakup in the Centurions."

Eaton agreed with that. "Believe me, we'd know about it if there was. Someone would be hurt by now. That's why I said I have no solid reason. But the Centurions summer ride has always been the club riders together. Now a few of them with Leo are taking the ferry from Harwich to Bremerhaven, toddling along to some biker meet in North Germany, then

283

riding down to join the others."

"Just sight-seeing a different route? Or meeting other bikers for a purpose, I wonder," Coombs asked, rhetorically. "Is this Motorrad100 a big event?"

DC Fellows responded. "Yes, but not a big one percenter event. It is more family-orientated. There's a big contingent that comes down from Scandinavia to that meet. Are the Centurions and another group doing business there?"

Coombs looked around his team; there were no answers or new ideas. He needed to move on down the list.

He concluded, "Pass that to the Germans and the Nordics; leave them to decide."

~~

Dr. Toth said, "I'm pleased with the results, as should you be. How long have you been on leave now?"

"Five and a half weeks. It took me a couple of weeks just to get my head out of things at the Met but since then I have settled. Regular exercise, but not pushing it; work at the pottery with my friends and more social stuff than I fitted in my life previously. Next week I am going back to Wales, to visit my parents and then Chris will drive down and we will go on to Cornwall, visit his family again. It's a different 'busy'."

At the end of the examination Dr. Toth said in conclusion, "Everything seems to be normal. Whatever you are doing, keep doing it and whatever you were doing last time and don't do now, keep it that way. No sudden passions to go running?"

Catrin shook her head. "I just take walks now; regular and steady. I miss the running but I can hold off."

Toth caught something in the document she was reading through on Catrin's patient profile. "At least I don't have to ask about smoking or alcohol consumption; you don't do either. I saw that last time."

Catrin nodded. "I never drank; my mother is a recovered alcoholic; it put me off. I tried smoking in my first year at university, but never got through my first pack."

Dr. Toth smiled. "Any cravings at all?"

For a seasoned police officer, Catrin suddenly looked guilty. "Custard tarts. Sweet ones, like my mum used to bake. There's a little baker's shop in Spitalfields that... well, I changed my walking route to make sure I don't pass it now."

Toth smiled. "I can't say anything about that; your blood work is good and your weight is fine. I'm your obstetrician, not your dentist."

~~

The biker meet that had Hilary Eaton's focus was held just south of Kiel, a large gathering of motorcycle enthusiasts from all over Northern Europe. Unlike the Bulldog Bash, which was mainly an adult gathering policed by the Hells Angels, the Kiel-Gaarden Motorrad100 was a large, public festival focused on motorsport and motorbike enthusiasts. There were exhibitors, bike dealers and companies selling an array of equipment.

It was held on the grounds of a former manor house and farm now popular for festivals, at least with the owners and the tradespeople in the Kiel-Gaarden area, if not with the local residents. But the summer festival events held there had their own professional security staff. The '100' tag had been there from its formation fifteen years earlier, a deliberate intent to counter the 99% and 1% separations of motorcyclists. It had no significant trouble and was family-orientated.

Leo and the five people with him; two patches and two prospects, one of which was Lyall and an 'old lady', the partner of one biker, melded into the crowd invisibly. Occasionally their jackets would get a second look. One Dutch biker came up and started talking with them enthusiastically about road trips in England, oblivious to the rule that you don't try to open conversations with 'one percent' bikers *en masse*. It they want to talk to you, they will make it clear; otherwise, don't bother them.

But it was fine. Lyall was happy as a kid in a sand box. The whole day was smooth and without issues.

It was early evening when Leo said he was 'taking a solo', heading out on his bike to the coast, just for a ride. No one offered to go with him; they had been drinking moderately and were accustomed to the occasional moodiness in the man these days. It was understandable.

Lyall looked a little put out but kept quiet; if Leo had told him they were going for a ride, he would have held off the beer. But he hadn't.

Leo appeared to wander a little during the ride, taking in the road and the sights and finally took a break along the Shönberger seafront at a small café near the historic railway museum. By chance, it seemed, if you were observing them, another biker more noticeable for being thin than for his height, was already having a glass of tea there. He looked something of a beanpole in leather.

They talked awhile. Then the beanpole rode away.

The following day, the second and last day of the Centurions presence at the event, the beanpole and Leo were around the site. But they never even spoke to each other or gave any sign of recognition that they had chatted on the Shönberger seafront.

~~

It was a week later, as Eaton was reading intently a report on the Motorad100 one percenter presence this year that DC Fellows asked, "Anything for us?"

She shook her head. "Nothing I would take up the ladder. But the list from Motorrad100 gives us Leo and his group."

"We know who went with him. What got your attention?"

She nodded. "Several names from Scandinavia and Germany, one-percenters. Nothing unusual, but they were there. They tend to know each other."

DC Fellows was still intrigued. "But something caught your attention."

"Leo knows Eric Sorensen, a Danish one percenter, I

know. Yet they were both at Motorrad and never talked to each other. Yet, according to this, they crossed paths twice on the grounds. Funny that."

She stood up holding the printout, heading to DI Coombs' office. "Funny enough to put him on a watch if he ever comes here. He's a tall, thin guy. The French think he doubles as a hit man but don't have the proof."

She crossed the work area. David Fellows had the impression that Coombs wouldn't be dismissive of this tenuous link after the M25 cock-up. He was right. Ten minutes later he was called in to Coombs' office.

"Dave, do some checking. We are keeping an eye on this man Sorensen, see if he comes here. Hilary is doing that. But check the planned movements of the Altman family, not just Leo. I want to see if the Altman-Sorensen paths line up at all in the foreseeable future, as best as we can assess. And particularly if they line up here. Just another job to add to your little list."

Dave Fellows would have taken it as a given that his instructions would include Lyall Beddows; he spent more of his time at Leo's home these days than his own. He wondered if Lyall and Leo's daughter, Renata were an item. Hilary didn't think so.

"He treats her more like a sister, I suspect. He's Leo's prospect now. He wouldn't make a move on Renata without Leo's blessing. Prospects are like slaves, at the beck and call of their patch twenty-four seven."

~~

Eaton was unwittingly correct about Lyall. Catrin Sayer was very much in Leo Altman's thoughts and Lyall was well aware of it.

After the discussion and the vote at the meeting that threw him out of the top position in the Centurions, Leo had said nothing for a moment then congratulated Stuart on becoming president. He was a good guy; had been his vice-president at one time. Several people had made awkward remarks, thanking Leo but making it clear they felt that a change was needed.

He didn't have a grudge against them. Now if Norm was still here... that would be different.

All he said to the assembled members was, "Have I ever let a fellow brother down... ever? Tell me?"

There were no answers but several headshakes; no one was disagreeing with him. He surveyed the room, his old sense of control coming to the fore. He added, "So do you think I would ever let a family member down; really?"

They spoke up, not in unison, their comments overlapping. Of course not. Leo was straight; a good guy, solid as a rock. Given good service. Loyal. It all came out.

But it was time for a change; it just hung in the air.

Norman Hart had left the Centurions shortly after the police raid. He had been thinking about a job offer in Ireland for a while, they all knew, so it was no surprise when he patched over to a Dublin club.

It was only later, over drinks and after Leo left that someone questioned the reason for Leo's last remark at the vote. "About family, why?"

"I think it's about that copper's remark; who put Stevie up to it, gave him the gun. Who knew where they were kept?"

"Well there is only Leo; and Stu now he is our president; they know where things are stored. And Skelly, of course. And Norm; he was sergeant-at-arms before Skelly."

It was a woman married to another patch who said, "When Stevie wanted in, it was Norm that he hung around a lot; before the vote, that is. Leo said the club, not he, should decide."

"What do you mean by that?" someone asked.

"Nothing," she said. "Just thinking, that's all."

Think it through yourself, she thought. Norm knew where the weapons are kept, Stevie was close to him and now Norm has scarpered over to Ireland. But she just smiled at the man.

In fact Leo felt guilty even though he hadn't given Stevie

the M9. He had wound him up; in fact, they had wound each other up about Obi, if truth be told, ignoring Renata's pleading for some commonsense. For him, it was reaction, tied to the grief of losing his wife. He hadn't foreseen how his son would react.

When he got the chance to talk to Stevie in the hospital afterwards, one on one, it came out that Norm had relented and given the weapon to him without checking. Stevie had convinced him that his dad had agreed to it, that Steve should be the instrument of the family's revenge. Leo's initial reaction was to say he would sort out Norm, but it was his son who convinced him otherwise.

"Just leave it, dad. I own this one; I'm taking the time for it. Leave me that. Norm's a good guy; not too bright, but I used him. Don't make it worse for me."

Norm leaving for Ireland had been a good thing. Leo wondered how he could have stomached having the man around the club if he had stayed.

But he had more important people for his revenge in his sights. Lyall was kept at his side, doing his bidding, watching his patch member obsess about 'justice'.

Lyall thought back to Seb's rib; he had no intention of going the same route. So when Leo set him the task of finding the home addresses of Catrin Sayer and John Obi, Lyall did as he was told without question.

Obi's was easy to locate. A Centurion from Tower Hamlets had let slip after the raid that Obi was from around there, somewhere along Thomas Road. It took a couple of days to locate the address; he had seen Obi in the street with his family and simply stayed on the wife and kids after Obi left them at the Underground station.

Some contact of Leo's had also found out that Sayer's husband worked at the Met and given Leo the name Chris Treneer, a computer specialist. Lyall had pulled up a photo of him on the internet from some old computer journal.

It took Lyall three consecutive days hanging around New

Scotland Yard before he saw the man. He was looking older than the photo but was clearly the same person. Treneer headed across to the Underground, followed by Lyall. Three hours later, the prospect was back in Leo's home with an address in Spitalfields.

Chris Treneer was a civilian computer expert. He had no idea he was being followed across London on the Tube, even by someone as amateurish as Lyall. Catrin, with her security background embedded, would have spotted Lyall within the first five minutes.

43 ST. PAUL'S

Catrin saw that the incoming call was from, of all people, Sophie Cartwright.

"Hello Sophie; how are you? What's up?"

Cartwright would never call her just to socialize.

"I need to talk to you. Can we meet? John tells me you are on leave?"

Catrin responded, "I am, so you should talk to him or Isabelle directly, though, instead. Is it an existing case?"

"I'm already in London; I arrived in Liverpool Street station half an hour ago. I was on the phone to John; Isabelle is in some meeting. I would prefer to meet with you, if possible, just to bounce an idea; possibly an important one. I've got a suggestion about the copyist I want to share."

Catrin looked at the clock; 3.00 p.m. And Sophie didn't know where she lived; that she was actually close by. She continued, "It's more logical if I come to see you. How about afternoon tea or something?"

There was a pause while Sophie decided. "Not here, though. There is nowhere nice in the station. But somewhere around here would be good."

The Crypt Café at St. Paul's Cathedral was busy, but with a

high turnover of tables as people began their commute home after a visit to the cathedral or a quick meeting with someone after work, in the same way that Catrin was doing. It was a small but functional meeting place next to the gift shop in the basement of the cathedral. The thick arched pillars of the structure divided the area up, giving natural alcoves for the tables.

"I like it. I have never been here before," Cartwright said, as they settled into a table. "I love these archways. You are looking relaxed, I must say. When they said you were on leave, I thought it was a holiday, not long-term. I'm sorry to have bothered you now, in a sense."

Catrin replied, "It fitted in for me OK; I happened to be nearby. I'm expecting, as you can see; I'm off work while I get through the first two trimesters, perhaps the whole pregnancy; I had problems last time."

"Congratulations; the very best for you. When is the baby due?"

"Around February, all being well."

Sophie asked, "Are you still doing ceramics?"

Catrin nodded. "Yes, moreso at present. Jean Hughes and I are making our gallery owner happy, for once. It's what I need; work that's absorbing and relaxing at the same time."

Sophie looked at her watch and got down to business. "This forger of the works in Norfolk. I have an idea."

Catrin looked neutral. "Fire away."

"I went back through the images I was given to review; on a whim, really. I think this person paints in such detail because he or she is naturally so highly-focused. As if the person is too fixed on minute detail or isn't normal somehow, not that I like that term. I'm not, that's for sure; I will admit that. But the differences I see in the paintings are tied to the difference in the person, I've decided, not simply an effort to copy the originals accurately. I am not quite sure how but it needs to be followed up."

"Have you mentioned it to DI Needham or DS Hollis, perhaps?" Catrin asked.

Sophie shook her head emphatically. "No, it needs a specialist to look into this; you or Isabelle or John, I thought. But it may give some leads."

She looked for some sort of affirmation from Catrin and got none. So she added, "Are you still looking? I've not heard anything."

Catrin replied with a deflection. "Nor should you; it's something I can't discuss. I am sure Norfolk appreciated your help and we did, certainly. But you know the rules. It's intriguing, what you say, but I am interested why you came here to discuss it in person, rather than just give me a call or send an email?"

Now Sophie looked to be on the defensive. "I'm not in London just for this. I have a commission for a copy of the 'Peter Peers and Benjamin Britain' portrait at the NPG. I'm not going to do that at the gallery, it is always too crowded. And I don't like their lighting. I have John Owens doing the photographs for me tomorrow and we will deal with the colour balance issue while I am there seeing it, then and I will paint it back in Aldeburgh. Take the boys back home, right?"

The portrait by Kenneth Green of the singer and his partner the composer on display at the National Portrait Gallery, she meant. Catrin recalled that the two musicians had lived in Aldeburgh. Someone at the NPG would be getting a lecture on gallery lighting tomorrow, she suspected.

Sophie pressed on. "Besides, it is hard to explain my thoughts about the copyist without being face-to-face with someone; it's not like the issue of this detail hits you straight off; it's very subtle."

Catrin sensed that her own deflection technique was now being returned from across the table.

"So which came first in your decision to visit? The NPG commission or the desire to talk to us about the forger?"

She knew the answer from Sophie's face.

"So why?" she persisted.

Sophie's voice lost the combative tone. "I'd like to meet the person, to ask why? I hoped you would let me do that, at some point. If they are so good, why do they just do copies? Why be like me, in a sense, not to blow my own trumpet; I don't do that. But when my Andrew died so did something within me, my creative spark. What went wrong in this person, I ask? I'd like to know."

She stopped, not looking defiant, just appearing more vulnerable now as she revealed her motives.

Because, if she can find the answer for that person, thought Catrin, perhaps she can find her own solution. She looked down at her teacup and said nothing for a moment. Sophie wondered whether the answer she had given had embarrassed this Welsh woman.

Then Catrin said softly, "So all this thing about you not painting anything original, the tests you put my people and others through, the banter with Neville about it in the past... it's not behind you, is it?"

It was Sophie's turn to look away.

"No, there are days when it still hurts. Actually, there isn't a day when it doesn't, at some point."

Catrin asked, "What if the cause in this other person is totally unrelated to your own; your loss of Andrew?"

"Then perhaps he or she would understand and... perhaps through talking, at least, we could help each other if we can't help ourselves. But I'd better go; it was just a wild idea. Now I've shared it out loud, I realise it's not very practical, is it? You have things to do and so do I; I have to get across to Chelsea. I am staying with a friend from the old days there and said I would buy her dinner, as a thank you. Thanks for listening - and for the tea."

She stood up, ready to run now; too much had been revealed.

Catrin did likewise and suddenly said, "Expect a call from me; I will see what I can do. In any event, I will give you a call with a yes or no, not leave you hanging. Don't talk to the Norfolk lot or to my team. Leave it with me."

As they left and Sophie headed for the Tube, on impulse Catrin walked around to the front of the building and into the cathedral entrance, counter to the flow of people leaving after Choral Evensong. A memory of a comment after the Malaysian incident from her psychologist, Dr. Herrington, had come out of nowhere.

"What is it about St. Paul's that works for you? You said that you are not a practicing Anglican, but I know you have this sense of finding peace there... you should go talk to someone at the cathedral, I suggest, and find out what it is they think that is working for you."

She would need to talk to the Norfolk team, and possibly Brendan's parents and even John Olson. But first she needed to get her own head straight. She walked into St. Dunstan's Chapel, to the quiet space that always seemed to bring her peace.

~~

Back in Scotland Yard, the people in the biker unit in Trident were not finding any peace and tranquility. An incident of road rage had a biker and Porsche driver both in custody for a fracas on the South Bank, caught nicely by CCTV. If the one percenter, a 'Satan's Slave', had left it alone or filed a complaint, he would have been the 'aggrieved party' as the Porsche had hit him first. Breaking the driver-side window with a glass-breaker on his knife and hauling the driver through it by his tie, however, changed the game.

Before heading out to follow up on the Porsche incident, DC Fellows reported to Coombs.

"There's nothing about Eric Sorensen travelling to the UK; nothing about the Altmans, other than they have a holiday in Spain booked. Renata and Lyall leave two weeks today from Heathrow; Leo the day after."

Coombs made a remark about bikers having more time and money for holidays abroad than coppers and got on with the next item.

It was later, when Hilary Eaton came back in and saw the status report that she asked herself, "Why, I wonder, aren't the

Altmans flying together on holiday, the same day?"

~~

Lyall Beddows had not only been asking himself the same question, he was pretty sure he had the answer, uncomfortable as it was, but he could never raise it with Leo. His 'patch' had become so withdrawn he was not the same man. At first Lyall put it down to grief at his loss - first his wife, then his son in prison, probably in there until well after Leo either died or became senile. All Leo had left was Renata.

Now Lyall saw Leo's problem as one of revenge. He knew that Leo had talked a couple of times to Oskar and Gerda and, in the back of Lyall's mind was the implication of several things he knew: locating the homes of the two police officers, the memory of Gerda's remark, 'we don't forgive - ever' and the name she gave him to pass on; 'Eric'.

But overriding it all was his desire to become a Centurion, to stay true to their world and as Gerda admonished, 'Look after Leo'.

It seemed that Lyall's job was to look after Renata, other than to keep up with Leo in trips to the clubhouse. Not that Renata needed much. She had her own car now, well, her mother's car. In a sense he was a substitute for Steve, Lyall thought. He and 'Ren' got along well, comfortable with each other; but she wasn't interested in him and, apart from liking her good looks, he wasn't really attracted to her.

He was looking forward to the trip to Spain with her, though; and with Leo. He hoped his mentor would revive a bit there, let go of the weight of the world and its bitterness. They would see. But still, Lyall was uncomfortable with Leo's decision to fly a day after them. Leo didn't bother to explain why or invent a reason; it was just the way it was going to be.

44 KINDRED SOULS

Ten days later, Melissa Nunn collected Catrin from the impressive entrance to Norwich Railway Station in a Norfolk Constabulary unmarked car. "Like old times, ma'am."

She had picked her up from the very same spot years ago. When they first met Melissa was a probationer and Catrin a detective sergeant.

Catrin replied, "Only now you are a DS, and I am long enough on leave to feel like a member of the general public."

Melissa responded, "But you are looking well, I must say. In the bloom, so to speak."

Catrin smiled. "My mother says life is a day at a time; I feel that these days. And I am looking forward to the cooler weather. It feels like I have my own internal heating supply switched on full."

Not too long now and her baby would be a viable 'preemie' at worst, perhaps. She had a big assessment next week with her obstetrician. Based on that she would decide whether she should return to work with light duties, mainly office-bound, or stay on leave.

DCI Wetherby had shown his dexterity in internal manage-ment issues, getting Derek Nkrumah on board yesterday. Both Isabelle and John had said their boss had become more 'hands on', electing not to have a temporary replacement for Catrin as John had passed his sergeant's exam. It was 'wait and see' now.

Catrin asked, "And you; was it the right decision?"

Months ago, following the events in Thornham, Melissa had gone to her meeting with Inspector Golding expecting to finalise her transfer to Great Yarmouth. Instead she was surprised by the first words.

"You've been making waves, I hear. Now you have another decision to make."

For one awful moment she thought that some sort of disciplinary issue was looming until she saw the woman smile.

"Superintendent Lubbock wants you in JMIT. But you have the position in Great Yarmouth, if you want; we think you would be a good fit there.

"Apparently he was impressed by the way you tracked down this forger but stood up for what you thought was in the interests of the service, even if he was blind-sided by the manner in which you dealt with it. He thinks you would add to his team. Not that I got any impression that it would be an easy ride - they are a strong-willed bunch. But it would be a different career. First thoughts?"

"I need to think about it, ma'am."

The senior officer persisted. "Nevertheless, I won't hold you to it; but what's your gut feel?"

Melissa only hesitated a moment. "I'd like to give JMIT a shot. If it doesn't pan out in the first month, then I would like to take the Great Yarmouth position, if you can keep it open for that time; to have my cake and eat it in a sense."

The older officer smiled. "We are on the same wavelength then; so go away and mull it over and give me an actual answer by Monday morning at the latest."

Melissa responded to Catrin, "So far it has been good; I enjoy the work and have had no run-ins with people, really. DS Hollis doesn't seem to hold any grudge; in fact, he is just the way he is. Every now and again I keep reminding myself that when I first met you, you were a DS too. I've come a long way, I feel."

And me, thought Catrin, thinking back to her own early days in Brixton.

~~

John Olson was with Hubert Atkin at the police head-quarters. It was a standard meeting room yet the Thornham man was ill at ease, it appeared.

When he saw Catrin, he said straight off, "Brendan still talks about you, you know? Joanne is with him today."

Mrs. Chalmers, the social services contact for Brendan, sat next to Hubert Atkin. DI Needham was there to represent the Norfolk Police, sitting alongside a representative of the Crown Prosecution Service. Needham was to chair the meeting, they had agreed.

"So, there is only topic, really," he began. "DI Sayer has made a proposal that an artist and art teacher, Sophie Cart-wright, who is already aware of the case, should be informed of the identity of Brendan solely with the intent of helping him artistically. That latter part is not our decision, but the decision on breaking the seal of confidentiality on the case rests with the court, who will seek our input."

He nodded at the CPS representative, showing they were together on that point. He added, "I understand that DI Sayer is not here in any official capacity; in fact she is on medical leave at present and has not discussed this with anyone at the Met. But she will inform her superiors of our decision if there is any change in the status quo."

"But it is a family decision primarily, I believe," said John Olson, "That of Mr. and Mrs. Atkin. They have first to agree before this question could be posed to the court."

Needham nodded. "Of course. But the primary purpose of sealing this case and not prosecuting further Mr. and Mrs. Atkin was in the interest of keeping Brendan safe from any biker retribution. That was a CPS decision. They have to be on

board, as we require court approval that confidential information should be released to a third party. We need a legal sign-
off on that."

Brendan's dad had obviously had enough of this. He spoke
up, quite loudly for the first few words but lowered his voice as
the room focused on him.

"Catrin, I'm going to call you Catrin because Brendan
does; why do you think this is a good idea; for Brendan, I
mean?"

Catrin responded, "Because Brendan and Sophie are kind-
red souls, artistically. I have known Sophie Cartwright for a
few years now. She stopped painting original works when her
partner died; she still grieves for him, I think. But she is
talented, very talented both as a copyist and as an art teacher.
Artistically, she is best placed to understand Brendan and she
has the technical qualifications and experience to help him
develop.

"She is also trustworthy; I have thought about that aspect. I
have reasons on another case to know she can keep information confidential.

"And, above all, as much as I am impressed by Brendan's
copies, I was more impressed by the brief look I had at his bird
paintings. Smaller, less professional, in a sense, but original.
But he stopped; you can see the arrested development there.

"I can't say whether it would benefit him or not. Mrs.
Chalmers or you and your wife are better placed for that decision. I can only see him as an artist, in the short time I had
with him and know what my own art means to me."

Brendan's father was nodding, but he said nothing; he
looked at Mrs. Chalmers.

She said, 'The truth is we won't know unless we try. It
could go wrong at the first meeting or... it could develop. But
the longer we leave it, the harder it will be for Brendan to
adjust. Where he is, as Mr. and Mrs. Atkin know all too well,
there is no coming back, no miracle cure. It is about any
attenuation of his condition and his personal fulfilment along
the way. Leaving aside the security concerns, I would like to try

it at least once; to be there with them both."

Needham said, "Which brings me on to another aspect. I requested updates on the potential threat areas from DCI Coombs."

He glanced at Catrin and added, "He was promoted yesterday, I gather?"

She nodded; she had heard too.

"They are being diligent, he assures me. Nothing from overseas, from people in Europe; they seem to have moved on. This man Altman, the biker that Brian Sleaman duped, seems to have gone quiet; become a little reclusive. He went to some biker events in Denmark and Belgium this summer but other than that he is at home; just him and his daughter there now. He goes to see his son in prison regularly."

John Olson asked, "So there is no indication of any effort by him to track down Sleaman's accomplice, as he sees it?"

Needham said, "None that they can see. Nor go after DI Sayer and her colleague, as his son tried to do."

Olson looked at Catrin, his expression acknowledging that he had overlooked the fact that she was also at risk.

Catrin couldn't think of anything to say. In her experience, you never know until it happens, but saying that wouldn't help at all.

It took a further hour, once they got into the review of the waiver requirements for the Norfolk Constabulary to release information. But it came together. It would need some time for formal sign-off by the court and a secrecy agreement signed with Sophie, but Catrin was given the job, at the right time, of telling the artist the truth; to see if she still wanted to go ahead herself.

Catrin had absolutely no doubt that she would; at the core of it were two artists with common needs.

At the end Hubert Atkin said, "I take it that you are heading back today; from what Sergeant Nunn said?"

Catrin smiled. "Yes, I need to. I have some medical tests tomorrow."

He glanced at her abdomen. "Well, every best wish to you. If you were staying a few days, I was debating whether or not it would be good for Brendan to see you, to be honest. He talks about you still, as I said. It was not the best of days when you came but for him, not the worst, by far. He really enjoyed your company."

Catrin glanced at Mrs. Chalmers and said, "I had some advice on that, too. It is probably best that I don't pop in and out of his life, I was told. But it was a special time for me, that day, I assure you. He is a very talented young man. I'm glad he is getting the chance to try to regain his own art; Sophie will be good for him in that regard, I think."

~~

On the train back to London, Catrin mused about the discussions and the satisfactory outcome. She was struck by the fact that after only a short period on leave the comments by Needham about Leo Altman's status had jarred, reminding her she hadn't been thinking like a police officer at the time. It brought home a comment from Li made a long time ago.

"Police officers think differently, Catrin. They have to, I suspect, to cope with the job."

There was some truth in that, she knew. Now she had to think more like a mother-to-be; a world away from the Centurions and their interests. She leaned back into the seat headrest and looked out the window. The next think she knew was the announcement that Colchester was the next stop, in five minutes. She had drifted off.

45 CONVERGENCE

There was a sea of charcoal grey suits and white irises, bunches of them; no colours were present. As Michael Yau had not reached the age of eighty before his death no colour was to be present. Symbolically, he had not achieved a full lifespan and by tradition, therefore, colours denoting happiness could not be worn at his funeral.

Li looked at the family, the formality of mourning clothes and armbands, the sense of reserve concealing heartbreak shown by Mrs. Yau and others, including Miele. In the crowd also were men with the look of sombre respect overlaying tough-looking exteriors. Whether they were Michael Yau's friends or enemies she would never know. At a triad funeral both business differences and old or new grudges were left outside for the duration.

She and James stood with her parents and Enlai and Yolande Lin, a small group in a crowd of people who knew each other but not them. That her mother, Eu-Meh, had attended surprised her; it was not a Christian funeral and... her mother at a gathering of major figures in the world of Hong Kong crime? But she was there primarily for Daniel, Li knew. He was hard hit by the loss of this friend.

Several people spoke to her father, though; male, complete

strangers to her and her mother. Then Li realised that they must be customers of Coulter & Yarrow. If Michael had bought his suits there, it was likely that others he knew would do likewise. It had never occurred that her dad would be a tailor to triad members, but… she restrained the smile. It would be unseemly.

Suddenly across the room she saw a familiar face; a woman from her past. Emily Chang has her eyes on Li and smiled briefly as Li's face showed she had recognized her. Emily was standing close to the Yau family. Then she saw Tak and Alex standing there, similarly formally attired. Li nodded at her to confirm her recognition, unsure of the next step. The only times they had met in person had been brief; an encounter in Wales and some years after, at a lunch in the White Moon.

Chang deliberately looked across to the entrance to the washroom areas of the hall, spoke briefly to Alex and walked over. After a few moments Li excused herself from her group and did the same, unsure why other than intuition that it was the right thing to do.

As she entered the hallway she saw Alex point; he had somehow got across the room behind Emily without Li seeing him. Li found Chang in a small area with a seat, an overflow sitting area of some sort.

Neither woman sat down.

"I'm sorry for your loss," Li said, almost automatically, driven by the expression on the older woman's face.

For a moment she could see the pain there then it was gone. Chang looked at her and gave a small smile.

"You decided to keep them after all; they do suit you."

The diamond earrings bought in Manchester for Li's use in Bangor years ago.

Li responded, "No; not keep them. I would wear them today I decided, in honour, in… memory. When we last met, Mr. Yau and I agreed that they would go at some time to Catrin Sayer. He was very happy with that."

Chang nodded. She too seemed pleased with the decision,

for some reason. But she said nothing.

Li's attention was caught by Chang's own earrings; diamonds, too; a small cluster mount but equally impressive. Change caught her gaze and smiled. "No, he did not give me these specifically. He gave me everything, in a sense, including the ability to make my own way in the world. And a big final gift; the chance to do something he wanted."

She paused. "Your friend is on leave, we hear; she is going to have a baby."

Li wasn't surprised that Chang was aware; probably Miele had mentioned it. "We hope so; she has had difficulties during pregnancy in the past."

Chang nodded. "She writes well. Miele showed me the sympathy card she sent to her. I appreciated seeing it. We put it with the others; look for the painted flower afterwards."

Li kept her face impassive. She hadn't realised that Catrin would do that but, on reflection, it was obvious that she would. Chang suddenly looked at Alex, who was now holding out a slim mobile phone, already connected.

Chang nodded. "Excuse me. Somehow the timing of this is so appropriate. But I must go outside; not disturb people."

Li understood. A business call at a funeral wake was inappropriate. It would disturb the spirits. But in any business, some calls were urgent.

"I quite understand. Goodbye, Emily."

Somehow she knew it was some form of closure. With Michael gone, there would be absolutely no reason for a triad operative and a respectable lawyer to cross each other's path again.

Emily smiled, acknowledging that reality, Li thought. Then she said something that quite surprised Li. "There are a lot of sparrows in the world, Jian Li. Some of them are guardian angels. Remember that."

Alex, normally silent, added, "Or they try to be." He glanced briefly at his wristwatch, his anxiety evident.

Chang gave a quick nod to Alex and they walked away rapidly, back into the crowd, heading to the exit. A few moments later, the announcement came that Michael's coffin would be taken to the hearse now to begin the funeral procession.

Li pondered a moment on the strange message, totally unclear as to its meaning. Whatever was pulling Emily Chang away at this moment in the funeral process must itself be very important, she thought - and time critical. It clearly couldn't wait.

She saw her parents with the Lin's, suddenly each locking their hands together in the time-honoured process of Christian prayer. She headed over to be with them. Michael Yau would now begin his last journey on earth and the band outside would play particularly loudly, to drive off evil spirits along the route. It was the funeral of a very important man.

~~

In Copenhagen airport the following evening, Eric Sorenson was about to board the last flight of the day to London; a ticket bought at short notice. All he brought with him was a small bag with a few clothes and his toiletries. Nothing there could alarm the security people.

He would buy everything else he needed with cash in England; cash supplied by Leo Altman, along with the weapon he was to use.

In their discussion near Kiel, Leo had asked whether an M9 would be suitable.

"It's as good as any, assuming it is in good condition. And I want a suppressor for it."

A silencer. Leo looked a little put out, stumped by that one. "I'll see what - ."

Eric said, "It's more complicated in the UK. You could machine an adjustment for a legal one, but I don't trust those; they can screw up and hurt you. I will get a guy who will call himself Nikki to call you. He is in Finland but can get an M9 suppressor over to you, at a price."

"It's a lot of trouble for one; why Finland?"

Sorensen shrugged. "Finnish law considers a suppressor as an accessory to a firearm; they are easier to acquire there. I don't use homemade silencers."

Waiting for the flight, Eric was thinking about the next step with Leo, who was flying out of the UK for a holiday in Spain while the job went down. They would meet briefly at a hotel near Heathrow. Leo had originally said he wanted one target, may be two, either together or near each other; he would let him know at the time.

When he took the contract on the Shönberger seafront, Eric had said, "One time; one place; whoever is there at the time. I leave no witnesses. Then I am out again."

He wasn't going on a chase around London. Twenty-four to forty-eight hours, then he would be on his way home.

~~

Catrin Sayer wasn't thinking about flying or travelling far. The train ride to Norwich had shown her that she needed to be careful with her energy level these days. She didn't normally fall asleep on trains in the afternoon.

Her plans for tomorrow were simple; stay home. The day following she wanted to go over to Liz's Place to meet a regular collector who was coming into town, an American who had bought Sayer-Hughes ceramics from the early days on.

So tomorrow she would take it easy and in the afternoon, prepare a nice dinner; Chris was finishing early, he said, assuming the panic alarms didn't go off over some crisis or other. Then they would take a walk together in the evening. She would not overdo it at all.

Not far away, in Tower Hamlets, John Obi had arrived home just in time to help put the girls to bed. For some reason, Hamishi, the younger daughter, had been a holy terror after school; Kaila was worn out. When her father came home, Hamishi was good as gold as he read the bedtime story.

307

John said, when he came downstairs, "It will be a long one tomorrow as well, but I will be home as soon as I can."

Kaila sighed. "It will probably be Deeba's turn to play me up; they'll take it in shifts to wear me down."

John smiled. "Now, they are not that bad; they are good girls."

Kaila gave him a penetrating stare. "You weren't here at supper time."

46 MASSAGE

The following morning Leo drove across to Heathrow Airport in his Vauxhall Insignia very early, to a long-term parking lot. From there he took the shuttle bus to the terminal. Lyall had taken the things Leo needed with him in Spain on the flight yesterday. The small grip bag he now carried would certainly not pass muster in a security check for his flight, so on arrival at the terminal he didn't go inside, he just moved across to the bus stop for the Hotel 'Hoppa', the bus system that serviced the outlying hotels around Heathrow. For £5 and a twenty minutes' bus ride, he was dropped off at the Sheraton hotel near the M4 as the bus worked its circuit.

Leo went straight up to the third floor, to the room number Sorensen had provided. He didn't plan to stay long; then he would be on his way to Spain and the pleasure of a very special holiday.

~~

In his recovery, Jim Hughes had changed his routine. When it came to things like lunch in his local he always had been consistent; he didn't often miss dropping into the Wheatsheaf. But now his plans included various medical visits and regular

309

massage therapy for his leg. His therapist was Polish, a bright young woman with a lot of expertise and even more ability to handle the ouches and groans of her clients.

But this morning, Lina wasn't on duty; she had called in sick, he was told. A Chinese masseuse called Ying, she said, was waiting for him, wearing the same uniform of the clinic. He hadn't seen her before.

As he came in from the changing room in his robe she smiled and closed the door firmly. He heard the lock click, which was unusual; it set him on edge. In his world, small things mattered. He stopped shuffling on to the treatment table as she pulled out a mobile phone and said something into it. The she spoke to him.

"No massage just yet today, Mr. Hughes. First there is someone we want you to talk with; someone you would very much like to speak to."

Later, Jim was to smile to himself about the gormlessly naïve response that he gave.

"And who might that be, young lady?" He had wondered who it was; someone in the clinic management, perhaps.

"The man who had you worked over; the reason why you need people like Lina and me. But first you need to know why. Wait; then I will give you this phone."

She said something in Chinese into the phone and listened. After a moment she said yes in Chinese; he understood that from the movies.

As she kept listening she explained to him. "Leo Altman was warned not to go after the police officers that his son tried to kill. We sent Jerry Prowse from New York to make it abundantly clear. Now Leo is in a hotel room with our people and Eric Sorensen. Sorensen and Altman were planning to eliminate one or other of those police officers. Do you know Prowse?"

Jimmy was absorbing it all, working out who 'we' were; Chinese organized crime of some sort.

"Of him - a Yank, an Outlaw - he was over here for a bit, rode with the Centurions. Never met him."

She waited, listening for about a further three minutes, a long time for nothing to happen, Jim thought. But his mind was now on Leo Altman and the fact that this woman was Chinese.

She said yes again, pressed a button on the phone and then handed it to Jim. He looked at the screen, at a video image on Skype of an over-bright window somewhere, facing out of the room as a blurry shadow moved into frame, stopped and the image stabilized.

It was Leo Altman.

~~

Leo had regained consciousness sitting in the armchair in Eric Sorensen's hotel room. The last thing he recalled was Sorensen going to open the door to tell the maid who knocked that he didn't want the room cleaned right now; he wasn't to be disturbed.

As his vision cleared and he became aware of his surroundings he saw Eric sitting in a chair by the small table. He appeared to be in pain, supporting his wrist with his other hand. It was broken or badly sprained, Leo concluded.

The three other men in the room were Asian. While none of them were the size of Leo or Eric, his first thought of making a fight of it was stopped in its tracks. His legs had been tied together at the ankles with a silk scarf. If he stood, he would fall.

No one said anything for a moment, so Leo asked, "What the hell do you want?"

Leo and Eric had reacted as soon as the men rushed through the door. One had used a stun gun on him, he remembered, as the other two took on Sorensen. The struggle was short and anything but sweet and his shoulder still hurt like crazy where the probes had been applied.

Being Asians, Leo thought, this must relate to the advice Jerry had given him, but someone needed to say something.

Eric said, "They don't say much."

Leo replied, "I need the bathroom."

"They'll understand that. But don't get smart."

He held up his damaged arm in his good one.

When he returned from the bathroom, Eric was now in the armchair. Leo was escorted to the small table and placed on a chair that had been moved over from the desk. His legs were not retied, though, this time; not yet at least.

One of the men in the room was now talking on a mobile.

On the table was a small laptop computer facing him and on the screen was the upper half of Jimmy Hughes in a white bathrobe watching Leo as he sat down.

Leo said, "So these people are yours. Payback time."

Hughes replied, "Not mine, no; I don't know who is there. I'm just an invited guest; as surprised myself as you look. I am supposed to be having a massage for the damage to my leg that Skelly gave me. I still can't ride, you bastard."

Leo saw a young Chinese woman's head appear over the shoulder of Jim Hughes slightly behind him.

She said, "They were just about to discuss which people Leo wanted Sorensen to kill, we understand."

Leo watched the Hells Angel absorb the situation, understanding what was happening. The message he had received from Jerry Prowse months ago had been on the mark. He wondered how far these people were going to go. Another warning or what? Elimination, he had been told.

Hughes said, "Sorensen, are you listening, too? Has Leo told you the target? Just a yes or a no will do?"

The Dane's deep voice came from across the room. "Not specifically, no. But it isn't Angels or any other MC. None of yours. Now, if you are playing games with us just get on with it, you Welsh bastard. It's boring sitting here with these Chinks hanging over me."

His arm may be damaged but he wasn't sounding cowed.

Hughes said simply, "It's not my show." He sat back and waited. It was getting interesting, better than his regular massage session.

One of the Chinese men present reached into the bag that Leo had brought to the room and pulled out the Beretta. He removed the magazine and cleared the chamber then handed it nonchalantly to Eric Sorensen, to his damaged right hand.

It must be sprained, thought Leo, abstractly.

It was so natural a move Eric accepted it before he realized why the man was wearing gloves; then he clued in as the weapon was lifted away again. But it was too late; his prints were on the weapon, in a pattern consistent with using it. The man took the gun away and gouged it into Eric's left palm, oblivious to the curse and short cry of pain from the big Dane. But now Eric's DNA and blood type were on the weapon, as if he had scraped his hand on the raised rear sight.

Eric said matter-of-factly, "They are setting me up to take this one for you, I think, Leo. Then they will shove it under my chin. Do we do remorse?"

Leo just looked at him, shaking his head. Bikers were more likely to blow their own brains out for fatigue or boredom than remorse.

The Chinese man proved Sorensen wrong. Placing the empty gun on the bed he took from his own pocket Eric's mobile and dialed a number on it. When it answered, he spoke first in Danish and then in English. What Leo caught was the last bit.

"Mr. Sorensen will not complete his assignment. In fact, he will need to go somewhere other than the UK or Denmark, we suspect. Talk to him."

He put the phone on speaker, but didn't give it to him, just held it close.

Then it was a Danish conversation with the Asian intently following. It was the Danish end that closed the call.

Eric said, "I have to go, right now; sorry, Leo. Wind in your hair, man."

Leo said nothing back. He knew his fate now. Within seconds, Eric and one of the Chinese men were out of the door. The killer that Leo had contracted was now carrying his small travel bag in his good arm, the other hanging down by his side. For a fleeting moment, Leo hoped that Eric would take down the smaller Asian and they would make a go of it. But the slope of the man's shoulders gave it away. The Dane was gone.

Leo looked at the computer screen. "Catch that, Hughes?"

"Enough, yes. You didn't listen. They sent Jerry Prowse all the way from New York to see you, I just heard, and you didn't listen to your own. I know why, it's in our blood not to comply, but I still don't know the reason. You had me beaten so badly I had to have my skull opened up to ease the pressure and I still can't walk properly.

"But other than your misunderstanding of my meeting with the two coppers from the Met, I don't know the real reason for all this; why you are still hanging on to it. Which one of them was the target? You couldn't count on both, could you? They don't spend the day driving round the M25 together."

Leo looked at the screen and sneered. "Does it matter now?"

Jimmy just looked at him. "Well, you sure as hell won't get much longer to tell anyone else, will you? You never heard of confession?"

That got to Leo, he saw, across the link. Leo suppressed a small smile, extraordinary under the circumstances, as if in defeat he had found a small victory.

He said softly, "Your friend, the Welsh bitch; or her husband. If I couldn't get her, she would learn what it was like to lose a spouse that fast. The black I was saving for later, a lot later, for myself, at the right time."

His tone had turned defiant at the end; his expression now angry at Jim, angry at these men with him. He kept on talking.

"That bitch and her partner invaded my home. She insisted that the black copper stay, even when Renée told him to leave. She as good as told me I was a fool for buying a fake, right there, in front of my family. Then the Germans were after me, wanting money back. And I thought you were feeding her

314

information, that's why. You weren't; Coombs said and you say, and I will buy that."

He took a deep breath and let it out.

"At the club during the raid she was running the show. I saw that. When Coombs baited Skelly it was her who sent the signal to one of the tactical people to look out for him. So she arranged all that shit there just to make me look small in front of my own club. And they all took it; hook, line and sinker. Kicking me out. Me!"

Hughes responded slowly. "They kicked you out as president because you misled them, Leo; that was what I heard. And Sayer probably just spotted the danger. I know what Skelly's like when he goes wild, don't I?"

He looked at the man on the other end of the link. They both knew they were done. Hughes tried to find something else to say, a token gesture; he could see what Leo was thinking and probably so could the men with him.

He said more softly, "One of mine said Stevie is holding his own, toughening up in there. Who knows, he may join your club in time, or even mine."

Leo laughed quietly, the bitterness showing. "My God, my son an Angel; no way... That's it, you bastard. I am done now."

Jim saw Leo's shoulder move as he reached over to the keyboard to close the call. He said, "I guess so. Adios, Altman."

Jim Hughes had heard what he wanted. As Eric Sorensen said, bikers don't do remorse. The link was closed.

Leo stared at the computer screen, taking in the final words. Adios; goodbye. Or ADIOS, a motto of the Outlaws but an acronym; 'Angels Die in Outlaw States'. Jim Hughes probably wanted him to think on it, part of the irony. It brought to mind the other Outlaw motto; God Forgives, Outlaws Don't. Leo was a Centurion; he had never become an Outlaw, but he had lived that way and now he was going to end it in the same fashion.

In the clinic, Hughes had seen the tension building in Leo Altman, knowing he was going to go down fighting if he was to go down at all; the biker way. Die as you live, control what you can and never give in. He simply held the mobile phone out to the masseuse.

"Wales one; England nil, I think," he muttered, more to himself, realising how close a call Sayer must have had. These Chinese were on top of things, but it could easily have gone completely wrong. More 'China one, England nil', was his afterthought.

Ying took if from him, her expression disdainful of the football analogy. This was work and she was a professional. She made sure the connection was closed and said, "You had better lie down. Angels don't talk to Outlaws, we know, but you are going to make another exception. You may well be getting a call from this man Prowse, if he wants confirmation after we talk to him. If so, when he asks, you confirm that Leo Altman was going after both the police officers and possibly the Welsh one's husband; that's all you have to do. He'll believe another patch; even an Angel."

For a moment, as she started to talk and he lay back on the table, he thought she was being solicitous about the shock of the event he had just participated in. But he realised that this group was using him, as well as giving him the satisfaction of seeing Leo's fate. Then he saw her getting ready, washing her hands; she was a massage therapist after all, it appeared.

"Lina will be here next time," she said.

In the Sheraton hotel room one of the men walked around the table; to pick up the laptop, Leo thought, from the way his right arm was reaching out.

Leo rehearsed his move in his mind; when the man was really close, it would be an elbow to his groin and then he would jump up, a back head butt to the chin. He would create hell with as much noise as possible and take on both of them, no matter what; a fighting chance. Timing was everything.

But as the right hand touched the computer, Leo suddenly

felt the air move by his neck. The man's left hand was at the other side of his head, he realised. Leo felt the prick of a needle and after that he had no time to react at all. It had been a feint; the right arm and hand were now wrapped tightly around his head, a steel band restraint. The second man had swiftly crossed the room to immobilize each of Leo's wrists. The biker had placed both hands on the table to provide purchase for his own action, so they were easy to trap.

These Chinese were a lot faster and stronger than he was, he realised belatedly. As the injection took effect and he felt the initial pleasure 'rush' and the growing heaviness in his limbs, his final thoughts were not of family but of the Welsh woman, Sayer. She had won.

47 COCKTAIL

The call to Catrin came in from DCI Wetherby. They hadn't really spoken much outside the odd work issue since she went on leave so his solicitousness about her current state of health raised her antennae.

"Is something wrong, sir?"

"No, but I would like to pop round, if I could, this afternoon? Would that be possible? Just some updates we should cover."

She wondered why he was trying to tiptoe through the tulips. She told him that would be fine.

When she opened the door, Wetherby was accompanied by DCI Coombs; so it was actually something that did affect her, she thought, not an issue of filling in performance reviews or other forms.

She accepted their compliments on her apparent good health and settled them down offering tea or soft drinks, which they accepted. She put the kettle on, waiting for the reason for the visit to unfold.

Wetherby got to the point. "There is some news; not that it affects us workwise. And I don't want to create any stress for you but we thought you should know. The Centurions case has taken a bad turn, in a sense. A death. We informed DC Obi this morning."

There was a pause. Wetherby looked at Greg Coombs, who said, "Leo Altman was murdered early this morning in an airport hotel near Heathrow. We are looking for a suspect, a Dane."

"Are you OK?" interrupted Wetherby.

She nodded.

Coombs went on. "He's a biker called Eric Sorensen, from Denmark. Sorensen is thought by the French to take on contracts; a killer for hire. From Leo's phone it appears that he and Leo were working together. A gun was found at the scene; we just had confirmation as we got here that it has Sorensen's prints on it so we suspect he was in the UK to take on a contract; he flew in late yesterday evening."

Coombs paused, letting her absorb it a moment then he continued. "The gun was local. The bag was Leo's and the traces inside show it carried the weapon. Also inside it was a suppressor. Leo probably brought them to the hotel for Sorensen to use, we think."

Catrin said, "Let me guess; a Beretta M9, same model as Stephen Altman used and as we found at the club?"

Coombs said, "You've got it; that accounts for three of the four stolen in Germany."

He went on, "Leo was due to join Renata and this prospect Lyall Beddows in Spain on holiday, to fly out this morning. A perfect alibi, perhaps. It appears that Sorensen flew to Spain instead, mid-morning. Where he is now, we don't know; we've been on to the authorities over there. But we were looking for the Dane as the news came in, anyway."

Catrin waited.

"Hilary had picked up some time ago that Sorensen and Leo had been at the same bike festival in North Germany. She had brought it to me and we put him on a travel watch list. The daily list this morning flagged it, putting him as arriving at the hotel late last night. Two of mine were on their way to see him, to let him know we were watching him and throw him off whatever he had in mind when the call came in. Someone beat us to it."

Catrin was impressed. "They were seen planning something at this festival?"

Coombs shook his head. "No, ironically. Hilary picked up they were ignoring each other, when she knew they had been in contact before. 'The dog that didn't bark in the night' sort of thing. I think she is really watching out for you after my screw-up previously."

Catrin didn't say anything, just looked away, thoughtful for a moment. "I'll call her and thank her. And thanks for letting me know that."

Wetherby's spoke up again, his voice changed as his throat tightened a little. "There is a chance, as DCI Coombs infers, that the targets could have been DC Obi or yourself. In that world, though, one never knows. The homicide team is currently searching Altman's phone and home to see if that sheds any light.

"But I don't want you stressed. We have no evidence that this scenario was the case, just speculation. It could also be that Brendan Atkin was the target, or it could be an entirely different person who had crossed Altman's path, some element of business that backfired.

"The last thing you need is to worry about is this; but Obi was concerned that you would hear the news on TV or something. So we came over."

Catrin said nothing for a moment, then asked, "The gun at the scene - was it used to kill him, can I ask?"

Coombs said quickly, "No, funnily enough; it wasn't the murder weapon. That was an injection in the neck; a heroin cocktail overdose. Pathology is still working out the mixture involved but heroin was there at a lethal level. We think the perpetrator wanted no noise. It was the room cleaner who found Altman. She went in with her supervisor after they received no answer on knocking."

I have a guardian angel, Catrin thought; not Hilary Eaton,

as Coombs inferred, but one I can never talk about.

She asked, "And CCTV at the hotel?"

"Coincidentally, we don't think, the recording across their entire hotel system has a blank spot for two hours early today. We are checking what we can from the rest and the reservations lists and witnesses there. But it is a Heathrow hotel. Most of last night's guests are in different countries by now or on their way back home to some other part of the UK. It will take time and won't be too productive, I think."

He sounded relieved to have conveyed the news. "How are you doing, handling it?"

For a moment, Coombs thought, Sayer looked lost; sad, it seemed. Then she brightened and she focused on Wetherby.

"A bit of a shock but… its nothing to do with us, though, as you said. I am glad we are out of that case. And thank you for dealing with it this way, coming round to see me; I do appreciate it."

Wetherby said, "That's the way, Catrin; don't let it play on your mind. You have someone far more important to think about now, don't you?"

Indeed I do, sir."

"We miss you in the office but all is well. Obi seems to be really serious about his new role, you will be glad to hear."

She smiled. "He calls me. I know. I'm glad you went along with it."

The conversation turned to her team and the Met in general, but Catrin could tell that they wanted to get away; Coombs obviously needed to get back on the case. Belatedly, Catrin realised that she hadn't complimented him on his promotion and when she did so, he was candid.

"I think a lot of it was to do with you; the Centurions raid. It made a mark with people up the chain, not just the bikers. I told Commander Moore as much, as well. So thank you."

"And Karen, what was her reaction?"

He smiled. "She paused, that mannerism of hers, with the slight turn of her head. Then she said, 'Glad to see that you recognize it. But you got it on your own merits'. You know how she is, always correcting things. I got the impression you are still in her sights, though."

Catrin said nothing. A new baby blanket was in the bedroom sent from Karen Moore, with a note to that effect.

It was only after her colleagues left, as she sat thinking about it, that she realised she really was not disturbed by Leo Altman's death. It was a relief, in fact; in the same way years ago that Nam Wu's death had lifted her spirits. That Yau's people did it, she was quite sure. The choice of a lethal injection was no coincidence. She had heard from the Malaysian police sometime after Nam Wu's death was finally confirmed of a rumour that he had died the same way.

She was sure that Li, who had instigated Michael Yau to take some action against Wu, knew that too, but she couldn't ask. Li was bound to secrecy on the matter.

If it was related to her and John being the targets, then Michael Yau had stayed true to the goal he had set himself after the Malaysian incident and Li's prompting. He had carried through on it not only in life but somehow from the grave, through his people. While it surprised her, it didn't shock her, somehow. And if it wasn't her and John in Leo's sights, it was nothing to do with her, as she said.

She touched her stomach, thinking of the child inside and the challenge they had ahead together. The revelation of Altman still seeking revenge made her realise that, despite being a police officer, there were some people the world was better off without.

She decided to talk to Jian Li and sent her a cryptic email. "Time to walk down Glanrafon Hill again." It was their code for matters to do with Michael Yau and her links to him. Catrin wanted to see if Li knew anything about this.

~~

Li said, "When I saw Michael for the last time, I told him about your miscarriage and that you had recently had a run-in with bikers; they had gone after you. He asked how you were doing. That was the extent of it. Why?"

Catrin said, "The father of the man who tried to kill John Obi and myself was found murdered in a hotel room. It was a professional job."

"You think Michael Yau arranged this?"

"I think so. He was killed with an injection of heroin."

On their Skype connection Li's face showed her surprise and concern and with it, her recognition of the significance of the method used. Catrin concluded that her friend did know about that aspect of Nam Wu's death, too.

Li suddenly asked, "When did it happen?"

"Early yesterday morning, our time. They think the person who was in the room with Altman at the time he was killed is now in Europe somewhere; he flew in from Denmark to Heathrow the day before. He is thought to be a killer for hire and Altman had brought him in for a job. Instead, Altman was killed."

Li thought it through rapidly, allowing for time zone differences. The man flying in from Denmark could have made his travel reservations at any time, she thought, but probably late on, at short notice. The Four Square triad focused on information theft and could monitor such things. It fitted in roughly with the events around Michael's funeral, perhaps; some development in monitoring these people that would cause Emily's remark of 'how appropriate it was' that Michael's protégé was being asked to make some decision at the time she was speaking to Li.

She may be making too much of it, she realised, but it was a possibility. Then the strange comment came back to mind. *"There are a lot of sparrows in the world, Jian Li. Some of them are guardian angels. Remember that."* She didn't follow the sparrow symbolism other than sparrows were everywhere. But now she was absolutely sure. And she knew what she must do.

She smiled at Catrin. "I think I will pop over to London, to see you and everyone, see if Miele wants to come over with me."

Catrin shot back, "Now, don't go complicating this. Glan-rafon rules, remember?"

Li said impudently, "Share what?"

That both Li and Miele Yau had wealth enough to hop on a plane to London, and not in economy seating either, was well understood by Catrin; it was the reason for the trip she worried about.

"I'm not to get stressed, remember that. So whatever you are up to - ."

"Nothing stressful at all, just a pleasant get-together. That's all. You should be pleased," interjected her friend.

Catrin smiled. "I am!!"

48 DINNER SERVICE

Catrin paid no attention as the shop door opened again and yet another customer came into The Cwmbran Kiln. Sitting in the workshop at the back, she was engrossed with her own design. Melanie was in the shop while the regular sales assistant was out on her lunch break and Jean was busy with Lili.

Jean glanced at the customer, a man who stood there resting heavily on a walking stick looking at her, smiling. A well-dressed woman was by his side.

"Well, who would have thought?" exclaimed Jean, getting up then walking through to the shop carrying her daughter. "Jim Hughes; I would recognize you anywhere."

Hughes said, "And you, too. This is my wife, Toni. Toni, this is Jean, our Euan's first girlfriend."

As Jean introduced Melanie she added, "And you didn't just drop in. What brings you here?"

Toni said, "To buy a dinner service, I think; for one thing."

"Oh, good," said Melanie. "Any friends of Jean are welcome; moreso if they want to buy!"

Catrin finished what she was doing and stood up too, putting down the brush she had just cleaned after use.

"Hi, Jim, Toni," was all she said, neutrally.

Hughes replied, "Hello Catrin; you are the other thing that brought me here, but all in good time. No rush."

"How's your mum and the family?" asked Jean, missing the context; but Melanie didn't. She gave Catrin a look which said, "What's up?"

Catrin shook her head slightly. "We know each other. And I met Toni a while ago, at the hospital where Jim was being treated after his injury."

Toni Hughes came over to her and held out her hand. "You were right. Thank you. It was the better way."

She turned to face Jean and Melanie. "Your police officer friend here got the two who beat up Jim to turn themselves in before Jim's friends gave them back what they did to him. It's like that."

She wasn't hiding it, she had decided.

Catrin took her hand and shook it gently; a peace of sorts, but she said nothing. Melanie and Jean looked at each other. Melanie wrinkled her nose a little. "Not her; not now. You must have made a mistake. She's a boring backroom copper on leave, she tells us, leading a quiet life. She wouldn't mix it with tough bikers."

She pointed to the two rings on Jim's right hand. "I've seen them before."

Jean gave her a look, showing her surprise. "Like where?"

Melanie replied, "Like before I met you. What bike do you have?"

She was sounding enthusiastic.

He smiled. "A Harley."

She said, "Yes, obviously. But which one? A Sportster; the Iron?"

He laughed. "No, not now. I had one or two in my time, though, Sportsters; now I have a Road King, a 2009 model. I have Toni on the back now."

Jean was looking at her partner in amazement.

He continued, "But not that I am riding, or will be for a while yet. But one day, I plan to again, when the leg strengthens. But I'd like to talk with Catrin, if I could, while Toni chooses what she wants."

He nodded at a bench in the open space outside in the enclosed market space.

Melanie said, "Well, come back in afterwards, see our baby and tell me more about your bikes."

Catrin followed him out, sensing the stiffness in the man was more than the injury to his leg. A Hells Angel speaking to a police officer voluntarily was unusual, to say the least. She was not going to make it any easier for him, though. He wouldn't appreciate mollycoddling, anyway. They were away from the social niceties of the Kiln now.

"My mother sends her regards - and her thanks. As does Donna," he said at last.

She nodded. "Tell them hello from me when you see them."

He looked unsure what to say next. He was examining her, trying to work out how to start, she thought.

"A 'boring backroom copper'? How did you get the scar?" he said suddenly, a quick movement, pointing with his finger then returning his hand to his thigh.

"An arrest that went wrong in Scotland. One of those things that come out of the blue."

She in turn parodied his pointing movement, her finger momentarily pointing at his leg. He nodded, accepting the comparison.

"Donna says you've had a couple of run-ins like that, had your mum worried stiff at times."

He went on quickly, "Me; I have my mum worried all the time, I know."

Catrin said nothing. From her encounter with Jim's mother at the hospital, while she thought the latter remark to be true, she had seen also that the woman was strong; it was Jim's life, not hers, she had said. She wondered where this was going, why this man was interested in her, bringing her outside for this stilted conversation.

"Spit it out; what do you want, really?" she said finally,

looking directly into his eyes.

"Are you involved with any Chinese at all?"

It was out there now, the real reason for his visit; looking at each other, they both could tell that.

It had been on his mind constantly since seeing Leo Altman get his final conversation in this life - with him, of all people. If Catrin Sayer was bent, had links to a Chinese gang, it intrigued him - ambivalently, it turned out. Part of him saw that it was open to exploitation; there were other police officers that one percenter clubs leaned on so she wouldn't be the first. They didn't last; it always turned ugly or painful. But her links to home and particularly to his aunt through her mother was the other part of it; he wasn't comfortable with the idea of pulling her down.

She looked away, caught suddenly by the directness and the unexpected nature of the question. What did this biker, this organized crime figure, know? If so, how?

She suddenly had a glimpse of a possible reason for his strange question. She decided not to ask the question that had come to mind; something along the lines 'why the hell was he asking'?

Instead, she replied deliberately, slowly; measuring her response carefully.

"It's none of your business, is it? But I'll tell you, anyway; make it explicitly clear. I have a very good friend in Hong Kong. I met her in Wales. Her brother was killed there during a port stop of his cruise ship; he was a crew member. I was part of the investigation team and our friendship grew from that. That's all."

She paused, reading his face now. "They say that a Hells Angel will die for a brother; take a bullet or a beating if need be. Is that true?"

Hughes nodded. "For a brother; yes. Any of us; it's the way we live. The bonds are that strong."

Catrin said, "Well, my friendship with the person in Hong Kong is something akin to that. And to answer your implied question; no, I have no contact with any Chinese people in your world, if that's what you really mean. I'm clean. And so is my friend in Hong Kong."

Not on the take, she inferred, her eyes now staring him out until he was the one to look away. Her expression had made it clear that if she saw herself as clean, she saw him as dirty, contaminated,.

She decided to change the subject. "So Skelton and Furneaux got prison time, I saw."

He replied, "Not enough. But you heard about Leo, obviously?" he asked, in return.

Catrin said, "Yes; they let me know."

"I got interviewed, as did Keith Parry and others in my chapter about our whereabouts. I was having treatment on my knee that morning in Tooting. It's understandable but aggravating; it wasn't us. We held by our agreement with you, to let the law handle it. We haven't back-tracked on that with any of the Centurions."

Catrin nodded. "I'm on leave. It's my third attempt to stay pregnant through to full term. So I am not really informed about any developments on that case."

He looked at her then down at the floor. "As a rule, Angels look after each other and don't get involved with others; with their business, their issues or their people. A Bandido goes after an Outlaw is their business, not ours. And so on. It's our code."

Catrin said, "But you helped Brian Sleaman; he wasn't one of yours - but I don't know where you are going with all this."

He had suddenly decided to tell her that he was glad she wasn't involved with triads or Chinese gangs, or his world. But he couldn't do that now. There was something about her that made him realise that the subject of Chinese links was a no-go area for her. And it wasn't what Angels did, anyway.

Instead, he said, "Thank you for the Centurions visit. Everyone says it was Coombs, but Toni told me that the idea was yours. I didn't need this -"

He looked down at his damaged knee.

"But I don't need my people doing time, either."

"And it stays that way, Jim; that was the deal. DCI Coombs led it, did what was necessary to get Skelton and Furneaux to turn themselves in. She and Parry promised; that's my expectation from you, too. Your wife is waving."

He looked across from the bench to the window of the pottery. She was at the door; waggling a credit card at him as she opened it. "Hopefully she saw what she wants."

Even if, he thought, he had only partially resolved his own question about Catrin Sayer. But he was now sure that she was linked somehow to the people who killed Altman yet equally convinced that she was a straight copper. He would take it no further.

Hughes stood up with difficulty, pressing hard on the cane, calling across to the doorway to his wife. "Found anything that works?"

Toni replied, "Yes, and I'm still spending, my lovely; I've seen something else. Come and see."

He moved forward in a limping gait but stopped and turned to Catrin. "Good luck. Smooth sailing with the rest of the pregnancy. I don't think anyone from my world will be troubling you again, will they? Steve is in gaol, Leo dead."

She nodded. "I really hope not."

There was something odd about the whole discussion, Catrin thought, that he was trying to find out if she was linked to Chinese criminal elements. His last comment had been revealing; that he should refer to her safety now, specifically. Then she thought back to his earlier comment about his massage appointment. It sounded as if it was very close to the time of Altman's death. But the Met had made no reference at all to the time of death; they never did in public releases. They would only comment on the time of discovery of the body, if they gave any timing at all. And in his interview, they would bracket the whole period around the death; it was standard practice.

Her mind started to work out the possibilities and - she

stopped. She didn't want to go there. She wasn't working, wasn't on the case; or any case, at present.

Hughes suddenly looked less serious, breaking into a smile. "Now I get to have a conversation about bikes, I think. I didn't expect that - it's a bonus."

One visit to the Kiln, Catrin thought; that's it. Despite Melanie's surprise enthusiasm for Harleys, no more. Hells Angels don't mix with others, particularly not coppers. She didn't want to spend any more time with him and, if need be, she would tell him that.

She followed Hughes into the shop and within moments she was lost in cuddling and playing with Lili as the others talked away about bikes and families while the purchases were wrapped and boxed. Jim Hughes was all smiles now. She could tell Melanie was vamping it a bit, winding up Jean with her latent knowledge of Harley-Davidson motorcycles that had re-surfaced.

It all went well but, notably, Jean did not invite the Hughes couple to stay for refreshments or give them any opportunity to linger. The goodbyes were friendly enough but when they were alone Jean gave Melanie one of her stares.

"Just making conversation, my lovely," parried Melanie, echoing Toni's term of endearment accurately. She was already reading her partner's expression and was on the defensive.

Jean looked across at Catrin, concerned. "OK?"

Catrin smiled. "Yes, but better now."

Jean nodded. "Me too. I don't want Jim Hughes around Lili. He's not the person I remember from when I went out with Euan. Money to burn, the pair of them and we made two good sales but there is something... hard and brazen about it all. His mother must wonder what happened to him."

Catrin said, "He's a Hells Angel, that's what happened."

Jean replied firmly, "Then I am even happier that you turned down that promotion. How's Myfy?"

Myfy; Myfanwy; Jean's special name for Catrin's baby.

Catrin smiled again. "Doing OK, she tells me. If you take

Lili, I'll make some tea."

Things were getting back to normal again in the Kiln, she felt, with Jim Hughes gone.

49 EARRINGS

It was two weeks after the call with Li that Catrin found out what the 'pleasant get-together' was really about, with the two women from Hong Kong sitting across from her, Miele holding out the gift.

On opening the outer packaging, Catrin found a handmade ceramic bowl with a lid, carefully wrapped. It delighted her, as intuitively she knew it would have been designed and made by Miele. And it was startling in its simplicity and workmanship. The potter who had spent a year in London had developed significantly in the time since she had returned home.

"It's wonderful. You really have - ."

Miele interrupted her. "Look inside."

Catrin took the lid off and saw a small square note, a piece of stiff paper with Chinese characters and at the end, the word 'Catrin'. As she removed the paper to look at it more closely, she saw the sparkle.

She said, "Oh, my ..."

Set on a fitted black velvet mount were two earrings; beautiful, expensive hoops of diamonds set in white gold. Catrin looked at Li.

"The last time I saw these was in Colwyn Bay. You were wearing them - for less than half an hour, it turned out."

Catrin said to Miele, "I love the bowl and will treasure it; and the earrings are beautiful, but I can't keep them. There are rules. I don't even know whether Enlai Lin or your grandfather bought these; but they should be Li's. Or yours, if they were your grandfather's."

Li smiled. "Yes, these are the earrings I asked Mr. Lin to borrow for me. He rented them, I thought, from Mappin & Webb in Manchester. I had no idea that Michael bought them. All I knew, as I sat across from the woman who caused my brother's death, was that she was a jewellery hound and she thought I was a student.

"When I met with Michael before he died, we talked about that and things I still can't talk to you about. But he also presented me with the earrings - in a case, not the bowl. I told him I couldn't accept them; they brought back the memory of that interview room, of sitting across from Lynn Williams; but I saw then exactly what he needed to do; to give them to you."

Her voice changed, controlling her emotions. "It's *guanxi*, Catrin, we have talked about that. You and me; Enlai, my dad and Michael; Jean and Melanie - and now Miele - we are all linked; in friendship, in support. Michael's gift to my dad was the bathhouse booking for him and Enlai, in perpetuity; God knows how much that costs; it can't be cheap these days but it's where the men talk about their lost sons. Dad said it would be good for his leg to keep doing it but I think it is good for his heart. Michael knew that."

"So these are yours, really?" Catrin said, trying to finesse her rejection of them delicately back into play.

"No," said Li, firmly. "Mr. Yau's gift to me was entirely different. You know what that was; one that was on-going, I now discover."

She pressed on. "Catrin, it's not a gift from Michael Yau; accepting these will be a gift to him, to his memory; a gift of friendship to a man who thought well of you and, in all honesty, helped you too; in a big way, you know that. You should have seen his face when I suggested it. Mr. Inscrutable was the happiest I have ever seen him; he had already thought of it himself. So, we are the messenger really, for him, but also for Miele and me.

"The bowl and its contents are a package; they are one present, from the three of us. To anyone else they are clearly a gift from Miele, for all the help you have given her. Keep or return them, as you wish; you will always be our friend, no matter what; we won't sulk. There is no stress in this; don't think of it that way; we aren't here for that. What do you want to do?"

Catrin said, "The note; what does it say, before Catrin?"

Miele responded, speaking very softly, "It says, 'to someone I can never repay enough; a token of my appreciation'; it is my writing but Grandfather told me what to write. And it is my message, too; I learned so much from you."

Catrin paused a moment and looked away into the distance, to something or somewhere that only she could see. The two visitors just sat it out, waiting for the response.

After a long silence, Catrin said, "I am quite literally knocked sideways by this. I can't thank you enough, either of you. Or Michael."

Her voice had taken on that strangled quality; tears or laughter were not far away.

"I will wear them at one of Neville Coltrane's fancy art galas; they would be just the thing there. And I will treasure them always. Both parts of the present. Thank you, both of you, for the gift - and your persistence in giving it."

Miele let out a big sigh, then looked surprised; she hadn't realised she was holding her breath.

Li said, "Well, I'm glad that's settled. She can be so difficult at times, don't you think, Miele?"

Miele just smiled, happy that her grandfather's wish had been fulfilled and that Li's idea for her to make the bowl had contributed to it. She said softly, "They will make a nice family heirloom, I hope. Something you can pass on to your daughter a long time in the future."

Later that evening after Li and Miele left for their hotel, as Catrin examined the bowl and tried the earrings yet again, Chris was perusing the paperwork Li had left behind; the proof of ownership. He said, "The documentation shows that they were originally bought in the UK so were exempt from import duty, but… do you know how much these things are worth, or were worth ten years ago?"

Catrin smiled. "I am an Art and Antiques expert, remember? That includes jewellery. I haven't looked at those papers yet, but I can guess."

"Go on then. Pick a figure."

Catrin walked over to give him a hug, shaking her head. "They are worth friendship. And that is priceless."

And it was true for her, she knew. Earlier she had looked at Li across the room, then into the distance, recalling the days back in Bangor when they first met. In her mind was the walk down Glanrafon Hill together when Michael Yau's name had first been mentioned to her, to explain the strange developments in the search for Li's brother. The recent conversation with Jim Hughes at the Kiln had also flooded back. 'I'm clean', she had told him; not in the pay of organized crime.

But she was, in a sense, in debt to a dead Triad member.

Michael Yau hadn't asked anything of her, hadn't at any time given her the impression of pulling her into his world or expecting any payback; his actions had been driven by gratitude. In the moments before she accepted the gift she had finally realised it was not a triad matter at all for her; it was *guanxi*, it was friendship.

"You will always be our friend, no matter what," Li had said. Always will be my friend, she meant, although she knew Miele held her in similar regard.

She hugged her husband, feeling the presence of three people in the room. She was at peace.

EPILOGUE. THORNHAM

The Opel came to a halt in the farmyard and Hubert saw a slim, middle-aged woman get out, open the rear door and pull out a small backpack and a large portfolio case. By then he had the front door open and was standing on the step. Joanne had gone to the kitchen to put the kettle on and check on her baking.

"Nice to meet you in person. A voice on the phone is not the same, is it?"

She smiled. "Well, I am Sophie. I found my way OK. I should use one of these satnav map things, I suppose. Can't be bothered. It's cooler up here than Suffolk."

Hubert smiled. He liked her already. "It's the wind; winter is on the way. Those satnav contraptions? Me neither. Playing around with those bloody things causes accidents."

She was looking into the house as she entered; Hubert could understand why. "Brendan is in his studio; it's the cottage at the back. He'll be over; he will have heard the car."

Joanne came forward with her hand out. "I'm Joanne, Brendan's mum."

As Sophie put down her things Brendan Atkin came in through the back door of the farmhouse, smiling. For a moment he said nothing and neither did Sophie Cartwright, as they assessed each other.

Brendan said, "Hi, you are Sophie. How is Catrin?"

He moved forward, his arm and hand outstretched formally, boyishly. Sophie smiled and shook hands, fitting in with his formal gesture and approach. "She's fine, I think. She was the last time we talked."

Catrin was doing well in late pregnancy, but had not gone back to work, she had heard.

Brendan said, "She was only here for a day. She's a police officer as well."

As well as what, wondered Sophie; does he think I am, too? She let that one go.

"Yes, she is," she replied, "but she is taking some time off at present."

"Doing her art, her pottery," said Brendan, with certainty.

Then he looked at his mother. "Can Sophie and I have our tea in the studio, so we can paint?"

He spoke to Sophie. "Mrs. Chalmers is over there already; she wants to watch."

Brendan had looked Sophie Cartwright up on-line. He knew an artist wouldn't want to waste time on small talk.

"It's good, but not as good as mine," he said some time later, having examined close up one of the copies of a painting Sophie had brought with her. She had already seen a number of his paintings in the studio.

Sophie replied, "It is not as accurate in the extreme detail as your copy of it, Brendan, that's true. But, I have been looking at your paintings for a while now. I can see how it is getting harder for you. You are almost down to brush hair linewidth in places."

He nodded, pleased that she had seen this. "Yes; it is. And I can't concentrate as long. Can I see the second painting now?"

"No, we have an agreement, right? We just talked about it. First I want to show you something else."

He smiled. "You sound a bit like Catrin."

I'll take that as a compliment she thought.

She pulled out her watercolour set and a pad of rough texture paper. He watched her set up and, as she mixed the individual pools of indigo and lemon yellow he said, "I can't do that; I can't control it."

She smiled and said, "Just watch."

Her first 'wet-into-wet' run was flowing nicely. Brendan looked intensely at the paper, seeing the colours mix and the web of blue tendrils enter the yellow, the boundaries blurring into a hazy edgeless pale green.

"What's happening?" she asked.

He answered, "The texture is growing. Turner could do that, he was good at it. Mists on the sea."

"Yes he was. And now this?"

She ran her second wash, adjusting strength by adding water to the run at critical points and waited on his answer.

"The texture develops then gets finer, fading into a single colour in places, leaving white puffy clouds in the unpainted bits. But that's what watercolours do!"

He sounded perplexed that she was showing him the obvious. One arm came up alongside his head and Harriet Chalmers leaned forward, catching Sophie's eye. Careful, her expression registered.

Sophie nodded to her and smiled at Brendan and the arm dropped down again. "What does that mean, though?"

He answered instantly. "You can control whether the paint surface looks coarser or smoother, whether there are hard or soft edges. It's obvious."

Sophie replied, "So let's look at my second painting. It's an oil painting, not a watercolour."

She pulled from her portfolio case the painting from Paris of her former partner Andrew Helmsley; her last original painting, the one that Catrin Sayer had latched on to on during her first visit to her home.

Brendan studied it intently. "I like this; it's much better than the other one; more interesting. I see what you mean about the control of detail and texture and its variation, as in the watercolour. But I see that in works I copy at times, too; it's very effective. Who painted the original?"

"I did. This is it."

He looked at her, a little startled.

She said, "If I worked with you, do you think we could do something original together?"

Harriet Chalmers seemed lost in her tablet but she looked up intently at Brendan as he glanced at Sophie, then back to the painting, then back to the woman. He said cautiously, "We can try, I suppose. I'd need help."

Sophie replied, "That's what I am here for."

Later, after Brendan announced he was tired and needed his nap, Sophie and Harriet sat down with his parents and explained what had gone on in the studio.

Sophie watched their faces and pre-empted Joanne's question. "I know the copies he is painting now could sell; as could any of his earlier originals, I expect. But I am not after money, I assure you. My own copies sell well, too. My home is paid for. I am financially stable. I don't need payment."

Joanne looked at her husband. "It's not that, although it had crossed my mind. It's… the uncertainty. I don't want him built up and then let down."

Hubert added, "It's a long way from Aldeburgh, though…"

Sophie responded, "It takes two hours driving; and I am not planning to be here a lot; I have my own life to lead, too. But I will commit to this, if you agree. I won't let him down."

Harriet Chalmers said, "It will not get easier, only harder, you realise? There will come a time…"

She let it trail open.

Sophie said firmly, some of her old obstinacy showing through. "There's now, and the time we have available to make art. To get him back to Titchwell Marsh, even, painting there, if we can. Who knows? But I'm no quitter. I'll stick with him on this."

Joanne said, reaching a decision, "Hubert, we should say

yes. I want to do it and so, I think, will Brendan. He's happy by himself but gets on easily with so few others. It looks as if he has made a good start with Sophie."

Chalmers smiled. "I'm glad. From what I saw, I really think this will be good for him."

For some reason, the social worker thought that it would be good for this Suffolk artist, too. It was in her expression, in her eyes.

~~

Lyall Beddows was self-conscious about his Centurion colours looking new, a different set from those of the one-percenters in the Demons clubhouse near Munich. Stuart and the two other patches had suggested the trip to him, inviting him along, part of building the relationship between the two clubs again.

While Stuart talked one-on-one later with Oskar, Gerda pulled Lyall away from the group of men and women, causing a witty comment or two. But she led him to a quiet spot and sat him down.

"You did well, through it all. But I have some questions."

'All' thought Lyall; the issues surrounding the death of Leo. He looked at her but said nothing, waiting.

"You worked out what Leo was doing, didn't you?"

Lyall just nodded then, as an afterthought, added. "I had a pretty good idea, but I didn't know - as in 'was aware of'.

"Would you have done it for him, if he had asked? If he hadn't involved Eric Sorensen?"

So that was her message, back at Renée's interment, he realised.

He answered her question with his own. "I'll tell you but first clarify for me; you gave Eric's name for the Centurions to go after the forger, did you not?"

She nodded. "Yes; exactly."

"Then the answer is - no, I wouldn't. I would have stood beside him and in front of him if needed but I would only do something like that for my club, if they asked me. If I could; the truth is I don't know if I could do that sort of thing, anyway. My loyalty is first to my club. Leo was my patch but his singlemindedness on revenge has caused a lot of problems for us. I love the man and his memory but I can't whitewash that, either.

"Does that answer your question?"

She didn't answer directly. She gave him an appraising look then called across the room. "Jon, Klara, Yves; look after our new friend here, Lyall. Take him out for a ride, perhaps, if he wants; show him around. And introduce him to some nice German girls; give him a very good time."

~~

"She painted this? I thought she was a ceramic artist," Mrs. Yau said.

Miele replied, "She is, commercially. But she paints for pleasure in watercolour. Her sister-in-law's partner is a well-known watercolour artist and he got her to take it up again some years ago."

"This is very good. Your grandfather looks so... it's that expression when he was thinking, hiding what he wanted to say, or trying to hold back a comment. It's him. She sent it to you, though?"

It wasn't that Michael Yau's widow was oblivious to the sensitivities of a British police officer sending a present to the family of a Triad member; she wondered why it was sent to Miele specifically.

"She had a request that I find a place to frame it professionally in a way that complimented the art but also fits our home. But it is for you. I like it - and you? Do you approve my choice for the mount and the frame?"

"Very much. It enhances the painting and... that has such character!! Your grandfather always looked either impassive or grinning on his photographs. This reveals more. Yet they saw each other only twice, so how did she get it so right?"

Miele smiled. "I asked that, too. One of the photos taken at Jian Li's wedding was the base, she said; and her memory of this expression during their discussion."

The older woman nodded, remembering the occasion.

And this signature; it's not her name, though."

"It's Welsh, Grandma; 'er cof'. It just says, 'in memory'.

The older woman thought back to the time she had first heard the name Catrin Sayer from her husband; his relief that Jian Li Yeung had not been injured or killed.

She said, "Their lives intertwined. I'm glad that, as a Westerner, she sent this message to me. It's fitting, too, for your grandfather. He thought well of her."

Miele Yau studiously avoided commenting on her grandmother's efforts to hide her tears; she had been taken to task on that previously. Grandma was as bad as her grandfather had been for concealing emotions; or trying to. Instead she looked around the reception room in their large home saying, "Now we have to find the right place to hang it."

"In my bedroom; it goes there. I will see him as I go to sleep each night," the older woman said emphatically.

NOTES

My wife Gill and my friends Jack Soule, Mike Stroud and Fred Grigsby each read drafts of the work and contributed significantly to the development of the story. I thank each of them. Any remaining errors are entirely my own.

As stated in previous novels in this series, the Metropolitan Police in London does have an Art and Antiques Unit within its Specialist Crime Command that was established back in 1969. During the course of writing this novel it was reported that the officers in the Art and Antiques Unit had temporarily been reassigned to other duties and later that the unit was being reformed. However, its people, structure and activities described herein are entirely my own creation. The same caveat applies to other units mentioned, including Trident, the Met Film Unit and the Stolen Vehicle Recovery Unit. The 'Art

Crime Unit' in the Metropolitan Police described in this series of novels is an invention that has no real-life counterpart.

The announcement that the headquarters of the Metropolitan Police, New Scotland Yard, would be downsized and moved from Broadway to reoccupy the Curtis Green building on the Embankment was made in October 2013. Considerable renovations had to be undertaken and the move occurred in October 2015. The change was cited partly as an economic measure and partly to take account of restructuring the headquarters group strength.

Shaun Greenhalgh, 'The Bolton Forger', wrote a book about his life called 'The Forger's Tale'. He produced forgeries that fooled many experts. Greenhalgh was sentenced to four years and eight months in prison in the UK in 2007, a reduction from a seven-year sentence for early co-operation and his guilty plea after his arrest.

The world of 'outlaw' motorcycle clubs differs according to the perspective of the individual; to some they are clubs of passionate motorcyclists who cut a different path in life and don't want interference from others. To law enforcement organisations, outlaw biker clubs are organized crime groups with their own, often violent sense of retribution and justice and a tribal sense of territoriality. Club patches are held in high esteem and remain the property of the club.

In 2009, eight members of the Hells Angels and the Outlaws in England were sentenced to substantial prison time for their part in a brawl, legally deemed to be a riot, in the Birmingham Airport Arrivals area. It had arisen after rival club members had spotted each other on an aircraft returning from Alicante, Spain and had called in reinforcements. According to reports, over thirty bikers were involved and weapons found included knives, knuckledusters, hammers, a club, a machete and a meat cleaver. All people jailed were family men in an age range between thirty-five and fifty-two.

ABOUT THE AUTHOR

Allan Jones lives in Ontario, Canada. He was born and grew up in Merseyside, England. By profession an industrial chemist, he worked for many years as a consultant on international chemical regulation. He has lived in or travelled to most of the regions featured in the Catrin Sayer novels.